Mendelssohn and Schumann

Mendelssohn and Schumann

Essays on Their Music and Its Context
Edited by Jon W. Finson *and* R. Larry Todd

Duke University Press   *Durham, N. C.*   *1984*

This publication has been supported by a subvention from the American Musicological Society. The Mary Duke Biddle Foundation provided a grant for the publication of the music examples.

Library of Congress Cataloging in Publication Data
Main entry under title:

Mendelssohn and Schumann : essays on their music and its
    context.

    Includes bibliographical references and index.
    Contents: Contemporary criticism: Schumann's critical
reaction to Mendelssohn / Leon Plantinga. Schumann in
Brendel's *Neue Zeitschrift für Musik* from 1845 to 1856 /
Jurgen Thym — Compositional process: A sketch leaf for
Schumann's D-minor symphony / Rufus Hallmark. The sources
for Schumann's *Davidsbündlertänze,* op. 6, composition,
textual problems, and the role of the composer as
editor / Linda Correll Roesner. Mendelssohn's late
chamber music, some autograph sources recovered /

Friedhelm Krummacher — [etc.]
    1. Mendelssohn-Bartholdy, Felix, 1809–1847—Addresses,
essays, lectures.   2. Schumann, Robert, 1810–1856—
Addresses, essays, lectures.   I. Finson, Jon W.
II. Todd, R. Larry.
ML410.M5M48   1984   780'.903'4   84–10120
ISBN 0-8223-0569-0

Contents

Contents

Acknowledgments

Research for this volume was undertaken with assistance from the National Endowment for the Humanities, the Mary Duke Biddle Foundation, and the Departments of Music at Duke University and the University of North Carolina at Chapel Hill. In addition the editors wish to acknowledge the kind assistance of several individuals who helped the volume through the various stages at the press. Among these we can only note in passing Stephen and Anne Keyl, for their meticulous copyediting, Frieda Woodruff, for her diligent preparation of the index, and Caroline Usher, Ken Kreitner, and Raymond Knapp, for their careful reading of the manuscript. We also wish to thank Professors Fenner Douglass and Tilman Seebass (Duke University), Margaret Crum (Bodleian Library), and Professors James Haar, James W. Pruett, and Howard Smither (University of North Carolina, Chapel Hill) for assistance of various kinds.

These essays appear with the support of two subventions from the American Musicological Society and the Mary Duke Biddle Foundation, which we gratefully acknowledge.

For permission to publish facsimiles of manuscripts and other material, we are indebted to several institutions: Biblioteka Jagiellońska, Kraków; Bibliothèque nationale, Paris; Bodleian Library, Oxford; British Library, London; Gesellschaft der Musikfreunde, Vienna; Heinrich-Heine-Institut, Düsseldorf; and Rare Book Room, William R. Perkins Library, Duke University.

April 1984

Mendelssohn and Schumann

Introduction

> Sunday, the seventh. A mild day, as in spring—memories, over-
> flowing ones of Mendelssohn—at three o'clock in the afternoon to
> Koenigstrasse—the great throng of people—the decorated coffin—all
> his friends—Moscheles, Gade, myself at the right, Hauptmann, David
> and Rietz at the left of the coffin, also Joachim and many others
> following—an interminable procession. . . .[1]

With these thoughts, and accompanied by the musical establishment of Leipzig, Robert Schumann escorted Felix Mendelssohn to his obsequies at St. Paul's Church in November 1847. It was altogether fitting that Schumann should have performed this last service for his friend. The two composers had shared Leipzig as the center of their artistic synergy for some twelve years when death overtook Mendelssohn; the constancy of the musicians' personal regard for one another is eloquent testimony to the greatness of both minds.

The first meeting between Mendelssohn and Schumann occurred during the fall of 1835, when Mendelssohn assumed his position as conductor of the Gewandhaus Orchestra in Leipzig. From the beginning Schumann had the highest praise for Mendelssohn's abilities both as musician and programmer. He clearly regarded Mendelssohn as a stalwart proponent of high musical values. Schumann actively supported the orchestra and its music director in a series of detailed reviews of the musical scene in Leipzig,[2] and he continued to promote the institution and its leader until he sold the *Neue Zeitschrift für Musik* in 1844. It is not too much to claim that Schumann's reviews greatly enhanced Mendelssohn's reputation as a conductor. By the same token, Mendelssohn often employed the orchestra to further Schumann's artistic projects and his career as a composer. It was Mendelssohn who conducted the Leipzig performance of Schubert's "Great" C-major Symphony at Schumann's urging, with the resultant publication of the work by Breitkopf and Härtel.[3] And Mendelssohn arranged the premieres of Schumann's first two symphonies, taking particular care in rehearsal to ensure the success of both works.[4] Much of the composers' mutual respect is best revealed in their activities surrounding the Gewandhaus concerts.

If the contact between the music critic and the conductor of the Gewandhaus is easy to document, it is more difficult to determine the purely artistic relationship between the two. It is often said that Schumann expressed an unwavering admiration for his friend, while Mendelssohn maintained some reserve toward Schumann.[5] In fact, the composers had a mutual appreciation for one another's music, but neither suspended his critical judgment on the other's account. Schumann was known through his articles in the *Neue Zeitschrift* as an outspoken admirer of Mendelssohn's works. Still, he noticed in Mendelssohn's music certain classicizing tendencies which isolated Mendelssohn from the mainstream of contemporary composition, a topic explored in this collection of essays at some length by Leon Plantinga. Mendelssohn, with his distinct disinterest in music journalism, would have had reason to remain aloof, for he knew Schumann initially more as a journalist than as a composer. Moreover, most concert-goers and musicians in Leipzig were either unacquainted with or puzzled by Schumann's musical output from the 1830s, and the strictly educated Berliner may have been no exception. But as Schumann began to produce his larger works in the 1840s, Mendelssohn and musical Leipzig in general became more enthusiastic about Schumann's compositions. When Schumann completed his *Paradies und die Peri* (1843), a major cantata based on exotic poetry by Thomas Moore, Mendelssohn wrote to the publisher Edward Buxton on Schumann's behalf, "I have read and heard this new work of Dr. Schumann with the greatest pleasure . . . and I think it a very impressive and noble work, full of many eminent beauties. As for expression and poetic feeling it ranks very high, the choruses are as effectively and as well written as the solo parts are melodious and winning."[6] Other actions of Mendelssohn evince his high regard for Schumann as a composer and musician. When Mendelssohn formed the Leipzig Conservatory in 1843, for instance, he asked Schumann to teach both piano and composition. For various reasons Schumann did not take to the role of teacher and abandoned the post after only a year of very sporadic instruction. Though Mendelssohn was willing to teach his craft, this activity brought no joy whatever to Schumann.[7]

Unlike Schumann, Mendelssohn had undergone a rigorous musical education in Berlin as a child. Schumann's early training in composition did not begin until he was in his early twenties, and even then it was not nearly so thorough as Mendelssohn's. This disparity in educational background necessarily influenced the two composers' individual approaches to compositional practice. Friedhelm Krummacher explores manifestations of the mature Mendelssohn's vast technique in some of the chamber works published posthumously, the autograph sources of which have just recently surfaced in Eastern Europe. And Marcia Citron views the critical relationship between Mendelssohn and his sister, Fanny Hensel, an accomplished composer and pianist in her own right. In their exchange of letters Felix invited and submitted to a kind of appraisal he would never have permitted an outsider. These glimpses of Mendelssohn's compositional practice contrast strikingly with Schumann's musical creativity as seen in Linda Correll Roesner's essay on the *Davids-bündlertänze,* one of his piano cycles from the 1830s. Roesner shows that Schumann ordered his copious outpourings of imagination by means of intuition and improvisation, not by use of an abstract technique. He relied more on literary than on musical models for his *Davidsbündlertänze.*[8] Only later in his career did he adopt a more traditional approach to composing, and Rufus Hallmark's essay shows the development of Schumann's craft. In a sketch for the D-minor Symphony (1841), Hallmark examines Schumann's systematic contrapuntal treatment and melodic transformation of some of the basic thematic material. Schumann's later approach is very similar to that of Mendelssohn, who customarily filled his sketches with detailed contrapuntal elaborations.

There may well be some merit to the claim that Mendelssohn exerted a strong influence on Schumann's later compositional development.[9] By 1835, Mendelssohn had successfully essayed almost every one of the major musical forms. While success in opera would continue to elude him all his life, the premiere in 1836 of the oratorio *St. Paul* proved Mendelssohn a composer with substantial dramatic talent as well as a defender of more traditional, "serious" musical values. Schumann, in contrast, limited himself almost exclusively to piano music during the 1830s.

The years from 1840 to 1843 may be viewed as Schumann's *anni mirabiles,* for during this time—at the height of Mendelssohn's concert activity in Leipzig—he broke with his earlier concentration on piano music. The output of the remarkable *Liederjahr* (1840) was followed by progressive concentration on symphonic (1841), chamber (1842), and choral works (1843). Whether by direct influence or by previous example, Mendelssohn must have been involved in Schumann's new burst of creative development. We know for a fact that Mendelssohn advised Schumann during the orchestration of the First Symphony.[10] And there is a striking affinity between Mendelssohn's chamber style and Schumann's Quartets, Op. 41, with their pronounced Mendelssohnian scherzi, lyrical slow movements, and contrapuntal preoccupation. Suitably enough, Schumann dedicated the quartets to Mendelssohn, who had finished his own set, Op. 44, in 1838. Schumann's D-minor Piano Trio, Op. 63 (1847) is indebted to Mendelssohn's great Trio, Op. 49 (1839), which Schumann had called in 1840 "the master-trio of the present."[11] In the last movement of his trio, Schumann even seems to have borrowed from the opening theme of Mendelssohn's D-major Cello Sonata, Op. 58 (1843). Surely this is a most striking and direct example of the affinity between the two composers' styles (see exx. 1 and 2).

Schumann was musically indebted to Mendelssohn in more general ways as well. Schumann viewed Mendelssohn as the originator of a new genre, the programmatic concert-overture.[12] The *Midsummer Night's Dream, Calm Sea and Prosperous Voyage,* and *Fingal's Cave* Overtures, based respectively on a play by Shakespeare, a pair of short poems by Goethe, and Mendelssohn's impressions of a Scottish seascape, deeply impressed Schumann. Schumann's later interest in the concert overture seems to reflect Mendelssohn's choice of subject in works like *Julius Caesar* (Shakespeare) and *Hermann und Dorothea* (Goethe). Moreover, Men-

Ex. 1. Schumann, Op. 63

Ex. 2. Mendelssohn, Op. 58

delssohn's intense interest in traditional counterpoint and works from the musical past stimulated Schumann's own interest in these subjects. It is true that in 1832 Schumann had perused Bach's *Well-Tempered Clavier* and a copy of Marpurg's *Abhandlung von der Fuge* (1754), a systematic treatise dedicated to the study of elaborate contrapuntal forms. But Mendelssohn's repeated performances of Bach's music in Leipzig were later to find direct resonance in Schumann's own successful performance of the *Johannespassion* in Düsseldorf after Mendelssohn's death. And as a result of their increased exposure to Bach's music, both composers paid compositional homage to Bach. For Mendelssohn this took shape in *St. Paul,* the *Reformation* Symphony, and the six sonatas for organ, Op. 65. As if in reply, Schumann brought forth the six fugues for organ on Bach's name, Op. 60, the *Ritornelle in canonischen Weisen,* Op. 65, and contrapuntal excursions in many other pieces.

In the most generous sense, then, the two composers were involved in an artistic exchange, with Leipzig as the central locus joining both men to common views of art and music. William S. Newman exposes just the tip of the enormous musical activity in Leipzig as part of a study which establishes the context of Mendelssohn's and Schumann's musical practice. Jurgen Thym's article on the editorial policy of Franz Brendel, Schumann's successor at the *Neue Zeitschrift,* reminds us that both Schumann and Mendelssohn were regarded as representatives of the "Leipzig School" (as opposed to what could be loosely characterized as the "Weimar School" of Liszt and Wagner). Both Mendelssohn and Schumann were members of an educated German upper middle class which eschewed extremity in any aspect of life. Ralph Locke's study portrays Mendelssohn's antipathy to the Saint-Simonian movement, quite in contrast to Liszt's fervent embrace of this Utopian sect.[13] (A similar tale could be told of the contrast between Wagner's active participation in the Dresden uprisings of 1849 and Schumann's choice in the same situation to flee the city and avoid the chaos of civil disorder.)[14] Essays on Mendelssohn's interest in Ossianic literature and Schumann's response to German *Shake-spearomanie* at the end of this volume also show that the composers were both affected by the important literary movements of their time. Both men attended a university at some length, both came from highly cultured families, and both maintained broad literary interests which marked their music in sophisticated ways. By later standards Mendelssohn and Schumann expressed German romanticism in a restrained manner, using the inherited language of the common practice in original ways but never seeking to transcend or challenge that language, as Liszt and Wagner were to do not long after Schumann's death. It is appropriate to speak of a Leipzig School and to view Mendelssohn and Schumann as its two principal members, linked by the bonds of friendship, by a common locale, by complementary activities, and by a similar artistic outlook.

With the present volume we intend to suggest a sense of the artistic commonality of Mendelssohn and Schumann. The essays serve, of course, only as a point of departure, ideally as an impetus for research which still awaits. The superabundance of unexplored source material for these two composers will surely contribute much to our understanding of Mendelssohn, Schumann, and their artistic milieu. We hope that the following essays will prompt a renewed interest in one of the most remarkable musical friendships of the nineteenth century.

Contemporary Criticism

Leon Plantinga

Schumann's Critical Reaction to Mendelssohn

When the twenty-six-year-old Mendelssohn appeared in Leipzig in the autumn of 1835 to assume leadership of the Gewandhaus orchestra, the warring musical factions of the city closed ranks, for a moment, to welcome him. Gottfried Wilhelm Fink, editor of the established and respectable *Allgemeine musikalische Zeitung*, hailed him as a master already much beloved of the Leipzig audience, particularly for his three concert overtures (these were the *Midsummer Night's Dream, Meeresstille und glückliche Fahrt,* and *Die Hebriden*)—all put out, he pointedly remarked, by Breitkopf and Härtel, the publisher for whom the *AmZ* was the house organ. It was a welcome innovation at his first concert, Fink continued, that for the instrumental works as well as the vocal music on the program Mendelssohn himself conducted from the podium. He observed, reasonably enough, "If the concert-master must do this, and act at the same time as the first violinist, he is faced with the necessity of dividing his efforts, of interrupting his playing to beat time."[1] And, casting a wary eye toward his opposition, he finished with the hope that this new undertaking should proceed "in a single spirit, in a pious love for art, free of the petty self-seeking that plagues only the weak."[2]

Robert Schumann, one year younger than Mendelssohn, and in his first year as editor-in-chief of the somewhat madcap *Neue Zeitschrift für Musik*, veiled his own comments about Mendelssohn's arrival and first concert in the novelesque *Schwärmbriefe*, promptly favoring him with a newly minted Davidsbündler name: "F. Meritis stepped forth and a hundred hearts flew to him in the first moment. . . . Meritis conducted as if he had composed the overture himself, and the orchestra played accordingly." (The overture was Mendelssohn's own *Meeresstille*.)[3] For his part, Schumann said, he was disturbed by Mendelssohn's conducting with a baton in the symphony (it was Beethoven's Fourth) and in the overture, for the orchestra should be "like a republic that recognizes no higher authority." He continued, "But it was a joy to see how Meritis anticipated with his eye the expressive turns of the music, from the most delicate to the most powerful, and as the most favored one proceeded ahead of the multitude. This instead of the sort of Kapellmeister one sometimes sees who threatens the score, the orchestra, and the public alike with blows from his scepter."[4]

Here began the ten-year history of Schumann's complicated relationship with Mendelssohn: as his friend and colleague, as a public commentator on a musical scene in which Mendelssohn was to play a central role, and as, in some sense, a competitor who was always decisively overshadowed by this vastly more celebrated resident of his own city.

Schumann's critical recognition of Mendelssohn had actually begun a bit earlier in 1835 with two appreciative reviews of his keyboard music: the second volume of *Lieder ohne Worte*, Op. 30, the Capriccio, Op. 5, and the *Charakterstücke*, Op. 7. And at the end of the year he added a review of the Piano Sonata, Op. 6. In these first assessments of Mendelssohn's early music, certain persistent themes in Schumann's perception of his work come to light. The *Charakterstücke*, he says, are an interesting witness to Mendelssohn's early development, when, still almost a child, he was much restrained by the chains of Bach and Gluck.[5] The Sonata, Op. 6, also seems like a preparatory exercise, one that points unmistakably to the greatness of Mendelssohn's future. And if parts of this sonata sound familiar—the first movement to the finale of Beethoven's Op. 101 and the last to various pieces of Weber—this should not be construed as weak dependency, but as a kind of "spiritual kinship."[6]

We can detect two recurrent motives in Schumann's criticism of Mendelssohn's music. The first is that Mendelssohn is more than usually dependent upon older models, in this case the works of Bach, Gluck, Beethoven, and Weber; his work never seems fully congruent with the expectations of present-day musical culture. The second is less tangible: a notion that Mendelssohn is a truly important composer of the modern age, but that somehow his greatness is never quite evident in the work at hand. His abilities, his intentions, his *Tendenz*, it seems, are often more impressive than his compositions. One reason for this impression in the reviews of 1835, perhaps, is the context in which Schumann's conclusions appeared. In two of these articles Mendelssohn's work is considered as part of a long series of compositions of roughly the same genre. It was Schumann's habit to save the best until last; thus Mendelssohn's Capriccio and *Charakterstücke* are taken up together with short pieces by Schubert and Chopin, and his youthful sonata is reviewed in proximity to Schubert's later sonatas in A minor, D major, and G major. In this company, Mendelssohn's music tends to come out second or third best.

In the years following, Schumann wrote formal reviews of a good many more instrumental compositions of Mendelssohn: two more sets of *Lieder ohne Worte*, the Capricci (Op. 33), the Preludes and Fugues (Op. 35), the Piano Concerto in D minor (Op. 40), the Sonata for piano and cello (Op. 45), the Piano Trio (Op. 49), the Overture to the *Schöne Melusine* (Op. 32), and the *Scottish* Symphony (Op. 56). All these reviews are favorable, or, in a couple of cases, at the very least respectful. Among the compositions mentioned, Schumann was perhaps least impressed with the Piano Concerto in D minor (Op. 40). He wrote in 1839:

Surely he always remains the same, always continues upon his familiar and good-humored course. . . . Thus Mendelssohn's compositions have an irresistible effect when he plays them himself. His fingers are only a means to an end, and might as well be invisible; the ear alone apprehends and the heart then judges. I often think that Mozart must have played like that. If then praise is due Mendelssohn because he consistently gives us such music to hear, we nonetheless could not deny that he often does so in a more casual [*flüchtig*] way in one work, in a more profound way in another. This concerto belongs to his most casual products. If I am not mistaken, he must have written it in a few days, perhaps in a few hours. . . . So let us enjoy this bright, unpretentious gift; it is like one of those works we know from the old masters done when they are resting from their more important labors.[7]

In his review of the Preludes and Fugues, Op. 35, Schumann pointed to what he considered one of Mendelssohn's special gifts, i.e., his facility in contrapuntal writing. It was the particular genius of Mendelssohn, Schumann said, to show that successful fugues could still be written in a style that was fresh and yet faithful to its Bachian and Handelian models: these fugues hold to the form of Bach, he felt, though their melody marks them as modern. While Schumann is at pains to convince his readers that these pieces represent serious composition and not only an exercise in antiquarianism, he really concludes that this is an unsuitable arena for the efforts of modern composers. Only Mendelssohn seems able to succeed here, and even his fugues must be judged by standards extrinsic to the genre.[8]

Schumann knew at least three of the five mature symphonies of Mendelssohn, but wrote a formal review of only one, the *Scottish;* this was toward the end of his career as a critic, in 1843. This work, said Schumann, seemed like Mendelssohn's first major accomplishment as a symphonist: the Symphony No. 1 in C minor was a very early work, the *Lobgesang* as a "symphonic cantata" didn't really count, and the others (i.e., the *Italian* and *Reformation*) remained unpublished and largely unknown.[9] Schumann had looked to this, a mature symphony of Mendelssohn, with the greatest anticipation, and now spoke of it warmly:

From a purely musical standpoint, no one could question its mastery. In beauty and ease of construction overall, and in the detail of its connective sections it is the equal of his overtures; in arresting instrumental effects it is no less rich. How splendidly Mendelssohn can reintroduce earlier ideas, ornamenting them such that they are cast in an entirely new light; how rich and interesting the detail without bombast and learned contrivances—of these things every page of the score provides new evidence.[10]

Yet the symphony was not quite what Schumann had expected: "The usual instrumental pathos, that customary massive breadth one does not find here, nothing that proposes to outreach Beethoven. It resembles much more, especially in its character, that symphony of Schubert [i.e., the "Great" C-Major Symphony that Schumann and Mendelssohn had brought to performance some four years earlier]."[11] And in the discussion that follows, Mendelssohn's symphony once more suffers by comparison with Schubert's music. In a summary description, finally, of the most salient traits of each symphony, Schumann attributes to Mendelssohn a "well-mannered grace," and to Schubert a "greater richness of invention."[12]

When Schumann wrote that in compositional technique the *Scottish* Symphony was the equal of Mendelssohn's overtures, he paid it no small compliment. For it was in Mendelssohn's cultivation of this genre, he said on more than one occasion, that the composer made his most distinctive and best contribution. Only one new overture of Mendelssohn's, his fourth, the *Schöne Melusine,* appeared during Schumann's tenure as a critic. This composition is assessed in his concert review of January 1836, a review, he tells us, that is based upon two hearings of the composition and a cursory glance at the score. Schumann begins this article with rather serious talk about the relation of the music to its program, tracing the tale of the ill-fated water-nymph and the mortal knight she loves back to its origins in a story of Ludwig Tieck:

With characteristic poetic grasp, Mendelssohn sketches here only the characters of the man and woman, the proud, knightly Lusignan and the alluring, devoted Melusine; but it is as if the swells of water joined in their embraces, overwhelmed them and divided them. . . . This, it seems to me, distinguishes the overture from the earlier ones—that such events, much as in fairy-tale, are recounted at a certain remove: the narrator keeps his distance.[13]

Later Schumann identifies the characters of the drama with specific passages of music: the "knightly theme" is the one in F minor; we can identify Melusine in the gentle, pliant theme in A-flat major. And the work begins and ends with that striking wave-figure in the clarinets that "has the effect of transporting one from the battleground of tense human passion to the sublime, all-encompassing universe of water."

The formal construction of the overture meets with Schumann's approval. In the exposition F major and F minor are immediately juxtaposed in the wave-figure and the resolute motive Schumann identifies with the knight. The further conduct of the overture must deal with this ambiguity. The principal modulation is to A-flat, relative major of F minor, where we hear the music Schumann associates with the character of Melusine. The effect of the opening motive is redoubled, Schumann observes, when it enters in the course of a modulation from that A-flat through G to C. This occurs at the end of the exposition, where the harmonic goal of C is deftly accomplished by shifting the function of G from leading-tone to dominant (ex. 1). We should also take note of one instrumental effect to which Schumann called special attention: "that beautiful B-flat in the trumpets, toward the beginning, that forms the seventh of the chord—a tone out of the distant past."[14] This sustained B-flat in the trumpets occurs in the opening section in F major (mm. 19–23), as the seventh of a dominant harmony; and as the music then makes a characteristically Mendelssohnian move at the climax of the phrase from dominant to subdominant, the B-flat can be retained (ex. 2).

Schumann has two quibbles to make about this overture. First, he had assumed upon an initial hearing that its meter was 6/8, and feels that this signature, with its implied faster tempo, is superior to the 6/4 shown in the score.[15] Second, in a passage deleted from the *Gesammelte Schriften* when he assembled them in 1854, he tempers his approval of the formal construction of the overture: "This latter, though, as well as the manner of instrumentation (especially toward the middle,

Ex. 1. Mendelssohn, Op. 32

where single instruments come and go in alternation), reminds us of things we have often heard before."[16]

Some of Schumann's most engaging commentary on Mendelssohn appears outside his formal reviews. The well-known discussion of the oratorio *St. Paul* together with Meyerbeer's *Les Huguenots*, for example, occurs in a sort of serialized feature article on the local musical scene entitled *Fragmente aus Leipzig*, written in 1837. Here Schumann gives full rein to his exasperation over Meyerbeer's hugely successful opera, a work, he said, that made him "weary and faint with anger." Its subject was for him revolting (all its action, he suggests, takes place either in a brothel or in church), its music superficial and eclectic—the whole a vulgar glorification of the contrived effect.[17] Pitted against this was Mendelssohn's most famous composition: his oratorio *St. Paul*, completed barely a year earlier, and now applauded throughout Germany and England as a revival of the glories of Bach and Handel.

Schumann begins his essay on *St. Paul* with considerable caution: it does not

Ex. 2. Mendelssohn, Op. 32

bear comparison, he says, with the Bach Passions or Handel's oratorios. These were written by God-like masters in their maturity; Mendelssohn is yet young. There are certain dramatic problems in the work, as in the disposition of persons and groups who have active roles and those that only observe. It is perhaps unfortunate that the dramatic weight falls mainly in Part I, so that Stephen emerges more important than St. Paul. And it has been remarked with some justification that the work is extraordinarily long.[18]

Midway through his article Schumann gets around to praising Mendelssohn: he speaks of "inner meaning, pure Christian spirit, musical mastery, elegant song—such freshness, such unquenchable color of instrumentation, an easy mastery of all musical styles." But then once again something of a sour note creeps in:

The music of *St. Paul* is for the most part of such a transparent and popular nature . . . that it seems as if in writing it the composer thought quite particularly about the impression it would make on the general audience. Admirable though this is, it could in future compositions detract from his music something of its strength and spirit, such as we find it in the works of those who present their material unimpaired, without special intentions and limitations. . . . Finally, one might recall that Beethoven wrote a *Christus am Ölberg,* but also a *Missa solemnis.* And we believe that, as the young Mendelssohn has composed an oratorio, the mature man will produce one too. Meanwhile let us be satisfied with what we have, learn from it, and enjoy it.[19]

In the *Gesammelte Schriften* Schumann added the observation that his prophecy had been fulfilled: ten years after *St. Paul* Mendelssohn had produced his *Elijah.*

In Schumann's writing about Mendelssohn we can detect a pattern that is a familiar feature of his criticism as a whole: a proneness to initial bursts of enthusiasm and high expectation—expectation that in the long run is never really fulfilled. This was also true of his criticism of Chopin and Berlioz. Both were largely unknown when he took up the cudgels on their behalf, and he expected both to be standard-bearers of a better future for European music. Neither developed fully in the ways Schumann had hoped, and his responses to their later music grew lukewarm. Of the composers Schumann championed, only one, Schubert, never disappointed him. Schumann the revolutionary, the spokesman for a new era, found his hopes best realized in the music of a composer who had been dead for years.

A reason for Schumann's frequent disappointment was that in his assessments of contemporary music he operated with a well-defined set of expectations, a kind of hidden agenda. He subscribed to a rather deterministic view of history in which a central tradition in music could be expected to develop in certain orderly and predictable ways. For him this tradition, for all practical purposes, had its beginning in Bach, the first in a series of monumental composers whose personal contributions comprised the locus of an inevitable line of progress leading to his own time. This line extended through Beethoven and Schubert to Schumann's own contemporaries. And a primary task of the critic, for him, was a sifting through of the evidence at hand to discover the continuation of this historical progression. He cultivated something of a messianic vision in which a single clear successor to Bach and Beethoven would one day be found—a vision that shone forth one final time when in his last public utterance, in 1853, he placed his hopes on the shoulders of the young Brahms: "I thought that after these developments one would and must suddenly appear, who is called to embody the highest expression of the time in ideal fashion, one whose mastery would not unfold in slow stages, but like Minerva, spring fully-armed from the head of Cronus. And he has come."[20]

In his review of the D-minor Trio, Op. 49, the one composition of Mendelssohn for which he expressed unreserved enthusiasm, Schumann said something of Mendelssohn's position in his historical scheme of things: "He is the Mozart of the nineteenth century, the most brilliant musician, the one who sees most clearly through the contradictions of this period, and for the first time reconciles them. And he will not be the last of such artists. After Mozart came Beethoven; this new Mozart will also be followed by a Beethoven—perhaps he is already born."[21] This is only one of several instances in which Schumann compares Mendelssohn's stylistic orientation and historical position with that of Mozart. Adjectives such as "clarity," "refinement," "grace," and "perfection" appear frequently in his commentary on both composers, and in his review of the Cello Sonata, Op. 45, in 1839, Schumann describes the progress of Mendelssohn's style as "ever more refined, enlightened, and Mozartian."[22]

It was in Schumann's generation that the notion of Mozart as a "classic" composer first gained currency. In the earlier 1830s the Hegelian historian and philosopher Amadeus Wendt, a professor at the University of Leipzig, wrote extensively about historical periodization in the arts, particularly in music. In his essay of 1836, *Ueber den gegenwärtigen Zustand der Musik besonders in Deutschland und wie er geworden,* he posited, perhaps for the first time, a "classic" period in music with Mozart at its center.[23] As this book was in preparation, Schumann named Wendt as one of the collaborators in the founding of the *Neue Zeitschrift für Musik*.[24] It may well have been from this source that Schumann derived certain of his lasting notions about the relation of music to history and the other arts.

But Wendt and Schumann subscribed to a distinctly Winckelmannian view of classicism—a view that the hallmarks of classic art are "ideal beauty," "grace," or "noble simplicity."[25] And language of this sort was easily transferable to the music of Mozart. In 1834 Schumann wrote, "Tranquillity, grace, ideality, and objectivity—these are the marks of ancient works of art, and of Mozart's school as well."[26] It was perfectly clear that in Schumann's grand design Mozart remained just outside the stately progression from Bach through Beethoven to the romantic composers of his own day. And Mendelssohn too, the "Mozart of the nineteenth century," Schumann said in his review of the D-minor Trio, stood somewhat outside the struggles of his time, was less embroiled than others in the "storms of the last few years."[27]

If Mendelssohn the composer never fully conformed to Schumann's expectations for contemporary musical style, he was in other ways, in Schumann's opinion, simply without peer: as a conductor, pianist, and organist, as the prime mover in the nascent Bach revival, as an improver of musical taste in Germany and a healthy influence upon younger composers. In a letter to Clara in 1838, Schumann offered a candid comparison of Mendelssohn's musical powers with his own: "How I compare with him as a musician I know exactly. I could still learn from him for years. But perhaps he could also learn something from me. Had I grown up in circumstances similar to his, destined from childhood for music, I would surpass them all."[28]

Schumann's view of Mendelssohn differs substantially from that of other critics of his time. At least until the early 1840s criticism of Mendelssohn in Germany and England was an unbroken litany of superlatives. In 1842 Carl Ferdinand Becker, the new editor of the *Allgemeine musikalische Zeitung* and formerly a regular contributor to Schumann's *Neue Zeitschrift,* stated something like a majority opinion: that Mendelssohn's stature was such that his works could only be contemplated, never criticized.[29] Schumann constructs a different and much more distinct portrait of Mendelssohn: a supremely accomplished musician whose music, always finely crafted, sometimes tends toward excessive facility, and often seems excessively dependent upon models from an earlier time. Schumann even hints at a reason for much of this: Mendelssohn's background and training were, to say the least, unusual. The elaborate, distinctly traditional education in music he received from earliest childhood was unique among leading composers of his period. Mendelssohn was brought up like a musician of the eighteenth century, and this was reflected in a certain removal from the dominant trends of his own time.

To that gallery of musical figures of the romantic period whom Schumann saw with particular clarity, drawing them more sharply into focus for following generations, we can confidently add the name of Felix Mendelssohn.

Jurgen Thym

Schumann in Brendel's Neue Zeitschrift für Musik *from 1845 to 1856*

Robert Schumann's activity as a music critic is widely known and has been well documented in Leon Plantinga's book, *Schumann as Critic*. But little has been written about Schumann, the founder and first editor of the *Neue Zeitschrift für Musik* (hereafter cited as *NZfM*), as he was viewed and reviewed in its pages after he had retired as a journalist in 1845. There still remain many questions about this phase of Schumann's dealings with the periodical, including his relationship with the new editor, Franz Brendel, his continued influence on the journal in general, and his occasional submission of specific articles, including his famous paean heralding Brahms. Under the leadership of Brendel, Wagner emerged in the pages of the *NZfM* as the strongest musical personality of his time, and this turn of events understandably affected the appreciation of Schumann in the journal after 1850.[1]

[*i*]

The relationship of Brendel to Schumann in the *NZfM* was inevitably a delicate one. If Brendel wanted to be more than a mere successor to Schumann, he had to acquire a profile of his own as an editor. This meant not only avoiding the welltried avenues explored in Schumann's criticism, but also providing a contrasting model of music criticism that would prove equally successful. But he had to do this with a staff of contributors and correspondents whom Schumann had gathered and who still may have felt an allegiance to the old *Davidsbündler* and his way of running things. Sooner or later Brendel would face a delicate political problem: he had to appear to continue the former tradition while actually changing it drastically in style and substance.

Another possible source of conflict was Schumann's music. Schumann had decided to retire as an editor in order to devote more time to his family and to composition. While Schumann had been an editor of the *NZfM*, the articles about his own music were necessarily few in number and written with restraint; the danger of their being interpreted as self-serving comments was simply too great. But how would the periodical view Schumann's work after his term as editor had ended? Schumann the critic had promoted the music of Schubert, Chopin, Mendelssohn, Berlioz, and other young composers and thus helped establish the romantic movement. The proper evaluation of Schumann the composer, however, in the context he actually helped create through his journal, was a matter to be tackled by his successor.

Brendel faced both challenges head-on in three major articles published in the first year of his editorship. In the first, his New Year's Day statement of 1845 and inaugural address, so to speak, he took issue with Schumann as a critic (see appendix 1).[2] As was typical of his editorials, he prefaced his prospectus with a long historical discourse in which he outlined the evolution of music criticism from the age of enlightenment to the present. He distinguished two contrasting types of criticism, one which limited itself to the technical side of music and which prevailed mainly in the eighteenth century (a type of criticism he considered representative of the "objective" contrapuntal compositions of Handel and Bach), and another more "subjective" type initiated by Rochlitz and the *Allgemeine musikalische Zeitung* around 1800, which focused mainly on describing the psychological content of music (a type he considered representative of the new emotional music beginning with C. P. E. Bach and Haydn). Although Schumann was not directly named, it is clear that Brendel viewed the man who had founded the *NZfM* more than ten years before as a representative of the second type of criticism, which— despite many merits and advantages over the former—led to "increasingly greater inconsistencies in its pursuit and arrived at a chaos of completely subjective notions and opinions."[3] In order to overcome the limitations of contemporary music criticism, Brendel envisioned a third approach which would preserve the search for psychological and emotional content in music (characteristic of the second type) while aiming for the objectivity of the first.

Brendel's solution, however, was not what we would expect from such a combination of critical methods—perhaps a kind of musical hermeneutics in which technical and analytical observations provided the basis for discussing the meaning of music. His educational background enabled Brendel to deal with music in its broad philosophical and historical ramifications rather than to analyze the structures and compositional procedures of specific pieces; in fact, some of his statements on individual compositions reveal errors in judgment which a more consummate musician would not have committed.[4]

Brendel was, first of all, a philosopher and historian; he had been an avid disciple of Hegelian philosophy during his years at the universities in Leipzig and Berlin and was eager to apply what he had learned there to his field of interest.[5] It is not difficult to see in Brendel's writings the application of dialectical principles (thesis, antithesis, and synthesis) to the history of music in general and of music criticism in particular. Hegel's philosophy, as the most advanced mode of modern science, helped Brendel to prove that music was not just a separate art, steeped in parochialism and isolated from other forms of human endeavor, but a manifestation of the

Weltgeist, of the universal spirit. Beyond that, Hegelian principles were not just useful tools to organize and conceptualize the music of the past: so sure was Brendel of the correctness of the dialectic law that he meant to be able also to predict and prescribe future developments. Musicology *(musikalische Wissenschaft)* was a discipline which, because it occupied itself with the study of the great art works of the past and their potential, was able to use the results of its research as guidelines for future creations; musicology had the obligation, as Brendel proudly put it in his New Year's Day message of 1851, "to further that great process of evolution which is the law of the world and which is called 'progress.' "[6] Music criticism must not just review and reflect music history passively, but should shape and steer it.

Schumann and Mendelssohn were to be the first objects (or victims) of this kind of criticism in a major article, published in installments from February to May 1845, in which Brendel interpreted the music of his predecessor in relation to Mendelssohn's work and the development of modern music in general (see appendix 2).[7] Brendel regarded Schumann as a composer who had inherited Beethoven's legacy; the bizarre humor and youthful enthusiasm of Schumann's early piano works especially showed him as an artist whose subjectivity (like Beethoven's) could not be cast properly in the confines of well-balanced classical forms. Brendel saw this as the reason for the lack of understanding which Schumann's music encountered with audiences. Mendelssohn, according to Brendel, was Schumann's antipode. The ease with which Mendelssohn handled the objective forms and genres of the past made him a successor to Mozart, a composer Brendel considered less profound than Beethoven. Most of the time, Mendelssohn was able to animate the established forms with subjectivity; but occasionally, when he did not succeed, he appeared dry and academic *(formalistisch).*

Brendel realized that Schumann had changed direction after 1840 with works such as the First Symphony, the String Quartets, the Piano Quintet, and Piano Quartet. He saw these compositions as Schumann's attempts to present his ideas now through the objectivity of classical forms; he viewed them as an antithesis—to use the Hegelian term—to Schumann's former mode of creation. Brendel, however, was not overly pleased with this turn of events and expressed concern that Schumann was in danger of losing himself to the Mendelssohnian manner, an avenue he considered unsuitable for Schumann.

The conclusions Brendel drew from this state of affairs were ambivalent. He doubted that either composer would have any significance for the future development of music in Germany—Mendelssohn because of the retrospective and academic tendencies inherent in his music, Schumann because he was meandering between different compositional approaches and lacked a clearly perceived goal. But what if the latest stage in Schumann's development should give way to a third phase of creativity, a synthesis which would combine the objectivity displayed in the larger instrumental works of the 1840s with the psychological refinement, humor, and fantasy characteristic of the piano music of the 1830s? After all, Brendel needed to prove that Hegel's law was applicable even in this case—and in his next major article, he stated his views on the genre in which the musical features just mentioned could perhaps be most successfully combined: opera.

This essay, one of Brendel's best, appeared in the journal in installments from July 1845 to February 1846, under the title "Opera—Past, Present, and Future."[8] For him the present situation of operatic composition in Germany was abysmal. While German composers had done quite well in the field of church and instrumental music, they were unable to build on the achievements of Gluck and Mozart and create a viable national opera. Instead, they left the field to foreigners who inundated the stages with productions that, instead of fulfilling the cultural needs of the people, entertained them with shallow vocal brilliance of Italian origin and cleverly designed sets based on French models. I suspect that Brendel was also thinking of certain matters that the censors would have prevented him from stating outright. Operatic production in Germany was dependent on the courts and their opera houses and therefore directly associated with political restoration and feudalism, forces retarding the powerful trends of the time toward national unity and democracy in the German states. Thus, the musical situation, especially operatic life, reflected and perhaps even reinforced an outdated political, social, and economic order.

Like most members of the educated middle class of the *Vormärz*, i.e., the time prior to the 1848 revolution, Brendel was a liberal who hoped for a unified Germany under the auspices of democracy as a solution to many social, economic, and political ills that resulted from the division into numerous larger and smaller states. Brendel felt that, as editor of a major music journal, he was playing an active role in the great political movements of his time. If music were to survive in the coming political upheaval, it was necessary that composers understand their own time and create works of art that were in sympathy with the great ideas of the era.[9] Composers needed to recognize that writing songs, piano pieces, and chamber music only reinforced particularity, parochialism, and isolation; at a time when the nation was gathering her forces for a powerful political movement, it was imperative for composers to stop indulging in romantic dreams and to face the challenge of addressing larger issues and larger audiences.[10] It was time to tackle the problem of a national opera.

Brendel did not limit himself merely to calling composers' attention to the establishment of a national opera as a patriotic duty; he also prescribed how this should be accomplished. His specifications were quite explicit and partly anticipated the results of Wagner's analysis of the operatic problem in *Das Kunstwerk der Zukunft* and *Oper und Drama* half a decade later. Brendel demanded first of all that libretti should more closely conform to dramatic laws. He denounced as unpsychological and undramatic the division of the whole work into small, self-contained pieces; instead he asked for larger structures which would accommodate smaller sections in an overriding musico-dramatic design. In its form, opera should be (and here Brendel quoted Rochlitz) "one single great finale where everything is in a state of flux, changing according to the [dramatic] moment."[11] Vocal virtuosity and spoken dialogue were anathema to Brendel's concept of opera as a musico-dramatic work of art.

Brendel was even able to specify the subject matter that would be best suited for establishing a national opera in the future: the Nibelungen legend. This suggestion actually had been advanced for the first time by the philosopher Vischer in his *Aesthetik* of 1844; Luise Otto, the peripatetic Meissen correspondent of the *NZfM*, had introduced this idea to the pages of the journal in August 1845 and, later in the year, followed up her proposal by publishing parts of a libretto for such an opera.[12] Despite these precedents, the following statement by Brendel is astonishingly prophetic in view of the future course of music history: "In my view a setting of the Nibelungen opera would indeed be a step forward, and I believe that the composer who could accomplish this task in an adequate manner would become the man of his era."[13]

I have felt it necessary to report in more detail on Brendel's first three major articles, because they set the philosophical framework and terminology for the discussion of Schumann's music in the years to come; they also set the stage for an even more radical change of direction to which Brendel subjected the *NZfM* in 1850 and 1851 and which deeply affected Schumann's reception in the journal. With this trilogy of essays Brendel established himself as an editor in his own right. He sketched a critique of the music criticism of the past, including Schumann's mode of operation from 1834 to 1844, and he provided two examples for applying Hegelian philosophical principles to music history. In one of them Schumann had not fared very well; although Brendel adopted basically a "wait-and-see" attitude toward the music of his predecessor, he really was in doubt whether Schumann would be able to lead music into the new era. He may have felt that Schumann's compositional talent did not extend to opera, the field he had clearly singled out for major innovative impulses in the years to come.

[ii]

There followed several years of debate on various issues raised by the editorials of Brendel's first year. He invited responses to his statements and soon the *NZfM* published concurring and dissenting contributions, the latter of which always elicited rebuttals from Brendel. These public discussions were intended to further the dialectical process and to lead to ever clearer insights, but often the debates were muddled and turned into an exchange of hair-splitting sophistries and polemics. One such discussion that filled the pages of the *NZfM* in 1847 concerned the function and significance of music criticism, with the participation of at least four authors. During the revolutionary year 1848 another such controversy took place, this time between Brendel and the *AmZ*, which had attacked Brendel on matters involving the *Tonkünstler-Versammlung,* a national conference of musicians founded by Brendel and furthered by the *NZfM* through publication of the minutes of the proceedings. Open dialogues and discussions in the journal became one of the hallmarks of Brendel's editorial style.

The debate on Schumann's music did not take the path of a formal exchange but found a quieter, though no less effective, outlet. The many reviews of Schumann's publications or of performances of his music gave various authors the opportunity to state their opinions. Some of the reviews were nothing but standard specimens of music criticism; they discussed Schumann's works mostly in verbal niceties but dropped a critical sprinkle here and there. By and large, they remained outside the discussion initiated by Brendel. Brendel himself reiterated his former critical position when reviewing a Leipzig performance of Schumann's Second Symphony in December 1846.[14] He hoped that Schumann's move toward the objectivity of classical forms as manifested in his recent output would be only a transitory stage necessary to counter the shortcomings of the earlier piano works. Alfred Dörffel, a student of Mendelssohn and Schumann, who had joined the staff of the journal in 1846, added a new element to the debate slightly later by stating that works such as the Symphony and the Piano Concerto were sufficient proof that the composer was, indeed, striving toward his third period and close to achieving a final synthesis.[15] The problem, therefore, was to determine the point at which Schumann finally crossed the threshold of greatness.

It was Dörffel who took the initiative in advancing Schumann's cause. Unfortunately, however, the announcement was hesitant, it was made piecemeal in several widely spaced reviews rather than in a single major essay, and—what is most important—it was never backed by a statement from the editor-in-chief himself. In other words, the chance to turn Dörffel's announcement into a public relations event was bungled. The half-hearted acceptance of Schumann as a second Beethoven was only a trial balloon and in no way resembled the journalistic fanfare with which Wagner was greeted as the champion of his age in the *NZfM* a few years later.

The events began to unfold in February 1848, when Dörffel reviewed Schumann's Second Symphony on the occasion of the publication of the score (appendix 3).[16] At first, he repeated Brendel's well-known image of a struggle between subjectivity and objectivity, between the forces of fantasy and form in Schumann's artistic development, but he added that in this work the composer had come so close to a synthesis that he surely would gain "the crown of laurels."[17] Dörffel saw Schumann's symphony as the immediate predecessor to a work that would combine Mozart's *Jupiter* Symphony and Beethoven's Fifth Symphony and thereby establish a synthesis of objective and subjective worlds.[18]

In the following months, Dörffel remained faithful to his decision on the symphony, even revising his estimation upwards in September 1848, when he reviewed the Piano Trio, Op. 63.[19] Now the symphony and the trio, especially the first movement of the latter, were elevated to the rank of major compositions, in which Schumann had succeeded in expressing the ideal of his era and providing models for works of art of the future. Five months later, in February 1849, Dörffel elaborated his conviction. Schumann had emerged victorious from the struggle between his individuality and the objective world and had indeed arrived at a successful synthesis in the symphony and the trio.[20] What Brendel and others had long expected and hoped for had now become reality. But the statement also contained an element of irony, because it was not made in the context of discussing a major work by Schumann, a symphony, an oratorio, or perhaps an opera. Rather, it appeared in a review of the *Album für die Jugend,* by no means a composition suited for announcing a landmark decision. It was an almost desperate attempt to reach out to the other contributors of the *NZfM* and invite them to share some of the journalistic burden of such a major pronouncement.

Dörffel's call for positive action on matters Schumannian went unheeded except in two instances. In April 1849, the Second Symphony was reviewed again on the occasion of the publication of the four-hand piano reduction, but the review was relegated to the *Kritischer Anzeiger,* a location traditionally reserved in the journal for discussing items of minor significance (appendix 4).[21] The writer did not sign the article, but the writing style and the enthusiasm for the work point to Dörffel; he now dropped all hesitancy in elevating Schumann to the rank of a symphonic composer with Beethovenian stature. "What the former [Beethoven] announced has been further elaborated and brought to a higher organic fulfillment in the Symphony of the latter [Schumann]. The great drama of the Ninth Symphony with all its magnificent aspects appears here again." A year later, in April 1850, Ernst Gottschald echoed this sentiment in a series of open letters to Dörffel,[22] discussing Schumann's Second Symphony in relation to Beethoven's works, especially the Ninth. He pointed out the artistic representation of universal love as the common denominator of both works: "Ludwig was not yet able to achieve it only with instruments, he needed to borrow the word from poetry. Robert accomplishes it for the first time with instruments alone."

[*iii*]

The remarks just quoted were not made simply in support of Dörffel's enthusiasm for Schumann's recent music. They also constituted a veiled response to a series of articles by Theodor Uhlig that had appeared earlier in the year in the *NZfM*.[23] In these articles, which dealt with the symphonies of Beethoven, Uhlig laid the foundation for a gradual shift in the direction of the journal. His basic thesis was that, instead of searching for a second Beethoven in the field of instrumental music, it would make more sense to look elsewhere, namely in the music dramas of Wagner. Beethoven had striven for an increasingly extra-musical content in his instrumental works and had even felt compelled to include poetry in the last movement of his Ninth Symphony. And in pursuit of the same goal, a later generation of composers had found it necessary to create the hybrid genre of descriptive music (e.g., the overtures of Mendelssohn, the symphonies of Berlioz). Would it not make sense to take those extra-musical aspects that appeal to the rational rather than the emotional side of humankind and transfer them to the visual action on the stage? A musico-dramatic work of art would render descriptive music superfluous while absolute music would retain its purity without borrowings from another art form. What Gottschald saw as an imperfection in Beethoven's Ninth Symphony, i.e., the need for joining poetry and music, was for Uhlig a milestone on the way toward the highest conceivable art work, in which the separate arts would be unified.

Uhlig, a young musician from Dresden, had been handpicked by Brendel with the specific purpose of reorienting the journal toward Wagner.[24] Brendel, after five strenuous years as editor of the *NZfM* and exhausted by his administrative work for the *Tonkünstler-Versammlung* between 1847 and 1849, decided to reduce his involvement with the journal for a while in order to spend more time writing his history of music. He continued to contribute some minor articles and reviews now and then, but by and large the journal was clearly dominated between 1850 and 1852 by the editorials of Uhlig. Uhlig brought to the *NZfM* not only greater expertise on Wagner but also far better musical skills, for Brendel always discussed music on a very lofty philosophical level, giving few if any analytical details. When Brendel returned to more active duty after Uhlig's death early in 1853, the journal had changed direction. Consequently, Brendel felt compelled to take remedial lessons by making pilgrimages to Weimar and attending Liszt's performances of Wagner's and Berlioz's music.[25] The book on music history which he had just completed during his partial leave of absence now needed to be revised because of recent developments in his own journal.[26]

Most of the editorials and front-page articles of the *NZfM* during those years were taken up with discussion of Wagner's operas and writings as well as responses to attacks from other music journals that had taken issue with the apparent change of direction; in pursuit of Uhlig's line, the periodical also had entered into vitriolic attacks on Meyerbeer and his recent opera *Le Prophète*, culminating in a sequence of anti-Semitic articles, including Wagner's infamous essay on "Judaism and Music," published in the summer of 1850 under the pseudonym K. Freigedank.[27] The *NZfM* became a mouthpiece for the causes of a composer who, ousted from his country after the failure of the revolution and neglected and misunderstood by music journalism in general, was in need of a platform for propaganda if he wanted to be remembered during his exile.

With the journal focused almost exclusively on Wagnerian issues, the Schumannian discussion was relegated mostly to the back pages. Only occasionally did the composer receive front-page attention, for instance after the first performance of his opera *Genoveva* in June 1850, in Leipzig. Brendel, who reviewed the opera for the journal in the summer of that year, was quite hesitant in forming a definitive judgment about it.[28] He did not think very highly of the libretto and attributed the failure of the opera basically to the choice of the subject matter. The world of medieval knighthood and quasi-pagan superstition appeared to him unsuited for a contemporary national opera. His attitude toward the music was more positive. The constant flux between recitative and aria made the work a milestone on the way to his ideal of a through-composed opera and thus to a better future.

A contrasting view of *Genoveva* was printed by the journal in the spring of the next year (appendix 5). The occasion was publication of the piano-vocal score.[29] Its author preferred to remain anonymous but the style of writing points to Eduard Krüger, a pedagogue at a *Gymnasium* and later at a teacher's college in Ostfriesland, one of the most remote corners of northwest Germany. Krüger made a sharp break with the judgments of Schumann's music that had prevailed in the pages of the journal. For the first time in the *NZfM* a correspondent openly stated his suspicion that Schumann "may have passed his prime" and that "the work at hand was not an intensification of the preceding compositions but a dimming of his genius."[30] Brendel's next statement on operatic matters—a short article of June 1851, in which he publicly admitted his conversion to the Wagner camp—did not go quite so far, but he compared both composers and concluded that in the field of opera Wagner held the edge over Schumann because he had more successfully solved the problem of combining music and drama.[31]

In November 1851, Uhlig extended the Schumann-Wagner comparison to the level of vocal music in general. The occasion for his more general remarks was a review of Schumann's *Lieder, Gesänge, und Requiem für Mignon*, Op. 98 (appendix 6).[32] He discovered a basic difference in the approach of both composers to text-music relationships. While Schumann superimposed the forms of absolute music on the text, Wagner's music seemed to be generated out of the word. Uhlig tried to capture this difference with the terms *Tondichter* and *Worttondichter*. Because of the more comprehensive talent of the latter, Wagner ranked higher as an artist than the more conventional Schumann. Uhlig's criticism of Schumann was not limited, however, to vocal music.[33] He also had little praise for Schumann's last instrumental works. For him, the Third Symphony and especially the First Violin Sonata were full of musical oddities and artificialities to such an extent that he felt compelled to call Schumann a mannerist.[34]

The framework and terminology for a discussion of Schumann's music had thus changed considerably. In the late 1840s, the question was whether Schumann had yet arrived at the third stage of his career, prescribed by the Hegelian system for his artistic development; after 1850, the question was simply who was a greater composer, Schumann or Wagner. Because of the simplistic categories of judgment with which the journalists of the *NZfM* approached his music, Schumann lost both rounds in the journal's campaign to shape, steer, and make music history. There was, however, to be a third round.

[iv]

The relationship between Schumann and the journal he once headed became strained, to say the least. Not only Schumann but also many of his friends and associates must have been taken aback by what they saw happening in the journal.[35] Many of the musicians who had been regular contributors during Schumann's time had been replaced by correspondents who were firm in their partisanship for the Wagnerian cause. Wagner's and Liszt's names appeared in the list of contributors that was published semi-annually. With Uhlig's death the most vociferous and venomous author of the *NZfM* had been silenced, but Bülow, Raff, Pohl, Cornelius, and Dräseke joined the journal in the 1850s, all of them associated with Liszt's *Ecole de Weymar*. Authors of a different persuasion had trouble getting their contributions published in Brendel's journal during those years; from some letters that Friedrich Wieck wrote to Brendel we know that Wieck's attempt to publish some chapters of his book *Klavier und Gesang* in the *NZfM* failed.[36] Brendel was determined to stick to his course, even to broaden the base now by opening the journal to discussions of the music of Berlioz and Liszt, composers whom he would in 1859 unite with Wagner under the odd label *neudeutsche Schule,* or "modern German school."[37]

There must have been some pressure on Schumann by his friends and associates to step forward, publicly call a halt to the journal's direction, and serve as rallying point and catalyst for a counteroffensive. Although by and large he had abstained from music journalism since 1844, his judgment still carried enormous weight in the music world.[38] Schumann waited for many years but finally made his move in October 1853, with the "Neue Bahnen" article,[39] in which he hailed the twenty-year-old Johannes Brahms, a composer from Hamburg who had not yet published any of his works, as the new messiah of music. This wonderful letter of recommendation is familiar enough, but I would like to call attention to the context in which it was published. After almost four years in which the readers of the *NZfM* were subjected to the Wagnerian water-torture, Schumann's paean to Brahms on the front pages of the journal must have appeared like an exotic bird; a voice like this had not been heard for a long time. The hymnlike, visionary style of prose seemed to recall the early years of the journal when *Davidsbündler* fought their battles against the Philistines. With "Neue Bahnen" Schumann also vented his anger over the recent editorial policies in a manner that was at once reserved and feisty. As if the whole Wagnerian cult in the journal had never existed, he pronounced that the young aspiring artists and the relevant musical production of the era had found recognition thus far only in limited circles. In order to make sure that he was fully understood, Schumann added a footnote in which he listed the names of those composers he considered promising. The artists championed by the journal in recent years were not among them—a provocative omission, indeed. Even as late as the fall of 1853, Schumann was still a sharp-witted journalist who knew that silence could be a more effective weapon than a lengthy rebuttal.

The answer to Schumann's attack came just two months later. The New Year's Day address had been used by Brendel in the past for statements of a programmatic nature. Its author this time, however, was Richard Pohl, a proponent of Liszt and Berlioz, who wrote under the pen name "Hoplit" in the journal (appendix 7). Brendel wisely refrained from being in the front line of attack in the controversy with Schumann.[40] In 1854, there was an especially good occasion for celebration: the *NZfM* turned twenty, reason enough to survey past and present achievements and to look ahead. Pohl's essay was clearly addressed to Schumann and the Schumannians. He began by quoting at length from Schumann's 1835 prospectus and concluded that the journal had been and still was faithful to the principles espoused by its founder. The *NZfM* was on track, twenty years old but still eager to support the new. It was not the journal that had aged, but rather those former contributors who now looked on in dismay at its present direction, and Pohl wrote them off as "fearful, one-sided, selfish, and opportunistic." He claimed that they were replaced by other well-known artists and their followers, who exerted a powerful influence on art and "led it down new avenues [*neuen Bahnen zugeführt*]."[41] Thus, the new avenues of Wagner, Liszt, and Berlioz were clearly set against those which Schumann envisioned for Brahms. Schumann's and Pohl's exchange set the stage for an aesthetic controversy that was to dominate musical life in Germany for the remainder of the century.

It is futile to speculate on how the debate between the journal and its founder would have been continued if Schumann had not suffered a physical and mental breakdown a few weeks later. The general controversy, of course, continued with ever wider repercussions in the following decades; Schumann's illness and death, however, created a moment of pause and relaxation in the ongoing strife. The magnanimous Liszt himself stepped forward with a lengthy article on Schumann, published in March and April 1855,[42] which was meant as a conciliatory gesture, if not to the Schumannians, perhaps to the composer himself who occasionally received issues of the journal in his asylum in Endenich. Liszt had the highest praise for Schumann the critic (forgiving him, of course, a few slanderous remarks about Italian and French music, namely that of Meyerbeer) and claimed Schumann the composer, because of his early piano works, as a champion of program music; a judgment about the last phase of Schumann's compositional output, Liszt decided, had to wait until all unpublished works had seen the light of day. Brendel himself wrote the obituary for Schumann when it was all over (appendix 8),[43] and now he stated more forcefully than ever the admiration which—in spite of his support of Wagner—he still felt for his predecessor in the journal: "Schumann has accomplished things immortal and the history of art sees him as one of Beethoven's greatest successors."[44]

Appendix 1

From Franz Brendel, "Zur Einleitung," *NZfM* 22 (1845): 1–12.

[10] So far I have described the two principal types of music criticism and presented examples from art itself to illustrate the discussion and provide a firm foundation through concrete documents. I now want to summarize what I have said previously: For quite some time, criticism has failed to fulfill its higher mission. It has become wavering, insecure, and—because it lacked a firm standpoint—lost in contradictory notions. It still succeeded many times even later on in individual cases, but these were isolated achievements; it limited itself

to clear-cut chores such as reviewing the works of the day without [however] presenting a large general viewpoint. . . .

The first type of criticism dwelt on technical matters; the second presented psychological descriptions of impressions. The first maintained a certain universality [*Allgemeingültigkeit*]; it was objective, but the spirit contained in these technical discourses remained hidden to perception. The second mode was subjective and wavering but more ingenious. The first was inclined toward the rational, the second tended toward enthusiastic sentiment and, for that reason, reached increasingly greater inconsistencies in its pursuit and arrived at a chaos of completely subjective notions and opinions.

The unifying synthesis, the combination of both standpoints, could be named (preliminarily and in short) as a challenge posed by our time. The solution of this problem, a third standpoint, would have to preserve the search for content (which characterized the second method) and aim for the objectivity of the first: it would have to be based on both methods but comprise them as views that have been superseded.

[11] It is one of the principal trends of the present time to subsume the various disciplines under general viewpoints, to bring together the individual fields which lead a separate existence disconnected from the Universal and to consolidate them into one large entity. The separation of individual disciplines (where one knew nothing of the other) has reigned supreme in Germany in science and life for a long time and has had the most unfortunate results. . . .

Music criticism has not been able to move the musical artworks out of the narrow musical sphere and to explain them in a way that would make them understood by the general intelligence. If the great works of the past are to be accepted by the intellectual awareness of the nation, and if contemporary music is to move closer to its true significance, it is now necessary that all who are able to write about music join ranks in bridging the chasm that separates science, literature, and music.

The results of modern science, [i.e.] the great progress in aesthetics, must also benefit music, and an attempt ought to be made to talk about music in such a way that its contents are raised to the level of general awareness. We must aim to recognize the relative significance of every artistic phenomenon in order to ban those numerous subjective idiosyncrasies, likes and dislikes; we must aim to replace them with a notion that has the potential of universality [*Allgemeingültigkeit*].

Appendix 2

From Franz Brendel, "Robert Schumann mit Rücksicht auf Mendelssohn-Bartholdy und die Entwicklung der modernen Tonkunst überhaupt," *NZfM* 22 (1845): 63–67, 81–83, 89–92, 113–15, 121–23, 145–47, 149–50.

[114] Schumann begins [his career as a composer] in an original way; he is highly subjective, occasionally almost bizarre, and it appears at times as if he has written only for himself, and we merely witness the play of the artistic spirit with its own content in disregard of the outer world. Mendelssohn begins in an objective way, but does not always succeed in animating this aspect and therefore much [of his music] remains rather formal. He masters [musical] form at an early stage and shows the ability to express himself in concrete terms, whereas Schumann's work is characterized by an inner life searching for expression and to a lesser extent by clarity in representing ideas. *On the one hand, we find an all-embracing foundation with the past evolution of art as a background; on the other, we find no immedi-*

ately noticeable background, no past, but a wide perspective on the future: in short, the future of art as perspective. The development of both composers goes in opposite directions. *Mendelssohn goes from the outside to the inside: from what is generally approved and established to self-recognition and poetry. Schumann moves from the inside out: he begins with his original personality; therefore, the law of evolution for him is to reconcile this individuality with the established forms and genres and to conquer them gradually.*

[149] Mendelssohn . . . is a representative of classicism in our time; for that reason he is not an expression of the present time in its entirety, least of all of future trends. Schumann is forced to strive for his ideal, the ideal of a younger generation, and to struggle for its manifestation. He is not yet finished with it and his direction is not yet clearly worked out. Both artists are unsuited to establish a school, to attract a circle of younger talents. Mendelssohn's students would work for the future even less than the master . . . and, in accordance with the whole movement, would degenerate into superficiality and formalism. Schumann's students would lack the essential element that a greater predecessor could provide: secure and firm guidance toward a clearly recognized goal. Schumann has changed substantially in the course of his compositional activity; he has come close to the objectivity of the opposite movement, perhaps even unconsciously influenced by external factors and his residence in classical Leipzig. However, the question is whether he can reach fulfillment following this avenue.

Appendix 3

From Alfred Dörffel, "Für Orchester: Robert Schumann, op. 61. Zweite Symphonie für grosses Orchester," *NZfM* 28 (1848): 97–101.

[97] With this work the composer has reached a new highpoint of his creativity. . . . If we look back at the instrumental works of the master and compare the G-minor Sonata (Op. 22), the last large-scale work before he devoted himself to vocal music, with the First Symphony (Op. 38), the three String Quartets (Op. 41), and the Piano Quintet (Op. 44), then it is evident that the constructive ability of the composer has increased in the latter works and that his technical skills have evolved to a point at which they are no longer subordinated to the force of fantasy but on a par with it. The structural side prevails in the Piano Quartet (Op. 47); foreign influences join in and undermine the original creative power of the master. These influences have not disappeared in the Piano Concerto (Op. 54); both forces, the inventive and the constructive aspects, fight against each other; the work contains traces of the upheaval which the composer underwent through this struggle. At the same time, it also shows passages where the limitations imposed on his personality disappear, where he achieves an objectivity of expression that may be considered the general language of the human heart, the utterance of a universal life.

The master has not found this expression in all sections of the symphony under review and has not completely overcome his individuality in surrendering himself to the general, but he has come closer to this goal in a way that we must salute as the most positive proof of his continuing progress toward gaining the crown of laurels [*Palme des Lebens*]. . . .

[100] If somebody is chosen to create such a work that combines the greatness of both compositions [Mozart's *Jupiter* Symphony and Beethoven's Symphony No. 5], then it is Schumann; no other contemporary master has yet been a match for him. [101] . . . The symphony under consideration is its immediate predecessor, and the future, when it gives birth to such a work, will look back at this composition and assign it its proper position in history.

Appendix 4

From "Für Pianoforte zu vier Händen: R. Schumann, op. 61. Zweite Symphonie
. . . Vierhändiger Clavierauszug vom Componisten," *NZfM* 30 (1849): 187–88.

[187] The greatness of this composition has been repeatedly pointed out in this journal. It is the *principal* work of the present time, another milestone on the way which Beethoven prescribed through his last works. The deep content of these compositions also lives in this work [Schumann's Symphony]. Schumann was designated as the first to gain and cultivate the soil on which his great predecessor walked. Who is still inclined to doubt Schumann's genius! Does Schumann not gain ground in ever larger circles and do not those who are touched by his flight increase in number every day? Deny these facts, you who want to belittle the spirit of his works: you only reveal thereby your immaturity and nearsightedness! What Beethoven wanted and completed in the works of his last creative period— compositions which hold open a distant future for music—that has been expressed by nobody else but Schumann. What the former announced has been further elaborated by the latter. [188] The great drama of the Ninth Symphony with all its magnificent aspects appears here again. The more we became familiar with the work, the more we were overwhelmed by this truth.

Appendix 5

From [Eduard Krüger], "Musik für das Theater: Robert Schumann, op. 81, Genoveva . . . Clavierauszug von Clara Schumann," *NZfM* 34 (1851): 129–31, 141–44.

[129] With his latest work, Robert Schumann has entered a path, announced for some time, longed for by many an admirer, and feared by many of his friends. The longing to see the friend at his highpoint is met by the fear that he may have passed his prime. Without wanting to decide this (because a firm judgment among contemporaries is impossible), we join the latter group. The work at hand is not an intensification of the preceding compositions but a dimming of his genius. . . .
[144] *Brendel's* review . . . concurs in principle, almost literally, with what we have found through a different avenue. We began from a different base and, for the time being, refrain from speculation . . . but we realize that the function of a true opera has not been fulfilled here, nor does the work represent the germ of a future opera. We speak so openly out of respect for our friend whom we want to steer away from the wrong path and out of respect for the poor scorned audience which never gets what it bargained for with this opera.

Appendix 6

From T. U. [Theodor Uhlig], "Kammer- und Hausmusik: Robert Schumann, op. 98, Lieder, Gesänge und Requiem für Mignon aus Goethe's Wilhelm Meister," *NZfM* 35 (1851): 219–21.

[219] Schumann and his works have always been appreciated according to their merits in this journal and discussed in such detail that their redeeming qualities need not be empha-

sized anew at every occasion. For several years, however, the composer pursued a path which—disregarding a few zealous partisans—has not been able to gain special sympathies among the connoisseurs of music. By stating this openly, we only repeat what other critics before us have said, Prof. Bischoff and Dr. Krüger among others. Nevertheless, the compositions under review appear not entirely to be suited to a detailed discussion of Schumann's latest style and thus to an explanation of our lack of sympathy. We postpone such a discussion for another occasion, and state for the time being only that we consider Schumann's present method of composition a musical mannerism rather than a style.

[220] Only one person lives who equals Schumann in artistic disposition but who ranks higher since his talent is even more encompassing: this is *Wagner*. One is led to comparisons involuntarily, as soon as both artists compose for the same genre, for instance opera or simply vocal music. Such a comparison reveals to the scholar a peculiar difference with regard to the mutual relationship of text and tone, of poetry and music, and we want to conclude our remarks here by sketching out this difference.

In Wagner's works, the vocal melody and, along with the accompaniment, the whole music (as long as the orchestra does not refer to a gesture or an action) appear as if they have grown out of the word. In Schumann's works, [221] on the other hand, the music appears to be imposed on the word despite obvious intelligent efforts to do justice to individual expression also in the vocal melody. Being an absolute musician, Schumann is not able to conceive of music other than within certain forms which have evolved in absolute, i.e. instrumental, music and which he now transfers to his texts.

Appendix 7

From Hoplit [Richard Pohl], "Zur Eröffnung des zwanzigsten Jahrganges der Neuen Zeitschrift für Musik," *NZfM* 40 (1854): 1–3.

[2] This was *Schumann's* and the New Journal's creed *twenty years ago*. Has it changed today? Has the journal ceased to fight vigorously against *mediocrity* on the rise? Has it ever made concessions to the *ungifted,* to the *commonplace talents,* to the *pen-pushers?* Has it not dared to take a *stand,* to put forth a decisive program and to stand up for it consistently? Has it ever tired of opposing the bad and the detrimental—in short, *the enemies of progress?* Has it ever ceased to be proud and happy when it was able to elevate *the beautiful, the great and the fine in art* and to support it, even to praise it without limitations? Did it not grasp its function and fulfill it according to its powers, i.e., *to prepare a new and magnificent future and* [3] *and to help speed up its development?* If it has not done all this, then, and *only then, may the journal declare itself defeated. . . .*

A quick glance at the records, however, tells us that the journal has done what it *should* have done; it has done what it *could.* And the addition, *"fortieth volume,"* in today's title tells us that the applause of the public and the sympathy of the artists and friends of art alike have not been lacking. This supported our decisive striving and enabled us to pursue it consistently. . . .

If we survey the list of those men who founded the first volumes of the journal with their writings, we see that only a few have remained with the journal until today. Some have died or disappeared; others gave up criticism altogether or devoted themselves exclusively to the job of production. Still others are alive and write as they did before, but they are dead for this journal, *because they did not want to realize or support—as living creators—any longer what is living and full of life. . . .*

Nothing, as we see it, has been lost with all those because they are *fearful, one-sided, selfish and opportunistic.* They have been replaced by others, among them names of which we need not be ashamed, because all of Germany knows these names. They have had a powerful impact on art and led it down new avenues.

Appendix 8

"Todesfälle," *NZfM* 45 (1856): 72 (August 8).

Robert Schumann died on July 29 in Endenich near Bonn. His wife, Joachim, Brahms and Dietrich were present at his funeral. As irreplaceable and painful as the loss is and as saddening as the news is, it hardly comes as a surprise to anyone. In view of the nature of his illness and considering all that was known about his situation, there was little hope for improvement from the very beginning. We have provided news about his condition only extremely rarely and, when we did, talked about improvement which we hardly believed to be possible. Even when the first sad news about his illness became known, we only hinted at it for no other reason than that our journal was sent to him continuously and, thus, we had to be very careful. What art has lost with him we (who were the first in taking a stance in favor of Schumann's recognition) do not have to repeat here. Until his resignation from this journal he was mainly recognized as a belletrist. Now nearly the whole public is convinced of what only a few felt positive about when we took over: Schumann has accomplished things immortal and the history of art views him as one of Beethoven's greatest successors.

Compositional Process

Rufus Hallmark

A Sketch Leaf for Schumann's D-Minor Symphony

"Auch kleine Dinge können uns entzücken."

Hugo Wolf, *Italienisches Liederbuch*
nach Paul Heyse

In a now famous article, Douglas Johnson challenged the assumption explicit or implicit in many manuscript studies that such studies can produce analytical insights into a finished musical work.[1] Johnson argued that pertinent observations are to be made without the aid of preliminary versions. He did not proscribe the study of composers' manuscripts, as the British scholar Eric Sams did, as an invasion of "music's privacy,"[2] but he simply doubted the value of such research for anything other than what he calls "biographical" information.

In a recent paper partly responding to Johnson, Joseph Kerman took up a line of argument he has voiced before.[3] He questioned the narrowness of what Johnson seems to mean by analysis and pleaded that a broader "critical" understanding of a work of art should not be limited to objectifiable or quantifiable data about technique and structure. In his view, "criticism" is well served by manuscript studies as well as by other areas of inquiry presumably extraneous to the musical work in Johnson's positivistic view.

I am in accord with Kerman's less exclusive view of what constitutes valid criticism; but in terms of analysis in the narrower sense, the idealism of Johnson's position is appealing. A musician should be able to learn all he needs to know about a musical work from the finished score. As teachers and scholars we ought to communicate that our primary interest and concern lie with the completed work, not with its preliminary sketches—and certainly not with the methodology whereby we deal with the latter. The axiom of basing analysis on the completed work has a corollary: to be valid any analytical observation arrived at through manuscript study must be evident in the finished score. This is logical. The further implication, however, that we can or should dispense with manuscript studies in preparation for analysis seems to me, in purely practical terms, like the aristocrat's naïveté about the quotidian concerns of lower classes. Although Johnson admits that "none of us is [an] omniscient critic,"[4] he still leaves the impression that analytical ideas or approaches based on sketch studies are vaguely suspect, even if persuasive, presumably because one should have been able to discern the reported musical phenomena in the finished work.

In a recent article, Lewis Lockwood demonstrated from sketch evidence that the opening theme of Beethoven's *Eroica* Symphony began its life as an offspring of the *basso del tema* from the Op. 35 Piano Variations.[5] In other words, the theme of the first movement in conception was closely related to the theme of what was to become the finale. The two themes, even in the finished work, share the melodic outline 1̂–5̂–5̂–1̂; so the analytical observation, though derived from sketch study, is relevant to the finished work. For the same reason, it is not an insight one could have gained only through an examination of the sketches, but in this instance the insight did stem from the manuscript evidence. Johnson argued that manuscript evidence can do no better than confirm musical relations that are present in the score. But it is one thing simply to confirm one's own analytical insight and quite another when that confirmation is provided by the composer's demonstrable intention to create the musical feature observed.

On a much more modest scale, a sketch leaf for Schumann's D-minor Symphony has suggested to me some thematic relations in that symphony which have not been noted before. The fragmentary nature of the sketches and the absence of other preliminary manuscript materials by no means allow one to infer compositional procedure to the extent that the *Eroica* sketchbook does; the context of the Schumann sketch is unknown and can only be hypothetically posited. The sketch leaf has nevertheless proved useful in raising old and new analytical questions. It also furnishes another instance of Schumann's penchant for contrapuntal experimentation and preserves rejected versions of two of the symphony's main themes. In this essay I shall present the following information and interpretation: first, a description of the manuscript and its contents and an attempt to ascertain its date; second, a comparison of the sketches with the final version and an hypothesis about their place in the compositional procedure; and third, a discussion of the implications of the sketches for analysis.

[*i*]

Until now, no sketch materials for the Fourth Symphony have been identified and discussed. Full scores, autograph or partly autograph, are known for all of Schumann's symphonies (including one for each of the two versions of the D-minor Symphony).[6] Extensive sketches for the First and Third Symphonies have been examined and evaluated; they consist mainly of continuity drafts.[7] Sketches of a presumably similar nature for the Second Symphony are in private hands and await scholarly study.[8] A single page of fragmentary sketches for the first movement of the Fourth Symphony can now be added to this list.[9]

Three sketches appear on one side of a single leaf in the Bibliothèque Nationale, Paris.[10] The other side contains a vocal sketch for the song "Flügel, Flügel!" which became No. 8 of the Rückert Lieder, Op. 37. The manuscript is catalogued only under the song's title, doubtless the reason why the symphony sketches have gone unnoticed. The sketches (see plate 1) are transcribed in exx. 1–3. Sketch 1 contains on the upper staff the lyric theme from the middle of the first movement. It is in the key of its initial occurrence in the symphony, beginning in F major and moving to D minor. Beneath the theme, on the second staff, are two ideas: (1) an eighth-note figure based on the movement's main theme, the very figure that accompanies the lyric theme in the first finished version of the symphony, and (2) a nearly canonic imitating voice. Sketch 2 is another essay at combining the lyric theme with itself contrapuntally, this time beginning in C-sharp minor and lasting only four measures. Sketch 3 is a preliminary version of the main theme of the movement, which differs considerably in details of melody, harmony and articulation from the final version of the theme.

Though it is not self-evident and cannot be proved beyond a doubt, common sense tells us that these sketches were made during the composition of the symphony, that is, in 1841 for the first version, not as a revision sketch for the 1851 version. It will be noted, for example, that in meter or rhythmic values the sketches are closer to the 1841 version than to the better known revision (see ex. 4).[11] In both versions, the meter is 2/4 (not the C or ₵ of Sketches 1 and 2); but in the 1841 score the main theme is in eighths and the lyric theme in dotted halves and quarters. Proceeding, then, on the fairly safe assumption that these sketches were written in 1841, can we be any more precise about their dating and about their location within the chronology of composition?

From Schumann's *Haushaltsbuch* and from the 1841 autograph score as well as from Clara's diaries, we have a fairly detailed chronological overview of the composition of the D-minor Symphony.[12] On May 31, 1841, Clara reported; "Yesterday [Robert] again started a symphony, which is to consist of one movement, but will nevertheless contain an Adagio and a Finale. I have heard nothing about it yet but I see Robert's activity and once in a while hear the D minor wildly sounding in the distance, so that I know in advance it is again a work created from the depths of his soul [*es ist dies wieder ein Werk aus tiefster Seele geschaffen*]."[13] According to Schumann's *Haushaltsbuch*, it was not one, but two days before, on May 29, that he had had a *Gedankenabflug* for a symphony.[14] From the various dates in the autograph, we know that Schumann began the score on June 7. Two months later, in August, Schumann made further sketches, and at the end of the month he finished the score of the first movement.[15] If we accept that sketching would have been completed before Schumann began to score the first movement, then we can take June 7 as a *terminus ante quem* for the Paris sketches.

The vocal sketch on the other side of the page does not help significantly with the dating of the symphonic sketches. The complete drafts of this song and six others of the Rückert Lieder are found in the third of Schumann's *Liederbücher* in the Deutsche Staatsbibliothek, Berlin, DDR.[16] There the first song is dated January 4,

Ex. 1. Paris, Bibliothèque nationale, Mus. ms. 342; Schumann, D-Minor Symphony, Sketch 1

Ex. 2. Paris, Bibliothèque nationale, Mus. ms. 342; Schumann, D-Minor Symphony, Sketch 2

Ex. 3. Paris, Bibliothèque nationale, Mus. ms. 342; Schumann, D-Minor Symphony, Sketch 3

Ex. 4. Schumann, D-Minor Symphony, main and lyric themes (1841 and 1851 versions)

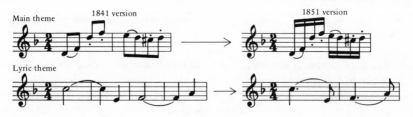

Plate 1. Paris, Bibliothèque Nationale, Mus. Ms. 342. (By permission of the Bibliothèque Nationale.)

1841. The vocal sketch in the Paris leaf resembles many other song sketches that preserve preliminary versions of the voice part and that precede the full drafts for voice and piano. In all likelihood, then, Schumann made the sketch of "Flügel, Flügel!" prior to January 4. The beginning of the year, however, is not a useful *terminus post quem* for the instrumental sketches on the other side since the reported sketching of the symphony did not begin for nearly another five months. About all one can say in this regard is that only after the page had served for the vocal sketch and was no longer needed for that purpose did Schumann use its blank side for his symphony sketches.[17]

The dating of the symphony's and of the song's origins, then, does not permit an exact dating of the sketch. We can infer only that the sketch was written after January 4 and before June 7, probably at the end of May. Thus from the external evidence we cannot learn how the sketch page relates to the composition of the symphony, and we must turn to interpretation.

[*ii*]

The third sketch contains a version of the main allegro theme that differs markedly from the final form. The melody in mm. 3, 4 and 7, the accompanying harmony (especially in m. 3), the articulation, and the string tremolo in the bass all make this sketch distinct from the theme in the finished work. The head motive (D–F–E–D–C-sharp–D) is already in place, but not the descent of the melody thereafter (see ex. 5). One might describe the evolution of the melody and the resulting effects as follows. The descending fourth in m. 3 of the sketch has been exchanged with the turning figure of m. 4. In the emended melody, the turn figure is now immediately repeated, and instead of a phrase structure of 2 + 2, the melody constitutes a four-measure unity. Now, too, the C-sharp is saved until m. 5 as the goal of the descending melody and at the same time the beginning of the rising line; the second phrase is thereby bound much more smoothly to the first.

As for the articulation, instead of Schumann's final decision to use a slur plus two dots throughout, the sketch often contains the reverse. A comparison of all the autograph sources—the sketch, the 1841 and 1851 scores—shows that the articulation underwent several changes, including two different versions within the 1841 score (see exx. 5a–c). From the straight eighth-note rhythm of the accompanying voices and from the reversed articulation after the midpoint, we can infer, perhaps, that when Schumann made this sketch, he had not yet conceived the motivic accompaniment rhythm of an eighth and two sixteenths that becomes so prominent later in the movement.

Sketch 3, then, appears to be simply an "idea sketch" for the D-minor melody that pervades the first movement as theme and as accompanying or articulating figure. It seems reasonable to conclude that it is a very early writing of this theme. But while Sketch 3 provides the basis for an interesting evolutionary study, the first two sketches are more provocative.

Schumann's interest in and study of counterpoint—especially canon and fugue—are well known. In his sketches and drafts of numerous works, Schumann often worked out fugal entrances of themes which he later rejected.[18] In her dissertation, Linda Roesner cites canonic passages in the continuity draft of the Third Symphony. In the first movement, where the main theme is repeated (from m. 57), Schumann originally wrote a canon at the unison; in the final version, we hear only an echo of this canon in the second phrase of the theme (from m. 62). He also planned a canon on the main theme of the second movement, but later abandoned it. As Roesner wrote, "The sketches for many of Schumann's works contain fugal or canonic trials in the margin or elsewhere that were not carried over into the final versions."[19]

In the Paris leaf we find canons or near-canonic imitations of the lyric theme which do not appear in the finished work. In Sketch 1, the theme is in the upper register and the imitating voice enters in the bass at a third (tenth) below; in Sketch 2, the theme appears in the bass, and the imitating voice begins at the second (ninth) above. From these two sketches, with their different registral presentations of the theme and different intervals of imitation, one can infer that Schumann may have been systematically trying out all the contrapuntal combinations of the theme.[20] Schumann would have quickly ascertained, either in his head or at the piano, that a canon on this theme would not be possible at most intervals; this would be clear from the first measure of imitation (see ex. 6). A canon at the unison or octave creates parallel fourths or fifths immediately (ex. 6a). A canon at the second below (or inverted at the seventh above) begins with a fourth and thereafter produces parallel perfect intervals (ex. 6b). Schumann would soon have discovered that a canon at the third below or sixth above—i.e., Sketch 1—would work until the third measure of imitation, where an exact canon would eventually lead to parallel octaves. So Schumann altered the imitating voice in its third measure (see ex. 6f). The only other interval at which the imitation can continue for more than a couple of notes is the second above or seventh below (ex. 6g). But when Schumann began to write out the canon at this interval—i.e., Sketch 2—he found that after three measures he would run into contrapuntal problems, and he stopped short.

The two sketches of the lyric theme differ also, of course, in their tonality. Sketch 1, as noted earlier, is in the key and sequential form of the final version. The tonal direction of Sketch 2 is less certain. It begins in C-sharp minor, but the chromatically altered notes and contrapuntal problems prevent us from being sure of its continuation, though we can postulate a goal of F-sharp minor. What is noteworthy, in contradistinction to Sketch 1, is that nowhere in the movement does the lyric theme occur in C-sharp minor. Schumann did not use this sketch merely to try out a canonic accompaniment for the entrance of the theme, but to try out the entrance itself, which he subsequently abandoned.

There is a passage where Schumann might well have considered using this theme in this key: as a transition between the two sequentially related halves of the "development" section, namely in place of mm. 171–74 (see ex. 7). After the lyric theme is stated once (mm. 147–54), a transition based on the figuration of the

Ex. 5. Schumann, D-Minor Symphony, main theme

a. Sketch

b. 1841 version

c. 1851 version

Ex. 6. Schumann, D-Minor Symphony; hypothetical canons on lyric theme

main theme moves us from D minor to A major by means of an augmented sixth chord to the dominant of the latter (mm. 155–58). A second cycle of the lyric theme follows (mm. 159–66), and then another transition, this time to G-sharp as the dominant of C-sharp (mm. 167–70). At this point, the three-stroke motive of the earlier D-flat theme (from mm. 121–46) combines with the main theme figuration, making a transition up a fourth from C-sharp to F-sharp (mm. 171–74). Following this, a solo trombone announces the beginning of the large-scale, transposed repetition of mm. 101–74. Sketch 2 might well have served in place of mm. 171–74 to make the connection between the large blocks of material. It would provide the culminating effect of a third, but considerably varied statement of the lyric theme and interrupt the regular four-bar phrase rhythm with a unit of five measures, if the imitating voice were completed.

This hypothetical function of Sketch 2 would explain its key and might suggest that the interval of the canon was chosen for a specific reason, not necessarily as a result of a systematic search by trial and error for possible contrapuntal combinations. Yet the two hypotheses are not mutually exclusive. Schumann could have recollected from his search that an imitation at the second above both would work and would bring about a tonal shift up a fourth (see ex. 6g).

We have yet to consider the eighth notes in Sketch 1. Whether or not the proximity of the two different themes on this one page was the impetus for the idea, it appears that it was at this sketching stage that Schumann conceived the lyric theme accompaniment figure based on the main D-minor theme. It is clear that he wrote this figuration after the canonic voice because the eighth notes of the former are squeezed in around the halves and quarters of the latter. There were, then, at least four different ideas for the presentation of the lyric theme: (1) the theme with a quasi-canonic bass line in the first layer of Sketch 1; (2) the theme with the canonic bass line and an accompaniment figure based on a motive from the main theme in the two layers of Sketch 1; (3) the theme with a revised, nonimitative bass line and the motivic accompaniment figure in the 1841 autograph score; and (4) the theme with the revised bass line and a neutral accompaniment figure in the final, 1851 version of the score.

To summarize: the Paris leaf contains a sketch for the main theme of the first movement of the D-minor Symphony which differs in many details from either of the final score versions, and yet bears the finishing touches of articulation. The leaf also includes a pair of sketches for the lyric theme. In these two sketches, the melody is in final form, but Schumann is experimenting with a canonic bass line and with an accompaniment figure and, in the second, with an additional and ultimately unused entry of the theme. These elements suggest that this sketch page served Schumann as scratch paper while he was writing his continuity draft. Such an adjunct working page is analogous to single leaves among the compositional materials of other works, but in other cases the continuity drafts to which such sketches correspond are preserved.[21]

Ex. 7. Schumann, D-Minor Symphony, reduction of development passage (with hypothetical use of Sketch 2)

[*iii*]

The order of the sketches on the page is intriguing in that the sketch of the main theme follows the sketches of the lyric theme. Without any corroborating evidence, of course, the order has no chronological significance. Schumann could have begun to write anywhere on the blank page, not necessarily on the uppermost staff. Roesner has persuasively used ink shades and pen nib size to distinguish various chronological layers.[22] If one could match the writing of Sketch 3 with the eighth notes of Sketch 1, one could show that Sketch 3 followed Sketch 1, since it is visually demonstrable that the eighth notes were written after the canonic voice. But one cannot distinguish different ink colors or pen thicknesses in these sketches.[23] Any attempt to ascertain the chronology of composition without further sketch materials is in vain.[24]

Regardless of the order of writing—which in any case would not prove the order of conception—the very appearance of these themes side by side is thought-provoking. There need be no particular reason for their proximity; it could be purely accidental. Yet the passing thought that Schumann might have conceived the themes the other way around—the lyric theme before the main theme—causes one to wonder afresh about their musical relationship. The sketch study prompts an analytical question.

Schumann's D-minor Symphony is, of course, a famous and standard instance of cyclical musical composition in the nineteenth century. The motivic relations within single movements and the thematic connections between movements have been remarked on since the first performance of the work. In most discussions, however (including Egon Voss's analysis in a recently published study score[25]), the lyric theme is regarded as essentially "new" and as related to the main theme only by virtue of sharing with it the turn figure. One published discussion goes so far as to declare that the two themes have five instead of just four notes in common,[26] but a miss is as good as a mile. The mention of the turn alone or even of five notes betrays the fact that neither analyst perceives the lyric theme *as a whole* to be present in the head motive of the main theme (see ex. 8). The main theme begins with a rising third and its repetition an octave higher followed by the turn; the lyric theme is a series of three rising thirds (the first inverted) that closes with a turn. The lyric theme thus is a melodic extension and rhythmic augmentation of the main theme's incipit.[27] The musical shape underlying the driving instrumental melody is transformed into the song-like tune.[28] The lyric theme, by virtue of this transformation, functions (i.e., is heard) as a strong musical contrast to the main theme, despite the motivic interrelation. Perhaps part of the reason Schumann eventually removed the motivic eighth-note accompaniment was in order to increase the contrast by relieving the movement momentarily of this otherwise pervasive figuration.

It is also frequently observed that the opening measures of the slow introduction have the five notes, F–E–D–C-sharp–D, in common with the main allegro theme. There is a less obvious but much fuller relation with the lyric theme. In outline, the first five measures of the symphony trace the same melodic curve as the lyric theme (see ex. 9); in fact, the pitches are identical to the second phrase of the lyric theme.

The sketch leaf reveals, it seems to me, another motivic relation. The interval of a minor sixth in the lyric theme, particularly as a harmonic interval in Sketch 2 (m. 2), is reminiscent of the transition figure played by the trombone (m. 103ff.), where the downward leap from F-sharp to B is followed by the rise of a minor sixth to G, which is harmonized by B a minor sixth below (see ex. 10). If one compares the trombone figure with the incipit of the lyric theme, one finds that both contain the same interval set—minor sixth, perfect fifth, and minor second—of which each theme is a different permutation. This is not to ascribe conscious proto-serial technique to Schumann,[29] but to acknowledge that present-day analytical methods may give us the conceptual framework and terminology with which to recognize and describe such a musical relationship.[30] The interrelation of these two ideas is clinched by their shared rhythm: the trombone figure is a simple augmentation of the dotted rhythm of the lyric theme. While the instrumentation of this figure and its function in the movement may be reminiscent of the trombone figure in Schubert's C-major Symphony,[31] it is nevertheless motivically related to the lyric theme of its own symphonic context.

Ex. 8. Schumann, D-Minor Symphony, main and lyric themes

Ex. 9. Schumann, D-Minor Symphony, Introduction

Ex. 10. Schumann, D-Minor Symphony, trombone theme and Sketch 2.

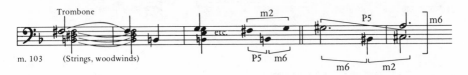

This perhaps makes more persuasive the contention that Schumann might have been considering Sketch 2 for the transition in mm. 171–74. The large-scale sequential repetition naturally begins with the trombone figure transposed from its model, and Sketch 2 would have provided not only the necessary tonal preparation but also a motivic harbinger of the trombone.

If one looks further, one finds that the other "new" theme of the so-called development section is also related to the lyric theme and trombone figure. The D-flat major theme shares with the others the dotted rhythm (in diminution in the D-flat theme), the melodic descent (bracketed in ex. 11), and the turn figure (intrinsic to the lyric theme and appended to the trombone figure and D-flat theme). These three themes, it should be noted, account for all the musical material of the "development" section, and all three share features that lie deeper than the foreground resemblances just mentioned. In each one, the tonic, dominant and subdominant chords (in different orders) are the primary harmonic ingredients, the descent through scale degrees $\hat{5}-\hat{4}-\hat{3}$ is prominent (either in the top voice or in the bass or both), and the mediant of the initial key is turned into the dominant of the key a minor third lower (see ex. 12). None of these features taken by itself would be suf-

Ex. 11. Schumann, D-Minor Symphony, development themes

Ex. 12. Schumann, D-Minor Symphony, development section, reduction

ficient cause to link these themes with one another at this level, but the presence of all the features in each theme seems (and sounds) significant. Is it possible that each half of the "development" section (mm. 103–76 and mm. 177–250) is a series of motivically interrelated yet highly contrasting transformations of an underlying melodic-harmonic model? From this vantage point, the question of the conceptual primacy of any particular theme seems less crucial than the common heritage of all.

This hypothesis has its problems, but it leads to the question one has about many apparently episodic compositions by Schumann (and other composers): what makes this order of events "right" and what holds it together? One can answer that the musical coherence in the present instance is due in part to a melodic line that runs through the three thematic areas. A continuous stepwise descent stretches from the B in m. 103 (in the bass) to the F-sharp in m. 175 (see exx. 12 and 7). Beginning in the bass at the trombone transition (mm. 103–21), the line moves to the upper register in the D-flat theme (mm. 121–34), into an inner voice for a moment in the latter half of this theme (mm. 134–46), and then once again to the top register in the lyric theme (mm. 147–75, ex. 7). This line recurs, a third higher, in mm. 177–250. Though not on the surface of the composition, this line is quite audible, and it acts as musical thread sewing the distinct episodes together.

[*iv*]

Douglas Johnson wrote, "I prefer to approach works from within."[32] So do I. But in numerous encounters with the D-minor Symphony "from within" I never noticed some of the relations to which the study of these sketches has led me. The sketch leaf does not by any means confirm these relations; it merely suggested to me the lines of investigation. The musical relationships themselves seem plausible and not at all remote in the finished work. If they are musically significant, I would be happy for them to be absorbed into broader analysis and criticism of the symphony and divorced from the sketches that engendered them, leaving the sketch study per se in the realm of the "biography" of Schumann's composition process in general and of the D-minor Symphony in particular.[33]

Linda Correll Roesner

The Sources for Schumann's Davidsbündlertänze, Op. 6: Composition, Textual Problems, and the Role of the Composer as Editor

On August 13, 1837, Clara Wieck gave a concert in the Saale der Buchhändlerbörse in Leipzig, the first time in two years that she had appeared publicly in that city.[1] Among the compositions she played were three of Robert Schumann's *Etudes Symphoniques,* Op. 13. Schumann was in the audience, and Clara's playing of his recently published work[2] was a declaration for him: since February 1836 the two had been completely cut off from one another, prohibited by Clara's overprotective father, Friedrich Wieck, from even exchanging letters. Later, Clara wrote to Schumann about her feelings on that day: "Hadn't you thought that I played that because I knew no other way to show you a little of my inner [feelings]? At home I was not allowed to do it, so I did it in public. Do you believe that my heart didn't tremble at that?"[3] Responding to Clara's gesture, Schumann proposed marriage in a letter dated the day of the concert, August 13. He asked Clara to consent to his intention to ask her father for her hand on September 13, Clara's eighteenth birthday.[4] Clara's affirmative reply is dated August 15—the name day of Eusebius.[5]

The second half of August through the beginning of September 1837 was thus a happy time for Schumann, and this happiness found expression in the composition of the *Davidsbündlertänze.* (He did not know, of course, that Wieck would reject him as a future son-in-law on September 13.)

Clara Wieck's association with the *Davidsbündlertänze* was musical as well as emotional. The first dance (Book I, No. 1) opens with a "Motto von C. W.," drawn from the first of the two mazurkas in Clara's *Soirées musicales,* her own Op. 6 (published in 1836).[6] Schumann reviewed Clara's Op. 6 in an article signed "Florestan und Eusebius" and dated September 12, 1837 (the day before Clara's birthday; the review appeared in the *Neue Zeitschrift für Musik* on September 15). Is it coincidence that Schumann's *Davidsbündlertänze*—the first edition originally published under the names Florestan and Eusebius[7]—should also have the opus number 6? When one considers that works Schumann composed and published several years earlier have higher opus numbers, it may not be too fanciful to suggest that Schumann, always attuned to lucky numbers, lucky days, mottos, ciphers, and the like,[8] and knowing that the opus number 6 was still available because of publishing irregularities, deliberately chose as a motto a theme from Clara Wieck's Op. 6 in order to form a union in yet another subtle way with his beloved.

The only surviving manuscript of the *Davidsbündlertänze* reflects several stages of the compositional process. The manuscript served as engraver's copy *(Stichvorlage)* for the first edition (Leipzig: Friese, January 1838),[9] yet it contains short sketches of a type that I shall call idea sketches (written-down improvisations); more extensive drafts, including one of a dance that Schumann never completed; and fragments of earlier finished versions of several dances that Schumann later revised and recopied. Actually, the manuscript as it survives today is really two manuscripts: an earlier one containing the sketches, drafts, and fragments in addition to some dances that were in sufficiently final form that they did not require revision and recopying; and a later manuscript, which Schumann intended as a fair copy. These two manuscripts-within-a-manuscript can be distinguished not only by the characteristics of the musical text that they transmit, but also by differences in paper. The earlier manuscript preserving the sketches and drafts survives only because of the finished dances it also contains. Originally this manuscript must have been more extensive than the present three leaves—a point to which I shall return. The fortunate circumstance that the earlier and later stages of the composition are on different papers also enables us to determine more precisely the chronology of the compositional process.

As a whole, the manuscript, in the Archive of the Gesellschaft der Musikfreunde in Vienna (Nachlass Brahms, MS A-281), consists of twenty-four pages in oblong format: ten individual leaves and one bifolio. It is unbound, and several leaves may be out of order. Schumann experimented with the order of the dances, and the present structure of the manuscript reflects this experimentation to a degree. The individual leaves give the impression of varying in size, color, and texture; several have been trimmed.[10] Close inspection of the paper and measurement of the staff lines, however, disclose only two papers: a 16-stave, medium weight, machine-made paper of a dirty cream color; and a 10-stave, coarse handmade paper, greenish light brown in color with prominent chain and laid lines but no watermark. The sketches, drafts, fragments, and several finished dances are on the machine-made paper, and this paper transmits the earlier stages of the composition. As the manuscript is presently structured, fols. 1–6 and 10–12 are handmade paper, fols. 7–9 machine-made paper. In addition, pieces of machine-made paper are pasted on to fols. 2v (hand paper) and 9r (machine paper). The structure and content of the manuscript are outlined in table 1.

The dates of composition for the *Davidsbündlertänze* cannot be precisely determined; but it is possible to arrive at a fairly accurate chronology with the aid of Schumann's correspondence, his entries in his diary, and evidence in the manuscript itself. Wolfgang Boetticher cites a retrospective entry in Schumann's *Tagebuch V* that lists the dates of composition of the *Davidsbündlertänze* as August 20

Table 1. Vienna, Gesellschaft der Musikfreunde, MS A-281

Fol.	Paper (Hand or Machine)	Contents ([　] = sketch, draft, or fragment)
1r	H	Title page
1v	H	I/9
2r	H	I/1, beginning
2v	H, M pasteover	I/1, conclusion; I/2 (on pasteover)
3r	H	I/3, beginning
3v	H	I/3, conclusion; [indications of placement (deleted) for "IV," "V," "VI"]; I/7, first section
4r	H	I/7, middle section (originally numbered "VIII"); I/8, beginning
4v	H	I/8, conclusion
5r	H	II/2; II/1, beginning
5v	H	II/1, conclusion
6r	H	II/3
6v	H	blank
7r	M	II/6; [beginning of unfinished dance in G minor, numbered "VI" (deleted)]
7v	M	[I/3, fragment (deleted)]; [I/6, sketch (deleted)]; II/5
8r	M	II/7; II/8, beginning
8v	M	[continuation of G-minor dance from fol. 7r (deleted)]
9r	M, M pasteover	II/8, conclusion (includes instruction to insert I/2 and, on the pasteover, the original coda of I/2)
9v	M	II/9; [II/1, sketch (deleted)]
10r	H	I/4
10v	H	I/5
⎧11r*	H	II/4, beginning
⎪11v	H	II/4, conclusion; I/6, beginning
⎨12r	H	I/6, continuation
⎩12v	H	I/6, conclusion

*Bifolio

to 31, 1837.[11] There are two dates in the manuscript: September 7 (crossed out) on fol. 5v (at the end of Book II, No. 1) and September 11 on fol. 3v (at the end of the first section of Book I, No. 7).[12] Significantly, both dates appear in conjunction with dances written on handmade paper, the paper representing the later, fair-copy stage of the manuscript. I suggest, therefore, that Schumann's diary entry refers to the sketching and drafting of Op. 6 from August 20 to the end of the month, and that the three leaves of machine-made paper (and the two pasteovers on machine paper) date from this time. The fair copy (handmade paper), then, dates from September and may have been progressing satisfactorily by September 11; on that day Schumann wrote to Walter von Goethe, the dedicatee, asking him to select the form in which he would like his name to appear on the title page.[13] The work in any event was finished by—perhaps on—September 21, as a letter Schumann wrote that day to Adolf Henselt suggests: "I have just written 18 *Davidsbündlertänze*— in the middle of my deeply agitated life. For that reason forgive me also for the bad scribbling."[14]

The sketches, drafts, fragments of dances, and complete dances on fols. 7–9 (machine-made paper) vividly reflect the way in which Schumann composed during the 1830s. He improvised at the piano, writing down ideas of various length as reminders. These idea sketches were then worked up into pieces or sections of pieces, often by linking the sketches together.[15]

The fifth system of fol. 9v contains an idea sketch for the first nine bars of Book II, No. 1 (see plate 1). Schumann has given it the number "V" and the caption "Balladenartig"[16] (this was changed to "Balladenmässig" in the fair copy, which appears on fol. 5r). The typical way in which the composer wrote down his idea sketches can be seen by the placement of the sketch on the page. He simply jotted down the sketch in the middle of what was then a blank page; the complete dance on the page, Book II, No. 9, continues around the sketch. The deleted Roman numeral, expression indication, and key and time signatures in the upper left-hand corner of the page ("X. Gemütlich," two sharps, 2/4) may indicate that Schumann originally intended to write on this page a full draft of Book I, No. 5. The caption and the key and time signatures fit this dance in its final manuscript form (in the first edition "Gemütlich" was changed to "Einfach"). An idea sketch for this piece exists on fol. 7v (plate 2). Here the sketch, marked "Leise," begins on the fourth system and continues on to the third system. This suggests either that the full draft of the dance at the bottom of the page (Book II, No. 5) was already present on the lowest four systems, forcing the composer to continue sketching Book I, No. 5, elsewhere, or that Schumann wrote down his improvisation of bar 17ff. of Book I, No. 5, the start of a chain of exquisite free variations (system three), before he noted down the theme as it appears at the beginning of the piece. The one possibility does not exclude the other, and either would be entirely characteristic of the young Schumann's compositional procedures.

Most, if not all, of the pieces in Op. 6 must have existed at one time in complete first drafts on the machine-made paper. Although fols. 7–9 are the only full pages of this paper remaining in the manuscript, two fragments of machine-made paper offer further clues about the original extent of the manuscript sources for Op. 6. Pasted over empty staves on the bottom of fol. 2v is a piece of the machine-made paper transmitting the text of Book I, No. 2. The verso of this pasteover contains bars 39–63 of a draft of Book I, No. 3. Because of the way in which the pasteover was cut, the lowest notes of bars 26–38 are also visible. Thus it is likely that a full draft of Book I, No. 3, existed on the machine paper. Furthermore, the last bar on the verso of the pasteover—bar 63 of Book I, No. 3—links up directly with bars 64–68, which appear on fol. 7v (see plate 2, system 1). This snippet of Book I, No. 3, at the top of fol. 7v is therefore not a sketch, but the continuation of the original complete draft of the piece. Schumann even considered using this draft as *Stichvorlage:* the instruction indicating a repeat of the beginning of the piece is ad-

Plate 1. Vienna, Gesellschaft der Musikfreunde, MS A-281, fol. 9v. (By permission of the Gesellschaft der Musikfreunde.)

Plate 2. Vienna, Gesellschaft der Musikfreunde, MS A-281, fol. 7v. (By permission of the Gesellschaft der Musikfreunde.)

Plate 3. Vienna, Gesellschaft der Musikfreunde, MS A-281, fol. 3v. (By permission of the Gesellschaft der Musikfreunde.)

Plate 4. Vienna, Gesellschaft der Musikfreunde, MS A-281, fol. 4r. (By permission of the Gesellschaft der Musikfreunde.)

dressed to an engraver ("Von A bis B auszustechen"; "to be engraved from A up to B"). Perhaps the composer's only reason for rewriting this dance on the handmade paper (on fol. 3r) was his decision not to recopy Book I, No. 2.[17] It appears to have been a relatively late decision, for Schumann had already begun to copy out Book I, No. 2, on fol. 2v. Its clefs, key and time signatures and expression indication ("Innig") were written on the page and are visible when the pasteover is lifted ("Innig" is visible even with the pasteover in place).

The verso of the pasteover on fol. 9r gives yet another indication of the scope of the earlier draft manuscript on the machine-made paper. It contains the beginning (bars 1–37) of the first piece of Book I with the caption "Motto von Clara Wieck" (in the fair copy on the handmade paper Schumann crossed out Clara's name and left only her initials).

The presence of large, fully drafted segments of Book I, Nos. 1 and 3, on the versos of the two pasteovers of machine paper; the six complete pieces on the machine paper in the manuscript (Book II, Nos. 5–9, and Book I, No. 2, the latter on the pasteover); and the sketches on the machine-made paper for three dances that appear in fair copy on the handmade paper (Book I, Nos. 5 and 6, and Book II, No. 1) suggest several conclusions about this earlier manuscript of the *Davidsbündlertänze*. First, it was originally much more extensive, presumably containing full drafts of all the pieces published in Op. 6 (the three extant leaves also contain a lengthy, though incomplete, draft of a dance that was not published).[18] And second, the manuscript probably also contained more sketches.[19]

[i]

Schumann experimented with the order of the dances in Op. 6. However, there is insufficient evidence in the manuscript as it exists today to detect how many changes in ordering there were, or even if there were several distinct stages. It is perhaps more accurate to say that the sequence of dances was in a state of flux until Schumann decided on the order as we know it. Certainly in the early stages of composition (on machine-made paper) the dances—both sketches and full drafts—were written down without consideration of order, in places where there happened to be space on the paper. Apparently Schumann had only a vague sense of the sequence the dances were ultimately to take while he was sketching them. This we can see from the few Roman numerals recorded in conjunction with this stage of composition: the dance that eventually became Book II, No. 1, is numbered "V" in the sketch, and the eventual Book I, No. 5, is numbered "X"[20] (in the later, fair copy on handmade paper this dance was at first numbered "VII"). When Schumann rewrote many of the dances in fair copy on the handmade paper, he did not initially number most of them at all. He added the numbers—almost always the final ones—during a late pass through the manuscript before submitting it for publication. (Inks can be unequivocally differentiated in this manuscript only in the case of some of these Roman numerals.) That the sequence of dances, particularly for Book II, was not clearly fixed in Schumann's mind until late in the compositional process can also be inferred from the fact that these dances, even those in fair copy on the handmade paper, appear on the pages in a sequence that only approximates their final order, and even this approximation of order may have been achieved by shuffling the pages around.

There is evidence, however, to suggest that Schumann began his fair copy on the handmade paper as a conscious fair copy with the dances in a definite order, one somewhat different from that of the published sequence. On fols. 2 and 3, Book I, Nos. 1–3 are in final order in fair copy, and the numbers of the dances were written at the same time as the musical text—at least this is true for Book I, Nos. 1 and 3. Book I, No. 2, as may be recalled, is the original full draft on machine-made paper pasted into position on the bottom of fol. 2v (but even here Schumann wrote the Roman numeral, expression indication, clefs, and key and time signatures on the main paper before pasting the insert into place). Schumann's next step in preparing this intended fair copy was to show by means of instructions for placement that three dances, IV, V, and VI, were to be inserted. Folio 3v (plate 3) contains these Roman numerals indicating placement, in one instance the expression marking "Zart" and a key and a time signature, and the directions "siehe Beilage," "siehe Beilage," and "siehe den Anfang auf der Beilage. Dann geht es weiter" ("see addendum" and "see the beginning on the addendum. Then it [the piece] continues"). The *Beilage* to which Schumann refers is fol. 7 of the manuscript, one of the leaves of machine-made paper containing full drafts of pieces that he did not intend to write out again. The dance on the lower half of fol. 7v (plate 2; fol. 7v was in all probability originally the recto side of a leaf) eventually became Book II, No. 5, but one can observe its original Roman numeral, "IV," crossed out. Since the other side of this leaf contains a dance originally numbered "V" and the beginning of a dance originally numbered "VI," we may conclude that the *Beilage* Schumann mentions on fol. 3v is indeed fol. 7. The dance at the top of what is now fol. 7r eventually became Book II, No. 6. The beginning of a dance at the bottom of the page with the number "VI," however, was not incorporated into the final form of the *Davidsbündlertänze*. On fol. 3v, Schumann's indications of the placement for this dance read "siehe den Anfang auf der Beilage. Dann geht es weiter." The piece continues on what is now fol. 8v (originally, I believe, a recto side), but Schumann never completed this dance, even though his inclusion of it in his conscious fair copy indicates that at one stage he fully intended to use it. This G-minor dance (ex. 1) is the only one to make overt use of the Clara Wieck motto of Book I, No. 1, here combined with the melodic and rhythmic patterns of Book I, No. 3. The harmonic progressions at the beginning of this dance are particularly striking and have some parallels with those of Book I, No. 1, especially in the move from G minor to B major (here notated as C-flat).

Slight differences in the inks and in the ways in which Schumann wrote the Roman numerals (e.g., "Nro. VII" instead of merely "VII") suggest that after these dances ("IV," "V," and "VI") Schumann temporarily omitted the numerals from

Ex. 1. Vienna, Gesellschaft der Musikfreunde, MS A-281, fol. 7r; fol. 8v. Schumann, Op. 6

(continued)

Ex. 1 (continued)

the dances that he wrote out in fair copy—probably because he realized that he would want to make changes in sequence. Therefore, to comment in hindsight on the effect of this early order of the first six dances on the tonal and aesthetic balance of the cycle as a whole would be inappropriate. We can observe, however, that when Schumann began his fair copy, he had a firm order in mind, even though this order soon broke down.

Schumann's fair copy also contains, on fol. 4r (plate 4), a dance in A-flat major that later became the middle section of Book I, No. 7. When the composer numbered this dance, in what I believe to have been a relatively late pass through the manuscript to fix the sequence of dances, he gave it the number "VIII." As can be seen in plate 4, the ordering "Nro. VIII (im ersten Heft)" is crossed out, and Schumann has added the instruction "NB. Dies Stück ist unmittelbar an Nro. VII im 1sten Heft anzuschliessen" ("NB. This piece is to be joined directly to No. VII in Book I"). The question of just when the composer decided to join the two dances remains open. On the one hand, the physical appearance of fol. 4r suggests that the decision may have been made while Schumann was numbering these dances: the dance at the bottom of the page bears only the Roman numeral "VIII" (it was not changed to "VIII" from "IX"). On the other hand, presumably later still, Schumann listed in Arabic numerals the correct sequence of dances on the title page as an aid for the engraver. Here the A-flat-major dance still appeared as No. 8, the C-minor dance (No. 8 in the final order) as No. 9, and the C-major dance (No. 9 in the final order) as No. 10. The listing of the A-flat-major dance is crossed out and the "9" in front of the C-minor dance converted into an "8." The C-major dance was inadvertently left as No. 10.[21]

Experimentation with the order of pieces in cycles of short pieces or in sets of variations was apparently Schumann's *modus operandi*. It is a continuation of a process of selection and refinement that began with the earliest sketches. Wolfgang Boetticher, for example, has amassed data indicating that the cycle *Papillons*, Op. 2, gradually emerged out of an enormous complex of sketches. Many of these sketches bear indications of order that have no relationship to the finished work.[22] I have shown elsewhere that the variation movement of the F-minor Piano Sonata, Op. 14, underwent several changes and projected changes in the order and number of the variations.[23] Many other examples of changes in the order of pieces could be mentioned.[24] Schumann's reluctance, therefore, to settle on a final order of dances in Op. 6 until very late in the compositional process is not unusual and must be viewed as an essential step in the composer's creative process. Only by constant thought and experimentation with the individual pieces could he ultimately arrive at an aesthetically "correct" sequence of tonalities, moods, and emotions.[25] It is worth emphasizing, especially since we now tend to attach much importance to a composer's choice of tonal plan, that Schumann did not have a firm tonal scheme in mind at the outset. This practice of waiting until the individual pieces were finished in order to assemble them into a final order has an analogue in Schumann's composition of his early works in large forms, the piano sonatas. Here substitutions and movings about of blocks of material, often with considerable effect on the tonal scheme and tonal balance of a movement, were made in otherwise complete drafts.[26]

[*ii*]

Although the Op. 6 autograph contains no engraver's markings, there can be little doubt that it served as engraver's copy for the first edition, which was published by Robert Friese in Leipzig in January 1838.[27] Throughout the manuscript there are instructions in Schumann's hand addressed to an engraver *(Stecher)* rather than to a copyist *(Schreiber)*, and several unusual engraving errors in the first edition can be traced to ambiguities in the manuscript.[28] Nevertheless, comparison of the manuscript and first edition reveals an astonishing number of changes in the expression marks, a term that I shall use to include everything but notes (i.e., all dynamic markings, accents, phrasing slurs, pedallings, captions, and so forth). These modifications involve more than two thirds of the measures in the entire cycle. Unless one is willing to accept the remote possibility of a lost manuscript—copy or autograph—that may have served as *Stichvorlage*,[29] one must conclude that these changes were made in proof.

I believe we are dealing here with an extreme case that nonetheless reflects Schumann's standard procedure in the 1830s and early 1840s in readying a work for publication. The Op. 6 manuscript, because of its dual nature as preliminary draft and fair copy, precipitated an unusually great number of changes in expression marks. But I should like to argue that Schumann not only habitually made changes in proof, as is well known,[30] but also often postponed a final decision about the placement of expression marks until very late in the process of finalizing a work.

The best evidence for this postponement is offered by the small but significant number of autographs dating from the late 1830s and early 1840s that Schumann submitted to copyists. In these manuscripts the composer directed that the copyist leave out all of the expression marks and copy only the notes.[31] Several of these copyists' manuscripts are extant, and the expression marks are indeed in Schumann's hand—not in the hand of the copyist.[32] Differences in ink shades between the notes and the expression marks in some of the autograph fair copies dating from the 1830s[33] may be another indication of Schumann's postponement of determining the expression marks. (In sketches, drafts and other "less finished" manuscripts of the same period, the notes and the expression marks are in the same shade of ink.[34])

I would like to suggest tentatively, therefore, that it was Schumann's reluctance to make final decisions about phrasing, dynamics, and so forth—and not solely a striving for accuracy—that prompted the composer in his early years to add expression marks last to many manuscripts intended to serve as *Stichvorlagen*. Moreover, the many changes in details of expression that one encounters between the various stages of composition in the works of the 1830s and early 1840s may be attributable to the possibility that Schumann continually "heard" the details differently.

Example 2 shows the phrasing in bars 1–16 of the right-hand part of Op. 6, Book I, No. 5, as it appears in the sketch (Vienna, Gesellschaft der Musikfreunde, MS A-281, fol. 7v), the autograph *Stichvorlage* (MS A-281, fol. 10v), and the first edition. Schumann's phrasings of this passage show not only progressive refinement from the four-bar units of the sketch, but also several fundamental differences between the *Stichvorlage* and the first edition, most notably the extension of the slur into the first beat of bars 3 and 7 in the *Stichvorlage*, and the different ways in which bars 9–12 and 13–16 are articulated in the *Stichvorlage* and the first edition. The articulation of bars 9–16 is especially interesting from a textual-critical point of view, because when the passage returns at the end of the dance (bars 49–56), the first edition has the reading of the *Stichvorlage* in bars 9–16. In the *Stichvorlage* the recurrence of the beginning of the dance (bars 41–56) is not written out; instead Schumann indicated that bars 1–16 be repeated. Evidently the composer changed in proof the phrasing of the first eight bars of the passage in both places where it occurs; but in the concluding eight bars of the period, although he changed the first statement (bars 9–16), he neglected to make the corresponding

Ex. 2. Schumann, Op. 6, Book 1, No. 5, mm. 1-16, right hand

changes in the second (bars 49–56). As we shall see, the same type of inconsistency appears in several of the dances of Op. 6.

The fragments that remain in the Op. 6 autograph of the complete first drafts of Book I, Nos. 1 and 3 (on the versos of the two pasteovers), also differ in many details (e.g., phrasing, accents, and dynamics) from both the *Stichvorlage* and the first edition. In addition, the fragment containing bars 1–37 of Book I, No. 1, includes numerous precise pedalling indications. In the *Stichvorlage* and the first edition Schumann indicated the use of the pedal simply by inserting the word "Pedale" at the beginning of the piece.[35]

Perhaps the hypothesis that Schumann heard the expressive details differently at different times is best tested by comparing two "souvenir" or autograph-album leaves with the published versions of the musical texts they transmit. An *Albumblatt* of "Des Abends" (No. 1 of the *Fantasiestücke*, Op. 12), written out by Schumann on August 18, 1837 and inscribed to his friend Ernst Adolf Becker, pre-dates the first edition by six months.[36] This early version of "Des Abends" not only contains more complete phrase markings than either the *Stichvorlage*[37] or the first edition[38] (bars 5–16 and 43–54 are unphrased in both later sources),[39] but also contains accents on the first beat of the right hand in bars 12, 33, and 50—accents that are present in the *Stichvorlage* but not in the first edition.

Another *Albumblatt* presents the opening section of Op. 6, Book I, No. 7,[40] and was written in the album of the Viennese collector Aloys Fuchs on November 8, 1838, ten months after the publication of the first edition. The details of expression in this manuscript differ in almost every bar from the *Stichvorlage* and the first edition (which also differ from each other, although not as radically). Example 3 shows bars 13–20 as they appear in the *Albumblatt* and the first edition. Of particular interest is the absence of the arpeggiation (*Albumblatt*, bars 13, 17–18); indeed, in the *Albumblatt* this melody is never arpeggiated as it is in the first edition (and its *Stichvorlage*), but instead it is marked with staccato dots within a slur. Also of interest are the changes in dynamics in the *Albumblatt* (bars 13–14, 18–20), the added *tenuto* (bar 14), the added accents (bar 16), and the changes in articulation (bars 16, 19–20). To be sure, it would be unrealistic to expect that during his visit to Vienna in November 1838—more than a year after the composition of Op. 6 and ten months after its publication—Schumann would write out a piece in Aloys Fuchs's autograph album accurately incorporating every detail of its published form. But the particular value of this *Albumblatt* lies in the evidence it supplies that in remembering his piece, Schumann "reheard" its details, and in effect reinterpreted the music.

Earlier I implied that one reason for the great number of changes in expression marks between Schumann's autograph *Stichvorlage* for Op. 6 and the first edition might be the fact that the manuscript is an assemblage of original working drafts and recopied dances. Such a manuscript, brought together relatively quickly, would not have provided Schumann with the time to reflect on the details of expression that he might have had under other circumstances.[41] There is also evidence to suggest that the engraving of Op. 6 began almost immediately upon the completion of the dances. In a letter of October 6, 1837, to E. A. Becker, Clara Wieck mentions that "Schumann has written a series of waltzes, which are now being printed."[42] Thus, Schumann's first real opportunity to rethink (and perhaps rehear) the details of Op. 6 would have coincided with his correction of the first proofs—a task undertaken, according to Schumann's entry in his diary, on October 13 and 14, 1837:

[October 13] Read proof on the *Davidsbündlertänze* for Friese . . .

[October 14] On the 14th (Saturday) got up cheerfully. Read proof on the *Davidsbündlertänze* all morning—then sent them to Clara with an open letter—[43]

Ex. 3. Schumann, Op. 6, Book 1, No. 7, mm. 13-20

The swift progression of Op. 6 toward publication may also account for the many inconsistencies in the expression marks within the first edition itself. The nature of these inconsistencies argues against attributing them solely to Schumann's rethinking or rehearing of details. Haste and a certain amount of carelessness on the composer's part, coupled with apparent inexperience on the part of the engraver,[44] must also have played a role.

Example 4 shows the first eight bars of Book I, No. 3, and their repeat later in the dance. In the *Stichvorlage* for the first edition the passage is written out only once; bars 69–76 are indicated with a written instruction to repeat bars 1–8. Both passages in the first edition (bars 1–8 and 69–76), therefore, were engraved from the one model. A comparison of bars 1–8 of the first edition with the *Stichvorlage* reveals the changes Schumann made in proof: revisions in details of expression, and corrections of apparent oversights in the *Stichvorlage*. In bar 4, for example, the articulation was altered, and in bar 8 the chord in the right-hand part was held for three beats. Both revisions appear to be examples of the rehearing or rethinking of details. The added slur in the right-hand part in bar 6 is an example of the rectification of an obvious oversight in the *Stichvorlage*, as is the addition of a staccato dot to the first beat in the left-hand part in bar 5. Measures 1–8 of the first edition thus appear to have been gone over thoughtfully in proof.

The parallel passage (bars 69–76), on the other hand, not only contains omissions on the part of the engraver that remained uncorrected (staccato dots in bars 3, 5, and 7; slurs in bar 6 of Ex. 4), but also reverts in two places to the reading of the *Stichvorlage*—after Schumann had changed the reading in the first statement of the passage (see the phrasing in bar 4 and the quarter rest on the last beat of bar 8 of ex. 4).[45] Bars 69–76 of the first edition also reveal new additions and alterations in the expression marks, nuances that Schumann had not included in bars 1–8. For example, crescendos have been added for the left hand in bars 1 and 5 of ex. 4. Also, the *forte* markings in bars 7 and 8 have been moved from below the left-hand staff to between the staves, presumably so that they would be perceived to be applicable to both hands. Separate (and often different) dynamic markings for the two hands are frequently a feature of Schumann's piano writing,[46] and perhaps one can posit that in reading through his composition Schumann felt the necessity for the intensified dynamic markings in bars 69–76. But when these modifications are coupled with the reversion of some of the phrasings to the reading of the *Stichvorlage* (after they had previously been changed), and also with Schumann's failure to correct obvious engraver's errors, we cannot easily escape the conclusion that Schumann did not so much read proof *against* an exemplar as read *through* his work in a creative way, rehearing the details as he went along. (Perhaps in reading through bars 69–76 he became so concerned with intensifying the dynamics that he totally neglected the other details of expression. In any event, the nature of the oversights suggests that carelessness also played a role.)[47] Such a view may seem antithetical to the commonly accepted image of the composer as a meticulous reader of proof,[48] and my intention is not to imply that Schumann was a poor proofreader; in the first editions I have examined, engraver's errors involving pitches are rare, and the composer's correspondence with his publishers shows his concern for achieving the best possible reproduction of his works.[49] But I would like to suggest that owing to the haste in which it was published, Op. 6 contains more traces in its printed form of the rethinking and rehearing of details—a process that in other works of the period was largely carried out over a longer period of time prior to publication. I would also like to suggest that consistency per se in the placement of expression marks in parallel passages was not something with which Schumann was overly concerned.

Remarking on the inconsistencies in the phrasing of parallel passages in Schumann's early piano music, Boetticher maintains that the different phrasings are de-

Ex. 4. Schumann, Op. 6, Book 1, No. 3, mm. 1-8 (69-76)

Stichvorlage for first ed., mm. 1-8 and 69-76

First ed., mm. 1-8

First ed., mm. 69-76

(continued)

Ex. 4 (continued)

Stichvorlage for second ed., mm. 1-8

Second ed., mm. 1-8

(continued)

Ex. 4 (continued)

Stichvorlage for second ed., mm. 69-76

Second ed., mm. 69-76

liberate.[50] But in parallel passages not marked as repeats, might not these differences be attributable more to casual reinterpretation than to calculated deliberation? With regard to exact repeats written out only once in the *Stichvorlage*, Boetticher's contention that the differences are intentional seems forced. In the first edition of Op. 6 every repeat so indicated displays differences in the phrasing and other expression marks when compared with the first appearance of the material. In all instances the second time the passage occurs, it contains many of the expressive details found in the *Stichvorlage* that Schumann had changed in the initial occurrence of the passage in the first edition. (See, for example, the discussion of ex. 2 above. Other examples include repeats in Book I, Nos. 6 and 7, and Book II, Nos. 7 and 8.)[51] In 1850, when Schumann went through the first edition with a critical eye before the appearance of the second edition, he regularized many of the discrepancies in the repeats. (See, for example, the four lowest lines of ex. 4. The *Stichvorlage* for the "Zweite Auflage" [Hamburg, Leipzig and New York: Schuberth, 1850/51; this edition used the plates of the first edition with some emendations] is a copy of the first edition now in the Gesellschaft der Musikfreunde, Vienna, with Schumann's corrections marked in pencil.)[52] Perhaps it might be argued that in later years Schumann paid more attention to inconsistencies, but the sources for the late works do not always bear this out. For example, both the autograph *Stichvorlage* and the first edition of the score of the E-flat-major Symphony (Op. 97, 1850; Bonn: Simrock, 1851) frequently display inconsistencies in the phrasing of parallel passages, some of which were indicated as repeats in the *Stichvorlage*.

A proper assessment of Schumann as editor of his own music will not be possible until the sources for a large number of works—from all periods of the composer's life—can be studied from this perspective. In particular, we need to learn more about the editorial standards of the era, the number and types of corrections and changes that were feasible to make, and so forth. The circumstances of publication vary from work to work, and this factor must also be taken into consideration.

The circumstances of publication of the first edition of Op. 6, for example, have never been adequately explained.[53] Why did Schumann give this work to Friese for publication so shortly after he had written it, and why did he give it to Friese rather than to a music publisher? Robert Friese had taken over the publication of Schumann's journal, the *Neue Zeitschrift für Musik*, in July 1837. Although he was not a music publisher, he undoubtedly had an interest in music and had in fact three years earlier published Schumann's *Allegro*, Op. 8.[54] Apparently Friese intended to become more active in music publishing, for according to Schumann's letters to W. H. Rieffel of July 24, 1837 and to Adolf Henselt of August 17, 1837, the idea of publishing musical supplements to the *Neue Zeitschrift* was Friese's.[55] Perhaps Friese solicited a work from Schumann to extend a friendly gesture toward his new editor and to give himself an opportunity to publish a work of music prior to the *Neue Zeitschrift* supplements, which began to appear in January 1838. This might explain the swiftness with which the *Davidsbündlertänze* went to press.[56] Unfortunately, most of the correspondence between Schumann and Friese has been lost,[57] and in any event, much of their communication must have been carried out in person.[58] A handwritten copy of a letter dated January 23, 1838 from Friese to Schumann survives, however, in the Robert-Schumann-Haus, Zwickau. It concerns the appearance in print of the first edition of Op. 6 and is interesting as a document of Friese's obvious esteem for Schumann:

My dear Editor!
The *Davidsbündlertänze* are finished [and] among other things delivered to those who ordered them. I hope that I as armorbearer of the king with the golden harp have looked after my affairs *well* and that the psalter of my David will float like an eternal tone around the sphere of Mother Earth, until it attains the historical age of the original singer David.[59]

Friedhelm Krummacher

Mendelssohn's Late Chamber Music: Some Autograph Sources Recovered

Recent biographical studies have shown that Felix Mendelssohn was not the *Glückskind* he has long been considered. Discussions of his music have proven convincingly the image of him as a mere imitator to be without foundation.[1] Still, we must recognize that there are those who question to this day Mendelssohn's significance in the history of music, and we must also recognize that their doubts will not be dispelled if we simply ignore them. We can refute these doubts, however, through a thorough and detailed analysis of the music itself, aided and enriched by an examination of the composer's sketches and autograph scores. These sources serve several functions: they can document the composer's creative process, give us new insight into the composer's intentions, and reveal the problems he encountered in his attempts to realize those intentions. Finally, they can help us make an aesthetic interpretation of the works themselves.

Even if we disregarded the autograph sources, analysis of the music would show quite clearly that Mendelssohn's compositional technique became increasingly subtle and complex in his later life. But the autographs help us to appreciate just how painstakingly and laboriously he struggled to achieve this heightened degree of subtlety and complexity. Previous investigations of Mendelssohn's autographs have concerned themselves primarily with the compositional evolution of the early and middle-period works.[2] The late works, for the most part, have remained unexamined, especially those works whose autograph sources are missing from the *Nachlass* housed in the Deutsche Staatsbibliothek and the Staatsbibliothek Preussischer Kulturbesitz in Berlin. We find these missing sources for Mendelssohn's late works among the volumes currently housed in the Biblioteka Jagiellońska in Kraków.[3]

Of all the questions these rediscovered sources might answer, the most important would seem to revolve around those works from Mendelssohn's last years published only posthumously. For we can—and must—ask whether Mendelssohn simply did not complete these works, or whether he intentionally withheld them from publication. For those compositions lacking authentic editions, the autographs take on even greater importance when we evaluate the posthumous editions. The question, then, is this: to what extent were these late works authorized by Mendelssohn?

My remarks will be confined to Opp. 80, 81, and 87, which as Mendelssohn's last chamber works are of special interest. The sources for the Piano Trio, Op. 66, and the Cello Sonatas, Opp. 45 and 58, are not available, as these works were already missing from Mendelssohn's original *Nachlass* of manuscripts. In any case, the composer supervised their first publication.

But before we investigate specific details in these late autographs, we should recall several premises that apply to Mendelssohn's compositional process. Otherwise, any description of the autographs runs the risk of becoming mired in a series of isolated details. If an examination of the autograph sources is to provide any new insight into the works, we must not lose sight of several historical and aesthetic considerations.

[i.] *The Historical and Aesthetic Premises*

In 1857, Karl Reinhold von Koestlin defined the aesthetic of chamber music—specifically, chamber music for strings—with the following words: "From the harmony of stringed instruments, we should not expect the full richness of life to unfold before us; nor should we expect an exciting fullness and variety of sound. Rather, we should expect a skillful intertwining of voices." Insofar as chamber music is "the most intellectual genre," it leads us "out of the noise and chaos of everyday life into the still and shadowy region of ideals, . . . into a world of the spirit liberated from the senses." It is "an intellectual music of the purest art" that does not resort to a "titillation of the senses." But because its essence is so spiritual, its content must be far richer than that found in other kinds of music. "The rich content of chamber music must compensate for its lack of external fullness and power. It is a dialogue of the (absolute) spirit with itself."[4]

The metaphysical demands of chamber music could scarcely be formulated more clearly. What Koestlin describes is a late and radical manifestation of an aesthetic idea promulgated in German Idealism since the time of Hegel. The concept of music as an autonomous art is crucial to this idea. Carl Dahlhaus has defined it as the "idea of an absolute music."[5] Even though Koestlin was writing after Mendelssohn's death, his text summarizes the ideas that dominated German music in the nineteenth century. And Koestlin, who was very close to Mendelssohn personally, considered his friend's works to be the last installment in the canon of works worthy of judgment.

The aesthetic paradigms had changed considerably since the Enlightenment. The long-undisputed supremacy of vocal music had been replaced by the new supremacy of instrumental music, now deemed the most potent medium in which music could demonstrate its artistic power. Vocal music remained bound to a text and was hindered by an inescapable obligation to that text.[6] But instrumental music, although freed from the external constraints of a text, made new demands of its own. If not linked to a text, how was it to be understood? As instrumental music came to be viewed more and more as an autonomous art, it became increasingly threatened by what Hegel called the loss of a comprehensible content. The danger of becoming overly esoteric was the price of its autonomy.[7]

To deal with this problem, one was obliged to cultivate a specifically musical idiom that would allow listeners to comprehend instrumental music as a kind of speech without words. The idiom of autonomous music had already developed a syntax and vocabulary of its own. Traditional genres and forms, together with conventions of thematic material and its development, were some of the more important principles that made instrumental music comprehensible. This idiom was eventually formalized in the *Kompositionslehre,* which in its theory of form, especially as codified in the writings of Adolph Bernhard Marx, appealed more to listeners than it did to composers. Aesthetic thinking revolved around the metaphysics of instrumental music, and the highest form of instrumental music was chamber music. Because it could not resort to any sensuousness of sound, chamber music necessarily concentrated on formal structure and the thematic process. One could consider a composition a work of art if it met the criteria of originality, individuality, and innovation. At the same time, somewhat paradoxically, these qualities contributed to the codification of a limited and rather rigid repertoire of normative works, for new compositions could scarcely be considered works of art if they were merely novel and of no lasting value. The demand for novelty on the one hand, and value on the other, led to the development of a distinct canon of masterpieces to which every aspiring composer was obliged to pay homage. The more general aesthetic norms were thus reinforced by the aesthetic norms of those very works that belonged to this canon and in turn so greatly influenced the *Kompositionslehre.*

A few examples must suffice here to show how deeply Mendelssohn's oeuvre was influenced by this aesthetic. We know that he attended Hegel's lectures, although we should not place too much emphasis on this fact. Nor should we take too literally Mendelssohn's avowed aversion to speculative debates.[8] The aesthetic categories were not empty formulations; rather, they were so all-pervasive as to influence both the creation and reception of music. An artist had to be prepared to take part in public debate about these categories: he could not escape public criticism, no matter how much he tried. And Mendelssohn's answer to Souchay's question about the meaning of the *Lieder ohne Worte* reads as if it were a catechism for the aesthetic autonomy of instrumental music.[9] In his reply, Mendelssohn speaks of his conviction that music is in fact an even more precise language than the imprecise spoken or written word. But this requires a mutual understanding between composer and listener that is possible only if there is a corresponding mutual understanding of historical conventions.

The struggle with this problem—how to make instrumental music comprehensible—is evident throughout Mendelssohn's works, and within his works nowhere more so than in the chamber music. That genre, more than any other, was bound to tradition, and Mendelssohn was remarkably consistent in his confrontation with the norms of that tradition. Like no other composer before him, Mendelssohn was steeped in the music of the past. He integrated the standards of the Classical era into his orchestral and chamber works; and in his vocal and organ music, he struggled with the self-imposed responsibility he had discovered in the legacy of J.S. Bach. Thus in his vocal music—from the lied to the oratorio—we find him struggling to free himself from an overriding obligation to the text and to incorporate this text into a more purely musical framework. But in his instrumental music more than in any other medium Mendelssohn strove to create a genuinely understandable idiom by combining the traditions of the past with new contributions of his own. In the autographs, we can follow an ever-increasing concern with the perfection of structure. And this concern is but one indication of the critical thoughts of a composer who was as aware of his historical position as he was of the aesthetic questions with which he was struggling.[10]

Beginning with the early string symphonies of the 1820s, Mendelssohn began to work his way through the history of music step by step from C.P.E. Bach to Beethoven. Only then—and the timing is significant—did Mendelssohn compose his first string quartet, in E-flat major, a work which, in spite of its large melodic debt to Mozart, still has its own character. In other early chamber works, Mendelssohn often made use of the wide range of sonorities he found in the piano, but it is in the Octet—a larger medium, and one in which Mendelssohn was not bound to any models—that he made the decisive breakthrough of integrating brilliance with subtlety. Having established as a new genre the poetic overture, Mendelssohn began work on the String Quartets, Opp. 13 and 12. With these two works, he renewed his study of Beethoven, particularly of the late quartets. From this point on, the autograph sources reflect the ever-increasing difficulties Mendelssohn encountered in his creative work.

The ensuing years of travel saw an interruption in the creation of any further instrumental works in cyclical format: a few were sketched, but none was completed. Mendelssohn turned his attention instead in other directions: to the *Lieder ohne Worte,* to the oratorio, and to music for the piano and organ. Only after his confrontation with the music of Bach did he feel confident enough in his mastery of tradition to take up once again the classic instrumental genres on a new and higher level.

Thus only after the years in Düsseldorf—after the success of *St. Paul* in 1836— did Mendelssohn actively return to chamber music. Especially significant among these works written in Leipzig are the String Quartets, Op. 44. These three works (1837–1838) were quickly followed by the Piano Trio, Op. 49, the unfinished Violin Sonata in F major, the two Cello Sonatas, and finally the Second Piano Trio, Op. 66. During this same period, Mendelssohn also finished the *Scottish* and *Italian* Symphonies, the *Lobgesang* and the *Walpurgisnacht,* the concertos, the psalms, and the organ sonatas. For Mendelssohn's late works, the three quartets of Op. 44 thus hold a position of key importance: having completed them, the composer felt free enough to assert himself in virtually every genre. And in these three quartets, we find more fully developed the compositional principles only tentatively or sporadically evident in earlier works. Mendelssohn's mature works depart significantly from these principles, and it is worth remembering them, if only briefly.

Mendelssohn did not disturb the classical canons of form and genre, but he was forced to reconcile these traditions with a thematic paradigm characterized by continuous, songlike melody. This *cantabile* ideal could not be easily integrated into the kind of periodic, discontinuous construction so basic to the music of the Classical era. In his earlier works—Opp. 20, 13, and 12, for example—Mendelssohn had experimented with isolated, individual solutions to this problem. But not until Op. 44 did he find guiding principles for reconciling these differences. His solutions, with some modifications, were equally valid for different types of movements. These solutions, in turn, led to a modification of structure that rendered the new characteristics of the music even more comprehensible. Among these procedures are the varied treatment of material; the derivation of contrasts from the thematic material itself; the introduction of contrasting *cantabile* episodes; the association of the various sections of each movement through integration of motivic material; the almost imperceptible linking of the various sections of each movement; the elucidation of motivic elements in accompanying voices; the synthesis of motives in the recapitulation and coda; and the thematic connection between the outer movements. These are only a few of the compositional procedures used to reconcile the conflicting principles of structure and melody. While it is true that these procedures are found primarily in the developed sonata and sonata-rondo movements, they are also present in the slow movements in ternary form (*Liedsätze*) in which we also find the influence of the *Lieder ohne Worte,* and in the subtle scherzi where Mendelssohn delighted in playing intricate games with the established norms.

These are the principles from which Mendelssohn began to deviate in his late works. These principles never disappeared entirely, for the late works are based on the same models as were the works of the middle period. But he did not follow the models as closely as before: the new works show less thematic concentration. This is especially true of the F-minor Quartet, Op. 80, written shortly before the composer's death in 1847. It is equally true of the B-flat major Quintet, Op. 87, a work composed as early as 1845 but one that remained unpublished at the time of his death.[12] What is new in these works is the lack of songlike thematic material, and a concentrated formal structure with little potential for contrapuntal voice-leading. This corresponds with an unbroken, almost undifferentiated structure in which extended passages are dominated by a single rhythm. We also encounter unexpected contrasts of tonality and dynamics between the various sections of each movement. But the new expressivity in Op. 80—especially in Op. 87—is achieved at the expense of subtlety. Transitional and developmental passages are not as closely woven as once before, and the remaining motivic development no longer permeates entire movements. Instead, we find sequences of figurations in unchanging rhythms that propel the movements along their way. What appears to be spontaneous in Op. 80 seems merely brilliant in Op. 87. While the thematic material of Op. 80 seems fresh, Op. 87 is based on rather conventional material never developed with any kind of intensity. Both works—and also the late movements from Op. 81—are thus ambivalent, insofar as their new qualities can also be viewed as latent flaws.

In any event, Mendelssohn authorized none of these works for publication. Are their new qualities a new path, a new ideal? Or are these works merely preliminary studies and unfinished attempts? Anyone familiar with Mendelssohn's autographs knows that copious corrections and variations are a sure indication of the composer's extreme care with his scores. From the autographs of these late works, then, we should be able to determine whether these late works were carefully polished or whether they were never definitively finished. We must ask ourselves whether these works remained unfinished or whether, if finished, they proclaim new intentions.

[*ii.*] *The Abandoned Attempt: Quintet, Op. 87*

In a letter dated January 26, 1844, Ferdinand David asked Mendelssohn to write "a new quintet, something I eagerly await."[13] The following year Mendelssohn did in fact write his second string quintet, in B-flat major; the autograph score is dated "Soden, July 8, 1845." Ignaz Moscheles found the Quintet "much more energetic" than other works of Mendelssohn, but wrote in 1846 that "we have also examined the B-flat String Quintet" and that "Mendelssohn himself maintains that the last movement is not good."[14] Nevertheless, the work appeared posthumously in 1850 as Op. 87 from Breitkopf and Härtel, the same firm that published Opp. 80 and 81. It is clear that Mendelssohn had sufficient time to see this work through the press. One could, of course, ask which is more important: the wishes of the composer or the interests of posterity.

On the whole, the autograph gives a very "finished" impression. It is a carefully written and very clean manuscript. One could almost believe that this is a fair copy rather than a working draft. In any case, the almost total absence of important corrections is striking. While there are minor corrections in the voice leading, they seldom affect the substance of the work itself. Corrections, deletions, and additions are the exception rather than the rule. The state of this manuscript is so different from what one finds in the autographs of the earlier works that one simply cannot help but be suspicious about this Quintet. Perhaps this really is a fair copy. Or did the composition of this work go so smoothly that there was little left to change? But if this is the case, then why did Mendelssohn withhold the work from publication? And how are we to take his own opinion that the Finale was "not good"? There is one more possibility: perhaps Mendelssohn considered the work to be so poor that it did not merit any further investment of his time.

The first movement shows only a few marginal corrections throughout the exposition, development, recapitulation, and coda. Not only the themes, but also the transitional and developmental modifications of those themes are notated practically without correction. Occasionally, some reductions were clarified (mm. 33–36), repetitions spelled out with the notation "bis" (mm. 177–78 = mm. 179–80), or groups of measures crossed out altogether (for example, three measures after m. 184 and single measures between mm. 259–260 and 261–262). But one discrepancy in the posthumous edition is all the more conspicuous alongside the minimal number of corrections in the autograph. Measures 137–40 of the development—an expansion of the opening in the distant B major—are crossed out in pencil in the autograph (plate 1). At the bottom of the page, in piano score, we find a possible substitution, also sketched in pencil, in Mendelssohn's own hand, demonstrating the authenticity of these alterations. Unfortunately, it is not possible to reconstruct this passage with absolute certainty, but the deletion clearly shows Mendelssohn's dissatisfaction with the entire passage. But this fact was completely ignored in the posthumous edition.

The second movement, *Andante scherzando*—Mendelssohn had originally marked it *Andante scherzando non troppo*—also shows few corrections in the manuscript. At the end of the coda, however, we find—again in pencil—six measures crossed out. But once again, the published edition ignores the unambiguous intention of the composer, who, at this point, was trying to eliminate a somewhat protracted return to the coda. The four final cadential measures should have followed after the fermata in m. 93 (plate 2).

In the *Adagio e lento*, we also find the form, substance, and thematic material largely unaltered in the autograph. As one would expect in such elaborate part-writing, there are a number of minor corrections in the voice-leading. In the cadence after the second subject, Mendelssohn lined through two measures of a solo violin cadenza (mm. 37–38). In the recapitulation, he eliminated two and then again three measures (mm. 60–61, 63–64); the measures in between were abbreviated and pasted in later, as can be seen from the rastration. But all the important elements of this movement—the harmony, the voice-leading, and especially the successive unification of themes in the coda—all of these are basically present in completed form in the autograph.

The state of the autograph up to this point can only increase our consternation. If the work was so polished, so complete, why did Mendelssohn withhold it from publication? We find the answer in an analysis of the Finale, and an investigation of the autograph confirms this analysis.[15]

In the published edition, the movement is a sonata-rondo form. It has a typical threefold statement of the rondo theme, with the refrain appearing in the tonic just before the development section. In the exposition, the couplet (or secondary thematic area) appears between mm. 41 and 59, but unlike the first movement, this episode does not appear in the development. It is also missing from the recapitulation. One would normally expect it to appear between mm. 154 and 155, that is, in a position analogous to its appearance in the exposition. Instead, it does not appear again until the coda (mm. 194–201). The result in the published edition is singularly nonsensical. What begins so clearly as a sonata-rondo quickly falls apart with a contrasting episode presented only once in the exposition and not again until the coda, almost as if it were a quotation. This contrasting episode without any thematic function is unique in all of Mendelssohn's oeuvre. Such a construction upsets the formal balance between the exposition and the recapitulation. And although it is true that recapitulations are often full of surprises, the complete absence of a contrasting episode is totally without parallel.

There are several possible explanations for this state of affairs. The first is that the contrasting section was stricken from the recapitulation as an afterthought. Its appearance in the coda would then have corresponded to the analogous passage in the development. Deletions such as these could have come from the composer's dissatisfaction with the substance of this thematic material, which, in point of fact, is exceptionally formal and rather characterless in profile. It would in any case be simple to reconcile such an explanation with the composer's own criticism that the last movement was "not good," for that might well have been reason enough to withhold the entire work from publication.

But the autograph does not confirm this hypothesis. There, the couplet was absent in both the development and recapitulation from the very start. Scrutiny of the autograph does, however, confirm our suspicion that Mendelssohn was unhappy with this contrasting episode. The autograph includes two variant passages ignored in the published edition, both of which coincide with the appearance of the couplet. Specifically, these passages present abbreviated versions of the exposition (m. 41ff.) and of the coda (after m. 170). Both variants point toward a total elimination of the couplet. On p. 109 we find mm. 39–61 of the exposition with the couplet and its transition back to the rondo theme (plate 3). But the verso of this leaf is empty, and the score does not pick up again until p. 111. At the top of p. 111, however, we find four measures missing from the published edition. These four measures are of great significance: they form the basis of a radically new version of the entire movement. The first two measures at the top of p. 111 correspond to the first two measures on p. 109, and the next two measures at the top of p. 111 correspond to the last two measures on p. 109. In other words, the four-measure variant at the top of p. 111 is nothing less than a reduction of all twenty-three measures on p. 109. The entire passage is shortened to four measures by a complete elimination of the entire couplet. The original editor, noticing that the first and last measures of p. 109 reappeared on p. 111, simply omitted the four-measure variant. Admittedly, Mendelssohn himself abstained from crossing out the twenty-three measures on p. 109, but his intentions for the new version are made clear by the fact that m. 62ff. on p. 111 agree not with the first version (mm. 60–61 on p. 109), but rather with the second, abbreviated, version on p. 111. In the latter, we find a new dotted rhythm in eighth-notes, a variant that reminds us of the original rondo theme, and one that is developed again later in the movement.

Our hypothesis—that Mendelssohn intended to delete the couplet—is confirmed by the recapitulation, which, beginning at mm. 154–155, p. 116, is consistent with the second version of the exposition in that it too eliminates the couplet.

Plate 1. Kraków, Biblioteka Jagiellońska, Mendelssohn Nachlass 40, p. 84; Op. 87/I (Development), measures 137–45. (By permission of the Biblioteka Jagiellońska.)

Plate 2. Kraków, Biblioteka Jagiellońska, Mendelssohn Nachlass 40, p. 98; Op. 87/II (Coda), measures 90–103. (By permission of the Biblioteka Jagiellońska.)

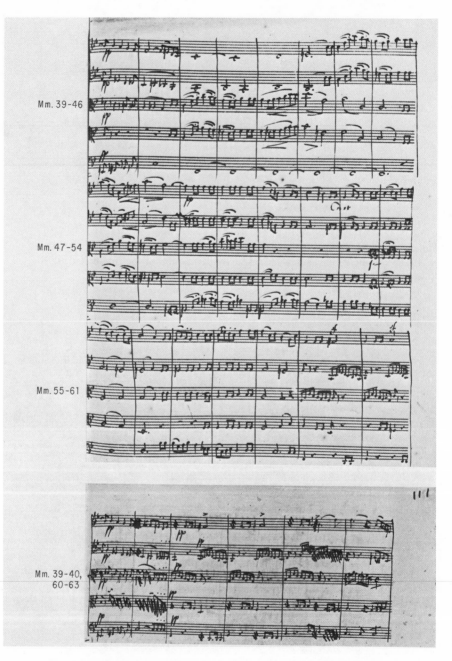

Mm. 39-46

Mm. 47-54

Mm. 55-61

Mm. 39-40,
60-63

Plate 3. Kraków, Biblioteka Jagiellońska, Mendelssohn Nachlass 40, pp. 109 and 111; Op. 87/IV (Exposition), measures 39–63, first and second versions. (By permission of the Biblioteka Jagiellońska.)

Plate 4. Kraków Biblioteka Jagiellońska, Mendelssohn Nachlass 40, pp. 119–20; Op. 87/IV (Coda), unpublished version. Measure numbers in parentheses do not correspond to the published version. (By permission of the Biblioteka Jagiellońska.)

(Mm. 189-194)

(Mm. 194-199)

(Mm. 200-207)

Plate 4 (*continued*)

Plate 5. Kraków, Biblioteka Jagiellońska, Mendelssohn Nachlass 44, p. 153; Op. 80/I (Development), measures 155–73. (By permission of the Biblioteka Jagiellońska.)

Plate 6. Kraków, Biblioteka Jagiellońska, Mendelssohn Nachlass 44, p. 156; Op. 80/I (Coda), measures 275–89. (By permission of the Biblioteka Jagiellońska.)

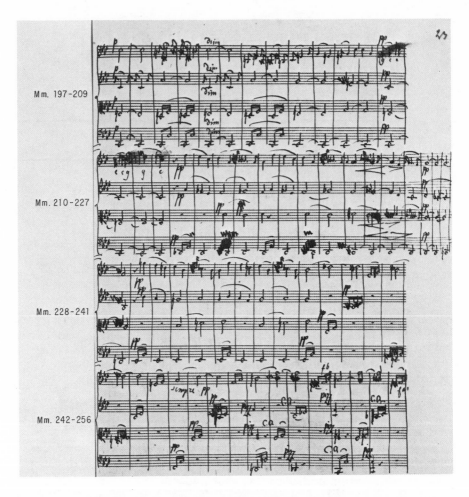

Plate 7. Kraków, Biblioteka Jagiellońska, Mendelssohn Nachlass 44, p. 171; Op. 80/ IV (Development), measures 197–256. (By permission of the Biblioteka Jagiellońska.)

This episode, it should be remembered, appears in the exposition only in the published edition and not in the autograph. The recapitulation in the autograph is clearly based on the still-unpublished "new" version. The dotted rhythm just mentioned reappears at the corresponding point of the recapitulation (mm. 155–56). The editor of the original publication chose the abandoned first version, with the couplet in the exposition. The resulting imbalance was made even more pronounced by the fact that the transitional passage (after the contrasting theme) appears in the first version in the exposition but in the second version in the recapitulation.

The two versions of the coda provide the final and most convincing piece of evidence. The published edition offers only the first version (pp. 117–18), completely ignoring the second (pp. 119–20, plate 4). This is especially odd, since at the end of the second version we find the date of composition in the composer's own hand (p. 120), indicating that the second version is the more authoritative of the two. The second version is almost as long as the first (mm. 172–207, compared with mm. 170–207), a fact which would demonstrate Mendelssohn's continuing concern with formal balance. Yet mm. 170–71 of the printed edition are not present in the first version: they were taken from the second. We can thereby be sure that the original editor was familiar with this second version. In the still-unpublished second version of the coda, the couplet, which had appeared in the first version (mm. 196–201), is eliminated, while the figurative material of the rondo theme is expanded. The thematic material needed for internal contrast is thus supplied by combining the second half of the rondo theme with the sixteenth-note figure in the outer voices. This also adds to the motivic intensity of the movement as a whole.

We must, for the time being, forgo any further examination of this second version and other differences between the autograph and the published score (for example, the figures in the transition and development, mm. 23ff., 84ff., or a deletion ignored in the published edition at m. 104). We can, however, make some general statements about the evolution of the Finale. Apparently, Mendelssohn originally conceived this movement as a normal sonata-rondo with repeated statements of the refrain and couplet. Doubts about the substance of the couplet arose shortly after he first committed his thoughts to paper. These doubts led him to revise this episode, and to omit it first from the development and then from the recapitulation. The only question is why it was brought back again in the coda at all, at least initially. Perhaps we should also ask ourselves if the movement could have been saved through a revision of the couplet. The fact that Mendelssohn did not cross through the first version would lead us to think that he may have considered it salvageable. In any case, the dated second version of the coda without the couplet would seem to represent the composer's final thoughts on the matter.

What remains is problematical, nevertheless. The movement was clearly conceived to be in sonata-rondo form; even the version without the couplet brings back the rondo theme in the tonic just before the beginning of the development. Moreover, the transitional passages leading up to this contrasting episode are left standing, even though the episode itself was deleted. These passages are thus robbed of their formal meaning. A rondo—which by its very nature relies on contrast—has been stripped of its contrasting material. The result is a monothematic finale unique in Mendelssohn's oeuvre. Mendelssohn might have attempted to substitute other material for the troublesome couplet, as he indeed had done once before, in the finale of Op. 44, No. 1. But his early decision not to make any further revisions in Op. 87 precluded such a substitution. It also reveals Mendelssohn's doubts about the rest of the movement as well, for the deletion of the couplet resulted in a monothematic *perpetuum mobile* whose thematic material, quite simply, was overtaxed.

We can now understand Mendelssohn's criticism of his own work, that this last movement was "not good." This dissatisfaction began with the finale but eventually spread to the rest of the work as well. As a result, he did not have it published. This self-criticism is testimony to the composer's own insight into the perils of his compositional approach to this particular work. Up to this point, he had always expanded his original thematic material. When he was forced to restrain its development, Mendelssohn came to rely all the more on the ability of the original thematic material to stand on its own. If the themes themselves were lacking in substance and character, the work was in danger of lapsing into a simple series of figurations.

At the same time, Op. 87 marks the beginning of a path Mendelssohn was to pursue in such later works as *Elijah* and the Op. 80 String Quartet, for the reduction of motivic interplay and counterpoint had also opened up new possibilities. Dynamic, tonal, and harmonic elements could all be intensified, even if intensity were achieved at the expense of subtlety. What we see in Op. 87 is, in fact, an attempt in a new direction. That this attempt was abandoned is due to the originally inadequate materials of the composition. One might well regret this, especially in light of the profound *Adagio*. But this newly-recovered source, it is hoped, will serve as an impetus toward a new critical edition.

[*iii.*] *The Perfected Late Work: Quartet, Op. 80*

During the summer of 1847, while working on *Loreley* and *Christus*, Mendelssohn wrote the F-minor Quartet. The work was published posthumously in 1850 as Op. 80. It is often linked with the sudden death of Mendelssohn's sister Fanny, or with Mendelssohn's premonitions of his own death. Georg Knepler has called it the "requiem of an era" and "a foreboding of new, stormy times." Moscheles was struck by its "extraordinarily somber mood." This uncharacteristically somber mood could not be reconciled with the more urbane image of the composer, and as a result, the work was neglected for years.[16]

The autograph (Mus. ms. Mendelssohn autogr. 44, pp. 149–176) is dated at the end "Interlaken, September 1847." The work thus was finished during the journey through Switzerland. With the aid of the last diary (Bodleian Library, Oxford, Ms. Mendelssohn G. 10, fol. 52r f.), the sketches for the second movement can be dated precisely to July 6, 1847. We can—and must—ask once again whether the work was truly finished. There was only a short period of time between the date on the manuscript and Mendelssohn's death, and during this brief period, the composer had begun yet another work for string quartet. The Variations in E major and the Scherzo in A minor appeared in 1850 as Op. 81. Breitkopf and Härtel issued these two movements with the earlier Capriccio in E minor, written in 1843, and the Fugue in E-flat major of 1827. Because these four movements do not belong together, the function of the two movements from the later period remains unclear. For in 1843, we find Mendelssohn planning "some caprices for quartet," of which the third movement of Op. 81 was one. And in 1844, David asks about "some small pieces for string quartet."[17] One could almost believe that these late movements for string quartet were part of an attempt to dissolve the classical cyclical structure by means of a series of miniatures, much as we find in Schumann's smaller chamber works.

The two late quartet movements are not dated in Mendelssohn's autograph. They follow the F-minor Quartet, but their location within the bound autograph volume cannot be taken as an indication of chronology, for this volume was assembled at a later time. In the manuscript of Op. 80 (p. 162), however, we find sketches for the first four measures of the theme for the variations from the first movement of Op. 81, written out in doubled note values. And Moscheles mentions finding next to the F-minor quartet "the first movement of another, unfinished quartet in D minor." He viewed these variations as "less somber, somewhat more comforting, and particularly distinguished harmonically."[18] Save for the tonality, this description could apply equally well to the variations of Op. 81. Thus, these variations might originally have been intended to serve as the first movement of a new quartet. In the autograph, the Scherzo in A minor is followed by a six-measure sketch for an *Allegro* in E major in 4/4 time (p. 188). According to these sketches, Mendelssohn was planning a work of at least three movements. A first-movement set of variations would have been unusual, especially in a slow tempo. Not since the early Viola Sonata (1823–24) had Mendelssohn incorporated a set of variations into any cyclical work. And an opening slow movement would have been equally unusual in the tradition of the string quartet.

It is not possible to draw any far-reaching conclusions from the autographs of either of these two movements. There are no developed sonata-form first movements to compare with other, earlier works. The *Scherzo-Allegro leggiero* is not sharply delineated from earlier scherzi, and as in earlier autographs, there are very few corrections (only between mm. 83–84 and 116–17 are two measures deleted). At the same time, this scherzo is not so much a typically subtle play of traditional forms as an intricate mosaic made up of the smallest building blocks imaginable.[19] This technique signals the beginning of a new tendency: the dissatisfaction with closed themes so characteristic of Op. 80 is even more prominent in this scherzo. Here, the themes have disintegrated into the smallest possible units. The confidence with which the movement is constructed, even down to the smallest detail, is thus all the more remarkable.

The variation movement also shows few variant readings from the autograph. The fifth variation, in E minor (*Presto*), is an exception. Measures 124–31 were pasted in later on a separate piece of paper. These measures heighten the sense of hectic tension, making the contrast between this E-minor *Presto* and the E-major *Andante* all the more pronounced.[20] The technique of variation is, of course, a hallmark of Mendelssohn's late works. The variation as a genre does not appear before 1841, with the *Variations sérieuses,* Op. 54, and is not taken up again until the comparable variations of Opp. 82 and 83. This renewed interest in the variation is not entirely surprising, for it is typical of the late works that different compositional elements take on new relationships to one another. While the use of variation is minimized elsewhere, here it forms the basis for an entire movement. The movements of Op. 81 can thus be seen within the context of the late works as a whole.

The autograph of Op. 80 shows a striking increase in the number of corrections; consequently, it should come as no surprise that we can learn correspondingly more about the evolution of this work than was possible with Op. 81. Even a quick and superficial analysis shows that the developmental and transitional passages of the outer movements are more figurative than motivic. It therefore seems doubtful that Mendelssohn left the work unfinished and in need of further revision at the time of his death. Indeed, the autograph shows that in his revisions, Mendelssohn made very little effort to intensify any of the motivic work. As in Op. 87, variants are absent. Instead, the corrections we find here were intended primarily to delineate the character of the themes more sharply and to emphasize the abrupt contrasts within the movement.[21]

The entry of the violins in the first movement, for example, was originally preceded by two measures of tremolo in the lower voices. Mendelssohn later reduced this to a single measure of tremolo, thereby intensifying the introduction of this statement (similarly in mm. 16, 96, etc.). The second subject was at first written over a prolonged pedal point in the cello that was later changed to a more forceful sequence of syncopated quarter notes. This rhythmic alteration is reminiscent of the agitation that characterizes the first subject (mm. 53ff., 57ff., and the corresponding passage in the recapitulation, m. 213ff.). On the other hand, the second two-measure phrase of the second subject was altered and transposed down a third in order to let the curve of the melody fade away (mm. 59–60). Connecting measures were eliminated at several points (before mm. 78, 99, etc.). At the end of the development, all of the lower voices originally provided a tremolo accompaniment to the first violin, and this tremolo passage quite logically prepared the way for the recapitulation (plate 5). Only later did Mendelssohn decide to intensify this transitional passage by replacing the tremolo with rhythmic counterpoint in the lower voices. Instead of a resolution of contrasts, the contrasts become even more accentuated. The beginning of the recapitulation also becomes more intense through the addition of a new upper voice presenting a fragment of the main theme. And in the coda, Mendelssohn eliminated four measures of violin arpeggiations just before the unison *Presto* (after m. 282). He replaced this passage with a five-measure segment, notated at the bottom of the page, that introduces the accelerando passage (mm. 283–89, plate 6).

Important changes such as these are not as prevalent in the two inner movements. In the trio of the *Allegro assai*, Mendelssohn modified the ostinato bass and the oscillating rhythm of the upper voices. In the *Adagio*, we find numerous minor corrections in the accompanying voices, but again no deletions. The embellishment of the theme through nuances of the dotted rhythm, however, is worth noting. The dotted rhythm in m. 4 of the first violin was added later, as was a series of dotted sixteenths where before there had been only rests (mm. 39ff., 70ff., 94ff.). Nevertheless, the formal structure of this movement remained unchanged.

The themes and structure of the finale were also firmly established from the start. This is especially true of the fragmentation of the structure into trill-like units not unlike the first-movement tremolos. The close of the main theme (m. 15), which originally featured a rather empty series of trill-like fragments in the cello, was made more striking by the abrupt contrast of the quarter notes. Mendelssohn also eliminated a number of repetitions he considered superfluous (four measures before m. 81, then two before m. 29 and again before m. 427, etc.). Of the few additions he made, the most important was the expansion of the contrasting *cantabile* episode in the development. Formally, the finale is in sonata form, with the secondary subject reduced to a series of breathless, two-measure fragments. It is scarcely coincidental that Mendelssohn at this point abandoned the *cantabile* quality otherwise so typical of his music. The sudden, almost parenthetical interpolation in *pianissimo* in the middle of the development, where we would have expected to find motivic development, is typical of this new approach. This passage is isolated and episodic; it does not return and has no thematic function—rather, it is a reminder of those earlier *cantabile* qualities. Because it has no connection with the rest of the movement, it creates a brief pause in the hectic course of events. As such, it anticipates the episodes that are so important in Mahler's music. Here Mendelssohn begins truly to shape the materials for the first time. This episode at first consisted of trill-like configurations in the cello (mm. 215 and 219) that were reminiscent of the main theme (plate 7). The fragments were then replaced by notes of longer value, and the episode was further stabilized by the addition of four measures (mm. 224–29). The closing portion of this phrase was then transposed down a third, reminding us of the changes already made to the secondary theme in the first movement. With these changes, Mendelssohn created a sense of rest, the first real pause in the entire movement.

These examples must suffice here to demonstrate how significantly Mendelssohn's corrections sharpened the contours of the work. The Quartet cannot be considered unfinished. On the contrary, the work was already polished when first committed to paper. Subsequent alterations sharpened the work's contours but did not intensify its motivic development. What is at first vexing about Op. 80 is its predilection for figurative rather than motivic elements. But this is not a symptom of incompleteness. Rather, it is the manifestation of an entirely new concept. An aesthetic understanding of this work can no longer be confined to the traditional ideal of *Ausgleich und Vermittlung*. It is more important that we consider instead the work's departure and distance from the traditional norms of the classical aesthetic.

It certainly must be conceded that an aesthetic judgment of any work of music should be based upon the work itself, and not upon the intentions of the composer or the state of the autograph. But in the case of works whose publication has not been authorized by the composer, the autograph sources become far more important. And an examination of the sources of Mendelssohn's late chamber music leads us to a re-evaluation of those works.

Although Op. 87 was never definitively completed, Op. 80 was. And although the Quintet was intentionally withheld from publication, the Quartet was not. One might at first think just the opposite from an examination of the autographs: the Quintet shows far fewer corrections than the Quartet. One might think that the Quintet was tossed off with very little effort, while the Quartet became a source of difficulties for the composer. A careful examination of the manuscripts, however, reveals exactly the opposite. It is the very absence of corrections in Op. 87 that shows that this work was abandoned, that the composer's doubts about its substance were simply too great. Op. 80, on the other hand, was important enough to warrant a great deal more time and effort. What puzzles us about this work are its new and unexpected qualities, its excursion into a new ideal. Other, earlier works had already pointed toward this new concept, particularly the Piano Trio, Op. 66, with its unexpected passionate outbursts, and *Elijah* in its more dramatic moments. While Op. 87 had relied upon an accumulation of tonal effects, Op. 80 followed the new path with greater consistency: its thematic material consists of contrasting elements rather than long melodic phrases. As a result, it tends toward divergence and dissolution rather than homogeneity and unity. The movements are held together by the inner dynamics of a constant rhythmic momentum that is generated from this new type of thematic material.

It would be interesting to know to what extent Schumann's music—with its distinctive thematic character and its formal concentration—disquieted Mendelssohn in the last years of his life. In its distance from the conventions of its day, Op. 80 establishes its own aesthetic criteria. If we accept it on its own terms, if we view its fragmentary elements as an innovation rather than as a defect, it becomes quite clear that the work is very far advanced for its time.

Contextual Studies

William S. Newman

Three Musical Intimates of Mendelssohn and Schumann in Leipzig: Hauptmann, Moscheles, and David

Anyone exploring the average terrain of Classic music—its run-of-the-mill symphonies, concertos, sonatas, and operas—must marvel at how far above and apart the masterworks of Haydn, Mozart, Beethoven, and Schubert stand. Similarly, anybody exploring the average terrain of Romantic music a generation or two later must wonder at the equally sharp contrasts. There are the symphonies of a Czerny, and there are the symphonies of Mendelssohn and Schumann.

What adds force to these generalizations, otherwise obvious, is the sharpness of the contrasts. From today's perspective, there seem to have been few intermediate figures who might at least reduce the abrupt gap between the ordinary and the great. To be sure, space and time tend to efface the accomplishments of such composers. For example, we retain today little interest in the vocal ballades of Karl Loewe, though they once brought him much esteem and success.[1] But in the 1830s and 1840s Mendelssohn and Schumann were not completely isolated as artists. We can pursue this argument more knowledgeably today, thanks to several recent studies partly replacing the rather nebulous nineteenth-century sources on which we all have had to depend.[2] Besides the three men to be discussed here—Moritz Hauptmann, Ignaz Moscheles, and Ferdinand David—there were over a dozen other musicians in Leipzig at the time who made conspicuous marks both locally and beyond. At this point nine of them should receive at least passing mention for their closeness to Mendelssohn and Schumann, as well as to Hauptmann, Moscheles, and David.

One was Johann Friedrich Rochlitz (1769–1842), critic and writer on music, as well as other topics. Rochlitz spent his whole life in Leipzig, yet exerted a much wider influence through his editorship of the influential *Allgemeine musikalische Zeitung* during its first twenty years, from 1798 to 1818, and through his further contributions to it as late as 1835. He had known both Mozart and Beethoven. Unfortunately, his highly imaginative recollections of those masters have since had to be largely, if not totally, discredited.[3]

Another of the nine musicians was the stern, much sought after pedagogue of the piano, Friedrich Wieck. Jealous father of the gifted Clara and begrudging father-in-law of Robert Schumann, he lived in Leipzig from 1817 to 1840. Clara herself achieved international renown as a recital pianist well before she moved away from her birthplace of Leipzig at the age of twenty-five. The year was 1844, four years and nearly three babies after she had married Schumann.

Many others are worthy of mention, among them the theorist, composer, and Kantor at the Thomaskirche Theodor Weinlig, who was in Leipzig from 1823 to his death in 1842. Among his more important pupils were Clara Wieck and, in 1831, Richard Wagner, after Wagner had matriculated at the Leipzig University. The prominent conductor and composer Ferdinand Hiller was in Leipzig much of the time between 1841 and 1844. During his last season he substituted as conductor of the Gewandhaus orchestra while his close friend Mendelssohn was often away in Berlin. But a break between the two men soon caused Hiller to move on to Dresden. From 1833 to 1845 and from 1847 to 1850 Albert Lortzing flourished in Leipzig, producing examples of the German comic opera, or *Spieloper,* with which his name is most associated. The distinctive Danish composer Niels Gade spent five years, 1843 to 1848, in Leipzig, including a period as associate conductor of the Gewandhaus concerts. Both Mendelssohn and Schumann received and supported him warmly. Wilhelm von Wasielewski, one of the first students—under Mendelssohn, Hauptmann, and David—was there when the Leipzig Conservatory opened in 1843. He became a first violinist in the Gewandhaus and Theater orchestras and a close friend of the Schumanns before he left Leipzig in 1850, later to publish the first standard biography of Schumann as well as pathbreaking historical studies.

Finally there was Julius Rietz, one of the first to follow Mendelssohn and Schumann in Leipzig. He served from 1847, after Mendelssohn died, to 1854 as a distinguished conductor variously of the Gewandhaus and Stadttheater orchestras as well as the Singakademie. Rietz further distinguished himself as a music editor, especially of Mendelssohn's works, but also of the Bach-Gesellschaft edition and of works by Classical masters.

All of these men worked in Leipzig in full cognizance of each other's activities, concentrating their efforts in the same principal organizations around which Leipzig's considerable music revolved: the Gewandhaus orchestra, which, under Mendelssohn's exacting direction, soon became one of the top German ensembles; the Stadttheater, the former Schauspielhaus, where operatic works by Spohr, Marschner, Weber, Lortzing, and others were produced; and the Singakademie, best known of several active choral societies. These organizations were interrelated, sharing each other's members as the lively concert life required. An organization that brought nearly all of these men together in one place in a shared mission was the eminent Leipzig Conservatory, founded under Mendelssohn's leadership in 1843. (The equally eminent University of Leipzig was not then a main center of musical activity.) These musicians could hardly have failed to know each other in such a small, concentrated center of German culture, where daily contacts were almost inevitable.

Although the population of Leipzig more than tripled over the next generation, in the 1840s it was no larger than it had been in Bach's day a century earlier when it numbered only about thirty thousand.[4] Other urban centers presented a different case. Beethoven and Schubert, for example, may have failed to meet in the Vienna of the early nineteenth century, which then already numbered nearly a quarter-million inhabitants and would grow another hundred thousand in the next generation, by the time Mendelssohn and Schumann were active in Leipzig. By then, even such prominent musicians might well have failed to meet in the other main music centers: Berlin, with a population comparable to that of Vienna; Paris, with more than a million citizens; and London, with a population of two million.

It becomes evident that the independent, self-governed city of Leipzig cultivated learning and the arts to a degree out of proportion to its population. It had a long and notable history in music, literature, and philosophical thought. A strong musical tradition can be traced back well before the construction of a Schauspielhaus and a first Gewandhaus in the eighteenth century and before the foundation of *collegia musica* in the seventeenth, well before the pinnacle achieved by Bach and the solid contributions of a composer like Schein before him. The earliest singing in the local churches, including that at a song school probably established in the Thomaskirche by the start of the thirteenth century, antedates the great stimulus in Leipzig of Luther's Reformation movement.

As for other cultural forces—going back from the powerful literary and philosophical stimuli of Schumann's youth—we can recall the names of such influential sometime residents of Leipzig as Jean Paul Richter, Goethe, Schelling, Fichte, Klopstock, Gellert, Gottsched, and, in the seventeenth century, even the young Leibniz.

In contrast to those nine musicians in Leipzig briefly mentioned earlier, Hauptmann, Moscheles, and David have been selected here for a fuller discussion of their contributions. Their choice from among the other minor figures reflects not only the extent of their contributions but also the degree of their involvement with Mendelssohn and Schumann and with each other. Indeed, each of these five men worked closely with each of the others at one time or another, whether in Leipzig or elsewhere. And all of them came together in Leipzig on occasion, although Moscheles did not establish residence there until 1846, two years after Schumann's departure in 1844. These musicians' periods of residence and most intensive activity in Leipzig are summarized in Figure 1. (Those periods are indicated in Figure 1 by solid lines and the years in other locations by broken lines; briefer absences from Leipzig are disregarded.)

It is also worth noting several interests and traits that these five men shared (with certain allowances for Schumann as something of a "loner"). All espoused the musical conservatism typical of many Leipzigers, taking special interest in the past masters of the nineteenth, eighteenth, and even earlier centuries, tolerating with difficulty Berlioz, Liszt, and Wagner.[5] All belonged to the teaching faculty of the Conservatory. All evinced high purpose and standards of achievement and a strong sense of discipline and the work ethic. All engaged in a ceaseless whirl of professional activities both in and away from Leipzig, often commuting on the new

Figure 1. Five Overlapping Careers in Leipzig

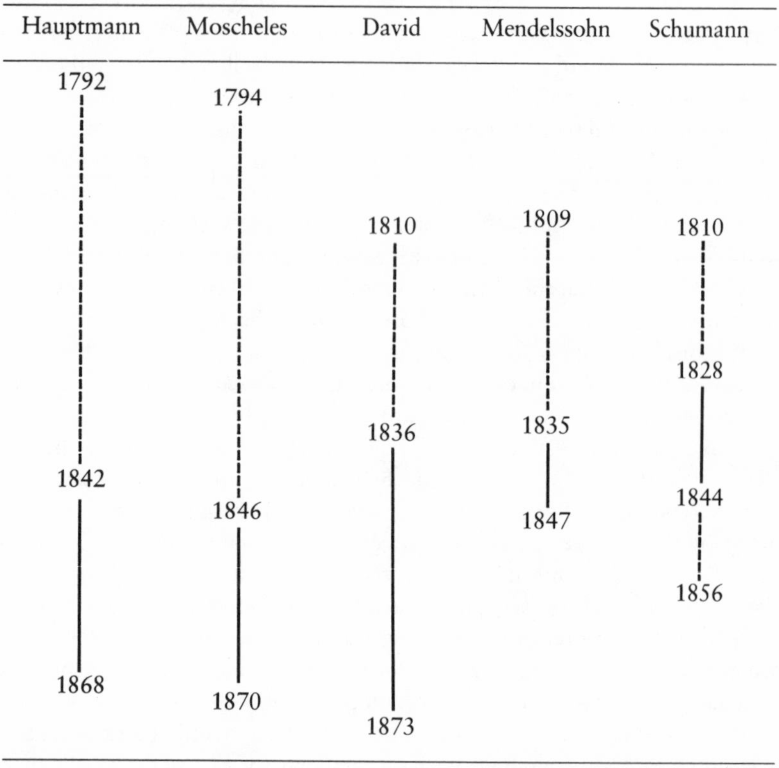

Hauptmann	Moscheles	David	Mendelssohn	Schumann
1792	1794			
		1810	1809	1810
				1828
		1836	1835	
1842				
	1846		1847	1844
				1856
1868	1870			
		1873		

Key: Solid lines indicate years spent in Leipzig, dotted lines years spent elsewhere. Briefer absences from Leipzig are disregarded.

trains within the two-hundred-mile radius that included both the Saxon and Brandenburg courts, in Dresden and Berlin. And all still managed to pursue a wide range of cultural interests and intellectual curiosities. What, then, distinguished these three musicians, Hauptmann, Moscheles, and David, from each other?

Moritz Hauptmann was the oldest of the three, having been born in Dresden in 1792. After early studies with Weinlig and others, he trained further with Ludwig Spohr in composition as well as violin. He then played under Spohr's direction while teaching both theory and composition at the Kassel court for twenty years. In 1842, Hauptmann accepted an invitation initiated by Mendelssohn to succeed Weinlig as director of music at the Thomaskirche in Leipzig,[6] and in 1843 to teach theory and composition alongside Mendelssohn at the new Conservatory. Not unhappy at discontinuing his violin assignment, Hauptmann further took over the editorship of the *Allgemeine musikalische Zeitung* in 1843 and became a chief founder and continuing mainstay of the Bach Gesellschaft in 1850.

These diverse activities and his outstanding students in theory and composition, including Ferdinand David, Joachim, Bülow and Jadassohn, brought Hauptmann wide recognition and much honor in his later years. His importance as an innovative, challenging, articulate theorist, of course, has remained assured. But his importance as a composer has been denied thus far by the judgment of time, even though a number of his numerous and varied compositions won the warm approval of his contemporary critics and listeners.[7] Hauptmann himself kept expressing doubts about his composing—as he did, to be sure, about all aspects of his musical activities. Those doubts crop up throughout his enlightening, entertaining, skillfully written, and often witty letters. He seems to have had least doubts about his lieder. One letter of 1837 to the excellent singer, his longtime friend Franz Hauser, offers a highly perceptive, if tentative, apologia for these lieder:

I have my doubts about the expediency of publishing them at all [the Italian songs, Op. 24, second series]. My music seems to me like one born out of due time—thirty years too late; everything is now so completely changed, that people will think it too simple—not spicy enough. . . . I must write as nature prompts me. I know my music is old-fashioned, and not being a pianist myself, I never could write brilliant piano-forte music. . . . who would care now-a-days to listen to a composition, which only modulates to the key of the dominant, without diminished sevenths? However, I wrote them [the songs] as a refreshment, after the agonizing stuff I have had to listen to.[8]

Representative of about a dozen sets of three to twelve lieder for solo voice and piano by Hauptmann is a set of six, Op. 26, published by Peters in Leipzig some two years before Hauptmann settled in Leipzig, about 1840, when he was fifty-one. These six lieder are settings of poems taken from the *Liebesfrühling* ("Springtime of Love") by the contemporary German poet Friedrich Rückert, a favorite of lieder composers. The first and sixth lieder of Op. 26 may serve as illustrations. Rückert's untitled text for the first—"Du meine Seele, du mein Herz"—was called "Mein Alles" by Hauptmann. This text is well known in the more impassioned setting by Schumann called "Widmung," composed in that same year of 1840. It would also be set by numerous other composers. Schumann took certain small liberties with the words.[9] Hauptmann took these same liberties, which suggest that one of them knew the other's setting. Hauptmann also made changes in the distribution of the lines and return of the first stanza. In fact, he changed somewhat more than he acknowledged in a letter of 1860 about other Rückert texts. After mentioning that "Rückert has been my librettist all along" and that his "two thick volumes abound in lyrics," he wrote, "I consider a slight transposition of words quite permissible with Rückert, who often omits the lyrical caesura, and I had rather make a small alteration here and there, than emphasize some unimportant word in a strophe. I know how poets resent this—but they have only themselves to blame for it."[10] The sixth and last song of Op. 26 Hauptmann called "Trennung," or "Separation." This time he reordered the lines but made no changes in the words of the text, which expresses the tears and sadness of a lover's parting, in spite of grief and entreaties not to part.

Schumann referred to Hauptmann as a "lieblicher Liederkomponist," a "delightful lieder composer."[11] A reviewer in the *Allgemeine musikalische Zeitung* of 1840[12] welcomed the *Sechs Lieder,* Op. 26, as the product of a sincere, genial, unpretentious but deep-feeling composer, one who preferred the simplest means, precisely controlled, to more lavish means, recklessly squandered. Thus, the reviewer was only echoing Hauptmann's own apologia for his style. One might add that the seemingly artless simplicity of Hauptmann's songs almost belies the skill of his voice-leading, the purity of his word-settings, and the rightness of his harmonizations. (In this combination of simplicity, directness, and musical depth, his writing recalls that of the theorist Georg Andreas Sorge, who had served in Lobenstein—not far south of Leipzig—about a century earlier.[13]) With reference again to lieder Nos. 1 and 6 of Op. 26, we may note that both songs are through-composed, fast and short, both restrict the vocal line to the range of a ninth, both modulate only to nearby keys, and both limit their chromaticism to a few passing notes and their harmonies largely to diatonic triads (ex. 1, from No. 6).

When we turn to the second oldest of our three minor masters, Ignaz Moscheles, we are blessed with one of the most valuable firsthand sources on music in the romantic era, one which is essential for research on Moscheles. It is the compilation of his lifelong diary entries, letters, and personal observations edited posthumously—with great devotion, restraint, and dignity—by his wife Charlotte.[14] It stands on a par with the similar compilation by Weber's son Max, with the autobiographies of Spohr, Berlioz, and Wagner, and with the more distantly related *Gesammelte Schriften* of Schumann. Moscheles—this gregarious, much loved, immensely successful pianist, conductor, and composer—seems not merely to have crossed paths with but to have built close friendships with nearly every important musician of his day. With Mendelssohn, younger by a half generation, he was first a piano teacher during a short but exciting, intensive period of lessons, then a kind of second father as the men exchanged visits at every opportunity, and ultimately more of a brother, confidant, and intimate musical companion. When Mendelssohn died at only thirty-eight in 1847, Moscheles, Hauptmann, David, and Gade were pallbearers at the Leipzig funeral, which marked an international tragedy and a lasting hurt not unlike that after John Kennedy's death in 1963. With Schumann, Moscheles stood, at least in name, as one model for aspiring young composers, although whether Schumann actually heard Moscheles play or knew much of his music before 1832 has recently been opened to question.[15] Thereafter, mutual respect must have developed, as suggested by reviews each did of the other's works, also by Schumann's dedication of his piano "Concerto without Orchestra," Op. 14, to Moscheles in 1836 and Moscheles's dedication of his Sonata for piano and cello, Op. 121, to Schumann in 1851. Even so, in 1849 Moscheles had to write his wife of Schumann's "extreme reticence; try as I will, I cannot inveigle him into a conversation about art."[16]

Among other friends whom Moscheles came to know not just casually but well were the pianists Hummel, Clementi, Cramer, Thalberg (who studied with him), Kalkbrenner, Chopin, and Liszt; the violinists Spohr, Paganini (with unhappy consequences), David, and Joachim; the composers Beethoven (whose late works, es-

Ex. 1. Hauptmann, Op. 26, No. 6

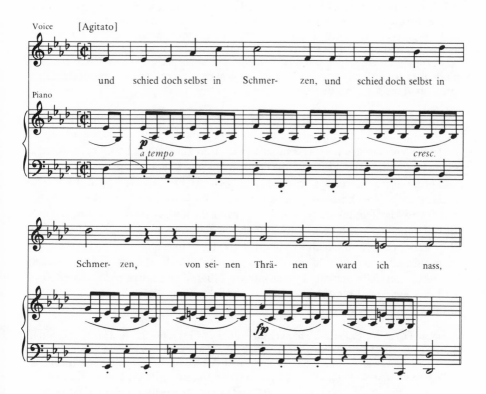

pecially the Ninth Symphony and last sonatas, Moscheles did much to make known and accepted before 1850), Weber, Rossini, and Meyerbeer; the singers Sonntag, Jenny Lind, Malibran, and Schröder-Devrient; and men of letters such as Sir Walter Scott, Heine, and the lieder poet Karl Klingemann.

Moscheles was born in Prague in 1794. During his long, busy life, he travelled often as a virtuoso. He established a first home base in London when he married in 1825 and a second, final one in Leipzig when he responded to Mendelssohn's call in 1846 to join the Conservatory faculty. As early as 1816, he had journeyed from Vienna to play in the first of many Gewandhaus concerts, and now in one year was to succeed Mendelssohn as director of the Conservatory. As a confirmed classicist, Moscheles evidently came much closer in his playing to Clementi and Hummel (of whom he was a friendly rival in his earlier years) than to Chopin or Liszt. The quality of his playing, both in technique and artistry, must have been on a par with the best, to judge by the almost universal praise that was lavished on him. As late as 1854 his Leipzig colleague Hauptmann wrote to Spohr:

Moscheles was at the piano, and I do not think his rendering could be improved upon. . . . Pianists who think they can equal Moscheles, or beat him hollow, are in number as the sand of the sea. . . . They have no eyes to see what a true artist he is, what a real master of his craft! No raw material for him; he works it all up into gold. It is often said that you cannot see the wood for the trees, but our young pianists cannot see the trees for the wood. Yet every tree, every little leaf upon every tree, has its own organization as part of the forest, as the condition of its existence. . . . With the ordinary *virtuoso*, a shake is a shake—a mordent a mordent. How different these things may be, occurring in different compositions, that artist alone can show, whose technical proficiency is made a means for the expression of truth, not for the display of execution.[17]

Moscheles showed interest in everyone and everything, all of which added experience, sophistication, and wisdom to his important teaching in Leipzig. He wrote in detail, with discernment and superior technical knowledge, about each make of piano he encountered. He took special joy in the music manuscripts of past masters and gradually acquired a fair number of his own. He became one of the first to present entire solo keyboard recitals (in the later 1830s, along with Clara Schumann and Liszt) and perhaps the first to revive the harpsichord in playing the music of Domenico Scarlatti and his contemporaries. And he still found time to worship Shakespeare and Goethe, to ponder over the classic philosophers, to study the sciences, and to relish his annual vacations abroad with his family. His comments on other musicians seem fair, accurate, and highly perceptive today. In 1849 he had this incidental remark to make about Schumann, Mendelssohn, and public taste in Leipzig:

How am I to understand this? The very same public which rationally and justly was enthusiastic in favor of Schumann's great work, the B-flat major Symphony, was now completely carried away by a lady-harpist and Parish Alvars' bravura playing! This is your so-called art-enlightenment audience! Again I was displeased with the lukewarm reception given to Mendelssohn's works. O Clique! as if in a city where the genius of a Schumann is worshipped, it should be necessary to cry down Mendelssohn as pedantic, and inferior to his brother in art! The public loses all judgment, and subordinates every feeling and musical instinct to one leadership, which cozens it as much as the Radicals do the German people.[18]

In spite of his enquiring mind, Moscheles might not have had much patience with today's musicologists. In later years he wrote from Leipzig, "I am sorry to say there are many students here who, instead of employing their time in composition, abuse it by writing pungent criticisms for the musical press, a practice which always reminds me of Mendelssohn's words: 'Why on earth do they talk and write so much? Let them compose good music instead!' "[19]

Like Hauptmann—and how many other creators in the arts, both great and small?—Moscheles expressed doubts about his own compositions. Thus, in a diary entry of 1838 he wrote, "I tried my [new] Pastoral Concerto [with its "shorter modern form in three connected movements"]; it pleased my friends but occasionally doubts arise in my mind as to whether my mode of composing on fixed principles does not spoil that easy flow and freshness which in my early youth was so attractive, and yet I am glad to show the musical world my greater earnestness and deeper aims, however short my present success may be of what I might wish."[20]

Moscheles's many published compositions include variations, etudes, fantasias, and sonatas for piano, as well as some lieder.[21] Among the most popular in his day seem to have been the duets for four hands at one piano, including several that he played with Chopin or Liszt at various times. Two of the most successful duets were large-scale sonatas. The earlier, Op. 47 in E-flat, he played so often with Chopin in Paris that it came to be known there simply as "La Sonate."[22] The other, Op. 112 in B minor, he wrote in Paris the year before his move to Leipzig, playing it first with his gifted daughter Emily for its dedicatee, King Louis Philippe, then soon after with Madame Pleyel for his emotional farewell concert in London, and finally with Mendelssohn in Leipzig. In each of these musical centers it was reviewed with much respect for its mastery of the duet setting and with considerable praise for its artistry, but also with gentle reservations about mature discipline supplanting youthful intuition,[23] thus seconding the doubts that Moscheles himself had expressed over his "Pastoral Concerto." Its title, *Grande Sonate Symphonique*, suggests Moscheles's serious approach to this four-movement work, with its extended outer movements which have interrelated slow introductions, and with an imposing chorale in the finale. In the slow movement delicate figuration prevails. In the third movement, entitled "Scherzoso alla tedesca antica," original harmonic turns, skillful counterpoint, ingenious rhythms, euphonious textures, and fresh technical demands raise Moscheles a clear notch above those run-of-the-mill contemporaries, as is at least hinted by ex. 2, from the opening. Pianists who still know his later etudes will agree that he was not simply a slavish imitator of Mendelssohn and that he revealed some classically neat Romanticisms of his own.

Ferdinand David, the third and youngest of our three musicians in the Leipzig of Mendelssohn and Schumann, left relatively less in the way of documentation, perhaps because he found less time for diaries and correspondence in his ceaseless, conscientious work.[24] Born in Hamburg in 1810, he went to Kassel at thirteen for violin training under Sophr and theory under Hauptmann. At fifteen he began wide recital tours with his sister, a concert pianist who was to settle in the London circles of Moscheles. And at fifteen he appeared in a Gewandhaus concert and in Berlin, where his lifelong friendship with Mendelssohn began. After service in Berlin and in Estonia, David responded in 1836 to Mendelssohn's invitation to serve as concertmaster of the Gewandhaus orchestra, making Leipzig his home thereafter. He soon became a kind of indispensable sergeant-at-arms under Mendelssohn, gradually adding the same duties at the Theater orchestra, then the directorship of church music in Leipzig, and, when the conservatory opened, the responsibility for the violin teaching. In 1835, shortly after Mendelssohn first met Schumann in Leipzig, David also met Schumann there. A warm professional friendship developed, as revealed in an exchange of informative letters between David and Schumann from 1840 to 1853.[25] A few typical sentences from one of David's letters, while the Schumanns were on their Russian tour in early 1844, gives a little insight into David's nature and current Leipzig musical life:

All is as before here, only four weeks later. The subscription concerts keep going at their calm pace, sometimes a bit too calm in the presto[s]. In the latest quartet evening I played

Ex. 2. Moscheles, *Grande Sonate Symphonique*

your A-minor Quartet; it pleased [everybody] greatly, especially me. At the Theater Mlle Masse guested in Huguenots-Robert-Templar-Norma and everything else spectacular that possibly can fit her voice and personality. The Milanollos [a pair of widely successful violinists, sisters from Italy] made a big hit, deservedly; they play most charmingly, especially the older one. . . . They have played three times in the Theater and once at the Gewandhaus . . . I visited Mendelssohn for a few days in Berlin and also heard a symphony evening; a Haydn symphony came off precisely, although rather dully; they played *Fingal's Cave* correctly, but without fire; however, the "Eroica" was ridiculous, erratic, shaky, cockeyed, without projection in the winds, without verve in the strings, without enthusiasm—indeed, without reaction by the audience—and [of all things] Mendelssohn conducted![26]

Ex. 3. Corelli, *Follia* Variations, Op. 5, No. 12

As one of the foremost violinists of his day David marked a transition from the classicists to the later romantic virtuosi. He not only introduced Mendelssohn's Violin Concerto in E minor, in 1845, but he had previously helped with its treatment of violin technique. He did much for violin pedagogy, too, including the teaching of both Joachim and Wilhelm, and much for greater refinement in the playing of both orchestral and chamber music. Alas, his sizable number of published compositions[27]—orchestral, chamber, solo instrumental, and vocal—made less impression, even while David lived. But his numerous transcriptions and editions did better. In fact, along with his pioneer performance edition of Bach's unaccompanied violin sonatas, one other of his editions remains the chief contribution that has kept his name alive at all. It is the three-volume historical collection entitled *Hohe Schule des Violinspiels,* started earlier but not published until 1867, by Breitkopf and Härtel. The historical significance of this edition today lies, of course, in its successful revival of early music rather than in its editing. The editing represents the need then felt to elaborate, enrich, and intensify the melody, harmony, passagework, and texture in order to make it all palatable to the tastes of the time. Like Bülow's editing of Beethoven's sonatas soon after, David's editing was a labor of love, carried out meticulously, expertly, and imaginatively, even though it is viewed as extreme and quite unacceptable in today's age of antiseptically pure editions. Some idea of that editing according to romantic tastes may be had by comparing the start of the final variation from Corelli's *Follia* of 1700 (Op. 5, No. 12), as realized by Antonio Tonelli probably by 1725,[28] with the version in David's virtual transcription (Ex. 3).

An unidentified reviewer, perhaps the teacher and composer Selmar Bagge, was much impressed by David's *Hohe Schule des Violinspiels* and both the historical and instrumental experience it implied. In consequence, he wrote a detailed analysis of each piece, from Biber to Mozart, spreading the whole over twenty-six columns, eight issues, and five months of the *Allgemeine musikalische Zeitung* in its second series.[29]

In Leipzig Hauptmann, Moscheles, and David defined quite respectable careers of their own. Each played essential roles in Leipzig's rich, concentrated musical life. If nearly a century and a half seems almost to have obliterated their activities and contributions, there still can be little doubt that each man made a conspicuous mark in his own day and that each enjoyed the mutual respect of the others and of Mendelssohn and Schumann.

Marcia J. Citron

Fanny Hensel's Letters to Felix Mendelssohn in the Green-Books Collection at Oxford

The Green-Books Collection—more than five thousand letters written to Felix Mendelssohn from 1821 until his death in November 1847—forms a major part of the rich corpus of Mendelssohniana in the Margaret Deneke Mendelssohn Collection of the Bodleian Library. Inherited by Felix's eldest son, Carl, after Cécile's death in 1853, the Green Books remained in the hands of Felix's descendants until his grandson, Paul Beneke, entrusted it to his friend Margaret Deneke. The Bodleian gained official possession of the Green Books in 1973, after the death of Margaret's sister Helena. Thanks to the recently published catalogue of the Collection prepared by Margaret Crum, the scholarly community at large now has bibliographical access to the wealth of source material housed within the twenty-six volumes of the Green Books.[1]

The significance of the Green Books to Mendelssohn research is clear: they form the largest extant collection of letters written to Felix over the course of his entire creative life. In the earlier volumes family letters dominate the correspondence, whereas a higher proportion of letters from friends and professional contacts occupy the later volumes. Felix's elder sister, Fanny Hensel (1805–1847), is represented by 279 letters, one of the largest groups of letters by any one correspondent. Many of her letters, especially those from Felix's early years, are parts of composite letters in which other family members—notably her sister, Rebecka, and mother, Lea—contributed substantial sections as well. As a group these letters provide insight into Felix's special relationship with his family and particularly with his musical confidante, "Fenchel." They also reveal the wit, perspicacity, and creativeness of this gifted woman musician at the center of a flourishing Berlin *salon*.

Fanny and Felix received similar musical educations from the leading Berlin pedagogues: study of piano with Ludwig Berger, and theory and composition with Carl Friedrich Zelter. The siblings naturally enough developed a lifelong closeness from their shared musical experiences. During these years the elder Fanny established herself as a mentor and guardian of her younger brother. As the children entered their teenage years, however, a clear decision was made by their parents about the future course of their children's musical training: Felix was encouraged to attain professional status, Fanny was not. Statements by Abraham Mendelssohn from the 1820s, quoted by Sebastian Hensel in *Die Familie Mendelssohn,* present the rationale for this decision, which nowhere points to a disparity in their musical abilities.[2] In fact, Fanny's musical talent earned high praise. Goethe, for example, asked to be remembered to "your equally gifted sister" in a letter to Felix from 1825.[3] Similar accolades later issued from other prominent figures, among them Ignaz Moscheles and Henry Chorley.[4]

In spite of her obvious creative abilities, both Fanny Hensel's life and her compositions are unknown to most performers and scholars.[5] The obscurity of her music may be readily explained: with few exceptions the published oeuvre has not been reprinted and is found only in a few libraries; hundreds of previously unpublished pieces remain in manuscript form, most of which are at the Mendelssohn Archive in Berlin; and an undetermined but a sizeable number of manuscripts in private collections are virtually inaccessible.[6] Source material illuminating her life and cultural position in Berlin has only been published peripherally in studies focusing on Felix. To date, Sebastian Hensel's pathbreaking biography of the Mendelssohn family—though marred by inaccuracies and uncritical transmission of documents—offers the most thorough published description of Fanny's life through excerpts from her diaries and letters.[7] Additional information may be found in the few published letters from Felix to Fanny, and in other published family correspondence. Surprisingly, Hensel's *Die Familie Mendelssohn* presents more letters from Fanny to Karl Klingemann and others than to Felix. As we know, Sebastian did not have access to the one very large collection of family letters to Felix which would have rounded out his account—undoubtedly, the Green-Books Collection.[8]

Statistically, the Green-Books Collection reveals an uneven distribution of letters from Fanny to Felix (see table 1). Volume 1 of the Green Books contains the greatest number of Fanny's letters—approximately one-fourth of the total of 279. Although this volume spans the nine years from 1821 to 1829, Fanny's sixty-two letters are not distributed evenly over this period: only sixteen were written between 1821 and 1828, for Fanny and Felix were generally together in Berlin, thus precluding the need for letters. Also, as Rudolf Elvers has suggested, Lea Mendelssohn may well have taken charge of letters addressed to Felix during his pre-adult years and thus removed letters which would have eventually been bound into the Green Books.[9] The great outpouring of correspondence begins during Felix's first extended solo trip, the journey of 1829 to England and Scotland. Both the quantity and contents of these letters attest to Fanny's strong emotional reaction occasioned by the siblings' separation. Her forthcoming marriage to Wilhelm Hensel on October 3 prompted a markedly intense production of letters in the immediately preceding weeks, culminating in a cathartic letter to Felix the morning of the wedding.

The years 1830 to 1833 are represented by the letters in Volume 2 of the Green Books; only twenty-nine letters from Fanny to Felix survive from this time. Nineteen are from 1830, the first year of Felix's European grand tour. But from August

Table 1. Distribution of Fanny Hensel's Letters in the Green Books

Year	No. of Letters	Year	No. of Letters
1821	4	1837	20
1825	4	1838	11
1827	5	1839	14
1828	3	1840	11
1829	46	1841	10
1830	19	1842	4
1831–32	*removed*	1843	11
1833	10	1844	7
1834	26	1845	11
1835	26	1846	12
1836	23	1847	2

1830 through all of 1832, no letters from any family member are present, as they and almost all others from this period were removed sometime after 1844.[10] Volumes 3, 4, and 5 cover the years 1834, 1835, and 1836 respectively; each is characterized by a fairly consistent flow of letters to Felix. The summer of 1835 produced a few letters from Fanny's vacation resort on the northern coast of France, Boulogne-sur-Mer. The letters of 1837 (Volume 6) are evenly distributed over the entire year except for a seven-week gap between April and June. These months marked the start of Felix's and Cécile's honeymoon: perhaps the couple was often unreachable; perhaps Fanny did not wish to intrude upon the newlyweds (not very likely); or perhaps any letters she did send to Felix were destroyed, or have since been lost. A more likely explanation, however, is that Fanny was still hurt because Felix had never introduced his fiancée to her and other members of the immediate family.[11]

The letters of 1838 are contained in Volumes 7 and 8. The lack of letters from the summer months is readily explainable by Felix's visit to Berlin. Less obvious, however, is the reason for the absence of any letters by Fanny from March, April, and May. The next two volumes, covering the period from August 1839 to June 1840, contain Fanny's lengthy and descriptive letters during her first trip to Italy. Most of the extended gaps in the remaining volumes result from the siblings' visits in Berlin and Leipzig, and from Felix's more stable residency in Berlin while he was court composer to Friedrich Wilhelm IV between 1841 and 1844.

The increased personal contact between Fanny and Felix during the years after 1840, however, does not account entirely for the smaller number of Fanny's letters from this period. The contents of the letters we do have give the clear impression that Fanny viewed her relationship to Felix in a different light after his marriage to Cécile. It is tempting to attribute the change merely to jealousy on Fanny's part, although this is too simplistic an explanation. Rather, there was a confluence of several factors: the elder Fanny no longer functioned as her brother's protector; Felix was firmly established as a celebrated composer; both Fanny and Felix now had their own individual family lives; and the old Mendelssohn family bond of their youth was weakened, first by the death of their father in 1835, and then by the death of their mother in 1842. In addition, the wounds resulting from circumstances preceding Felix's marriage in March 1837 probably left a permanent scar that had its effect on their future relationship.

Another factor may well have involved Fanny's reaction to Felix's lack of support for a number of her musical projects. This issue surfaced in 1836 and 1837. In January 1836, Fanny wrote to Felix, "I'm very sad, although truly not out of vanity, that I haven't been able to be grateful to you in such a long time for liking my music. Did I really compose better in the old days, or were you merely easier to please?"[12] Later that year, Fanny began to seek Felix's recommendation about having her music published: "In the recent past, I've been frequently asked, once again, about publishing something; should I do it?" (GB 5, No. 132; October 28, 1836). Apparently Felix responded negatively, for Fanny broached the subject again one month later in a letter dated November 22: "With regard to my publishing I stand like the donkey between two bales of hay. I have to admit honestly that I'm rather neutral about it, and Hensel, on the one hand, is for it, and you, on the other, are against it. I would of course comply with the wishes of my husband in any other matter, yet on this issue alone it's crucial to have your consent, for without it I might not undertake anything of the kind" (GB 5, No. 139; November 22, 1836). Felix eventually did give his approval to a publishing venture—a lied included in a Schlesinger anthology—but only after the anthology was issued, early in 1837. The matter of Fanny's publishing reappeared the following summer. This time, Lea penned a letter to Felix in which she urged him to encourage Fanny to publish her music (GB 6, No. 44; June 7, 1837). His negative response to this request makes it clear that he wished Fanny to remain an amateur rather than a professional composer.[13] Felix's failure to encourage his sister contributed to Fanny's modified posture toward him and, perhaps, to the decrease in letters from Fanny in subsequent years.

The Green-Books Collection documents in detail what in any case must have been a close musical and personal relationship between Fanny and Felix.[14] The letters also reveal Fanny Hensel as a major participant in the musical life of her time and as a composer of stature in her own right. Her letters present detailed comments on Felix's works in progress, witty descriptions of cultural figures, and occasional disclosures of the challenges which confronted her as a gifted female musician.

Fanny Hensel's letters supply valuable information about Felix Mendelssohn in several areas: his relationship with his family, the dissemination of his music in Berlin, the chronology of his music, and the various compositional stages of a given piece. Fanny frequently functioned as a kind of mail-order critic for Felix—for many pieces, in fact, his chief critic. Most of her comments consist of relatively brief, generalized remarks, such as we read in a letter of May 11, 1834: "I like your

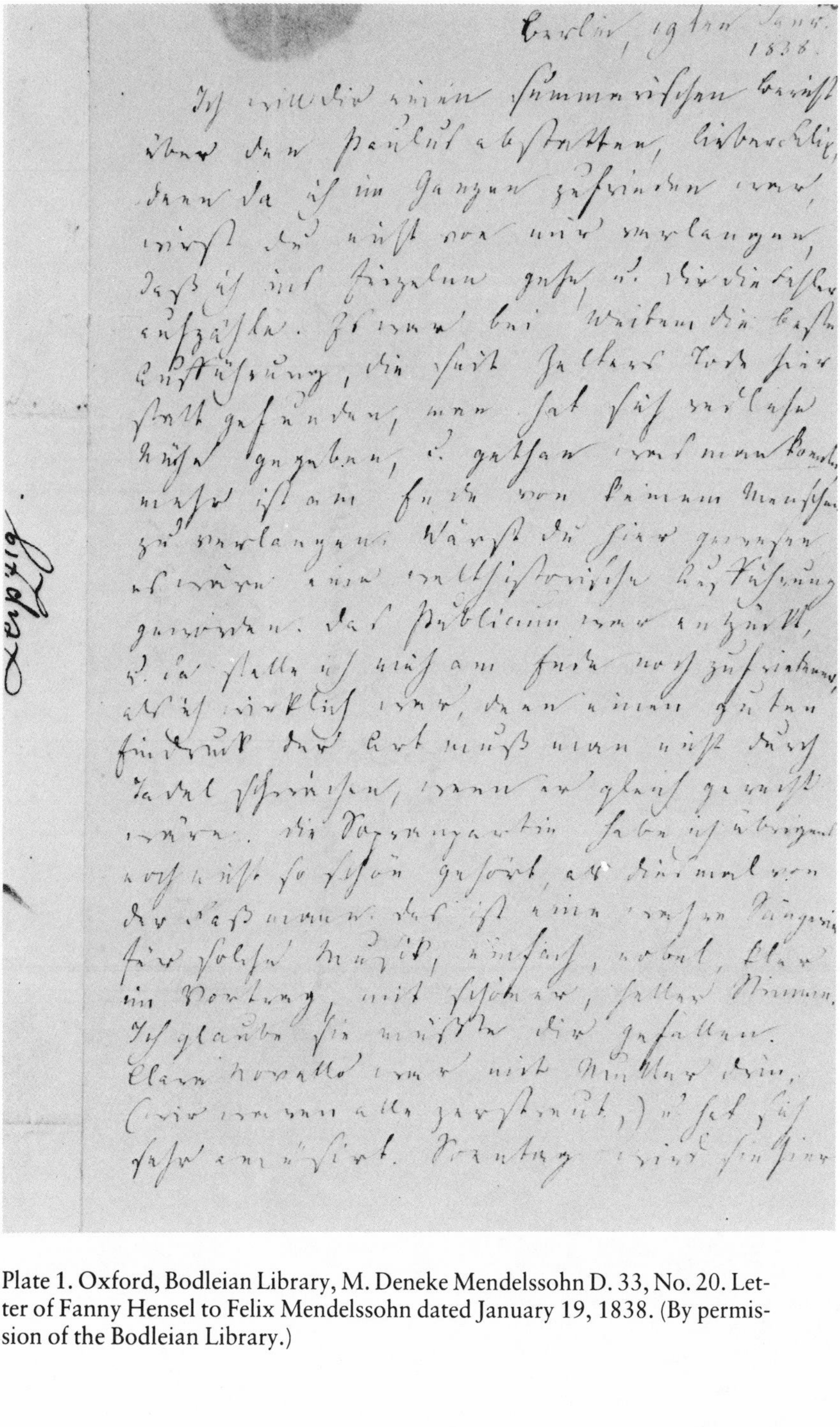
Berlin, 19ten Jan.
1838.

Ich will Dir einen summarischen Bericht
über den Paulus abstatten, lieber Felix,
denn da ich im Ganzen zufrieden war,
wirst Du nicht von mir verlangen,
daß ich ins Einzelne gehe, u. Dir die Fehler
aufzähle. Es war bei Weitem die beste
Aufführung, die seit Zelters Tode hier
statt gefunden, man hat sich redliche
Mühe gegeben, u. gethan was man konnte,
mehr ist am Ende von keinem Menschen
zu verlangen. Wärst Du hier gewesen,
so wäre eine welthistorische Aufführung
geworden. Das Publicum war entzückt,
u. ich stelle mich am Ende noch zufriedener,
als ich wirklich war, denn einen guten
Eindruck der Art muß man nicht durch
Tadel schwächen, wenn er gleich gemischt
wäre. Die Sopranpartie habe ich übrigens
noch nicht so schön gehört, als diesmal von
der Faßmann. Das ist eine rechte Sängerin
für solche Musik, einfach, nobel, klar
im Vortrag, mit schöner, heller Stimme.
Ich glaube sie müßte Dir gefallen.
Clara Novello war mit Mutter drin,
(wir waren alle zerstreut,) u. hat sich
sehr amüsirt. Sonntag wird sie hier

Leipzig

Plate 1. Oxford, Bodleian Library, M. Deneke Mendelssohn D. 33, No. 20. Letter of Fanny Hensel to Felix Mendelssohn dated January 19, 1838. (By permission of the Bodleian Library.)

Sonata in F-sharp very much. I'm working at it diligently, for it is, *à la* Felix, very difficult. Thank you very much for it"[15] (GB 3, No. 140; May 11, 1834).

In contrast are the extended, often minutely detailed treatments of a few pieces, especially the *Melusine* Overture, Op. 32, and the oratorio *St. Paul,* Op. 36. Fanny's discussions of *St. Paul,* which span almost two years, from February 1836 through January 1838, are representative. Her comments address a variety of concerns. In February 1836, as the oratorio was nearing completion (Mendelssohn finished Part I on April 8, Part II on April 18), Fanny responded to Felix's request for a musical critique:[16]

On the whole I wouldn't want to abandon anything: the pieces are well ordered and follow each other nicely and naturally. My criticisms only concern details. . . . A few of the recitatives (in which the strength of the whole work resides) are pointless or too modern. The first one and the following chorus, chorale and second recitative are grand and beautiful and I wouldn't want to omit any of them.[17] The entire first part of the aria in B minor, from "Herr, thue meine Lippen auf" through the *tempo primo,* is marvelous. I find the return of the words weak. The ending is again very lovely.[18] The start of the following recitative is very nice—so serene and cheerful and calm, and it's one of my favorite passages up through "denn siehe, er betet." I find the subsequent text through *tempo primo* too trivial and modern. Don't you think *Allegro con moto* too quick a tempo for this passage?[19] The next piece contains the passage about which Devrient and I disagree: the entrance of the altos with the text "denn der Herr hat es gesagt," with the sopranos in imitation two bars later.[20] Together with the accompaniment, this passage doesn't really seem stern, and I think you invented the theme merely to serve as a countermelody to the first. Later on the theme sounds lovely with the accompaniment, as well as when it's alone and followed by the entrances of the other voices. Only this double entrance on the same notes doesn't sit well with me. And finally, I still want to express my opposition to a passage in the last soprano recitative: the musical treatment of "und ging hin und liess sich taufen" doesn't measure up to the importance of the text[21] (GB 5, No. 21; February 4, 1836).

The public premiere of *St. Paul,* which Fanny attended, took place at the Lower Rhenish Music Festival in Düsseldorf on May 22, 1836. Following the performance, Fanny herself became involved with organizing a performance of the first part of the oratorio in June. In July, she described some later rehearsals and referred to Mendelssohn's insatiable habit of revising:

I held two very pleasant rehearsals of *St. Paul* while Decker was here.[22] But now everybody is scattered in all directions, and so I think the entire matter will have to be postponed until the fall. I'm truly sorry that you've had such a difficult time with the piano arrangement; had you given me even one part of the job, I would have gladly worked hard on it.[23] Furthermore, I am liking the oratorio more and more as I know it better. The weak passages, or those that appear so to me (which we've discussed), are few in number, and I'm very curious about the most recent changes. For example, have you really omitted the first chorus as well? I hope not "Der du die Menschen"—that aria has grown on me[24] (GB 5, No. 112; July 30, 1836).

And, shortly before Christmas of the same year:

I agree with most of your changes, but not all of them. I would have gladly taken a slap on the face rather than the change in one of my favorite passages, "welcher gemacht hat

Himmel und Erde und das Meer."[25] Furthermore, I can't understand why you've excluded the soprano aria that I like so much. I could have done without the one in F major or the alto aria.[26]

On the other hand, I'm glad that you've distributed the dialogue between bass and tenor at the epiphany, [27] and am especially grateful for the change at "denn der Herr hat es gesagt." Why haven't you also inserted a lively chorus at the end, as you intended? (GB 5, No. 149; December 19, 1836).

If Fanny questioned some of Felix's revisions, her intimate knowledge of the score placed her in a good position to report to him about another concern, the preparation for the Singakademie performance of the oratorio.[28] A letter from January 15, 1838, provides a witty description of the rehearsals leading up to the concert:

By the way, the story concerning *St. Paul* is really fascinating. If nothing else, in my role as adviser I was able to avert great disaster for the noble apostle. I understand that Mother wrote you that Rungenhagen[29] had sent me a request to attend the rehearsals and enlighten him with my opinions. So I went there last Tuesday and was quite appalled, just as you have described it. I was suffering and champing at the bit, just like you, as I heard the whining and Grell's dirty fingers on the piano.[30] I thought to myself, "If you were only up there everything would be fine." Lichtenstein sat next to me and heard my sighs. They started "mache dich auf" at half the right tempo, and then I instinctively called out, "My God, it must go twice as fast!"[31] Lichtenstein invited me to show them the way but told me that Schneider, the music director, had assured them that one cannot be ruled by a metronome marking.[32] Then I assured them that they could be ruled by my word, and they'd better do it for God's sake. I went back on Friday, this time to the small hall in the Academy. I hadn't been there since Zelter's death and encountered all sorts of living and deceased ghosts. Then Rungenhagen himself came up to me after each chorus and asked me whether it was correct, and I told him honestly yes or no. But overall, I was pleasantly surprised to find such an improvement and started to become hopeful. On Saturday Rungenhagen was here for over an hour and had me listen to all the solo numbers. Friday I also spoke to Ries, who asked, among other things, how I'd feel about adding a tuba to the organ part, as has been done in churches.[33] Now, said tuba is a monstrosity; it transforms all passages in which it appears into drunken beer brewers. Thus I fell on my knees and asked them to spare me and leave the tuba at home.[34] Rungenhagen lifted me up and granted my plea. Yesterday was the first large rehearsal, which far exceeded my expectations. To my great satisfaction, I can tell you that I was thoroughly delighted with everything. The choruses, now taken with the correct tempo (a few perhaps too fast), were performed with fire and power, and enunciated as well as one could wish. The good old blockhead really went all out, and everyone was astonished at his liveliness. Many people realized from which direction the wind was blowing. But I've been calmly restraining myself so as not to seem like the Don Quixote of *St. Paul*. I hope I haven't made any enemies—unless you count the tuba player. . . . It's a shame, however, that you are not conducting this performance; it would have been splendid and required only a minimum of effort on your part[35] (GB 7, No. 17; January 15, 1838).

Fanny's reports on the progress of *St. Paul*, covering almost two years, represent her most substantial written involvement with Felix's compositions. From her perspective in Berlin she surveyed not only her brother's successes and disappointments, but also a broad cross section of the musical life of her time. In her letters to Felix she sharpened her critical views for the benefit of her absent brother. Here is an excerpt from May 1829, in which she coolly commented on Paganini, then the rage of Europe:

Yesterday Paganini was the embodiment of the devil. He played a so-called *Canto appassionato* in E-flat minor with the orchestra in broken tremolos. Suddenly he takes the whole thing into E-flat major, in order to fall back immediately into minor.[36] It was very beautiful and seemed as though he were plumbing the depths of his soul and yet simultaneously ripping the heart out of the poor violin. The *Hexen* Variations, in which he imitates the chatter of hoarse old women, are disgusting. He finished in a very ordinary way, which was a shame (GB 1, No. 66; undated, probably May 6, 1829).

Occasionally she took up the problem of musical fashion. In a letter of December 27, 1834, she waxed philosophic about changing tastes in music:

One can't deny that times change, and with the times the taste, and with the taste of the times we also change. There is definitely also a positive Good in the arts. I don't believe that what we have recognized as the highest and always will recognize as such can be subject to fashion, and I hope you would never think me crazy enough to be capable of such beliefs. Little Hanna in the *Seasons* will age as little as Alceste or the evangelist Matthew. But now there appear an unbelievable number of gray areas within that Good. Since two times two doesn't always equal four in aesthetic matters, there will be a point (in criticism primarily regarding performance interpretation) where the outer world, or the changeability of time, or the *fashion* (get around the word as you wish) will exert its influence. You remember as well as I that there was a time when we were thoroughly charmed by Spohr's music. Now we no longer feel that way. His music hasn't changed and we are still the same people, but our relationship to him has changed. Let's take the case that we've considered before— violinists. Spohr certainly possesses infinite positive Good in his playing, which won't fade away, but he also has a certain sweetness that perhaps contributed to his fame at the time. Now along comes Paganini who plays in a wild, fantastic, and powerful way. All young violinists strive to imitate him and tear the G string. Then, after several years, I hear Spohr again and his sweetness is instinctively more noticeable than before because my ears are now exposed to a totally different style. The public at large is chiefly susceptible to this influence, individuals more or less, but no one is immune to it. It wouldn't be difficult for me to cite many other examples of things or people who were pleasing in the past and now seem dull and boring, or bizarre and unbearable. Such change naturally affects the highest and best of its kind. But I am convinced that even the Good will appear more or less good within the context of time. Respond to this, Clown! (GB 3, No. 341; December 27, 1834).

To some extent, change in musical fashion was determined by the cult of virtuosity. Mendelssohn, like Hensel, a distinguished pianist, appreciated these comments from a letter of June 1837. Here Fanny discussed concert pianists and the virtuoso style:

The musical eccentricity that you mocked stems from the fact that there was hardly any music during the winter, and then three virtuosos—Döhler, Wieck, and Henselt— appeared in a row. . . . Henselt played a pair of Chopin *Etudes* in his concert, as well as a very nice pair of his own. These two were played very delicately and quickly and were the best things on the program. He also performed the somewhat boring trio by Hummel in the same manner that we used to perform it in the old days, the one we had dubbed

"Schmöckerio."[37] . . . Henselt played some of his own variations at the end of the concert.[38] In spite of their difficulties, there was so little that was brilliant, yet so much that was ugly, that I became disgusted, as I generally am with this type of concert. Not one of these three pianists had a regular concert; none played with accompaniment, but only solo etudes, variations, etc. Next they'll go before the public and give a lesson (GB 6, No. 43; June 2, 1837).

Fanny Hensel's descriptions of her own musicales disclose the favored repertoire of one major segment of Berlin's musicians. There is in her letters a decided preference for the music of Bach, Mozart, Beethoven, and Handel, a sympathy that doubtless won Felix's favor. Her letter from December 12, 1837, offers a glimpse into the musical fare at her Sunday musicales:

Vieuxtemps, who plays wonderfully, performed here a week ago Sunday, when he played variations by Bériot, and then Beethoven's trio in D major with Ganz and me.[39] Then came [Mozart's] *Davidde penitente* in which Decker sang the soprano part brilliantly. The aria in B-flat major was unbelievably brilliant and the long cadenza that I composed for her created a furor.[40] There were between 120 and 130 people here, and it was one of our most brilliant morning musicales. Little Vieuxtemps pleases me in many respects. He is unassuming and obliging, traits that are very admirable in someone who, since the age of seven, has been dragged around the world as a *Wunderkind*. Here they create enormous difficulties and intrigues against him, i.e., Möser and company[41] (GB 6, No. 151; December 12, 1837).

Fanny Hensel's letters to Felix provide another perspective on musical life in Berlin in the 1830s and 1840s and especially highlight the contribution of the *salons* to the formation of musical taste in the first half of the nineteenth century. But the letters also reveal much of Fanny's own musical life as composer and performer. Just as Felix sought the critical reaction of his sister to his music, so did Fanny discuss her compositions in her letters to him. Sometimes the references are very brief, such as the following excerpt from an early letter dated October 29, 1821: "The first movement of my F-major Sonata is copied.[42] The corrections are a pain in the neck and proceed slowly. Meanwhile, I hope they will all be made by the time you come home" (GB 1, No. 5; October 29, 1821).

In other letters, the deep influence of Felix on Fanny is evident, as in these letters from 1836, written when Fanny began seriously to consider publishing her music:

As the strict taskmaster has ordered, I've continued to compose piano pieces, and for the first time have succeeded in finishing one that sounds brilliant. I don't know what Goethe means by the demonic influence, which he mentioned very often near the end,[43] but this much is clear: if it does exist, you exert it over me. I believe that if you seriously suggested that I become a good mathematician, I wouldn't have any special difficulty in doing so, and I could just as easily cease being a musician tomorrow if you thought I wasn't good at that any longer (GB 5, No. 112; July 30, 1836).

You ask what I've composed and I answer, half a dozen piano pieces, as per your instructions. . . . If you have time, play them through sometime, or have one of your students play them, and let me know what you think. I bear such a great similarity to your students that I always find it most profitable if you tell me to do this or that (GB 5, No. 132; October 28, 1836).

Felix's admiration for these new pieces pleased Fanny,[44] as we learn in her letter of November 16: "You can imagine how happy I am that you like my piano pieces, for it leads me to believe that I haven't gone totally downhill in music. Only please return them; I want to have them copied for you" (GB 5, No. 135; November 16, 1836).

Felix's positive reaction to these piano pieces was typical of his high regard for Fanny's compositions. He consistently encouraged her to write music, yet the encouragement stopped short of recommending publication—Felix was opposed to Fanny's aspirations to become a professional composer. During the summer of 1846, Fanny wrote to Felix to inform him of her firm plans for the publication of her music. Her letter of July 9, 1846, is singularly revealing of the lifelong closeness and tensions between the two:

Actually I wouldn't expect you to read this rubbish now, busy as you are,[45] if I didn't have to tell you something. But since I know from the start that you won't like it, it's a bit awkward to get under way. So laugh at me or not, as you wish: I'm afraid of my brothers at age 40, as I was of Father at age 14. Or, more aptly expressed, desirous of pleasing you and everyone I've loved throughout my life. And when I now know in advance that it won't be the case, I thus feel rather uncomfortable. In a word, I'm beginning to publish. I have Herr Bock's sincere offer for my lieder and have finally turned a receptive ear to his favorable terms.[46] And if I've done it of my own free will and cannot blame anyone in my family if aggravation results from it (friends and acquaintances have indeed been urging me for a long time), then I can console myself, on the other hand, with the knowledge that I in no way sought out or induced the type of musical reputation that may have elicited such offers. I hope I won't disgrace all of you through my publishing, as I'm no *femme libre* and unfortunately not even an adherent of the *Young* Germany movement. I trust *you* will in no way be bothered by it, since, as you can see, I have proceeded completely on my own in order to spare you any possible unpleasant moment, and I hope you won't think badly of me. If it succeeds—that is, if the pieces are well liked, and I receive additional offers—I know it will be a great stimulus to me, something I've always needed in order to create. If not, I'll be as indifferent as I've always been and not be upset, and then if I work less or stop completely, nothing will have been lost by that either (GB 24, No. 3; July 9, 1846).

The frustration and bitterness that emerge between the lines of the above letter were acknowledged by Fanny, and then softened to some extent, in the following passage in a letter from either late August or September 1846:

If your letter were my only pleasure from the publishing of my lieder, I wouldn't be sorry. It's very kind and has made me happy the last three days, even if I weren't so already. Why didn't I address the lieder to you? In part I know why, in part I don't. I wanted to enlist Cécile as a go-between because I had a sort of guilty conscience toward you. To be sure, when I consider that ten years ago I thought it too late and that now is the latest possible time, the situation seems rather ridiculous, as does my long-standing rage at the idea of starting Op. 1 in my old age. But since you're so amenable to the project now, I also want to admit how terribly uppity I've been and tell you that six four-part lieder, which you really don't know, are coming out next.[47] I gladly would have shown them to you, but you didn't come, and sending them to you is hardly feasible. My Friday singers have enjoyed singing them, and supported by the good advice that is here at my disposal, I have made every effort to make them as good as possible. I will take the liberty of sending Dr. Mendelssohn a copy (GB 24, No. 205; undated, after August 26, 1846).

Fanny's allusion to her old age proved justified, as she died suddenly of a stroke the following May—approximately six months before Felix succumbed to a similar fate. In any case, the tone of this letter, one of Fanny's last in the Green Books, reveals an independent spirit nevertheless influenced by conflicting feelings toward her formerly acknowledged guiding star. Not only does it supply essential information about their changing relationship, but it also attests to the special problems and frustrations facing gifted female composers of the period who might have aspired to professional status through the publication of their music.

The outpouring of emotion displayed in the previous two letters should not give us the wrong impression: most of Fanny Hensel's letters confront everyday family matters and mutual concerns in a straightforward manner. Disappointment and sadness naturally surface from time to time, but anger and bitterness only rarely. A special sisterly concern, growing out of this very special sibling relationship, colors the entire correspondence and is on occasion especially touching.

Letters always tell much about the character of their author: in this case, a mixture of wit, humor, knowledge, perceptiveness, outlook, sophistication, affability, and warmth. Fanny, like her brother Felix, emerges a shrewd and insightful chronicler of the world around her. Her wit animates these letters and makes them a delightful reading experience for both scholar and layman. Their eventual publication[48] should prove a welcome and vital addition to Mendelssohniana, to cultural history, and to the burgeoning interest in one of the nineteenth century's most gifted female musicians.

Ralph P. Locke

Mendelssohn's Collision with the Saint-Simonians

In memoriam Jerald C. Graue

During the winter of 1831–32 Felix Mendelssohn spent four months in Paris. There he came into repeated contact with members of the Saint-Simonian movement—perhaps the most prominent, influential, and controversial of the various "pre-socialist" or "utopian socialist" movements.

He was not the only professional musician to become involved with Saint-Simonism. Indeed, several musicians actually enrolled in the movement and placed their musical talents at its disposal. The most notable of these was Félicien David, future composer of *Le Désert* and various operas on exotic subjects. His propagandistic chansons and choruses for the movement number some two dozen, and he even joined the charismatic Saint-Simonian leader Enfantin on a mission to Egypt.[1]

Mendelssohn's involvement, as one might expect, was far more limited. It more closely resembled, in this respect, the involvement of five other prominent musicians: Berlioz, Halévy, Ferdinand Hiller, Adolphe Nourrit (leading tenor of the Opéra), and the young Franz Liszt.

But there the resemblance ends. These five were all Parisians, whether by birth or adoption, and each of them reacted for the most part positively to the movement and its doctrines. Berlioz, for example, let himself be courted by the Saint-Simonians for nearly a year, and Liszt remained sympathetic to their social and religious ideas his whole life long.[2]

Mendelssohn, in contrast, was not at all Parisian in outlook. And, partly for that reason, his relationship with the movement ended abruptly and soon, having produced little but distress. A "collision" it may well be called, for, like objects or vehicles physically colliding, the two parties in this brief encounter were coming from opposite points on the compass and, as they hurtled toward each other with a bit too much momentum, neither showed the least inclination to yield the right of way.

The story of this collision has never been adequately told, primarily because the relevant passages in Mendelssohn's letters have until now remained unpublished or, at best, been published in abridged and censored form. For the present study, I have transcribed them all afresh and in full. (The three most extensive and important passages are included entire in the appendices.) These new and fuller texts provide us with a good deal of unsuspected information about Mendelssohn's encounter with the Saint-Simonian movement.[3] And when the evidence from the letters is then interpreted in light of the movement's history and certain of its publications, we can finally comprehend why the encounter had to end in collision.

[*i*]

Before we examine Mendelssohn's references to Saint-Simonism in his letters, it will be helpful to look briefly at the Saint-Simonians themselves and at some of their most basic social and aesthetic doctrines. (Certain more specific doctrines and tendencies will be enlisted later as tools in the interpretation of Mendelssohn's letters.)

The Saint-Simonian movement was founded in 1825 by the disciples of the recently deceased social philosopher Henri Saint-Simon.[4] Though the Saint-Simonians intended to spread their master's ideas, in the process they necessarily adapted and altered them; even their own views on certain issues underwent some dramatic transformations during the years in which they were most active, 1825 to 1835.

Nonetheless the central tenets of Saint-Simonian doctrine remained fairly constant. Foremost among these was the belief that French (and, more generally, European) society needed to be reorganized to serve the interests of "the poorest and most numerous class." The Saint-Simonians (following Saint-Simon) called upon the leaders of government and industry to abolish "all privileges of birth, without exception"—including the aristocrats' right to inherit income-producing lands—and instead to reward and foster the work of those "men of talent" who were truly productive, whether they produced with their hands or their heads. An individual's social position would thus be based not on accident of birth, but on his or her native abilities and willingness to use them. "To each according to his calling; to each according to his works," proclaimed the masthead of their newspaper, *Le Globe.*[5] Saint-Simon and the Saint-Simonians hoped that the resulting new social structure would be organic and meaningful, that class antagonisms would thereby disappear, and that the economy would prosper, benefitting people on all rungs of the social ladder. Similarly, all nations would join hands in "the peaceful exploitation of the globe" instead of hacking away at each other in needless bloody conflict.

When Saint-Simon himself spoke of the "productive" members of society, what he most often had in mind was what he called the *industriels*: farmers, artisans, factory owners and workers, merchants, and all others who produce and distribute necessary goods and services. Artists and scientists, in his view, do not by themselves produce anything of great social utility, but they can, indeed must, contribute to the "public welfare" by placing their skills in the service of the *industriels*. "The industrial class must occupy the first place [in society], because it is the most important of all. . . . The other classes must work for it, because they are its creatures and it keeps them alive. In a word, since everything is done *by* industry, everything must be done *for* industry."[6]

Thus the artist was assigned a subordinate position in Saint-Simon's social hierarchy. Subordinate, of course, does not mean expendable or unappreciated. Saint-Simon and his early disciples repeatedly urged artists to join efforts with them. (We shall use the term "artist" here—as they did—to indicate anyone involved in literature, music, or the visual arts.) But their proposed social scheme, with *les industriels* perched securely on top, seems to have made *les artistes* wary, and few responded to the call.[7]

Several years after Saint-Simon's death in 1825, though, his disciples began to shift the emphasis. They still aimed at improving the lot of the poor (and of course the middle class) by rewarding people according to their works, but they also began to feel that people would only take up that message if it were presented to them in an emotionally appealing way: "Reasoning can only convince, whereas feelings persuade and stir people [to action]."[8] Their solution was to turn their movement into a new industrial religion and—since art can work upon people's feelings—to seek out artists willing to aid them in the tasks of persuading and stirring. At times certain of the Saint-Simonians went so far as to suggest that artists would be not just the priests of the new religion, but its prophets and leaders. Emile Barrault, for example, echoing the Romantic exaltation of the creative genius, declared that "the artist is not a weak bird repeating in its cage the tunes which its master has taught it," but rather an eagle "which soars aloft freely and glides high above the earth. A neighbor to the heavens, it is from that spot that he lets his inspired and often prophetic voice be heard. . . . The artist alone, through the force of that sympathy which allows him to embrace God [above] and society [below], is worthy of leading humanity."[9]

This new exaltation of the artist was undoubtedly intended to be more appealing to people in the arts, and—to an extent—it seems to have succeeded. (All seven of the musicians mentioned earlier, including Mendelssohn, became attracted to the Saint-Simonians during the two years that followed publication of Barrault's brochure.) But hidden beneath the captivating imagery lay strong hints that even Barrault still expected artists to "propagate ideas" (i.e., ideas of the Saint-Simonian *pères* or priests), not to develop ideas of their own. "When . . . we [the leaders] announce the advent of a new world, . . . [the artists will know how to find] the songs to revive half-hearted souls, to instill courage, to rouse us to spread open all our sails." The movement's leaders expressed it more bluntly in February 1831: the artist is "[the] agent . . . the *word* and the *gesture* of the priest."[10]

In short, the artist (in the view of the Saint-Simonians) was not at all a free-flying bird, but rather—as Mendelssohn would learn—the servant-songster of a new, Saint-Simonian master.

[*ii*]

Mendelssohn had made two trips to Paris as a youth, in 1816 and 1825, both times accompanied by members of his family. On this third visit, in 1831, he was twenty-two years old and traveling alone. Paris was one of his final stops on a two-year tour of the main cultural centers of Europe; his aim on this journey was to make himself better known and to gather the information and the impressions that would help him select the country and city in which he (as he put it) "would like to live and work" *[wohnen und wirken]* as a composer, pianist, and conductor.[11] The French capital must not have semed very promising in this regard. True, Mendelssohn arrived full of liberal, pro-French sentiments, at least as regarded politics. (He greatly admired what he called the "sublime" revolution that had overthrown the Bourbon regime during July of the previous year.)[12] But in the area that concerned him most—music—he harbored grave doubts. He could not forget the rather dreadful works of Auber and others that he had heard in Paris when he was sixteen.[13] Still, he was willing to give the city a try, if only to prove to the satisfaction of his father that Paris was indeed not the place for him "to live and work."

He arrived on December 9, 1831, and promptly renewed contact with two childhood friends, Ferdinand Hiller and Gustave d'Eichthal,[14] as well as members of the Rodrigues family, friends of his father. Hiller, d'Eichthal, and the Rodrigueses' son Olinde were all Jews, and they were all actively interested in the Saint-Simonians. This was not coincidental. A number of Jews found the Saint-Simonian doctrine attractive because it promised them a position in society according to merit, unimpeded by the religious intolerance that had flourished under the Bourbons.[15] D'Eichthal and Rodrigues were in fact among the leaders of the Saint-Simonian movement, and Hiller, though not a member, eagerly attended its meetings.[16]

Mendelssohn's letters from his first few weeks in Paris are full of annoyance at having to spend the whole winter in the frivolous and superficial French capital.[17] His feelings about the Saint-Simonians during these early weeks seem similarly distant and disapproving, as if he preferred not to get to know the movement and its ideas: "By the way, [Father,] I wanted to ask you if you want me to visit Rodrigues. Olinde has become a raging Saint-Simonian *[ein wüthender Saint-Simonist]*; and his wife, too. They try in every way to convert anyone they run into, so I'm not too inclined [to call on them]. But I don't know if you are as friendly with him as you are with his father and so I ask you to tell me what *you* want."[18]

After a month of grousing, though, Mendelssohn began to loosen up and enjoy the city, perhaps in spite of himself. On January 11, 1832, he wrote to the dramatist Karl Immermann, "I thoroughly enjoy and admire Paris, and am becoming better acquainted with it. . . . I have thrown myself right into the whirlpool, and do nothing the whole day long but see new things: the Chambers of Peers and Deputies, paintings and theaters, dio-, neo-, cosmo-, and panoramas, social gatherings, and so forth."[19]

The "and so forth" included the Saint-Simonians. In a longish letter written on

January 14, 1832 (appendix 1), Mendelssohn reported that he had recently had discussions with Gustave d'Eichthal, had been given brochures by Olinde Rodrigues to distribute in Germany, and had attended a meeting at which Olinde presided in authoritarian manner. Mendelssohn responded to all this with very mixed emotions:

Eichthal has moved out of his parents' house into the rue Monsigny, where he now lives body and soul. His entire household is unhappy about it, and rightly so, but I cannot see an end to it, for it is an *idée fixe* with him. I have an appeal to all people by Olinde Rodrigues, in which he presents his confession of faith and calls upon everyone to give a portion of his fortune, as small as one may wish, to the Saint-Simonians. The call also goes out to artists to devote their art henceforth to this religion: to make better music than Rossini and Beethoven, to build temples of peace, to paint like Raphael or [Jacques-Louis] David. I have twenty copies of this appeal, which I am supposed to send to you, dear Father (as Père Olinde instructed me). I will leave it at *one*, and you will find it quite enough; and that one only when the opportunity presents itself, of course.[20]

It is a bad sign of the state of the public mind here that such a monstrous idea, in such detestable prose, should ever have come into existence and that a good many of the pupils of the *Ecole polytechnique* have taken part. You would not believe how it can be possible, since they approach the matter in a purely external way, promising honor to some, fame to others, a public and applause to me, money to the poor; since, in short, they want to reward everyone according to what he deserves; since they [would] therefore destroy all striving and desire for advancement with their perpetual, cold estimation of capacity.

But then from time to time certain ideas appear—e.g., ideas of universal brotherly love, of disbelief in Hell, the devil, and damnation, of the annihilation of egoism—all ideas which in our country spring from nature, and which prevail in every part of Christendom, ideas without which I should not wish to live, but which they regard as a new invention and discovery.

And when they constantly repeat that they seek to transform the world and to make men happy; when Eichthal tells me quite calmly that they do not need to improve themselves, but others only, for they are not at all imperfect but, on the contrary, perfect; when they do nothing but praise and compliment each other and anyone whom they wish to win over; when they admire the talent or capacity [which you possess] and lament that such great powers should be lost through adherence to all the worn-out notions of duty, vocation, and activity, as they were formerly interpreted—when I listen to all this, it does seem to me a sad mystification.

Last Sunday I attended a meeting at which the Fathers sat in a circle, high up [on the stage]. Then came the highest Father, Olinde Rodrigues, who called them to account, praised and blamed them, addressed the assembled people and issued commands—it was the first time that I have seen him since seven years ago, and to me it was almost ghastly [*schauerlich*]! He too has renounced his parents and lives with the Fathers, his subordinates, and is endeavoring to organize a loan for their benefit. Enough of this![21]

On January 22, a week after writing this first long letter on the Saint-Simonians, Mendelssohn wrote a second one (appendix 4), this time directed mainly to his elder sister Fanny. The letter indicates that Hiller, d'Eichthal, and Olinde Rodrigues were in the custom of calling on him at his lodgings, that there was still much talking of things Saint-Simonian, and that Rodrigues had recently offered some shocking "disclosures" about the movement that now made it seem utterly repulsive to Mendelssohn. (Also, the reference to a copy of his Piano Quartet in B minor, Op. 3, suggests that he had at some point attended at least one soirée at the Saint-Simonians' headquarters, 6 rue Monsigny, and perhaps taken part in a performance of the Quartet there.)

[I am always being invited here and there.] So when am I to compose? In the forenoon, perhaps! Yesterday, first Hiller came, then Kalkbrenner, then Habeneck. The day before that, Baillot came, then Eichthal, then Rodrigues. Perhaps early in the morning! Well, I do compose then—so you are wrong, you witch.

. . . .

Rodrigues was with me yesterday, talking Saint-Simonism, and because he thought I was either stupid enough or smart enough, he made disclosures that shocked me so much that I resolved never again to go to him or to the other accomplices. This morning Hiller rushed into the room and told me that he had just witnessed the arrest of the Saint-Simonians. He wanted to hear their sermon; the Popes do not arrive. All of a sudden soldiers make their way in and request everyone present to disperse as quickly as possible, since Herr Enfantin and the others have been arrested in the rue Monsigny. In the rue Monsigny a party of National Guards and other soldiers are standing in formation. Everything gets locked up and now the trial will begin. They will have a difficult case, because the new jury, which no longer consists of the candidates of [liberal leader] Odilon Barrot, supports the ministry [of Auguste Casimir Périer] and has already given out several very harsh verdicts. My B-minor [Piano] Quartet, which is lying in the rue Monsigny, gets locked up as well; only the Adagio movement belongs to the *juste milieu*, all the others are *mouvement;* I shall eventually be obliged to play it before the jury. But seriously, I feel extraordinarily sorry for the Eichthals. Gustav [sic], who is in London, will probably have a tough case, and in the end it will become apparent that he has been the [Saint-Simonians'] chief dupe.[22]

Rodrigues's "disclosures" must indeed have shocked Mendelssohn greatly. He seems to have held to his resolve never again to visit the Saint-Simonians. He did continue to see Gustave d'Eichthal socially—he even went to the theater with him.[23] But his attitude toward Olinde Rodrigues and the movement now became firmly ironic and distant: "I've seen Rodrigues, the father, several times. He is in no way a Saint-Simonian, and the apostlehood of his son and of his daughter seems to give him little joy. A few days ago his daughter married the Saint-Simonian preacher [Henri] Baud in a simple civil exchange of vows, not with church, organ, benediction and that sort of outdated rubbish *[und dergleichen veraltetem Zeug]*."[24]

On February 19, about a month after the catastrophic visit from Olinde, Mendelssohn wrote a little-known letter to the editor of *Le Globe* that marked the definitive close of his rather uncongenial encounter with the Saint-Simonian movement:

Monsieur,

My friend, M. Gustave d'Eichthal, undertook several days ago to ask you no longer to send me your newspaper *Le Globe,* since all my ideas are too opposed to all those which you espouse. In spite of this, I have continued to receive it since that time, and I am therefore writing to ask you yourself no longer to send me a newspaper whose sole aim is the propagation of your new religion, and which, since I have read it, has only served to alienate me from it [your religion] irrevocably.[25]

[*iii*]

What, one cannot help wondering, led Mendelssohn to such a negative view of the Saint-Simonians? Any answer to such a question can at best be only partial. We are dealing here with the relationship between a very complex, sensitive individual and a social movement whose leading representatives all had their own favorite ideas, their personal quirks, and so on. The best evidence is found in Mendelssohn's two letters on the Saint-Simonians from January 14 and 22, in certain Saint-Simonian publications from around that time, and in what is known more generally of the views and personal characteristics of Mendelssohn and of the Saint-Simonians.

The passage from Mendelssohn's letter of January 14 consists almost entirely of negative remarks. One of these can be partly reinterpreted in a positive sense. Mendelssohn lists several essentially religious ideas of the Saint-Simonians with which he agrees, objecting only that these ideas are not at all novel: "universal brotherly love; disbelief in Hell, the devil, and damnation; the annihilation of egoism." I can find no satisfactory explanation for Mendelssohn's curious claim that these ideas "spring from nature [in Germany] and . . . prevail in every part of Christendom." True, Mendelssohn's own family, with its roots in the German Enlightenment, held firmly to such ideas as religious tolerance and public service, specific instances of two of the principles that Mendelssohn cites here (brotherly love, annihilation of egoism). But the Mendelssohns were hardly typical, as the young musician himself had discovered on many occasions. He cannot honestly have been convinced that religious superstition (e.g., belief in the devil) was entirely a thing of the past and that humanitarianism already existed everywhere and no longer needed to be preached.[26] Perhaps he simply could not become accustomed to the Saint-Simonians' willingness to attack such problems head-on, even insolently; certainly no social or political movement back home in Prussia would have dared to do so.

The remaining negative remarks in the letter of January 14, truly negative ones now, refer to two basic issues: the movement's views on the social role of art, and the movement's authoritarian tendencies. Mendelssohn attacks first the movement's aesthetic views as promulgated in what he calls "an appeal to all people by Olinde Rodrigues." The brochure in question is clearly the *Appel* which Rodrigues wrote in November 1831 to announce a fund-raising bond drive. The specific passage to which Mendelssohn must have been referring is the following (the original text may be found in appendix 2). It contains the very phrases which annoyed him: about Rossini and Beethoven, Raphael and David, and "temples of peace."

I call upon artists who love the people. . . .

Where is he, the poet who truly loves the people, who—proud of having sung [the praises of] Napoleon and the people's flag—will henceforth sing the hope of a hard-working people, a people which wishes no longer to make war? When will I hear the people sing the hymn of peace, more electrifying than the awesome "Marseillaise," more joyful than the simple "Parisienne"? Where is he, the Saint-Simonian Béranger, the Tyrtaeus of peace, whose accents will halt the horrid battle and will convert the masters and the workers to the new faith?[27]

Let him appear, too, the musician whose intoxicating and powerful music—richer than that of Rossini and Beethoven—will seize hold of the emotional power unique to music through all its melodies, through all its variations, in order to accompany the hymn of the future.

Painters, do not soil your brushes any longer by offering to our eyes a debauched and bleeding liberty. Worthy heirs of Raphael and David, be inspired by the sufferings of the daughter of the people, cause us to admire the woman of the future, throwing her life and her faith into the midst of the combatants in order to win them over to the love of God and humanity.[28]

Sculptors, let the Moses of peace burst forth from the marble.[29]

Architects, where are your plans for the temple of peace?[30]

Political writers, journalists . . .[31]

A "monstrous idea" in "detestable prose," thought Mendelssohn. Rodrigues's suggestion that composers should stand on the shoulders of Rossini and Beethoven must have been particularly distasteful. Rodrigues, to be fair, may have been trying to allude to the then current idea that the music of the future would combine the melodic fluency of the Italians with the harmonic and orchestrational subtlety and power of the Germans.[32] He may even have had in mind the fashionable composer who was doing just that: Giacomo Meyerbeer. But Mendelssohn was raised to respect, even worship the great masters. The idea that anyone might be able to surpass Beethoven must have struck him as unlikely. But to seek actively to surpass Beethoven—that was worse. It was "monstrous."

The larger idea which Rodrigues was pushing in this passage was that—as Mendelssohn put it—artists should "henceforth devote their art to this religion." Mendelssohn objected later in his letter to an even stronger version of this thought: "They admire the talent or capacity [which you possess] and lament that such great powers should be lost through adherence to all the worn-out notions of duty, vocation, and activity, as they were formerly interpreted." Such laments mixed with admiration (or flattery) can indeed by found in Saint-Simonian writings, for example in a speech by Emile Barrault (appendix 3), whose text Mendelssohn may well have known: "Artists and poets—you men of desire and independence—listen to us! . . . Come to us without mistrust. Outside of us what can you do today? Extol or repudiate the past, blaspheme or sing [the praises of] the present, repeat what Lamartine, Byron, and Béranger have done."[33]

The patronizing, blustering tone that marred such pronouncements was certainly unfortunate; what is more, it was unnecessary. The movement's desire to attract artists was, in fact, not as narrowly defined as such categorical rhetoric implied. Though the Saint-Simonian leaders were particularly eager to find a "court composer" who would sing the praises of an organic, industrial future and willingly write propagandistic and ceremonial hymns for both internal and external use (they eventually found such a composer in David), they would no doubt have been happy to receive artistic support of a more modest or conventional nature: a benefit concert, for example, such as Berlioz seems to have been planning on their behalf in July 1831, or an oratorio or opera based on a libretto which even faintly echoed their sentiments. It is not inconceivable that Mendelssohn would have given a public performance or composed a piece in honor of a social movement. Indeed, in 1828 he had already written a cantata for a major gathering of scientists and doctors, and the text, using images not unlike those favored by the Saint-Simonians, conjured up visions of a blessed future in which men together harness the forces of nature to "shape and build the magnificent world."[34] Nonetheless, the disrespectful tone in the Saint-Simonians' approaches to him would in itself have gone far toward souring any enthusiasm he might have had.

This lack of respect for artists was symptomatic of a more general authoritarian tendency which Mendelssohn found perhaps even more disturbing: "Last Sunday I attended a meeting at which the Fathers sat in a circle, high up. Then came the highest Father, Olinde Rodrigues, who called them to account, praised and blamed them, addressed the assembled people and issued commands. . . . To me it was almost ghastly!"

The new Saint-Simonian religion had adopted a hierarchical structure analogous to that of the Catholic church. Private and even public confession (calling to account), as Mendelssohn observed, was regularly practiced by the leaders and, in the opinion of some members, abused.[35] Indeed, the very existence in this religious movement of a few infallible Fathers giving orders to their subordinates went so directly against Mendelssohn's individualistic, liberal Lutheran ideals that he could not possibly have remained interested for long.[36]

The final break, though, came for other reasons, reasons that Mendelssohn hinted at in his second letter (January 22). Rodrigues, he wrote, made certain "disclosures" that so "shocked" him that he resolved never again to visit Rodrigues or "the other accomplices." This is harsh language. What could Rodrigues have said to upset Mendelssohn so?

The history of the Saint-Simonians suggests two possible shocking "disclosures," one dealing with legality, the other with sexuality.

The Saint-Simonian movement had come under government suspicion in 1831. An investigative team began to seek to prove that the movement, which had proselytized in Lyons, was somehow responsible for the recent uprisings of the weavers in that city. Nothing could have been further from the truth. The Saint-Simonians had always preached firmly against strikes and other unilateral, antagonistic actions on the part of the workers. Perhaps the government wanted to act tough, and thus may have needed a victim, in order to intimidate further acts of opposition. Quickly frustrated by the evident innocuousness of the Saint-Simonians' political doctrines, the investigators redirected their search, hoping to find evidence of something even remotely prosecutable: financial irregularities, "immoral" doctrines, or disobedience of the repressive Article 291 of the penal code, which prohibited most gatherings of more than twenty persons.

The Saint-Simonians were eventually acquitted on most of these counts. But, as reported (worriedly?) by Rodrigues on the morning of January 21, the accusations may have sounded rather ominous to Mendelssohn. (He called the Saint-

Simonians "accomplices" as if they were known criminals.) Ominous it was. The very next morning, January 22, government troops shut down the Saint-Simonians' headquarters and lecture hall and confiscated some of their papers.[37]

The other disclosure which Rodrigues may have made and which would have been more than enough to occasion a violent reaction from Mendelssohn concerned the movement's sexual doctrines. The Saint-Simonians had for some time been preaching against the low social status of women and inveighing against the hypocritical sexual mores of those bourgeois and aristocratic men who zealously guarded their daughters' virginity yet purchased sex for themselves from women too poor to resist. This dreadful state of affairs, the Saint-Simonians felt, derived from the Catholic church's denigration of the body, its glorification of celibacy, and—ultimately—its promise of paradise in the hereafter. The Saint-Simonians thus began to speak publicly of the "rehabilitation of the flesh," by which they meant a new appreciation of all activities of the flesh: manual labor as well as love-making, the achievements and joys of the here-and-now, paradise on earth.[38]

This aspect of Saint-Simonian thought struck a resonant chord with Félicien David, Heine, Liszt, and others in the movement or on its fringes. We can well imagine, though, how uneasy it made Mendelssohn feel. He was prudish about sex—his letters from Paris make that amply clear—and hedonism of any sort struck him as vaguely immoral. Still, his reaction to Rodrigues's "disclosures" seems remarkably intense. The most likely explanation is that Rodrigues, for some reason of his own, divulged to Mendelssohn certain details of the new sexual code that one of the movement's two "Pères Suprêmes," Barthélemy-Prosper Enfantin, had for some time been proposing privately to his disciples. Enfantin felt that since marriage can be such an oppressive institution, it must be modified to allow people whose sexual natures are unusually "mobile" to obtain a divorce easily and move on to a new marriage, followed perhaps by another marriage, and another.

What Enfantin was proposing here was something akin to what exists in many societies today: liberal divorce laws, and full legal protection for any and all sexual activities between consenting adults. This was already too much for people in the 1830s. The newspapers began to report that the Saint-Simonians wanted to replace marriage with free love. Within the movement, objections ran so strong that in late November 1831, a substantial group, including the other "Père Suprême," Saint-Amand Bazard, reviled Enfantin and left for good.[39]

Undeterred, Enfantin continued to elaborate his vision with ever juicier details. In private letters he suggested that the high priests of the new religion—namely himself and a future high priestess—would be the very opposite of the chaste clergy of the Catholic church. They would be unusually "mobile" and would use their whole sexual being to comfort and guide their confused or troubled followers.[40] Even to us today such a suggestion may sound offensive, foreshadowing the sexual promiscuity of certain modern cult leaders such as Charles Manson and Jim Jones. What Mendelssohn would have thought of it may well be clear from his letter of January 22.

[*iv*]

Rodrigues's disclosures, we have seen, caused Mendelssohn to break off all contact with him and the other Saint-Simonian "accomplices"—except Gustave d'Eichthal, who was presumably too close a friend—and to insist that they stop sending him their newspaper. Thus ended the collision.

Curiously, Mendelssohn came into contact again with Enfantin and his friends some ten years later. In 1842 Charles Duveyrier, one of the movement's leaders, desiring to establish himself as a librettist, tried to interest Mendelssohn in an opera libretto. On the face of it, he was making a perfectly reasonable gesture in proposing a collaboration with Mendelssohn. But the details and tone of his proposals smacked of the disrespect for art that Mendelssohn had objected to ten years earlier. Duveyrier at first suggested an opera on the life of the prophet Mohammed, a subject which no doubt had for him the advantage of being both *religieux* and symbolic of the Saint-Simonians' latest project: cutting a canal through Suez to improve trade and international relations.[41] Mendelssohn replied that he was not interested in composing a grand (five-act) opera, an opera for Paris, or an opera on Mohammed. He wanted to write a more modest work, in three acts, and he wanted to write it for the German public.[42] Duveyrier assured him rather heavy-handedly that he understood "the political, moral, artistic, and religious reasons why Mohammed is more a Spanish or Italian subject than a German one," and he quickly came up with another suggestion: Schiller's *Jungfrau von Orléans*, whose heroine (Joan of Arc) embodies "patriotism, exaltation, simplicity, modesty." In support of his proposal he dredged up "the memory of the few moments that we [met]" and launched into a paean to the essential blood-tie between the French and the Germans ("le sang Saxon"),[43] which was of course remarkably insensitive, considering Mendelssohn's Semitic origins. The composer's response to Duveyrier's letter is not known.

A year later, Duveyrier, attempting to salvage the Joan of Arc project, wrote to suggest that the opera could stress the "marvelous" rather than the historical and that, in particular, the character Lionel could be transformed into "a true demon, a true amorous devil," citing the success of Scribe's libretto for Meyerbeer's *Robert le diable*. (Mendelssohn, he did not know, had in fact detested *Robert* in 1832 and ridiculed Scribe's devil.)[44]

Arlès-Dufour, a prominent banker and a close friend of Enfantin's, wrote next in support of Duveyrier's ideas and pressed Mendelssohn to write the opera for Paris; he promised that if Mendelssohn accepted the task, he would ask another of Enfantin's business associates, Louis Jourdan, to do the versification. Arlès-Dufour waxed poetic about the proposed subject: "Joan, the daughter of the people, she whom God raises above kings, princes and nobles"; Joan, who would be applauded not just by "the elite of a single city" but by "the people *en masse*" of all Europe. Furthermore, Arlès transmitted some comments of Enfantin, such as that "Joan would necessarily have an ecstatic vision of the future."[45] Mendelssohn must have been aghast at this onslaught of suggestions, instructions, and shards of Saint-Simonian philosophy, and nothing ever came of the project. Félicien David flourished under similar conditions; indeed, *Le Désert* (1844), his enormously successful oratorio, was in some ways the culmination of Duveyrier's Mohammed project. But a stronger artistic personality could only have felt stifled.

In 1845, when David was making a concert tour of Europe conducting *Le Désert*, Mendelssohn, to his credit, received the young Frenchman with all possible kindness. David was preceded by letters of recommendation from Enfantin and from Duveyrier.[46] Enfantin closed his letter with "the feelings of *religious* admiration that are wished for you by this old friend of some good friends of your father," meaning the Rodrigues and d'Eichthal families.[47] Enfantin could not resist inserting, and underlining, a bit of the old dogma ("les sentiments de *religieuse* admiration"), but his main appeal was to Mendelssohn's sense of loyalty to family and social circle. There was no longer any use pretending. Enfantin recognized clearly enough that Mendelssohn, despite all efforts at converting him, neither was now, nor had ever been, *"ein wüthender Saint-Simonist"*—"a raging Saint-Simonian."

Appendix 1

Excerpt from Mendelssohn's letter to his family, January 14, 1832

Eichthal ist aus dem Hause seiner Eltern in die *rue Monsigny* gezogen und lebt nun mit Leib und Seele dort. Sein ganzes Haus ist unglücklich darüber und wohl mit Recht, aber ich sehe kein Ende davon ab, denn es ist eine fixe Idée bei ihm. Ich habe einen Aufruf an alle Menschen von Olinde Rodrigues, worin er sein Glaubensbekenntniss ablegt und Alle auffordert, einen Theil ihres Vermögens, und sei er so klein er wolle, den St. Simonianern zu geben; auch an die Künstler ergeht der Aufruf, ihre Kunst künftig für diese Religion zu verwenden, bessere Musik zu machen als Rossini und Beethoven; Friedenstempel zu bauen; zu malen wie Raphael und David. Diesen Aufruf habe ich in 20 Exemplaren, die ich Dir, lieber Vater, zuschicken soll, wie Père Olinde mir auftrug. Ich werde es bei einem bewenden lassen, und Du wirst genug daran haben; auch das eine nur bei Gelegenheit, versteht sich. Es ist ein schlimmes Zeichen für den Zustand der Gemüther hier, dass eine solche monströse Idee in ihrer abschreckenden Prosa entstehen konnte, und dass von den Schülern der Polytechnischen Anstalt sehr viele Theil nehmen. Man würde nicht begreifen, wie es möglich sei, wenn sie die Sache so von aussen anpacken: den Einen Ehre, den Andern Ruhm, mir ein Publikum und Beifall, den Armen Geld versprechen, kurz wenn sie Jeden nach seinen Verdiensten belohnen wollen—wenn sie also alles Streben, alles Weiterwollen vernichten durch ihre ewige kalte Beurtheilung der Fähigkeit; aber dann kommen zuweilen Ideen vor, von allgemeiner Menschenliebe, von Unglauben an Hölle, Teufel und Verdammung, von Zerstörung des Egoismus,—lauter Ideen, die man bei uns von Natur hat und im Christenthum überall findet,—ohne die ich mir das Leben nicht wünschte,—die sie aber wie eine neue Erfindung und Entdeckung ansehen; und wenn sie sich jeden Augenblick wiederholen, wie sie die Welt umgestalten, wie sie die Menschen glücklich machen wollen, wenn Eichthal mir ganz ruhig sagt, an sich selbst brauche man gar nicht zu bessern, sondern an den Andern, denn man sei gar nicht unvollkommen, sondern vollkommen,—wenn sie einander und Jedem, den sie gewinnen wollen, Nichts als Complimente und Lobpreisungen machen, die Fähigkeit und Macht bewundern, und bedauern, dass so grosse Kräfte nun verloren gehen sollten durch alle die abgebrauchten Begriffe von Pflicht, Beruf und Thätigkeit, wie man sie sonst verstand:— so will es Einen wie eine traurige Mystifikation bedünken. Ich habe vorigen Sonntag einer Versammlung beigewohnt, wo die Väter oben im Kreise sassen; dann kam der oberste Vater, Olinde Rodrigues, forderte ihnen Rechenschaft ab, belobte und tadelte sie, redete zum versammelten Volke, gab Befehle;—es war das erste Mal, dass ich ihn wiedersah, seit 7 Jahren, und mir war es fast schauerlich! Auch er hat sich von seinen Eltern losgesagt, lebt bei den Vätern, seinen Untergebenen, und versucht eine Anleihe für sie zu machen. Genug davon!

Appendix 2

Excerpt from *Appel* by Olinde Rodrigues

J'appelle les artistes qui aiment le peuple, et les femmes qui toujours ont voulu la paix entre les hommes, qui toujours ont contribué à adoucir la brutalité des hommes, à calmer les souffrances du vieillard, à consoler l'orphelin délaissé.

Où est-il le poète qui aime vraiment le peuple, qui, glorieux d'avoir chanté Napoléon et le drapeau populaire, chantera désormais l'espoir du peuple qui travaille et ne veut plus faire la guerre? Quand entendrai-je le peuple chanter l'hymne de la paix, plus électrisant que la terrible *Marseillaise,* plus joyeux que la simple *Parisienne?* Où est-il le Béranger Saint-Simonien, Thyrtée de la paix dont les accents arrêteront l'horrible bataille, et convertiront les maîtres et les ouvriers à la foi nouvelle?

Qu'il paraisse aussi le musicien dont la musique enivrante et puissante, plus riche que celle de Rossini et de Beethoven, en accompagnant l'hymne d'avenir, s'emparera par toutes ses mélodies, par toutes ses variations, de la puissance d'émotion réservée à la musique.

Peintres, ne salissez plus vos pinceaux en offrant à nos yeux une liberté débauchée et sanglante; dignes héritiers de Raphaël et de David, inspirez-vous des souffrances de la fille du peuple, faites-nous admirer la femme d'avenir, jetant sa vie, sa foi, au milieu des combattants, pour les rallier à l'amour de Dieu et de l'humanité.

Statuaires, faites jaillir du marbre le Moïse pacifique.

Architectes, où sont vos plans pour le temple de la paix?

Ecrivains politiques, journalistes . . .

Appendix 3

Excerpt from a published speech by Emile Barrault

Vous donc, hommes de désir et d'indépendance, artistes, poètes, écoutez-nous! . . . Venez donc à nous sans défiance; hors de nous, que pouvez-vous aujourd'hui? célébrer ou renier le passé, blasphémer ou chanter le présent, refaire Lamartine, Byron, Bérenger [sic]. Quoi? lorsque le peuple souffre, s'agite, et se pousse à des destins nouveaux, ne sentez-vous pas qu'une tâche nouvelle vous appelle? Artistes, qui que vous soyez, vous êtes du peuple; car vous aimez votre liberté et vous sympathisez avec tous les désirs d'émancipation!

Appendix 4

Excerpts from Mendelssohn's letter to his family, January 21 [recte 22 or 21-22], 1832

Also wann soll ich componieren? Vormittags! Gestern kam Hiller, dann Kalkbrenner, dann Habeneck. Vorgestern kam Baillot, dann Eichthal, dann Rodrigues. Also Morgens früh! Na ja,—da componir' ich auch.—Du bist widerlegt, Drude.

. . . .

Gestern war Rodrigues bei mir, sprach St. Simonismus und machte mir, indem er mich entweder für dumm oder für klug genug hielt, Eröffnungen, die mich so empörten, dass ich mir vornahm, weder zu ihm, noch zu den andern Complicen wieder hinzugehen. Heut' früh stürzt Hiller in's Zimmer und erzählt, wie er eben der Arrestation der St. Simonianer beigewohnt habe; er wollte ihre Predigt hören; die Päpste kommen nicht. Plötzlich treten Soldaten ein, und man wird gebeten, sich schleunigst fortzubegeben, da Herr Enfantin und die übrigen in der *rue Monsigny* arretirt seien. In der *rue Monsigny* stehen Nationalgarden und andere Soldaten aufmarschirt; Alles wird versiegelt, und nun wird der Prozess anfangen. Sie werden einen schlimmen Stand haben, denn die neue *Jury,* die nicht mehr aus den Odilon Barrot'schen Candidaten besteht, ist ministeriell, und hat schon mehrere sehr strenge Aussprüche gethan. Mein *H moll-Quartett* ist in der *rue Monsigny* liegen geblieben und wird nun auch versiegelt; nur das Adagio ist vom *juste milieu,* alle anderen Stücke vom *mouvement;* ich werde es am Ende vor der *Jury* spielen müssen. Aber im Ernst bedauere ich Eichthals ungemein; Gustav, der in London ist, wird wohl einen schlimmen Stand haben, und am Ende wird es sich zeigen, dass er der Haupt-*dupe* gewesen ist.

Appendix 5

Mendelssohn to the editor of *Le Globe,* the Saint-Simonian newspaper

Monsieur,

Mon ami, Mr. Gustave d'Eichthal s'est chargé, il y a quelque[s] jours, de vous prier de ne plus m'envoyer votre journal, le Globe, toutes mes idées étant trop contraires à toutes celles, que vous professez. Malgré cela [the word "j'ai" is crossed out] je l'ai toujours reçu depuis ce tem[p]s, et je viens donc vous prier vous même de ne plus m'envoyer un journal, dont le seul but est la propagation de votre nouvelle réligion, & qui n'a contribué, depuis que je l'ai lu, qu'a m'en éloigner irrévocablement. Agréez l'assurance de ma parfaite considération

avec laquelle je suis
votre tres devoué
Felix Mendelssohn Bartholdy

Paris ce 19 fevr.
[18]32

[Address:]   À la redaction du *Globe*
rue Monsigny no. 6

Literary Influences

Jon W. Finson

Schumann and Shakespeare

The influence of William Shakespeare on nineteenth-century Europe is one of the most interesting and well-explored subjects in all of modern scholarship, and surely a whole book might be written on the relationship between nineteenth-century "Shakespearomania" and contemporary composers, among them Berlioz, Nicolai, Weber, Mendelssohn, and Verdi. The name of Robert Schumann would hardly be prominent in this context, but there is some evidence that Shakespeare was every bit as important to Schumann as to the other composers I have just mentioned. Shakespeare's plays ultimately provided little material for Schumann's published works; but Schumann did undertake some composition based on the dramas at each important juncture of his life. Schumann's occasional use of Shakespearean material betokens a wider familiarity with the plays, and this familiarity in its turn places Schumann as part of a German class holding certain common values manifested in the appreciation of Shakespeare's works. For this reason, it will be appropriate to examine Shakespeare's role in eighteenth- and nineteenth-century German culture as well as the poet's significance to Schumann in particular.

[1]

In his book *Shakespeare in Germany, 1740–1815,* Robert Pascal traces the reception of the poet's work among German critics, and he suggests that the German attitude toward Shakespeare "does not belong merely to the history of German literary taste. It is the epitome of the outlook of the successive leaders of German thought in [the] period, of those who most profoundly affected the forms of art and life in their own and following generations."[1]

For Pascal and other historians,[2] Shakespeare is the "touchstone" of a transformation in aesthetic criteria for the arts in Germany. Moreover, the poet's elevation became a symbol for a progressive and learned professional class of which Schumann was ultimately a member. German Shakespeare criticism, according to Pascal, provides a history of the values of "professors, tutors, clergymen,"[3] and others educated in German universities of the time: "It is a record of the most significant aspect of their intellectual struggles, and is closely linked up with the practical situation of these professions in German society. In the eighteenth century this professional section is the moral leader of the middle class in Germany."[4] If this final assessment of the professional middle class's function is familiar to Schumann scholars, it is simply because men like Schumann and his law professor, Thibaut, did in fact form the musico-aesthetic conscience of their respective generations through their writings. As a member of the professional middle class, Schumann inherited his view of Shakespeare from class members who had begun to formulate their position beginning in the eighteenth century.

The initial reaction to Shakespeare in eighteenth-century Germany was negative. When a series of translations of individual plays appeared during the 1740s,[5] German critics applied the aesthetic standards of Aristotelian poetics. As a result, most commentators frowned on Shakespeare's intermixture of farcical and tragic characters, and they found the plays to be aimless and structurally incoherent. Still, Shakespeare fascinated German readers, and to account for the poet's attraction, writers like Johann Elias Schlegel invoked a kind of cultural relativism. According to J. E. Schlegel, Shakespeare's virtues and vices lay in the nature of English drama, which was concerned more with the "imitation of people" than with the "imitation of a particular action."[6] While the Aristotelian unities might be expected in Greek tragedies or in the neoclassical French theater of Corneille and Racine, the English theater was dominated more by a "spontaneous spirit" than by rules of coherent dramatic action.[7] Friedrich Nicolai was to summarize this view of Shakespeare in 1755: "Shakespeare, a man without knowledge of rules, without erudition, without order, owes to the variety and strength of his characters the greatest part of the fame which his and all other nations accord him to this very moment."[8] Shakespeare's ability to portray the differing states of man excused his defective plots; and many of his other faults, especially the banal language of certain characters like Falstaff or Polonius, also served his characterizations, or so German critics reasoned. To these middle-class writers, the depth of Shakespeare's characterizations must have been appealing, if only because the poet suggested that virtue or vice are inherent in particular individuals, not in particular classes of men. Nobility has no patent on virtue in Shakespeare; in fact, aristocrats are often portrayed with the normal faults of ordinary men, a condition which had been long suspected by the middle class.

It was not long before some critics in Germany began to explore the mechanism employed by Shakespeare to achieve depth of character in his plays. In 1758, Moses Mendelssohn suggested that the poet's characterizations were the product of dramatic contrast:

Nobody is as successful as Shakespeare in deriving advantage from the most common of circumstances, ennobling them by means of a fortunate change. The effect of this ennoblement must be that much stronger, the more it overtakes us unexpectedly and the less one foresees such important and tragic results from trivial causes. I will give a few examples of this from *Hamlet*. The king has entertainments presented in order to divert the prince from his melancholy. Plays are performed. Hamlet sees the tragedy "Hecuba" performed. He seems to be in a good mood. The company leaves him, and—now one is astonished at the tragic consequences that Shakespeare is able to draw from this commonplace. The prince says to himself:

> O what a rogue and peasant slave am I! etc.

What a masterstroke! . . . Shakespeare's Hamlet and his Lear are full of the same unexpected transitions, at which the spectator can only be amazed.[9]

Mendelssohn suggests that the depth of Shakespeare's insight into human nature is communicated by means of contrast, both in situation and between characters. To the relativism of critics like Nicolai, Mendelssohn adds a notion of dramatic contrast.

For the generation just following, Mendelssohn's assessment was particularly fortunate, for the "Sturm und Drang" movement placed a premium on sudden dramatic contrasts in literature. During the time of Herder, Goethe, and Lenz, Shakespeare was elevated to a position of pre-eminence among playwrights. The expanse of Shakespeare's drama and its resulting ability to unify seemingly disparate events clearly won the admiration of Herder in 1773: "That time and place always go together like the hull and the kernel need not be brought to mind, and yet over just this the loudest outcry has come. Shakespeare invented the god-like concept of encompassing a complete world of the most disparate occurrences in one event; naturally, for the verisimilitude of his events it is appropriate to idealize every place and time, in order to create an illusion."[10] Herder found the Aristotelian stricture of unity in time and space to be artificial and stilted on stage. For the playwright must create the illusion of time passing as it would in our perception, sometimes dragging, sometimes flying. In the freedom of his action, Shakespeare creates a more natural impression for the spectator.[11] And in the process, Shakespeare can portray much more of the variety of human existence. Goethe's reaction is much the same:

I did not hesitate a moment to foreswear the conventional theater. Unity of place seemed to me so prison-like and fearful, unity of action and time [seemed] tedious shackles on our power of imagination. [When I beheld Shakespeare,] I sprang in the free air and only then felt that I had hands and feet. And precisely then, when I saw what an injustice the gentlemen in their holes with rules had done to me, how many free souls still were weighed down with them, my heart would have ruptured, if I had not informed them of my feud and sought daily to demolish their towers.[12]

Freed from the strictures of Aristotelian poetics, Shakespeare could create a new world, divorced from the truth of real time and physical reality, but true to the inner workings of man and his perception of the natural world around him. The episodic construction of his dramas was not at all objectionable to Herder and Goethe. They were the means by which the poet portrayed the complexity of human nature and also the complexity of human perception.

If Herder and Goethe raised Shakespeare to an unprecedented rank as a dramatist, it was left to critics and translators like August Wilhelm Schlegel to codify and
articulate the actual workings of Shakespearean drama. Schlegel gives his view of
consistency and structural integrity in Shakespeare as part of a 1798 issue of the
Athenäum:

In the nobler and more original sense of the word "correct," which means intentional development and conformation of the core and detail of a work according to the spirit of the
whole by practical reflection of the artist, probably no modern poet is more correct than
Shakespeare. Thus, he is also systematic like no other: sometimes through antitheses, contrasting individuals, masses, even whole worlds in pictorial groupings; sometimes through
musical symmetry on the same large scale, through gigantic repetitions and refrains; often
through parody of the literal and through irony beyond the spirit of romantic drama, and
always through the highest and most perfect individuality and its manifold representation
by all degrees of poetry from physical imitation to spiritual characterization. [13]

And so by the turn of the nineteenth century, Shakespeare was firmly established in
the German dramatic pantheon, and through the translations of Tieck and Schlegel, he became ensconced on the German stage. Shakespeare could be called a
"classical" playwright in the sense that his plays were perfect examples of their
type; this kind of cultural relativism appealed to a liberal, university-educated middle class interested (and motivated to some extent by self-interest) in promoting
pluralism in all aspects of society. Moreover, the content of Shakespearean drama,
with its admixture of banality and elegance, commoner and king, was concerned
with many classes of men, focusing on the characters of individuals; and the structure of the poet's plays, with their juxtaposition of contrasting events and characters, allowed for a dramatic flexibility which in itself promotes an artistic plurality.
These are some of the reasons, simplified of course, why Germans of the late eighteenth and early nineteenth centuries held Shakespeare in such esteem, and it is not
an exaggeration to say that Shakespeare's dramas exerted a powerful influence, in
their freedom of content and structure, on German dramatists like Goethe and
Schiller. [14]

[ii]

The example of Shakespeare was not lost on early nineteenth-century German critics in other artistic disciplines, and one of the most prominent to invoke the English
poet as an example was Anton Friedrich Justus Thibaut. Thibaut's book, *Ueber
Reinheit der Tonkunst,* was designed to do for "classical" composers (by these I
mean Palestrina, Lasso, Victoria, Handel, Bach, the originators of various German
chorales, and many others) what literary critics had done for Shakespeare. In fact,
Thibaut appeals to Shakespeare's example in the opening pages of his moralizing
tract, first published in 1824:

Never has it been so generally recognized as now, that historical study and familiarity with
the available classics should be the foundation of all well-founded knowledge. For sure

progress can be made only if one seeks to promote the good with new zeal, instructed by the teaching of others. . . . Men of true genius, like Plato, Raphael, and Shakespeare, are very rare occurrences; but they can dominate generations and exert a beneficial influence throughout millenia; therefore, it is the most distressing of all presumptions to banish oneself from the studio of the classical, trusting to one's own capabilities, declaring in reality that one believes he may be compared with the great intellects of earlier times.[15]

Shakespeare is mentioned in many of the ensuing pages as one of the prime examples of a "classical" genius, and Thibaut continually laments the fact that students of music neglect earlier masters of their art.

One of Thibaut's comparisons between an earlier composer and Shakespeare immediately annoyed the young Robert Schumann, who had come into Thibaut's Heidelberg circle just a few years following the appearance of *Ueber Reinheit der Tonkunst*. After an evening spent in Thibaut's home on February 25, 1830, Schumann wrote in his diary, "The first part of *Samson* by Handel was fresh and lively, but performed without precision. Thibaut unjustly compares Shakespeare with Handel. Handel stands between Shakespeare and Klopstock. Handel is Götz von Berlichingen, he does not dance, thinks Thibaut; for that very reason [Handel] is unlike Shakespeare, who always dances and saw the world through different glasses from Handel with his one-sided greatness."[16] Schumann goes on in his diary to list Mozart, Michelangelo, and Shakespeare together as "universal geniuses." He declares his basic sympathy for Thibaut's book as well, suggesting that it would cause the downfall of Rossini and Czerny if it were widely read. Though it is clear that Schumann did not learn of Shakespeare from Thibaut, he shares the same special regard for the poet and the same attitude toward the works of the "classical masters."

The source of Schumann's early acquaintance with Shakespeare seems to have been his father's publishing business, for August Schumann undertook many translations of English classics into German and began a series of "pocket" classics by a wide range of authors.[17] In fact, Leon Plantinga observes that Schumann's childhood training in literature was stronger than his grounding in music, and in one of the brief autobiographical sketches written around 1840, the composer lists at least as many playwrights, poets, and novelists as musicians among the influences on his formative years.[18] The direct evidence shows that Schumann attended performances of Shakespeare's plays during his stint at the University of Leipzig,[19] but he knew many more plays than he had seen by 1831. On July 17, 1831, the composer recorded in his diary the names of almost thirty plays by Shakespeare, with a list of their female characters, suggesting that he had access to copies of all of them in translation. Chief among the list are *The Tempest, Twelfth Night, Macbeth, Cymbeline, Julius Caesar,* and *Romeo and Juliet.*[20]

The first practical result of Schumann's early fascination with Shakespeare seems to have been initiated when Schumann moved to Leipzig to begin his career as a professional musician. Two surviving drafts of a "Sinfonia per il Hamlet" appear in the Bonn sketchbooks, the first (ex. 1) in Bonn, Universitätsbibliothek Schumann 13, surrounded by piano exercises probably undertaken for Friedrich

Wieck; and the second (exx. 2–4) in Bonn, Schumann 15, surrounded by counter-point exercises for Heinrich Dorn.[21] The first sketch can be dated tentatively between October 1830, when Schumann began to study with Wieck, and June 1832, when he seems to have discontinued study.[22] This initial sketch consists of only eight measures in piano score, with brief instrumental indications. The short theme is built by repeating a rising eighth-note figure which is increasingly compressed in time by successively shorter rests between each repetition. The second fragment of a "Hamlet" overture (ex. 2), clearly related to the first fragment, was probably recorded between 1831 and 1832, when Schumann studied counterpoint with Heinrich Dorn.[23] This sketch begins in piano score, and is actually marked for the "Pfte;" but as it progresses, the sketching expands to four staves, and instrumental designations are given in almost every system. The sketch contains a great deal of scholastic counterpoint (see ex. 3), not inconsistent with Schumann's course of study at that time, and as the composer reached the second key-area (see ex. 4), he lost interest in the draft.

It is not clear what Schumann had in mind for these sketches of a "Hamlet" overture, nor can we specify how the composer related the music to the Shake-spearean drama. We know Schumann was familiar with *Hamlet*. He had attended a performance in Leipzig as early as October 1828; following the presentation he apparently read (or reread) the play.[24] The composer comments only once in his diaries about the use of Shakespeare as a source of inspiration, writing in July 1832, "Why should there be no operas without texts: that would be just as dramatic. In Shakespeare there is much for you."[25] Did Schumann imagine a concert overture following Mendelssohn's example, as the sketches suggest, or did he have something akin to Berlioz's *Romeo and Juliet* in mind as an ultimate goal? Of course, we cannot say. Like so much of his early compositional activity, his piano quartet and the G-minor Symphony, for example, plans for a "Hamlet" overture or for some longer work based on Shakespeare's play were neglected in favor of composition for piano solo and the *Neue Zeitschrift*. Taken as a whole, the evidence from early diaries and sketchbooks suggests Schumann's familiarity with, and admiration for, Shakespearean drama.

During the years just following the sketch for the "Hamlet" overture, the evidence of Schumann's high regard for Shakespeare continues to accumulate in small increments. The poet's special rank is reaffirmed in the pages of the *Neue Zeit-schrift* as part of an 1835 review by Schumann: "There are many things in the world about which one is left speechless; for instance, the C-major Symphony with fugue by Mozart, much by Shakespeare, and individual things by Beethoven."[26] Shakespeare received a kind of praise given to no other artist, and lines from his plays were occasionally quoted on the masthead of the *Neue Zeitschrift*. We might speculate that the structure of Shakespearean drama, as it was understood by Germans of Schumann's time, provided part of the model for the composer's piano output. Pieces like *Carnaval* and *Papillons* are freely formed dramatic entities which employ contrast of mood and juxtaposition of banality and elegance to achieve a larger cohesion. But there is no specific evidence that Shakespeare provided a direct model for one of Schumann's piano pieces from the 1830s; in fact,

Ex. 1. Sketch for Schumann's "Sinfonia per il Hamlet" (Bonn, Schumann 13, fol. 39r)

Ex. 2. Sketch for Schumann's "Sinfonia" (Bonn, Schumann 15, fol. 65r)

only one piece, *Papillons,* traces its inspiration directly to a literary model, in this instance a scene from a novel by Jean Paul.[27]

Schumann's next direct compositional encounter with Shakespeare came at a highly significant juncture of his career, in 1840. This is the so-called *Liederjahr,* and Schumann chose to initiate this phase of his song-writing activity with a philosophically comic text from the *Twelfth Night,* translated in German under its subtitle, *What You Will* or *Was ihr wollt.* As the first text of the *Liederjahr* Schumann selected Feste's closing song, titled "Schlusslied des Narren," in the translation by Schlegel and Tieck, with extensive changes made by the composer in the last verse.

Ex. 3. Continuation of Sketch for the "Sinfonia" (Bonn, Schumann 15, fol. 65r)

Eric Sams dates the song from February 1840, though its publication (as part of Op. 127) was delayed until 1854. Sams says that it constitutes an "odd choice of serious debut,"[28] but the selection contains a kind of irony which is consistent with Schumann's later choice of certain texts by Heine. Shakespeare's Feste sings of the basic indifference of the universe to his various plights in different stages of life, constantly repeating the refrain, "For the rain, it raineth every day" (see appendix). This seems at first to be a non sequitur, but its commentary in the context of the Clown's narrative about his youth and manhood is clearly pessimistic and provides a good example of the intermingling of comic character with rather more profound sentiment for which Shakespeare was famous in Germany. Schumann sets only

Ex. 4. Second Theme from Sketch of "Sinfonia" (Bonn, Schumann 15, fol. 65v)

three of the five verses of Shakespeare's text, preserving the progression from child to young man ready to marry, and then moves to the moral of the song which asserts the purpose of the present entertainment in the face of an indifferent creation. By this selection, Schumann preserves the basic irony of the text (one wonders whether the irony of Schumann's choice to begin his serious career as a song writer was intentional), and the setting basically preserves the strophic form of the original. The choice of Shakespeare for his "serious debut" and his particular selection of an ironic text is not so puzzling in the light of Schumann's deep acquaintance with the poet and the composer's penchant for irony. But the fact that Schumann never set another text from a Shakespearean drama is very curious and, I would add, unfortunate. We can only imagine what the composer of "Mondnacht" (Op. 39, No. 5) might have done with "Serenade to Music" from Act 5, Scene 1 in *The Merchant of Venice,* for instance. It seems that Schumann was hesitant about setting Shakespeare, perhaps because he disliked dealing with the poet's texts in translation, or perhaps owing to some deference to the poet's special artistic position.

There is some evidence suggesting that Schumann did not find any composer living during the 1840s equal to the perfection of Shakespeare. Schumann's extraordinary regard for the plays prompted him to write of his first encounter with Mendelssohn's incidental music for *A Midsummer Night's Dream:*

Many, I can assure you, probably viewed Shakespeare in order to hear Mendelssohn; for me it was just the reverse. I know quite well that Mendelssohn did not want to do as bad actors do when in incidental stage business they play very broadly; [Mendelssohn's] music (with the exception of the overture) seeks only to be an accompaniment, an intermediary, a bridge equally between Bottom and Oberon, without which a transition into the kingdom of the fairies would be almost impossible, [and music must] also have played this role in Shakespeare's time. Who expects more from the music will be found to have been disappointed; it recedes markedly [in comparison with] "Antigone," where the choruses of musicians certainly compelled richer productions.[29]

The virtue of Mendelssohn's music lay in refraining from intrusion into Shakespeare's comedy, and though Schumann goes on in his commentary to praise the overture in extravagant terms, he disparages just slightly Mendelssohn's decision to end his incidental music with a passage borrowed from the last part of the overture. Even Schumann's favorite living composer could not rival Shakespeare.

It is clear from Schumann's review of Mendelssohn's music that Schumann regarded the concert overture as the most appropriate musical bridge to Shakespearean drama. And when Schumann finally addressed the concert overture seriously during his last orchestral efflorescence in the 1850s, he chose a Shakespearean historical drama, *Julius Caesar,* as a source of inspiration, immediately following a similar project based on Schiller's *Die Braut von Messina.* The overture based on *Julius Caesar* was sketched from January 23 to January 26, 1851, and orchestrated from January 26 through February 2.[30] Following a long-established pattern, Schumann completed the initial work on the piece in short order, only to revise it by trial and error over a much longer period of time. The initial rehearsal for the Overture to *Julius Caesar* took place on October 31, 1851,[31] but no performance of the work was scheduled. Instead, Schumann used the rehearsal to revise the orchestration, and he was not satisfied with the piece until July 30, 1852, when we read in his household accounts, "the overture to *Julius Caesar* from afar and suddenly decision and joy."[32] Schumann's "decision" involved a performance of the overture which took place on August 3, 1852, at the yearly song festival in Düsseldorf.[33] Even after the premiere, the composer was not satisfied with the composition; he held the score several months before sending it to Peters on January 2, 1853.[34] Peters must have rejected it, for Schumann sent the overture along with a number of other compositions to Litolff in Braunschweig in September 1853,[35] and it was Litolff who finally published the piece as Opus 128 in 1855.[36]

If Schumann had trouble finding a publisher for the Overture to *Julius Caesar,* it may have been because it was not one of his more articulate symphonic compositions. It suffers from many of the idiosyncrasies that became increasingly pronounced in Schumann's later orchestral style. The composer provides a surfeit of contrapuntal detail using themes too rhythmically intricate to produce a clear effect. If the texture is slightly opaque, the opacity is increased by a heavy and unrelenting orchestration. The surface of the overture is not sufficiently varied to make it attractive.

Whatever its ultimate merits, the overture constitutes evidence of Schumann's persistent regard for Shakespeare, and the sketch of the piece provides a special demonstration of the composer's attention to the play. Plate 1 shows the first page of the sketch housed at the Heinrich-Heine-Institut in Düsseldorf under the call number 74.256. At the top right-hand side of the first page of sketching stands the motto, " 'Dies war ein Mann!' Antonius von Brutus in J. Cäsar ["This was a man!" Antonius about Brutus in J. Caesar]," a quotation from the very end of the play which may lend a certain irony in the context of a heroic concert overture entitled *Julius Caesar.* At the bottom of the same page we see what appears to be a brief

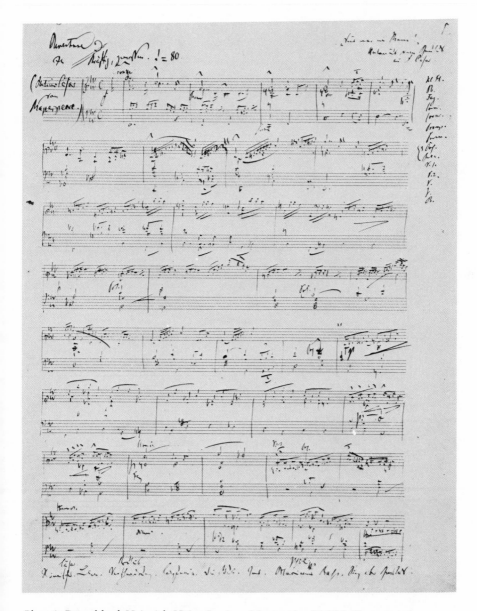

Plate 1. Düsseldorf, Heinrich-Heine-Institut, Manuscript 74.256. (By permission of the Heinrich-Heine-Institut.)

summary of elements from the play, including "Cäsar. Römisches Leben. Brutus. Verschwörung. Calpurnia. die Idus. Tod. Octavius' Rache. Sieg über Brutus. [Caesar. Roman life. Brutus. Conspiracy. Calpurnia. The Ides. Death. Octavius's revenge. Victory over Brutus.]" This brief summary was not a program which determined the progress of the overture: Schumann's piece is not a potpourri overture presenting a succession of unconnected episodes juxtaposed for dramatic effect. The sketch shows that the composer had a three-part sonata form firmly in mind. Like all of Schumann's orchestral sketches from this period, the adumbration for *Julius Caesar* was written on the outer pages of several bifolios. The inner pages were left blank for expansions and revision of the initial continuity draft. For this overture, Schumann sketched the continuity draft on the outside of one bifolio, numbering the pages 1 and 2; he then moved to the outside of a second bifolio where he finished the development (at rehearsal "H" of the complete edition), but the recapitulation trails off, and the next segment of the continuity draft is marked "Schluss" and continues with the prelude to the coda (just before rehearsal "N"). As in many other drafts by Schumann, the omission of some large portion of a draft was usually a token of a literal repetition, and in fact, the composer makes this explicit in a revised sketch for the end of the development. On a third bifolio of sketching, he expanded the pedal point before the recapitulation and numbered the measures 108 to 115 which brings us to the double bar after rehearsal "H." The composer then drew a double bar and entered the number 1, signifying a repeat of the exposition. Schumann explicitly thought of the overture in terms of a purely musical form, and the summary of events at the bottom of the first page of the sketch must have been used, then, for general inspiration. The composer conjured the mood of Shakespeare's play by invoking its events in order to endue the overture with the proper spirit. This sketch reminds us that form and content (the spirit of a composition) were separable entities in Schumann's view; "absolute" music was not devoid of spiritual content, and it was perfectly plausible for Schumann or Mendelssohn to write an overture in sonata form based on a Shakespearean drama. It is in this sense that we might interpret what seems to have been Schumann's last reference to Shakespeare. It comes in a letter to Joseph Joachim concerning the violinist's *Hamlet* overture:

Many thanks for your lovely letter, as well as for the music that was enclosed, above all for your overture, which aroused my deepest interest from the first measures. I was very surprised;—I expected, because you did not mention the title of the tragedy, to find a cheerful concert overture, and instead found something quite different. While reading, it was as if the scenes unfolded before me from page to page, and Ophelia and Hamlet appeared in physical form. There are quite moving passages in it, and the whole is presented in so clear and magnificent a form as is appropriate to such a lofty undertaking.[37]

To the end of his life (this letter is dated June 8, 1853), Schumann obviously cherished a special regard for Shakespeare and the music connected with his drama.

Schumann's actual employment of material from Shakespeare was very minor, though quite real, and it is clear that his regard for Shakespeare as a dramatist far exceeded his specific musical involvement with Shakespeare's plays. The token efforts examined above are simply marks of the composer's membership in the class of liberally educated, university-trained professional people who dominated social, political, and intellectual life in early nineteenth-century Germany, especially in towns like Leipzig. They believed in a "classical" culture, in which "classicism" was not confined to any one historical period or to a particular national group. Their outlook was cosmopolitan in principle, and they had no qualms about adopting styles and structures from the past as part of their work, because directed artistic progress rested for them on a firm knowledge of historical masters. They used Shakespeare to free themselves from the shackles of Aristotelian poetics, and thus they did not gain their freedom at the expense of history. Rather, by studying the history of art, literature and music, they discovered many new stylistic options which would have been unavailable otherwise. For this reason, it is possible to see Schumann and Mendelssohn as progressive in one light, or as conservative in a different light. This ambivalence resulted from the acculturation of the two composers as members of a particular German class which held as one of its common values an appreciation for Shakespearean drama.

Appendix

Two Versions of Feste's Song from Shakespeare's *Twelfth Night*

Original version	*Schlegel's translation*
When that I was and a little tiny boy,	Und als ich ein winzig Bübchen war,
With hey, ho, the wind and the rain,	Hop heisa, bei Regen und Wind!
A foolish thing was but a toy,	Da machten zwei nur eben ein Paar;
For the rain it raineth every day.	Denn der Regen, der regnet jeglichen Tag.*
But when I came to man's estate,	Und als ich vertreten die Kinderschuh,
With hey, ho, the wind and the rain,	Hop heisa, bei Regen und Wind!
'Gainst knaves and thieves men shut their gate,	Da schloss man vor Dieben die Häuser zu;
For the rain it raineth every day.	Denn der Regen, der regnet jeglichen Tag.
But when I came, alas! to wive,	Und als ich, ach! ein Weib thät frein,
With hey, ho, the wind and the rain,	Hop heisa, bei Regen und Wind!
By swaggering could I never thrive,	Da wollte der Müssiggehn nicht gedeihn;
For the rain it raineth every day.	Denn der Regen, der regnet jeglichen Tag.*
But when I came unto my beds,	Und als der Wein mir steckt' im Kopf,
With hey, ho, the wind and the rain,	Hop heisa, bei Regen und Wind!
With toss-pots still had drunken heads,	Da war ich ein armer betrunkner Tropf;
For the rain it raineth every day.	Denn der Regen, der regnet jeglichen Tag.
A great while ago the world begun,	Die Welt steht schon Jahr ein, Jahr aus,
With hey, ho, the wind and the rain,	Hop heisa, bei Regen und Wind!
But that's all one, our play is done,	Doch 's ist all Eins, das Stück ist aus,
And we'll strive to please you every day.	Und so wolln wir gefalln euch jeglichen Tag.*

*Indicates verses set by Schumann; his final two lines read: "doch das Stück ist aus, und ich wünsch euch viel Heil, / und dass es euch künftig gefalle!"

R. Larry Todd

Mendelssohn's Ossianic Manner, with a New Source—On Lena's Gloomy Heath

> "Ossian hat in meinem Herzen den Homer
> verdrängt."
>
> Goethe, *Die Leiden des jungen Werthers*

The Ossianic craze from the latter part of the eighteenth century onward left a profound impact on European culture with far-reaching ramifications. James Macpherson's inauthentic renditions of allegedly ancient Celtic poetry, though quickly judged by the ever-skeptical Samuel Johnson as an "impostor from the beginning,"[1] were widely read, translated, and assimilated into the literature, painting, architecture, and music of the time. There were many reasons for the great appeal of the fragments. These purported "translations," manipulated by Macpherson into a simple prose with a discernible poetic meter and rich Homeric imagery, seemed to exude a beguiling essence of authenticity. Here was the poetry of a primitive people, an art previously unknown, now salvaged; here was the legacy of a barbaric yet noble society, formerly assumed to be uncultured.

The "discovery" of Ossian aroused an international curiosity, just as the excavations at Herculaneum and Pompeii had earlier in the century, when artifacts of Roman culture were uncovered. But the Ossianic awakening engendered a different response: Ossian came to be acknowledged as an alternative source for the Western classical tradition. This recognition occurred at a crucial time, when critics were attempting to understand and codify the historical divisions of literature. Friedrich Schlegel, for one, asserted the need to discover cultural roots in his *Gespräch über die Poesie*, which appeared in the *Athenaeum* in 1800: "It is an essential quality of all art to follow closely what has already been formed. Therefore, history goes back from generation to generation, from phase to phase, always farther back into antiquity, to its original source."[2] Of course, Schlegel thought he had discovered the *fons et origo* of modern literature in the epic poetry of Homer. The principal effort of the modern poet, he advised, would be to reconcile the great classical tradition with the onset of romanticism; this goal, he predicted, would be achieved by Goethe.

The "discovery" of Ossian, however, provided a challenge for this historiography of literature. Already Klopstock, eager to establish roots for modern German literature, had sought in Celtic heroes such as Fingal and Ossian substitutes for Homer's Achilles and Hector; Herder had viewed Ossian as a source for German folk poetry. Another recognition of Ossian was presented by Johann Georg Sulzer in a lengthy article on Ossian for the *Allgemeine Theorie der schönen Künste,* which appeared in the 1770s, only some ten years after the publication of Macpherson's first edition. Macpherson's Caledonian barbarians were treated by Sulzer with a respect not accorded Homer's cultivated Greeks, who were, after all, more interested in fame and glory than honor ("sie waren dabei mehr ruhmräthig und prahlerisch, als ehrbegierig").[3] In Sulzer's phrase, "Fingal was the better Achilles."[4]

This reception of Ossian, no doubt, owed something to nascent German nationalism. Klopstock, convinced of Ossian's Germanic stock, fervently rewrote some of his own poems and carefully rooted out references to Greek mythology, which he replaced with Ossianic allusions.[5] Dithyrambs yielded to the songs of Ossianic bards. In France, too, Ossian was exploited for nationalistic purposes; a veritable Ossianic fever raged throughout France. The bard became a favorite subject for paintings,[6] and at least two operas on Ossianic subjects, LeSueur's *Ossian, ou les bardes,* and Méhul's *Uthal,* were premiered (1804 and 1806, respectively).[7]

Later in the nineteenth century, these nationalistic yearnings gave way to an extra-national impulse—exoticism. The idea of a primitive, heathen culture effaced by the ravages of civilization became an international theme in literature. Two fresh waves of influence broke over a susceptible Europe. Sir Walter Scott, who published anonymously for a while and enjoyed such sobriquets as "the great unknown" or "the wizard," chronicled in his *Waverly* novels fundamental social changes in Scottish history—chiefly, the inevitable displacement of an outmoded society based upon clans by a more modern and urban society. The passing of the old was treated by the "American Scott," James Fenimore Cooper, whose American Indians were depicted as a race doomed by the expanding American frontier and by contact with Western civilization.

The effect of these fresh influences was far-reaching. Willibald Alexis exploited Scott's anonymity and published his own historical novel, *Walladmor,* in Scott's name. Goethe corresponded with Scott and read Cooper.[8] The poet Nikolaus Lenau, eager to experience the American frontier firsthand, visited Niagara Falls and reflected Cooper's work in his own poem "Die drei Indianer."[9] Three Indians, survivors of their race, symbolically sing a *Sterbelied* as they propel their canoe over the precipice of the falls. Here, seemingly, were living legends—tokens of a past civilization, in-the-flesh examples of Rousseau's noble savage or Chateaubriand's René.

These experiences were absorbed vicariously by the reading public of Europe, which devoured new translations of Scott and Cooper. We have a critical reaction from Mendelssohn's mother, Lea Mendelssohn Bartholdy, who compared Scott and Cooper in a letter written to Karl Klingemann on December 28, 1827. "Scott causes quite a nuisance," she announced after reading *Ivanhoe;* for her the novelist concerned himself too much with insignificant figures ("um jede Lumperei bemüht man historische Personen") and not enough with central characters such as Rebecca or Richard the Lion-Hearted. Cooper, on the other hand, was more appealing: "But I would rather struggle with Cooper, who despite his insufferable prolixity offers the advantage of producing American scenes of the last century and depicting graphically American life."[10]

Not surprisingly, Macpherson's Ossian, Cooper's Chingachgook, and Scott's Rob Roy cut across international lines—all reinforced the new urge to rediscover an exotic past, an alternative to the classical Greek heritage. Occasionally, these literary stimuli were mixed together. Thus, Stendhal, who attended the premiere of Rossini's *Donna del lago* (based upon Scott's *Lady of the Lake*), described his initial impression in this way: "The *décor* of the opening scene showed a wild and lonely loch in the Highlands of Scotland, upon whose waters the *Lady of the Lake,* faithful to her name, was seen gliding gracefully along, upright beside the helm of a small boat. . . . The mind turned instantly towards Scotland, and waited expectantly for the magic of some Ossianic adventure."[11] Scott availed himself of Ossianic figures and allusions by using bards as the narrators of his longer poems; he incorporated a direct reference at the beginning of *The Lady of the Lake* to the "harp of the north," an instrument almost inevitably associated with Ossian. Chateaubriand contrived to have René meet the bard in the wilderness of America. And could not Cooper's *Last of the Mohicans,* with the eloquent, clipped metaphoric speech of Chingachgook, have had the same appeal as Scott's *Lay of the Last Minstrel,* or Macpherson's *War of Inisthona,* in which Ossian dreamed of heroic ages long past?[12]

Ossianic subjects appealed greatly to nineteenth-century composers, even after Macpherson's work was generally recognized as a forgery. Not the least of these was Mendelssohn, who travelled to Scotland in 1829, where he found the germinal ideas for his *Fingal's Cave* Overture and *Scottish* Symphony. These are only two of several works on Scottish subjects or texts which are listed in table 1. On stylistic grounds alone these works form a distinct group or "manner" in Mendelssohn's oeuvre, even though not all the compositions have patent ties to Ossianic poetry. Among these are the *Sonate écossaise* (ca. 1829–1833), eventually stripped of its vague title and published as the *Phantasie,* Op. 28; a series of six Scottish folksongs arranged by Mendelssohn in 1839 (though only recently edited, by Rudolf Elvers);[13] and the duet, Op. 63, No. 5, set to a text of Robert Burns.

Strictly speaking, we may claim only two works by Mendelssohn with direct links to Ossianic literature: the *Fingal's Cave* Overture, by the association of the cave on the Isle of Staffa to Fingal, and—even more directly—*On Lena's Gloomy Heath,* an unpublished concert scene composed in 1846, with its text drawn from Macpherson's epic poem *Fingal.* Along with these two we may group the *Scottish*

Table 1. Mendelssohn's Scottish Compositions

Title	Year(s) composed
Die Hebriden (Fingalshöhle) Overture, Op. 26	1829–1835
Sonate écossaise (Phantasie), Op. 28	ca. 1829–1833
Jagdlied, Op. 120, No. 1 (Scott)	1837
Sechs schottische National-Lieder	1839
Scottish Symphony, Op. 56	1829–1842
Duet, Op. 63, No. 5 (Burns)	1842
On Lena's Gloomy Heath (Ossian)	1846

Symphony; though its programmatic meaning is unclear, it has some compelling relationships with one other Ossianic work, Niels Gade's *Ossian* Overture. Finally, Mendelssohn's *Jagdlied,* a part-song for male chorus published posthumously as Op. 120, No. 1, is based upon a poem of Scott; its text brings to mind images of *The Lady of the Lake,* and, by association, of the Ossianic poems. These four works, spanning the years from 1829 to 1846, represent what we may propose as Mendelssohn's "Ossianic" or "Scottish" manner: Mendelssohn here achieves his most romantic expression and captures forcefully the exotic.

[i]

Mendelssohn and Klingemann were among many notable tourists who flocked to the Scotland popularized by the writings of Macpherson and Sir Walter Scott. The aging Samuel Johnson, escorted by Boswell, visited the Hebrides Islands as early as 1773, and surveyed the ruins of the Columban order on the island of Iona.[14] (Nearby Fingal's Cave, only discovered for all purposes in 1772, was not yet accessible to would-be sightseers.) Ludwig Achim von Arnim visited Scotland in 1803 but curtailed his journey due to financial straits. Washington Irving made a pilgrimage to Abbotsford to visit Scott in 1817, just as Scott's mansion in medieval style, described by the American as a "huge baronial pile,"[15] was being erected. Ignaz Moscheles followed in 1828, a year before Mendelssohn's visit, and celebrated the "great wizard of the North" in his *Anklänge von Schottland,* Op. 75, a medley of Scottish folk tunes.[16] And Turner, after consulting with Scott about some illustrations for his poetry, set out on two tours of Scotland in 1831 and 1834, which took him, like Mendelssohn, to Fingal's Cave.[17]

The Hebridean tour was one of the highlights of Mendelssohn's journey; from it came his first substantial work based upon his impressions in Scotland, the *Fingal's Cave* Overture. Characteristically silent about the programmatic meaning of his overture, Mendelssohn provided little commentary in his letters—only the celebrated musical sketch for the opening, notated with coloristic orchestral details,[18] and a pen and ink drawing of a view toward the Hebrides, with prominent ruins on

a cliff and an indistinct—though not exactly Turneresque—seascape.[19] Klingemann, who co-authored the stream of letters sent to Mendelssohn's family in
Berlin, was more communicative. His letters of August 1829 are replete with rich
descriptions and, more importantly, with allusions recognizable to readers of Ossian and Scott. Some examples:

Iona, one of the Hebrides-sisters—there is truly a very Ossianic and sweetly sad sound
about that name. . . .

I shall think of Iona, with its ruins . . ., the graves of ancient Scotch kings and still more
ancient northern pirate-princes. . . .

Smoky huts were stuck on cliffs, . . . cattle herds with Rob Roys now and then blocked up
the way. . . .

Finally, as the two departed from the Hebrides:

. . . we start for Loch Lomond and the rest of the scenery which ought to be published and
packed up as supplements to Sir Walter Scott's complete works.[20]

Klingemann thus included in his letters a general reference to Ossian and more or
less explicit references to such works of Scott as *Rob Roy* (1817), or the poem *The
Lord of the Isles* (1815).

But can we argue for connections between such references and Mendelssohn's
Fingal's Cave Overture? For an answer, we should take into account a common
interpretation of the cave on the island of Staffa. Discovered in 1772, this formation hollowed-out by the sea, with its symmetrical basaltic columns, was viewed as
a unique spectacle, a kind of natural temple or cathedral which humbled man-
made counterparts. Thomas Pennant provided two engravings of Staffa in his popular *Tour in Scotland* of 1774 (one is reproduced as plate 1). Joseph Banks, who
was among the first landing party in 1772, commented, "Compared to this what
are the cathedrals or the palaces of man! mere models . . .," and, "What had been
added to this by the whole Grecian school?"[21] In *The Lord of the Isles,* which
Klingemann and Mendelssohn probably knew, Sir Walter Scott waxed eloquent as
he described

> that wondrous dome,
> Where, as to shame the temples deck'd
> By skill of earthly architect,
> Nature herself, it seem'd, would raise
> A Minster to her Maker's praise!
> Not for a meaner use ascend
> Her columns, or her arches bend;
> Nor of a theme less solemn tells
> That mighty surge that ebbs and swells,
> And still, between each awful pause,
> From the high vault an answer draws,
> In varied tone prolong'd and high,
> That mocks the organ's melody.
> Nor doth its entrance front in vain

To old Iona's holy fane,
That Nature's voice might seem to say,
'Well hast thou done, frail Child of day!
Thy humble powers that stately shrine
Tasked high and hard—but witness mine!'[22]

For Scott, too, the cave surpassed the work of Greek temples or Gothic cathedrals. Fingal's Cave, in short, dwarfed the monuments of the Western architectural tradition, just as Ossianic myths seemed to supplant their classical counterparts.

In his overture Mendelssohn deliberately avoided the traditional and instead set out to evoke the exotic. Some unusual features of the overture include aspects of its thematic construction and registration, scoring, and structure. Quite striking is the very opening, with its consecutive fifths and undulating figures in the lower strings. The first few bars outline a direct progression by parallel fifths, a forbidden construction by any rules of conventional voice leading (see ex. 1).[23] Here Mendelssohn indeed expressed something primitive, uncultured.

Also pronounced is Mendelssohn's concern for tone color, which sometimes takes precedence over other musical considerations. A good example is provided by bars 21 and 22, a short passage which interrupts the presentation of the first theme in the violins (ex. 2). These bars are an intrusion of orchestral timbre: Mendelssohn surely inserted the shimmering prolongation of a diminished-seventh harmony here as a special coloristic effect, one which does not bear on the basic thematic material.

Finally, we may mention an aspect of the thematic treatment. The opening figure in the strings, from which the other thematic material of the movement is derived, suggests an arpeggiation of the B-minor triad with an embellishing tone, in the position, F-sharp–D–B–F-sharp. But a few measures later the same octave is divided differently into two tetrachords: F-sharp–C-sharp–B–F-sharp, a division with a distinctly modal flavor (ex. 3). This arrangement is similar, in fact, to some of the gapped scales common in Scottish folk music. In art music, it became a cliché. Brahms, inspired by Schumann's setting in the *Myrthen Liederkreis* of Burns's "My Heart's in the Highlands," included a melody in the finale of his C-major Piano Sonata with the same two divisions Mendelssohn used—in this case, transposed to E–A–B–E and E–A–C–E (ex. 4).[24] In addition, his well-known Ballade, Op. 10, No. 1, inspired by the Scottish ballad "Edward," displays prominently the same sort of melodic division (ex. 5).

Mendelssohn's overture, then, contains clear signs of special effects, no doubt intended to convey some programmatic effect. When we turn to the chronology of the work, which underwent extensive revisions and changes of title between 1829 and 1835, we find further evidence which might help us to unveil Mendelssohn's programmatic purpose. The composer began with *Die Hebriden* (1830), but then turned to *Die einsame Insel* (1830), *The Isles of Fingal* for an English performance (1832), and finally, when the work was published in score, to *Fingalshöhle* (1835).[25] Clearly, here is a progression from the general geographical location of the Hebrides to the cave on Staffa—a gradual defining of the scope of the overture. But what of *Die einsame Insel*? Did Mendelssohn mean to capture musically the

Plate 1. Engraving of Staffa from Thomas Pennant, *Tour in Scotland and Voyage to the Hebrides, MDCCLXXII*, vol. 2. (By permission of the Rare Book Collection, Duke University Library.)

Plate 2. London, British Library, Additional Manuscript 48597. (By permission of the British Library.)

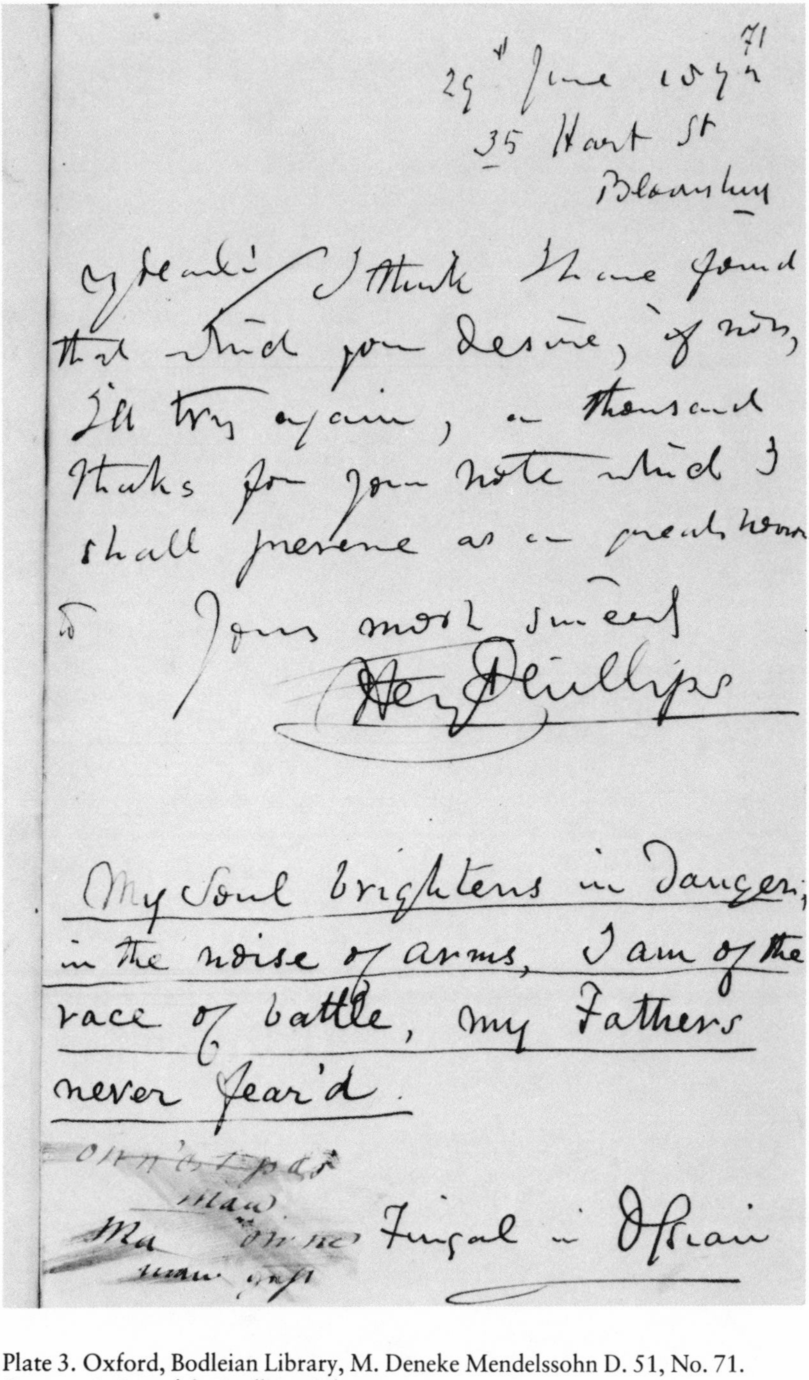

29ᵈ June 1842
35 Hart St
Bloomsbury

My dear L[ ] I think I have found
that which you desire, if not,
I'll try again, a thousand
thanks for your note which I
shall preserve as a great honor
to

Yours most sincerely
Hy Phillips

My Soul brightens in Danger;
in the noise of arms, I am of the
race of battle, my Fathers
never fear'd.

Οἰτήσπαρ
(Μαω)
Μα [ ] Fingal in Ossian
μαω γηρι

Plate 3. Oxford, Bodleian Library, M. Deneke Mendelssohn D. 51, No. 71.
(By permission of the Bodleian Library.)

Ex. 1. Mendelssohn, Op. 26

Ex. 2. Mendelssohn, Op. 26

Ex. 3. Mendelssohn, Op. 26

Ex. 4. Brahms, Op. 1

Ex. 5. Brahms, Op. 10, No. 1

indescribable loneliness of the Scottish seascape, with the ruins of an earlier civilization on the neighboring island of Iona, or something more?

We do not have a direct statement from the composer, but we do have some intriguing evidence from Scott's poetry which might bear on *Die einsame Insel.* The image of a lonely island is central to *The Lady of the Lake;* the second canto, in fact, is entitled *The Island,* and concerns the isolated hiding place of Helen and Douglas, outcasts from the court of James V of Scotland. More strikingly, at the beginning of *The Island* a song sung by the harper Allan—himself an Ossianic figure—presents the image as a recurring refrain:

Then, stranger, go! good speed the while,
Nor think again of the lonely isle.
. . . .
And lost in love and friendship's smile
Be memory of the lonely isle.
. . . .
Remember then thy hap ere while,
A stranger in the lonely isle.
. . . .
But come where kindred worth shall smile,
To greet thee in the lonely isle.

As we know, Mendelssohn knew *The Lady of the Lake,* if not in the original version, then in German translation. In 1820 he actually set two famous passages of the poem, Helen's "Ave Maria" and "Soldier, rest! thy warfare o'er" (the same two, incidentally, were set by Schubert in Adam Storck's translation as "Ave Maria, Jungfrau mild" and "Raste Krieger, Krieg ist aus!"; D 839 and 837). Mendelssohn's unassuming songs are more childhood exercises than expressions of a juvenile yearning for Scottish climes. The "Ave Maria," in fact, reveals Mendelssohn as a studious imitator of Bach and Handel in a marvelously naive interpretation of Scott's poetry.[26] Certainly by 1829 the cultured young man appreciated Scott's poetry on a much more sophisticated level. If he did not know Schubert's settings, he might well have known Rossini's opera on the subject, *Donna del lago*; and he might have had reason to reread the poem when it was freshly translated into German by Willibald Alexis in 1824 as *Die Jungfrau vom See*.[27] In 1829, before setting out for Scotland, Mendelssohn copied Moscheles's *Fantaisie sur des Airs des bardes écossais,* Op. 80, which was dedicated to Scott.[28] Mendelssohn's title, *Die einsame Insel,* probably alludes to more than Fingal's cave. It is an appropriate image linking Scott and Ossian, and summarizing Mendelssohn's impressions of Scotland.

A final bit of evidence again ties the overture to literary sources. When Mendelssohn returned to Berlin in December 1829, he brought with him the score of his *Singspiel, Die Heimkehr aus der Fremde* (Op. 89), based upon a delightful libretto by Klingemann for the silver wedding anniversary of the composer's parents. The plot, about a soldier who has returned from abroad to the shelter of home, deliberately was constructed to parallel Mendelssohn's own return from the wilds of Scotland. In the *Singspiel,* Mendelssohn's military alter ego, Hermann, has returned unrecognized to reclaim his sweetheart, Elizabeth. The lovely strophic lied, "Wenn die Abendglocken läuten," sung by Hermann to serenade Elizabeth, contains a contrasting section which tells of the forlorn soldier in a distant campaign on his solitary watch. The text is striking: "But the lad is on the battle field, assigned to a forlorn post" ("Doch der Gesell ist im Feld, weit auf verlornen Posten gestellt"); and, "When the trumpet and horn call out at night, he thinks of her on his lonely sentry post" ("Ruft die Trompet' und das Horn zur Nacht, denkt er an sie auf einsamer Wacht"). Even more striking, though, are the fanfares in the score, bringing to mind the overture with a direct citation (exx. 6 and 7). Here, finally, is an unambiguous link between the overture and a specific text. The idea of a distant campaign in an exotic land, with a soldier on a lonely watch—surely all this evokes the rich imagery in Scott's *Lady of the Lake* and Macpherson's Ossianic poems.

This evidence, of course, has certain limitations: we cannot presume to establish a specific program for the overture. Mendelssohn himself was characteristically reluctant to do so. He was unwilling, for instance, when asked by the firm Breitkopf and Härtel, to provide a program for the *Midsummer Night's Dream* Overture for distribution to audiences. Unlike Berlioz, who had taken such great care with the program for the *Symphonie fantastique,* Mendelssohn put little stock in such props: "To set down the sequence of my ideas for the composition on a program is certainly not possible for me, for this train of ideas *is* my overture."[29]

Notwithstanding Mendelssohn's reticence, some would have interpreted the *Fingal's Cave* Overture as conveying an Ossianic meaning. Indeed, the work directly influenced the *Echoes of Ossian* Overture by the young Dane, Niels Gade, composed in 1840. In this case, Gade was more obliging for the would-be program seeker: in addition to the title, he inscribed a motto from the poem "Freie Kunst" by Uhland. Here Gade found a veritable call for a new art, one free from formulaic constraints—and outworn classical models:

Formel hält uns nicht gebunden, Formulas will not constrain us,
Unsre Kunst heisst Poesie.[30] Our art is named poesy.

Uhland had sought a new source for art, an alternative to the classical tradition. That he found in nature: "Sing, you who are endowed with song, in the German forest of poetry!" ("Singe, wem Gesang gegeben, in dem deutschen Dichterwald!"). The call for the regeneration of art was put even more clearly in the closing lines:

Nicht in kalten Marmorsteinen,
Nicht in Tempeln dumpf und tot,
In den frischen Eichenhainen
Webt und rauscht der deutsche Gott.

Not in rigid marble stones, not in the temples of antiquity, but in the oak groves was the natural divinity to be worshipped. For Gade, Ossian indeed met these requirements: not in temples did the bard sing his epic poems, but by the stream of Luba, or in oak forests.

Gade's overture is gratifyingly rich in programmatic allusions. In addition to the motto, we have the use of the harp, a literal reference to the bard's preferred instrument (too obvious for Mendelssohn, who characteristically eschewed direct references). In addition, there are three themes in the exposition with more or less specific programmatic connotations. The second, a fiery *agitato* figure accompanied by martial fanfares, suggests a raging Ossianic battle (ex. 8). The first, as Finn Mathiassen has shown, has its origins in an early setting by Gade of Goethe's ballad "Der König in Thule."[31] Gade was inspired to create a ballad-like melody, with modal, even pentatonic features (ex. 9).[32] In the overture this ballad theme is often accompanied by the harp and thus is tied to the bard. Gade's third theme, a lyrical melody in F major, was reused in his cantata *Comala* of 1846, a work based on the

Ex. 6. Mendelssohn, Op. 89

Ex. 7. Mendelssohn, Op. 26

poem of the same name by Macpherson. Comala, in love with Fingal, dies of grief when she erroneously imagines he has been killed in battle. The melody from Gade's overture is revived in the cantata in the same key just before the text, "There, lonely, sits Comala, she gazes down in the vale where went her loved one," where part of the melody is reused again (exx. 10 and 11).

These references to the bard Ossian, the warrior Fingal, and the forlorn Comala almost mask the influence of Mendelssohn's *Fingal's Cave* Overture on Gade's overture. Gade's freer approach to sonata form is underscored in the *Ossian* Overture by its use of cyclical thematicism. The exposition is expanded formally, and the three themes—three, instead of the expected two—are recapitulated in a re-arranged order, with the work ending as it began with the ballad of the bard. The composition is framed by a slow introduction and a coda. More than this, Gade occasionally combined themes, as for instance, when Ossian's theme is pitted against the *agitato* subject, as if a poetic comment upon some distant battle (ex. 12). This new, flexible approach to thematic structure—a musical answer to Uhland's plea—also has some precedent in Mendelssohn's overture, in which the first theme, its accompaniment, and the second theme are closely related and com-bined (ex. 13).

Ex. 8. Gade, *Ossian* Overture

Ex. 9. Gade, *Ossian* Overture

Ex. 10. Gade, *Ossian* Overture

Ex. 11. Gade, *Comala* Cantata

Ex. 12. Gade, *Ossian* Overture

Ex. 13. Mendelssohn, Op. 26

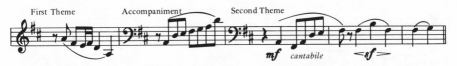

Telling, too, are some specific musical correlations between the two works, which clarify our programmatic appreciation—or at least Gade's—of *Fingal's Cave*. Three comparisons may be offered. The first concerns a passage which closes the presentation of the first theme in both works. Gade and Mendelssohn employed the same cadential progression, iv–i $^{5-6}_{3-4}$–V^7–i (see exx. 14 and 15). Gade's scale-like accompaniment is surely borrowed from Mendelssohn's passage. Gade also had the sound of *Fingal's Cave* in his ear when he conceived the many fanfares of his overture. In a *fortissimo* flourish before the graceful Comala theme, Gade scored his brass to allow the trumpets to pierce the texture, with an effect strikingly similar to the close of Mendelssohn's exposition (exx. 16 and 17). Finally, the *pianissimo* conclusions of the two works are suspiciously similar. Mendelssohn counterposed the two themes (flute against clarinet) with *pizzicato* strings; Gade presented a descending arpeggiation of A minor with *pizzicato* accompaniment. Gade's figure, an appropriate echo of Ossian's harp, nevertheless seems like a deliberate echo of Mendelssohn's first theme (even to the detail of the final fermata), which outlines a similar descending arpeggiation from the fifth scale degree (exx. 18 and 19). The closings suggest a fleeting glimpse of a vanishing, heroic, Ossianic world which recedes into obscurity just as quietly as it had materialized.

[*ii*]

Mendelssohn's *Fingal's Cave* Overture thus provided some specific points of departure for Gade. No doubt, the Ossianic evocations of the earlier overture—vague as they may be—were an impetus for Gade to explore again an Ossianic theme, this time with more explicit programmatic references. We may detect a reverse direction of influence in Mendelssohn's second major Scottish work, the

Ex. 14. Mendelssohn, Op. 26

Ex. 15. Gade, *Ossian* Overture

Ex. 16. Gade, *Ossian* Overture

Ex. 17. Mendelssohn, Op. 26

Ex. 18. Gade, *Ossian* Overture

Ex. 19. Mendelssohn, Op. 26

Scottish Symphony, first sketched in 1829 but not finished until 1842, two years after the appearance of Gade's overture.[33] Several features of the symphony, particularly in the first movement, betray a kinship with Gade's *Ossian*.

An obvious point of similarity concerns the structure of the symphonic movement and the overture. Mendelssohn's first movement is framed by a slow introduction; its return at the close of the movement is similar to Gade's recall of the opening few bars in his overture. In addition, there are three themes in Mendelssohn's exposition instead of the customary two; perhaps this thematic expansion was encouraged by Gade's use of three themes. Perhaps most revealing, the first and second themes in the symphony are bridged by a *fortissimo* transition with trumpet and horn calls, effectively bringing to mind Gade's second subject. Part of Mendelssohn's bridge, in fact, centers around the same diminished-seventh harmony employed by Gade (cf. exx. 20 and 8). Other similarities may be noted in passing, including the same key for the two works,[34] and *piano* openings scored for the lower strings.

Beyond these specific comparisons, Mendelssohn's movement strikes one as a concerted response to the motto of Uhland used by Gade. Mendelssohn took great pains to produce in his symphony a tightly knit, organic structure. He insisted there be no pauses between the movements; in addition, his carefully marked tempi—as in the first movement, *Andante con moto, Allegro un poco agitato,* and *Assai animato*—assured a fluent continuum. Mendelssohn also recycled his thematic material. Like Gade, he resorted to combinations of themes (e.g. bar 125 ff. in the first movement), but, as in the *Fingal's Cave* Overture, went beyond this by deriving the bulk of his material from a common germinal idea. Thus, the opening of the introduction is closely allied to the first theme; the material resurfaces in the scherzo as part of a pentatonic gapped scale; and part of it in a different order appears in the finale. This tight thematic unity was quickly noticed by critics. The *Allgemeine musikalische Zeitung,* for instance, reported that "all four movements are very closely related to one another, and are bound by an inner connection."[35] Very possibly Mendelssohn's concern for the unity of the symphony owed something to Gade's earlier, thematically compact overture.

If Mendelssohn was indebted to the *Echoes of Ossian,* then perhaps that debt extended beyond musical matters to programmatic considerations. Once again, what evidence we have leads to Ossian and Sir Walter Scott. To begin with, the

Ex. 20. Mendelssohn, Op. 56

composer's first sketch for the symphony was written on July 30, 1829, while he was visiting the ruins of Holyrood Palace in Edinburgh, where Mary, daughter of James V of Scotland, was crowned Queen of Scotland. In a letter to Berlin, Mendelssohn described the ruins: "The chapel close to it is now roofless, grass and ivy grow there, and at that broken altar Mary was crowned Queen of Scotland. Everything around is broken and mouldering, and the bright sky shines in. I believe I found to-day in that old chapel the beginning of my Scotch Symphony."[36] The ruins and nostalgic longing for the past must have provoked as strong a reaction in Edinburgh as at Fingal's Cave.

The next day, July 31, Mendelssohn visited Abbotsford, the baronial mansion recently built by Sir Walter Scott—a new monument to the past. This anachronistic residence, with its relics of the past, impressed Washington Irving as a place where a "little realm of romance was suddenly opened. . . ."[37] And not far away was Melrose Abbey, also in ruins, and memorialized in Scott's *Lay of the Last Minstrel.* In the poem the abbey is described by the minstrel as a scene which should be visited in the solitude of night:

> When the cold light's uncertain shower
> Streams on the ruined central tower;
> Then go—but go alone the while—
> Then view St. David's ruin'd pile.[38]

Scott's minstrel is again reminiscent of Ossian, for like the bard he

> spoke of former days
> And how old age, and wand'ring long
> Had done his harp and hand some wrong.

Surely Mendelssohn would recall Melrose Abbey when he and Klingemann approached the ruins on Iona in August 1829.

But did Mendelssohn musically relate his experiences at Staffa with his visits to Holyrood, Abbotsford, and Melrose? Some evidence would suggest just that. Many stylistic features of the *Scottish* Symphony recall the *Fingal's Cave* Overture. These include the beginning in the low strings, frequent octave doublings, disjunct lines, and open spacings. There is a suggestion, too, that Mendelssohn had in mind to revive something of the opening of the overture, with its sequential bare fifths. The first theme of the *Allegro* traverses three harmonic levels—A minor, C major, and E major—just as the first theme of the overture is given in B minor, D major, and F-sharp minor (ex. 21). Of course, in the symphony, the direct progression by thirds is broken up by the intervening voice leading, in contrast to the opening of the overture, which presents stark fifths and octaves. But something just as exotic as that opening occurs in the development of the symphony, which Mendelssohn initiated by directly moving a third from a unison on the dominant E to C-sharp minor, without mitigating motion (ex. 22). And in the following bars, with bare fifths in the winds and octave doublings in the strings, he shifted unexpectedly from C-sharp minor to B minor, before eventually reaching C minor, an altered mediant, as his point of departure for the development. The approach to C minor is nearly as striking as the opening of the overture; we have, in short, a similar attempt to capture the primitive, the unconventional.

One other possible link in the symphony to Ossian is the horn call, the symbol of the hunt. This stock figure recurs throughout the symphony (ex. 23). A common romantic literary subject, the hunt of course figures prominently in Ossian and Sir Walter Scott. Fingal, having vanquished Swaran, enjoys a hunt in the concluding book of the epic. In *The Lady of the Lake,* Ellen sings a song for the tired hunters (also set by Schubert; see above). Scott also wrote a "Hunting Song," "Waken, lords and ladies gay" (1808), which Mendelssohn composed as a part-song for male chorus. Replete with imitations of horn calls, his *Jagdlied* (ex. 24) displays the same exuberant spirit as the second movement of the symphony, which concludes with fleeting references to the hunt.

These connections—especially those tying the symphony to *Fingal's Cave* and Gade's *Ossian* Overture—allow us to propose the *Scottish* Symphony as another example of Mendelssohn's Ossianic manner. With its connected movements, pentatonic melodies, and dark scorings, the symphony—whatever its programmatic meaning—is an extraordinary work for the composer. It represents another example of Mendelssohn's intent to avoid the traditional and to explore the unfamiliar.

[*iii*]

Mendelssohn was to have one more encounter with an Ossianic subject, the result of which was a setting for bass solo and orchestra of *On Lena's Gloomy Heath.* Finished in 1846, barely a year before his death, this work remains unpublished.[39] It was commissioned by Henry Phillips, an English bass whom Mendelssohn met at the Philharmonic concerts in London during one of his several visits. An account of the work is given in Phillips's autobiography, a delightful source which preserves several letters from the composer concerning this concert scene.[40] Phillips asked Mendelssohn for a composition as early as June 1842, around the time of the English premiere of the *Scottish* Symphony, conducted by Mendelssohn on June 13 in London. For the text Phillips selected passages from the third and fourth books of *Fingal.* For various unknown reasons, Mendelssohn procrastinated in finishing the commission. In two letters of January 1843 and June 1844, he apologized to Phillips for the delay, but assured him that the score was nearly complete. Not until

Ex. 21. Mendelssohn, Op. 56

Ex. 22. Mendelssohn, Op. 56

Ex. 23. Mendelssohn, Op. 56

Ex. 24. Mendelssohn, Op. 120, No. 1

September 22, 1846, however, did Phillips receive the autograph, a few weeks after the premiere of *Elijah* at the Birmingham Music Festival. According to Phillips, he rehearsed the work privately with Mendelssohn. Phillips premiered the work at a Philharmonic concert on March 15, 1847; a second performance was given in London on November 15, only a week after Mendelssohn's death.[41]

Mendelssohn was not pleased with the work and did not consider its revision or publication (in his presentation note to Phillips he even relinquished his claim to a copy of the work). The executors of Mendelssohn's estate respected these wishes—they did not publish the work, even though they did include among the posthumous Opp. 72 through 120 many early, immature works. Apparently, the Mendelssohn family actually attempted to reclaim the autograph from Phillips.[42]

Though the autograph has disappeared, two undated manuscript copies of the work do survive, enabling us to add this work to the Mendelssohn catalogue. One copy, preserved at the British Library (Add. Ms. 48597, plate 2), bears the personal owner's stamp of Sir Charles Santley (1834–1922), an English baritone who perhaps had access to the work through Phillips. A second copy is in the Margaret Deneke Mendelssohn Collection at Oxford (Cat. C. 50). These two copies are the only known sources for the work.

The main body of the text Phillips chose is from Book IV of *Fingal*. It describes the sleeping Ossian, who is awakened by a vision of his deceased wife, Everallin. She calls upon him to rescue their son, Oscar, trapped in an ambush:

On Lena's gloomy heath the voice of music died away. The inconstant blast blew hard. The high oak shook its leaves around. Of Everallin were my thoughts, when in all the light of beauty she came; her blue eyes rolling in tears. She stood on a cloud before my sight, and spoke with feeble voice! "Rise, Ossian, rise, and save my son; save Oscar, prince of men. Near the red oak of Luba's stream he fights with Lochlin's sons." She sunk into her cloud again. I covered me with steel. My spear supported my steps; my rattling armor rung. I hummed, as I was wont in danger, the songs of heroes of old. Like distant thunder Lochlin heard. They fled; my son pursued.[43]

The passage is the quintessence of Ossian: solitude, gloom, natural imagery, apparitions, a distant battle, nostalgia for the past—all set in a driving, unrelenting iambic prose.

There is little wonder that Phillips excerpted this particular passage; the image of the sleeping Ossian was a favorite theme in the visual arts. In particular, Ingres, who was commissioned to paint an Ossianic scene for Napoleon, created a major work in his *Songe d'Ossian*.[44] The painting was actually inspired by another dream of Ossian, this one from Macpherson's short poem *The War of Inisthona*. Here the slumbering bard reminisces about the past and conjures up visions of his father, Fingal; his son, Oscar; and the heroes of old:

Daughter of Toscar, take the harp, and raise the lovely song of Selma; that sleep may overtake my soul in the midst of joy; that the dreams of my youth may return, and the days of the mighty Fingal. . . . I see the heroes of Morven; I hear the song of bards: Oscar lifts the sword of Cormalo; a thousand youths admire its studded thongs. . . . The bard of other times holds discourse with his fathers! the chiefs of the days of old! Sons of the chase, stand far distant! disturb not the dreams of Ossian![45]

Ingres's painting presents the bard resting on his harp by a body of water. Hovering on the right in the middleground is the armed figure of Oscar; on the left, the figure of a woman, perhaps Malvina, his wife; and behind her, receding into the clouds, Fingal and a host of other heroes. Several figures are playing harps.

Ingres also left some sketches for *Le Songe d'Ossian* with some significant variations. One in particular has the figures grouped together, without the clear separation in the finished painting. Winds blow through the clouds, and at the top of the sketch stars are visible.[46] Perhaps here Ingres had in mind the well-known poem of Macpherson, *The Songs of Selma,* which Goethe extracted in translation in *Werther.* Here is the opening of *Selma:*

Star of descending night! fair is thy light in the west! . . . The stormy winds are laid. . . . Let the light of Ossian's soul arise! . . . I behold my departed friends. Their gathering is on Lora, as in the days of other years. Fingal comes like a watery column of mist! his heroes are around: and see the bards of song, gray-haired Ullin![47]

The passage is indeed close to that from *Fingal,* "On Lena's gloomy heath."

Ingres's work, with its tones of French patriotism—these Caledonians, after all, had their counterparts in Napoleon's *grande armée*—could almost be interpreted to represent Ossian's dream in *Fingal,* the subject of Mendelssohn's *scena.* The compelling effect of Ingres's painting and its supernatural elements are pictorial expressions of the same moods captured by Mendelssohn in his Ossianic works. As we might expect, in Mendelssohn's concert setting we find many of the same stylistic features from the works already discussed.

The extract from *Fingal* suggested to Mendelssohn a tripartite division: an introduction to establish the mood and locale; a central portion to present Everallin and her plea; and the final section to gird Ossian for battle. As Phillips noted in his memoirs, the composer was not satisfied with the ending of the text, the unsuccessful "My son pursued," and he asked for an addition, which "could be repeated several times, had an energetic expression in itself, and gave a point to the last part of the music."[48] Phillips obliged with a short passage from Book III of *Fingal:* "My soul brightens in danger, in the noise of arms. I am of the race of battle. My fathers never feared."[49] Though the text here concerns another hero, Calmar, and has nothing to do with Ossian, Phillips appropriated it and sent it to Mendelssohn on June 29, 1842. Phillips's note accompanying these lines survives in the Green-Books Collection of the Margaret Deneke Mendelssohn Collection at Oxford (plate 3).[50] In Mendelssohn's hands, the supplementary passage became a stirring, if somewhat prosaic, march in G major designed to form the culmination of the work.

Mendelssohn devoted the beginning of the composition to several soft wind fanfares accompanied by a slowly descending series of trills in the lower strings (ex. 25). The chromatic bass line is a particularly deft touch—it suggests tonal ambiguity and achieves an atmospheric effect comparable to the mood of Ingres's *Songe d'Ossian.* Mendelssohn's introduction also looks ahead to the marvelous opening of Liszt's first tone poem, *Ce qu'on entend sur la montagne,* based upon a mystical

Ex. 25. Mendelssohn, *On Lena's Gloomy Heath*

poem by Victor Hugo. Hugo's supra-natural sound, "un bruit confus," is portrayed in Liszt's score by chromatically oscillating trills in the lower strings (ex. 26), also ambiguous and atmospheric. In Mendelssohn's score atmosphere yields to a move to the dominant D major, with *fortissimo* bursts from trumpets and horns and then a *pianissimo* pause as the voice enters.

The first line, "On Lena's gloomy heath," is set to a melody which quite strikingly recalls the thematic construction of Mendelssohn's earlier Ossianic works (ex. 27). The first phrase spans an octave on D, the fifth scale degree, a construction similar to the technique in *Fingal's Cave* and the *Scottish* Symphony. The shape of the phrase, moreover, suggests divisions of the octave either into a simple arpeggiation of the tonic G minor, D–G–B-flat–D, or into the (now familiar) pentatonic arrangement, D–G–A–D. The open spacing of the chords and subsequent repetition of the melody in octaves by the violins bring back some other salient features of the *Scottish* Symphony.

Mendelssohn's setting of "the inconstant blast blew hard, the high oak shook its leaves" is a good example of word painting, with its *sforzando* blasts from the horns (ex. 28). But it also echoes a passage from Gade's *Ossian* Overture, thus further tying the work to the group of compositions we have discussed. Example 29 gives the passage in question from the overture; both figures, melodically very similar, appear over a dominant pedal point (strings in Gade's passage, sustained horns in Mendelssohn's). For the appearance of the imploring Everallin Mendelssohn shifted the tempo without interruption to *Animato*. Everallin's speech, "Rise, Ossian, rise and save my son," is presented over an ascending chromatic sequence, with dramatically rising tension. Tonally, the passage rises, too, from D major to E

Ex. 26. Liszt, *Ce qu'on entend sur la montagne*

Ex. 27. Mendelssohn, *On Lena's Gloomy Heath*

Ex. 28. Mendelssohn, *On Lena's Gloomy Heath*

minor, and then further away toward F-sharp minor, before reaching the tonic G minor. One of the most successful portions of the work (ex. 30), the passage serves as a transitional tempo between the opening *Moderato* and the concluding *Allegro vivace* of the march. The whole complex demonstrates the same kind of fluent control of tempo exhibited in the *Scottish* Symphony.

The following march in G major, "My soul brightens in danger," is almost predictable in view of the impending fray and rescue of Oscar; musically it is largely

Ex. 29. Gade, *Ossian* Overture

Ex. 30. Mendelssohn, *On Lena's Gloomy Heath*

Ex. 31. Mendelssohn, *On Lena's Gloomy Heath*

unsuccessful. We should note, however, that the march tune is derived from the first phrase of the composition: the beginning of the march spans the same arpeggiation based upon D (ex. 31). Here again Mendelssohn has linked thematically the structural areas of the work, just as he and Gade had experimented with cyclical thematic schemes in the *Scottish* Symphony and *Ossian* Overture. The march is interrupted by the return of the opening trills in G minor; a short coda concludes triumphantly with the pursuit of the fleeing foe.

On Lena's Gloomy Heath is not among Mendelssohn's best efforts; we may not claim here the recovery of a major work. It is important, though, not only as a new addition to the catalogue of Mendelssohn's works, but as a work representative of the composer's Ossianic manner. In it, as in the *Fingal's Cave* Overture and *Scottish* Symphony, Mendelssohn succeeded in unleashing his romantic imagination. These works force us to consider afresh the essential conflict in Mendelssohn's music between two pulling forces—those of romanticism and musical tradition. To be sure, Ossian did not dominate Mendelssohn's imagination—the bard did not replace Homer, so to speak, as he did for Werther. Mendelssohn could compose fugues in imitation of Bach or choral works in emulation of Handel, just as fervently as he could set down some exotic experiences in his Ossianic works. In the final summary, we have in his music a balance which Lord Byron struck in his own Ossianic poem, "The Island":

> Long have I roamed through lands which are not mine,
> Adored the Alp, and loved the Apennine,
> Revered Parnassus, and beheld the steep
> Jove's Ida and Olympus crown the deep:
> But 'twas not all long ages' lore, nor all
> *Their* nature held me in their thrilling thrall;
> The infant rapture still survived the boy,
> And Loch-na-gar with Ida look'd o'er Troy,
> Mix'd Celtic memories with the Phrygian mount,
> And Highland linns with Castalie's clear fount.
> Forgive me, Homer's universal shade!
> Forgive me, Phoebus, that my fancy stray'd;
> The north and nature taught me to adore
> Your scenes sublime, from those beloved before.

Notes

Introduction

1. Robert Schumann, *Memories of Felix Mendelssohn-Bartholdy*, trans. James A. Galston (Rochester, N.Y., 1950), p. 53. (*Erinnerungen an Felix Mendelssohn Bartholdy*, ed. Georg Eismann [Zwickau, 1948], p. 23.)

2. "Rückblick auf das Leipziger Musikleben im Winter 1837–1838," *Neue Zeitschrift für Musik* 8 (1838), nos. 27–29; and "Musikleben in Leipzig während des Winters 1839–1840," *NZfM* 12 (1842), nos. 38–40.

3. *Robert Schumanns Briefe. Neue Folge.* ed. F. Gustav Jansen, 2nd ed. (Leipzig, 1904), pp. 424–26; see also O. E. Deutsch, "The Discovery of Schubert's Great C-Major Symphony: A Story in Fifteen Letters," *Musical Quarterly* 38 (1952): 528–32.

4. See especially the account of the rehearsals for the premiere of the Second Symphony in Joseph Wilhelm von Wasielewski, *Schumanniana* (Bonn, 1883), pp. 16–17.

5. For instance, a version of the viewpoint can be seen in Walter and Paula Rehberg, *Robert Schumann. Sein Leben und sein Werk,* 2nd ed. (Zürich and Stuttgart, 1969), p. 134. Only at one time, though, was the friendship apparently strained. In a letter to Karl Klingemann of January 31, 1847, Mendelssohn alluded to some difficulties, unfortunately without specifying the nature of the problem (*Felix Mendelssohn-Bartholdys Briefwechsel mit Legationsrat Karl Klingemann in London,* ed. Karl Klingemann [Essen, 1909], p. 320). In any event, this did not influence the admiring tone of Schumann's memoirs of Mendelssohn.

6. Felix Mendelssohn, *Letters,* ed. G. Selden-Goth (New York, 1945), p. 331. From the original in English.

7. For some views of Mendelssohn as teacher, see Eric Werner, *Mendelssohn: A New Image of the Composer and his Age,* trans. Dika Newlin (London, 1963), pp. 386–87.

8. This literary connection is best explored by Bernhard Appel, "Schumanns Davidsbund: Geistes- und sozialgeschichtliche Voraussetzungen einer romantischen Idee," *Archiv für Musikwissenschaft* 38 (1981): 1–23.

9. This is not an entirely new idea, of course; see Gerald Abraham, *A Hundred Years of Music* (New York, 1938), p. 69.

10. Eugenie Schumann, *Robert Schumann. Ein Lebensbild meines Vaters* (Leipzig, 1931), p. 290.

11. *NZfM* 13 (1840): 198.

12. "Hector Berlioz, 'Episode de la vie d'un Artiste'. Grande Symphonie Fantastique," *NZfM* 3 (1835): 34.

13. Ralph P. Locke, "Liszt's Saint-Simonian Adventure," *19th Century Music* 4 (1981): 209–27.

14. For an account of Schumann's behavior during this period, see Rehberg, *Schumann,* pp. 319–24.

Leon Plantinga / *Schumann's Critical Reaction to Mendelssohn*

1. *Allgemeine musikalische Zeitung* 37 (1835), cols. 688–89.
2. Ibid., col. 689.
3. Robert Schumann, *Gesammelte Schriften über Musik und Musiker,* ed. Martin Kreisig, 5th edition (Leipzig, 1914), 1:117.
4. Ibid., 1:118.
5. Ibid., 1:111.
6. Ibid., 1:124.
7. Ibid., 1:387–88.
8. Ibid., 1:252–54.
9. Schumann of course knew nothing of the twelve symphonies (eleven of them for strings alone) the young Mendelssohn had composed by the age of fifteen.
10. *Gesammelte Schriften* 2:133.
11. Ibid., 2:132.
12. Ibid. It might be mentioned in passing that in this review Schumann made something of a gaffe. He reports having heard "at third hand" that the symphony in question originated during Mendelssohn's stay in Rome, so he fancifully compares it to the description of an Italian journey in Jean Paul's *Titan.* It was of course the *Italian* Symphony to which that report referred; preparatory work on the *Scottish* Symphony occurred during Mendelssohn's visit to that northern wilderness in 1829. The drone-like sounds that Schumann heard only as a *Volkston* were meant to remind him of heather and kilts.
13. Ibid., 1:143. Mendelssohn himself disparaged certain attempts to make specific connections between the overture and an implied program: "Many persons here [in Leipzig] consider 'Melusina' to be my best overture; at all events, it is the most deeply felt; but as to the fabulous nonsense of the musical papers, about red coral and green sea-monsters, and magic palaces, and deep seas, this is stupid stuff and fills me with amazement." Mendelssohn to Fanny Mendelssohn Hensel, January 1836, *Mendelssohn's Letters,* ed. G. Selden-Goth (New York, 1945), p. 257.
14. *Gesammelte Schriften* 1:144.
15. This despite his impression that the "knightly theme" in F minor would gain in "pridefulness and significance" if its tempo were *slower.* Ibid.
16. *Neue Zeitschrift für Musik* 4 (1836):7.
17. *Gesammelte Schriften* 1:318–21.
18. Ibid., 1:322.
19. Ibid., 1:323.
20. Ibid., 2:301. Schumann of course got this familiar bit of mythology somewhat wrong. Minerva (or Athena) sprang from the head of Jupiter (Zeus); Cronus (or Saturn) was the father of Zeus.
21. Ibid., 1:500–501.
22. Ibid., 1:398.
23. Amadeus Wendt, *Ueber den gegenwärtigen Zustand der Musik besonders in Deutschland und wie er geworden* (Leipzig, 1836), pp. 3–4.
24. *Jugendbriefe von Robert Schumann* (Leipzig, 1885), pp. 209–10.
25. See, e.g., J. J. Winckelmann, *Geschichte der Kunst des Alterthums* (Weimar, 1964), pp. 263–67. This book was first published in 1764.
26. *Gesammelte Schriften* 1:9.
27. Ibid., 1:500.
28. *Jugendbriefe,* p. 283.
29. *Allgemeine musikalische Zeitung* 44 (1842), col. 1.

Jurgen Thym / *Schumann in Brendel's* Neue Zeitschrift für Musik

The present article has appeared in Italian as "Schumann e la critica al suo pensiero: La 'Neue Zeitschrift für Musik' di Brendel, negli anni 1845–1856," in *Musica/Realtà* 11 (August 1983), pp. 135–61.

1. Surprisingly little has been said about these matters in the musicological literature of the past. C. F. Glasenapp records the various encounters of Brendel and his journal with Wagner in *The Life of Richard Wagner*, trans. W. Ashton Ellis, 6 vols. (London, 1900–1908), but his volumes—because of their one-sided function as Beyreuth court biography—do not do justice to Schumann's side of the story. Wolfgang Boetticher's monumental tomes on Schumann touch on several aspects of the topic under consideration, particularly the relationship between Schumann and Brendel and the image of Schumann in contemporary criticism in general: *Robert Schumann: Einführung in Persönlichkeit und Werk* (Berlin, 1941), pp. 274–79, 355–98; *Robert Schumann in seinen Schriften und Briefen* (Berlin, 1942) also contains excerpts of letters from Schumann to Brendel. Boetticher's selection and interpretation of the documents, however, were guided by the cultural politics of Nazi Germany. As a result, he tended to downplay the friendship between Mendelssohn and Schumann, to overemphasize the connection between Schumann and Wagner, and to give the impression that Brendel and Schumann worked together to bring about the triumph of Wagner in music history.

2. Franz Brendel, "Zur Einleitung," *NZfM* 22 (1845): 1–12; also published under the title "Ein Program" in Brendel's *Gesammelte Aufsätze zur Geschichte und Kritik der neueren Musik* (Leipzig, 1888), pp. 29–56.

3. Ibid., p. 10. Almost ten years later, Brendel restated his objections to Schumann's criticism more clearly in a review of Schumann's *Gesammelte Schriften;* see *NZfM* 41 (1854): 165–66: "In comparison with this standpoint, Schumann's criticism seems infinitely more insightful, ingenious, and penetrating. It is to Schumann's lasting credit that he prepared the new epoch in art with this journal. However, in comparison with the more solid former accomplishments, for instance . . . of Rochlitz, his criticism also reveals shortcomings. Schumann is fantastic in his criticism, he often exaggerates by leaps and bounds, . . . [his criticism] lacks firm stability, [and] he often fails to hit upon the target but rushes beyond it."

4. Brendel's discussion of Schubert's "Erlkönig" in his programmatic introductory article is a case in point, *NZfM* 22 (1845): 8–9. He considered the setting a failure, especially because the voice of the Erlking is represented through lovely (*lieblich*) and pleasant (*angenehm*) melody that presumably lacks the essential element of eeriness.

5. Johannes Besser, "Die Beziehungen Franz Brendels zur Hegelschen Philosophie: Ein Beitrag zur Musikanschauung des Schumann-Kreises," in H. J. Moser and E. Rebling, eds., *Robert Schumann 1856/1956* (Leipzig, 1956), pp. 84–91.

6. Franz Brendel, "Zum neuen Jahr," *NZfM* 34 (1851): 1–2.

7. Idem, "Robert Schumann mit Rücksicht auf Mendelssohn-Bartholdy und die Entwicklung der modernen Tonkunst überhaupt," *NZfM* 22 (1845): 63–67, 81–83, 89–92, 113–15, 121–23, 145–47, 149–50.

8. Idem, "Vergangenheit, Gegenwart und Zukunft der Oper," *NZfM* 23 (1845): 33–35, 37–39, 41–43, 105–8, 109–12, 121–24, 149–52; *NZfM* 24 (1846): 57–60, 61–64.

9. Ibid., p. 63: "The nation—I am afraid—will drop music as a part of the great movements of the present era, if music hesitates much longer in aspiring to higher ideals and linking herself to the historical trends of the time. Is it not a most ominous sign that many advocates of the liberal party are unfavorably disposed toward our art, calling it useless for the shaping of things to come?"

10. Ibid., p. 62: "However beautiful and lovely the special German inwardness and coziness [*Gemütlichkeit*] may have been, and however excellent the achievements that Germany alone has produced under their auspices, idealistic day-dreaming can no longer establish the content of art at the present time. The people have become more practical; it is legitimate to demand that art reflect this turn of events. However, all my remarks are only indications or different wordings for one thing, the solution to the problem, which I now state outright: namely, loyalty to the people and democratic conviction in a higher sense. These alone will enable us to reach this goal. . . . Opera, however, the genre to which all parts of the people have access in equal measure, is called upon above all to realize this progress."

11. *NZfM* 23 (1845): 111.

12. Luise Otto, "Die Nibelungen als Oper," *NZfM* 23 (1845): 49–52, 129–30, 171–72; and idem, "Die Nibelungen, Oper in fünf Acten," *NZfM* 23 (1845): 175–76, 181–83.

13. *NZfM* 23 (1845): 124.

14. Franz Brendel, "Leipziger Musikleben. Abonnementsconcerte," *NZfM* 25 (1846): 177, 180–82.

15. "Für Pianoforte: Robert Schumann, op. 54, Concert mit Begleitung des Orchesters," *NZfM* 26 (1847): 17–19.

16. Alfred Dörffel, "Für Orchester: Robert Schumann, op. 61. Zweite Symphonie für grosses Orchester," *NZfM* 28 (1848): 97–101.

17. The phrase *Palme des Lebens* had been borrowed from an article by Eduard Krüger on Mendelssohn's *Elijah* published two months earlier in the journal, "Über Mendelssohn's *Elias* (Bruchstücke aus einem Briefwechsel)," *NZfM* 27 (1847): 265–68, 277–82, 289–93. Krüger named Schumann, Chopin, Löwe, Hiller, and Gade as the most important composers of the time and continued his statement in the following enigmatic way, stopping short of singling out Schumann as the champion: "Among those five, there are two more refined talents, and among those there is one for whom the crown of laurels is in store, if he—but stop, that is enough now! Your own wits (not I) will tell you whom I mean" (266).

18. Schumann, who occasionally commented in his letters to Brendel on articles in the *NZfM*, was quite pleased that the journal had advanced the discussion of his music with new vigor and enthusiasm. On July 3 [recte 5], 1848, he wrote to Brendel that he enjoyed reading Dörffel's review of the Second Symphony, and previously (on February 20, 1847) he expressed his delight in a similar way about Dörffel's account of the Piano Concerto (see n. 15). Both letters are published in Boetticher, *Schriften und Briefen*, pp. 417–18 and 438–39.

19. Alfred Dörffel, "Für Pianoforte und Streichinstrumente: Robert Schumann, op. 63, Trio für Pianoforte, Violine und Violoncell," *NZfM* 29 (1848): 113–15.

20. Idem, "Für Pianoforte: Robert Schumann, op. 68, Album für die Jugend," *NZfM* 30 (1849): 89–91.

21. "Für Pianoforte zu vier Händen: R. Schumann, op. 61. Zweite Symphonie. . .Vierhändiger Clavierauszug vom Componisten," *NZfM* 30 (1849): 187–88.

22. Ernst Gottschald, "Robert Schumann's zweite Symphonie, zugleich mit Rücksicht auf andere, ins besondere Beethoven's Symphonien: Vertraute Briefe an A. Dörffel," *NZfM* 32 (1850): 137–39, 141–42, 145–48, 157–59.

23. Theodor Uhlig, "Beethoven's Symphonien im Zusammenhange betrachtet: Ein Beitrag zur Auffindung des Wahren," *NZfM* 32 (1850): 29–30, 33–34, 45–47, 53–54, 69–71, 77–78.

24. See Brendel's postscript to J. Rühlmann's obituary for Theodor Uhlig, *NZfM* 38 (1853): 33–37: "Until then I knew Wagner's achievements only very little and only his first two writings [*Die Kunst und die Revolution* and *Das Kunstwerk der Zukunft*] opened my eyes and made me realize the artistic greatness that had existed unrecognized in this man. Now I asked Uhlig to take up the matter, since I knew how familiar he was with the Wagnerian direction" (p. 36). Always eager to point out the continuity of tradition in the journal, Brendel added that it was Schumann who introduced Uhlig to him as one of the most qualified music journalists.

25. Brendel reported on his Weimar trips in several essays: "Ein Ausflug nach Weimar," *NZfM* 36 (1852): 37–40; "Ein zweiter Ausflug nach Weimar," *NZfM* 36 (1852): 120–21; and "Ein dritter Ausflug nach Weimar," *NZfM* 37 (1852): 225–27, 237–40, 251–54.

26. Idem, *Geschichte der Musik in Italien, Deutschland und Frankreich: Fünfundzwanzig Vorlesungen* (Leipzig, 1852); Brendel published revised editions in 1855, 1860, and 1867.

27. K. Freigedank [Richard Wagner], "Das Judenthum in der Musik," *NZfM* 33 (1850): 101–7, 109–12.

28. Franz Brendel, "R. Schumann's Oper: Genoveva," *NZfM* 33 (1850): 1–4, 17–18.

29. "Musik für das Theater: Robert Schumann, op. 81, Genoveva. . .Clavierauszug von Clara Schumann," *NZfM* 34 (1851): 129–31, 141–44.

30. Ibid., p. 129.

31. Franz Brendel, "Einige Worte über Richard Wagner," *NZfM* 34 (1851): 264–66.

32. T[heodor] U[hlig], "Kammer- und Hausmusik: Robert Schumann, op. 98, Lieder, Gesänge und Requiem für Mignon aus Goethe's Wilhelm Meister," *NZfM* 35 (1851): 219–21.

33. Idem, "Kammer- und Hausmusik: Robert Schumann, op. 105, Sonate (in A-moll) für Pianoforte und Violine," *NZfM* 37 (1852): 117–20.

34. Ibid., p. 117: "We find Schumann's new sonata in connection with his last symphony [the Third] to be eminently suited to serve as a convincing proof that Schumann at present is a musical mannerist if there ever was one among the composers." It is almost ironic that Uhlig described Schu-

mann's works of the 1850s with a vocabulary similar to that applied to Schumann's "bizarre" piano music in the 1830s.

35. Brendel admitted in a postscript to an article about his third Weimar trip (see n. 25) that because of the journal's support of new trends in music, a rift had been growing between the *NZfM* and its founder: "I am thinking here especially of Robert Schumann and the position which this journal formerly assumed toward him. It is known that for a long time we considered Schumann the most significant musical personality of the present time among the artists then on the rise. Lately our paths have taken somewhat different directions and individual correspondents of this journal have occasionally carried on against him in a polemical way. Even if our position now is somewhat polemical, it is always based on the conviction that Schumann accomplished great and beautiful things. We stand by what we have said before; the change in judgment is only temporary." *NZfM* 37 (1852): 254.

36. Ralph P. Locke and Jurgen Thym, "New Schumann Materials in Upstate New York: A First Report on the Dickinson Collection, with Catalogues of Its Manuscript Holdings," *Fontes Artis Musicae* 27 (1980): 160–61.

37. Franz Brendel, "Zur Anbahnung einer Verständigung," *NZfM* 50 (1859): 265–73; also in his *Gesammelte Aufsätze,* pp. 147–67.

38. After his retirement as editor, Schumann's contacts with the journal did not cease. His name appeared in the list of contributors until 1855; beginning in 1847, the title page for each volume carried not only the name of the current editor but also Schumann's name as founder, a tradition the journal has continued to the present time. However, he wrote very little for Brendel's journal between his retirement and the "Neue Bahnen" essay: "Curiosum, den englischen Nationalcanon: *Non nobis Domine* betreffend," *NZfM* 28 (1848): 226–27, clearly a peripheral piece of music journalism; and "Musikalische Haus- und Lebensregeln," an addendum to the May 3, 1850, issue of the *NZfM.* His influence on the journal after 1844 was covert rather than overt; what has come down to us from extensive correspondence between Schumann and Brendel (see n. 1) suggests that Schumann functioned de facto as a senior advisor to his successor for the journal, especially during the first years. In his letters to Brendel, Schumann often commented with praise or criticism on articles and reviews that had appeared in the *NZfM,* exerting some influence on editorial policies. In the early 1850s, of course, this influence all but disappeared. The correspondence with Brendel ceased in October 1853, i.e., at the time of Schumann's article on Brahms.

39. Robert Schumann, "Neue Bahnen," *NZfM* 39 (1853): 185–86.

40. Hoplit [Richard Pohl], "Zur Eröffnung des Zwanzigsten Jahrgangs der Neuen Zeitschrift für Musik," *NZfM* 40 (1854): 1–3.

41. Ibid., p. 3.

42. Franz Liszt, "Robert Schumann," *NZfM* 42 (1855): 133–37, 145–53, 157–65, 177–82, 189–96.

43. "Todesfälle," *NZfM* 45 (1856): 72.

44. Ibid.

Rufus Hallmark / *A Sketch Leaf for Schumann's D-Minor Symphony*

1. Douglas Johnson, "Beethoven Scholars and Beethoven's Sketches," *19th Century Music* 2 (1978): 3–17.

2. Eric Sams, "Making a Song," *Musical Times* 122 (1981): 382–83.

3. Joseph Kerman, "Sketch Studies," *Musicology in the 1980s. Methods, Goals, Opportunities,* ed. D. Kern Holoman and Claude V. Palisca (New York, 1982), pp. 53–65; a version of the same essay is published in *19th Century Music* 6 (1982): 174–80.

4. Johnson, "Beethoven Scholars," p. 16; he quotes the phrase "omniscient critic" from Philip Gossett's "Beethoven's Sixth Symphony: Sketches for the First Movement," *Journal of the American Musicological Society* 27 (1974): 261.

5. Lewis Lockwood, "Beethoven's Earliest Sketches for the *Eroica,*" *Musical Quarterly* 67 (1981): 457–78.

6. These sources are: First Symphony, Library of Congress, ML 96.S415 Case; Second Symphony, Breifkopf und Härtel Archiv, Leipzig (lost), photocopy in Österreichische National Bibliothek, Vienna, Photoarchiv 1281; Third Symphony, Staatsbibliothek Preussischer Kulturbesitz, Berlin, Mus. ms. auto. R. Schumann 12; Fourth Symphony (1841 version), Gesellschaft der Musikfreunde, Vienna, A-292; (1851 version), Staatsbibliothek Preussischer Kulturbesitz, Berlin, Mus. ms. auto. R. Schumann 17.

7. Sketches for the First Symphony are bound with the score in the Library of Congress. Sketches for the Third Symphony are in the Bibliothèque nationale, Paris, Mss. 329 and 334. For description and discussion of the manuscript materials of the symphonies, see Linda Correll Roesner, "Studies in Schumann Manuscripts: With Particular Reference to Sources Transmitting Instrumental Works in the Large Forms," 2 vols. (Ph.D. diss., New York University, 1973); and Jon W. Finson, "Robert Schumann: The Creation of the Symphonic Works" (Ph.D. diss., University of Chicago, 1980).

8. Sketches for the Second Symphony are listed by Wolfgang Boetticher as part of the Wiede Collection, in Robert Schumann: Einführung in Persönlichkeit und Werk (Berlin, 1941), p. 632; the same listing is given by Georg Eismann in "Nachweis der internationalen Standorte von Notenautographen Robert Schumanns," Sammelbände der Robert-Schumann-Gesellschaft 2 (1966): 16. This manuscript is presumably still part of the collection.

9. Two other sketches for this symphony have been erroneously listed by Boetticher. In Einführung, p. 636, he cites "Skizzen und Verbesserungen in der ersten Niederschrift. Fragment. 3 Blatt, 6 beschr. Seiten" for "IV. Sinfonie in D-Dur [sic]" at the Gesellschaft der Musikfreunde, Vienna. Eismann in his "Nachweis" makes no mention of these, and Linda Roesner informs me that no manuscript fitting this description exists at the Gesellschaft today. Boetticher also describes an incipit of the main theme in a travel diary as a "Themenstudie zur D-Moll Sinfonie," in Robert Schumann in seinen Schriften und Briefen (Berlin, 1942), p. 364. The diary, however, was written during a trip Schumann made in the late winter and early spring of 1842, some months after he had completed the score of the D-minor Symphony. The diary in question is the Reisenotizbuch V. Hamburg, 1842 (Robert-Schumann-Haus, Zwickau, 4871 VII A/b, 5A3). Martin Schoppe and Gerd Nauhaus of the Schumann-Haus have suggested to me the likelihood that Schumann wrote the theme incipit down in order to show it to some fellow traveler.

10. Bibliothèque nationale, Ms. 342. The paper (23 × 28.5 cm) is printed in vertical format with 16 staves. The staff is 0.6 cm. wide and 18.3 cm. long; the space between staves is 1 cm., and the total staff span is 24.1 cm. From the relative size of the margins, it appears that the side of the leaf bearing the song sketch is the recto side. This same side carries Clara's inscription at the bottom right corner, "Handschrift von Robert Schumann beglaubigt v. Clara Schumann."

11. For discussions of the two versions of the symphony, see Donald Francis Tovey, Essays in Musical Analysis (London, 1935), 2:56–62; Gerald Abraham, "The Three Scores of Schumann's D Minor Symphony," Musical Times 81 (1940): 105–9, repr. in Slavonic and Romantic Music (London, 1968), pp. 281–87; Mosco Carner, "The Orchestral Music," Schumann: A Symposium, ed. Gerald Abraham (London, 1952), pp. 214–19; Asher G. Zlotnik, "Die beiden Fassungen von Schumanns D-Moll-Symphonie," Österreichische Musikzeitschrift 21 (1966): 271–76; and Marc Andreae, "Die Vierte Sinfonie Robert Schumanns, ihre Fassungen, ihre Interpretations-Probleme," to be published as part of the Schumann Symposium held in Düsseldorf, June 1981.

12. See Gerd Nauhaus, "Zur Edition der Haushaltsbücher Robert Schumanns," 1. Schumann-Tage des Bezirkes Karl-Marx-Stadt (Zwickau, 1977), pp. 26–33; Finson, "Symphonic Works," pp. 182–209; Egon Voss, Robert Schumann, Sinfonie Nr. 4, d-moll, Op. 120: Einführung und Analyse (Mainz, 1980), pp. 137–68.

13. Berthold Litzmann, Clara Schumann: ein Künstlerleben nach Tagebüchern und Briefen (Leipzig, 1920), 2: 32–33.

14. Nauhaus, "Zur Edition," p. 29.

15. Ibid.

16. Deutsche Staatsbibliothek, Berlin (DDR), Mus. ms. auto. R. Schumann 16/3, pp. 66–80.

17. A reverse situation is found in Bibliothèque nationale, Ms. 334. First used for sketches for the third symphony, the page later served for recording two drafts of songs ("Die Fensterscheibe," Op. 107, No. 2, and "Jung Volkers Lied," Op. 125, No. 3). See Roesner, "Studies," 1:77ff.

18. Boetticher, Einführung, pp. 572–85.

19. Roesner, "Studies," 1:225.

20. The plausibility of this idea is strengthened by a page of five fugue beginnings Schumann wrote in the third of his early sketchbooks (Universitätsbibliothek, Bonn, Schumann 15, p. 75). Each

of five different subjects is imitated at a different interval: "Im Einklang," "In der Sekunde," "In der Terz," "In der Quart," and "In der Quinte."

21. For an example, see n. 17.

22. Roesner, "Studies," 1:204ff.

23. The question of chronology did not occur to me while I was looking at the manuscript in Paris, unfortunately. I am indebted to François Lesure for examining the sketch again and communicating to me by letter that all the writings look alike.

24. Many tantalizing and unanswerable questions remain. There is, for example, the anomaly of the meter. In Sketches 1 and 2, which contain a melodically finalized theme, one finds a "foreign" meter; yet Sketch 3, which is in many ways distant from its final form, has the meter of the finished work. Perhaps the simplest explanation is that Schumann wavered (possibly more than once) in deciding on the metrical notation of the rhythms; after all, he changed his mind again for the 1851 version. A further puzzlement is that the time signature of Sketch 3 looks as if it was originally 3/4. In the lower signature, one can discern a stroke turning the 3 into a 2, while the upper signature appears unemended. This may, of course, be nothing more than a careless if curious error.

25. Voss, *Einführung und Analyse,* p. 185.

26. Brian Schlotel, "The Orchestral Music," in Alan Walker, ed., *Robert Schumann: The Man and his Music* (London, 1972), p. 301.

27. Jon Finson also came to the conclusion that the lyric theme "is really an augmented variation of the 'main theme' of the movement," "Symphonic Works," p. 208.

28. The melodic curve of a minor sixth down and half step up is a common ingredient in Schumann's songs; one encounters it frequently at the beginnings of phrases, and it is also a favorite cadential melody. A phrase in "Du Ring an meinem Finger," Op. 42, No. 4 (mm 9–10 and 11–12) has the same contour as the lyric theme as a whole. When the lyric theme returns in D major near the end of the movement (mm. 297–304), its new extension bears a strong resemblance to a passage in the song "Dein Angesicht," Op. 127, No. 2, mm. 22–26 (composed in 1840).

29. Cf. Hans Keller, "Strict Serial Technique in Classical Music," *Tempo* 37 (1955): 12ff.

30. In *Carnaval,* the Sphinxes As–C–H and [A]–Es–C–H can be understood as similar note play achieved by different means with the interval set minor second, minor third, and major third.

31. Cf. Schubert's "Great" C-major Symphony, first movement, mm. 199–227. This similarity was noted by Hermann Kretschmar, *Führer durch den Konzertsaal,* 1. Abteilung (Leipzig, 1921), p. 324.

32. In his rebuttal to the replies from Sieghard Brandenburg and William Drabkin to his original article; see Douglas Johnson, "Viewpoint," *19th Century Music* 2 (1978): 278.

33. I am indebted to Hugo Weisgall and the Queens College Orchestra for generously taking the time to read through the sketches (in an orchestration based on that of the 1841 version of the symphony). I also gratefully acknowledge the stimulating and helpful reactions of William Caplin, James Haar, Lillian Pruett, Linda Roesner, Jurgen Thym, and Nancy van Deusen. Finally, thanks are owed to Peter Gülke, Akio Mayeda, Gerd Nauhaus, and Martin Schoppe for their responses to an earlier form of this paper presented at the Schumann-Symposion (Leipzig, December 2–4, 1981).

Linda Correll Roesner / *The Sources for Schumann's* Davidsbündlertänze

1. See the reviews of the concert in the *Allgemeine musikalische Zeitung* 39 (1837), col. 657, and the *Neue Zeitschrift für Musik* 7 (1837): 71–72.

2. Vienna: Haslinger, June 1837. See Kurt Hofmann, *Die Erstdrucke der Werke von Robert Schumann* (Tutzing, 1979), p. 31.

3. Berthold Litzmann, *Clara Schumann. Ein Künstlerleben: Nach Tagebüchern und Briefen,* 2nd ed. (Leipzig, 1903–1908), 1:117. Litzmann does not give the date of this letter, and thus far I have been unable to find it in another source. Litzmann's statement that the Schumann work that Clara played was the F-sharp-minor Sonata, Op. 11, is not borne out by the contemporary reviews of the concert cited above.

4. Ibid., 1:119.

5. Ibid., 1:119, n. 2.

6. Roger Fiske has pointed out some of the ways in which the motto theme influences the dances in Schumann's Op. 6. See "A Schumann Mystery," *The Musical Times* 105 (1964): 574–78.

7. A *Titelauflage* under the composer's own name appeared in October 1838; see Hofmann, *Erstdrucke*, p. 15. Each dance in the first edition is signed by F[lorestan]. and/or E[usebius]. or contains a caption identifying its "author" (Book I, No. 9; Book II, No. 9). The "Alter Spruch" on the title page ("In all' und jeder Zeit/ Verknüpft sich Lust und Leid:/ Bleibt fromm in Lust und seyd/ Dem Leid mit Mut bereit.") may have been intended as a message for Clara. In the "Zweite Auflage" of Op. 6 (Hamburg, Leipzig and New York: Schuberth, 1850/51) Schumann omitted the "Alter Spruch" and all references to Florestan or Eusebius but one: the "F." at the end of Book I, No. 8, which he neglected to cross out in the copy of the first edition that served as engraver's copy for the second edition (Vienna, Gesellschaft der Musikfreunde, MS A-282).

8. See Eric Sams, "Schumann and the Tonal Analogue," in Alan Walker, ed., *Robert Schumann: The Man and his Music* (London, 1972), pp. 390–405.

9. See below, n. 27.

10. Cf. Wolfgang Boetticher's description of the manuscript in *Robert Schumanns Klavierwerke: Neue biographische und textkritische Untersuchungen, Teil I, Opus 1–6* (Wilhelmshaven, 1976), pp. 168–69. Boetticher's study of the sources for Op. 6 is often misleading and contains many errors, some of which are discussed in my review of his book in the *Journal of the American Musicological Society* 31 (1978): 160–63.

11. Boetticher, *Klavierwerke,* p. 162.

12. This was originally the entire piece; its middle section had been a separate dance (see below). The present study follows the first and second editions in numbering the dances. The division into two books of nine dances each highlights structural parallels in a way that the more recent continuous numbering from 1 to 18 does not.

13. *Robert Schumanns Briefe: Neue Folge,* ed. F. Gustav Jansen, 2nd ed. (Leipzig, 1904), p. 96.

14. *Robert Schumann's Leben: Aus seinen Briefen geschildert,* ed. Hermann Erler (Berlin, 1886), 1:127.

15. See Wolfgang Gertler, *Robert Schumann in seinen frühen Klavierwerken* (Leipzig, 1931), pp. 11–13; Wolfgang Boetticher, *Robert Schumann: Einführung in Persönlichkeit und Werk* (Berlin, 1941), p. 527; Helmuth Hopf, "Stilistische Voraussetzungen der Klaviermusik Robert Schumanns" (Ph.D. diss., Göttingen, 1957), p. 226.

16. Schumann later crossed out the sketch in red pencil so that it would not confuse the engraver of the first edition.

17. See my review of Boetticher, *Klavierwerke,* in *JAMS* 31 (1978): 161.

18. The presence of three early page numbers in Schumann's hand is another indication of the original size of this earlier manuscript: "5," "6," and "7" appear on what are now fols. 8v, 8r, and 9r respectively.

19. There are no sketches for Op. 6 in Schumann's five sketchbooks (Bonn, Universitätsbibliothek), which predominantly date from an earlier period. Boetticher (*Klavierwerke,* p. 166) posits the possibility of additional sketchbooks dating from the period after 1835, but Schumann's own comment in his Sketchbook II suggests that he did not use a sketchbook to record his *Davidsbündlertänze* ideas. See the facsimile of Sketchbook II, fol. 10r, in Boetticher, *Klavierwerke,* Tafel XV.

20. These numbers may reflect the order of composition.

21. In November 1838, Schumann wrote out the first section (G minor) of Book I, No. 7, in the autograph album of Aloys Fuchs (see below). This album leaf does not contain the A-flat-major middle section, a circumstance that Boetticher regards as an atypical memory slip on Schumann's part; see Wolfgang Boetticher, "Neue textkritische Forschungen an R. Schumanns Klavierwerk," *Archiv für Musikwissenschaft* 25 (1968): 59. But perhaps one could also argue that Schumann continued to regard the G-minor section of Book I, No. 7 as complete in itself. The linking together of pieces originally separate also occurs in one of Schumann's early manuscripts of the *Etudes Symphoniques,* Op. 13 (Morlanwelz-Mariemont, Belgium, Musée Royal de Mariemont, Ms Aut. 1132c). In this manuscript the variation later published as No. V of the posthumous variations had its original independent numbering crossed out and was converted into the middle section of the variation that was to become—but without this middle section—Etude X of the first edition.

22. Boetticher, *Klavierwerke,* pp. 61–77.

23. Linda Correll Roesner, "The Autograph of Schumann's Piano Sonata in F minor, Op. 14," *The Musical Quarterly* 61 (1975): 114–16.

24. See, for example, Robert Münster, "Die Beethoven-Etuden von Robert Schumann: Aus Anlass ihrer Erstausgabe," *Die Musikforschung* 31 (1978): 55–56; Werner Schwarz, *Robert Schumann und die Variation* (Kassel, 1932), pp. 51–54; Rufus Hallmark, *The Genesis of Schumann's "Dichterliebe"* (Ann Arbor, 1979), pp. 110–28. An autograph manuscript of the *Romanzen* for women's voices (Opp. 69 and 91) in the Pierpont Morgan Library, New York (Lehman Collection), shows much evidence of the rearrangement of the order of pieces; see in this regard Schumann's letter of August 7, 1849, to the publisher Simrock, in Wolfgang Boetticher, *Robert Schumann in seinen Schriften und Briefen* (Berlin, 1942), p. 451. The early sources for the *Etudes Symphoniques,* Op. 13, are of particular interest from the standpoint of changes in the order of the pieces. For a discussion of these manuscripts see my study of Brahms's editions of Schumann, to appear in the proceedings of the 1983 International Brahms Conference, Washington, D. C.

25. As late as 1850, when preparing the second edition of Op. 6, Schumann even considered omitting Book I, No. 3, and had in fact gone so far as to cross it out in the copy of the first edition that served as *Stichvorlage* for the second edition (Vienna, Gesellschaft der Musikfreunde, MS A-282).

26. See Linda Correll Roesner, "Schumann's Revisions in the First Movement of the Piano Sonata in G minor, Op. 22," *19th Century Music* 1 (1977): 97–109.

27. Hofmann, *Erstdrucke,* p. 15, gives the date of publication as the end of December 1837; but see Schumann's letter to Clara of January 5, 1838 (Litzmann, *Clara Schumann,* 1:169) and the unpublished letter from Friese to Schumann of January 23, 1838, cited at the end of this article.

28. For example, in bar 79 of Book I, No. 3, the engraver mistook a dash in "ri—tar—dan—do" for a tie; consequently, in the first edition of Book I, No. 3, there is an erroneous tie linking the g's in the left hand in bar 79. In his study *Die Davidsbündler: Aus Robert Schumann's Sturm- und Drangperiode* (Leipzig, 1883), p. 44, F. Gustav Jansen opined that Schumann's elaborately drawn title page may have prefigured the decorative Gothic portal on the title page of the first edition.

29. Chronological factors discussed below as well as textual considerations argue against a lost manuscript.

30. See the statement made by Roitzsch, the proofreader at C. F. Peters, to Hermann Erler, in Erler, *Robert Schumann's Leben,* 2:124. A comprehensive study of Schumann's first editions and their *Stichvorlagen* has yet to be undertaken. A small sample comparison reveals that some first editions differ in many details of expression from their *Stichvorlagen* while others do not. For instance, many differences can be observed in the following: Piano Sonata in F-sharp minor, Op. 11, finale only (autograph *Stichvorlage:* Berlin, Deutsche Staatsbibliothek, Mus. ms. autogr. Schumann 20; two addenda in Vienna, Österreichische Nationalbibliothek, MS 18411; first edition: Leipzig, Kistner, 1836); *Frauenliebe und Leben,* Op. 42 (*Stichvorlage* in a copyist's hand with Schumann's corrections: New York, Pierpont Morgan Library, Cary Collection; first edition: Leipzig, Whistling, 1843). There are few differences in the following: *Concert sans Orchestre,* Op. 14 (autograph *Stichvorlage:* London, British Library, MS Add. 37056; first edition: Vienna, Haslinger, 1836); *Waldscenen,* Op. 82 (autograph *Stichvorlage:* Paris, Bibliothèque nationale, MS 344; first edition: Leipzig, Senff, 1850). A middle ground between the two extremes can be seen in: *Papillons,* Op. 2 (autograph *Stichvorlage:* Paris, Bibliothèque nationale, MS 315; first edition: Leipzig, Kistner, 1831); *Fantasiestücke,* Op. 12 (*Stichvorlage* in a copyist's hand with expression marks and corrections in Schumann's hand: Düsseldorf, Heinrich-Heine-Institut, MS 71.126; first edition: Leipzig, Breitkopf & Härtel, 1838); and Symphony in E-flat major, Op. 97 (autograph *Stichvorlage* of full score: Berlin, Staatsbibliothek der Stiftung preussischer Kulturbesitz, Mus. ms. autogr. Schumann 12; first edition of full score: Bonn, Simrock, 1851).

31. Examples include: an early autograph fair copy of the *Etudes Symphoniques,* Op. 13 (Morlanwelz-Mariemont, Belgium, Musée Royal de Mariemont, MS Aut. 1132c), on fol. 1r the directive "Ohne alle Vortragsbezeichnung [*sic*] abzuschreiben"; the mostly autograph score of the 1841 version of the D-minor Symphony, Op. 120 (Vienna, Gesellschaft der Musikfreunde, MS A-292), at the beginning of the scherzo, "Ohne alle Vortragsbezeichnungen zu copiren"; autograph score of the *Fantasiestücke,* Op. 88 (Paris, Bibliothèque nationale, MS 312), on fol. 1r, "Ohne alle Bezeichnungen abzuschreiben, *nur Noten*"; the autograph of an earlier version of the G-minor Piano Sonata, Op. 22 (Berlin, Deutsche Staatsbibliothek, Mus. ms. autogr. Schumann 38), on fol. 1r, "Ohne alle Vortragbezeichnung [*sic*] zu copiren," and on fol. 4r, "Ohne alle Bezeichnungen zu copiren"; the autograph of the *Fantasie,* Op. 17, sold by Sotheby's in London on November 23, 1977 (on p. 1, "Der Herr Notenschreiber wird ersucht *nur die Noten* zu schreiben." See the facsimile in Sotheby's *Catalogue of Important Musical Manuscripts . . . 23rd November 1977,* facing p. 42). In the autograph *Stichvorlage* of the finale of the F-sharp-minor Piano Sonata (Berlin, Deutsche Staats-

bibliothek, Mus. ms. autogr. Schumann 20), Schumann instructed the engraver to omit the pedal indications from the first proofs: "Alle in dieser Abschrift vorgezeichneten 'Ped' und ' ⊕ ' bitte ich beim ersten Stich wegzulassen."

32. Examples of expression markings in Schumann's hand in copyists' manuscripts copied from some of the autographs cited in n. 31 can be found in the following: Vienna, Gesellschaft der Musikfreunde, MS A-284 (Op. 13, copied from the autograph in Morlanwelz-Mariemont); Budapest, Széchényi Library, Ms. Mus. 37 (Op. 17, copied from the autograph listed in Sotheby's 1977 sale; facsimile of p. 1 in Alan Walker, "Schumann, Liszt and the C Major Fantasie, Op. 17: A Declining Relationship," *Music & Letters* 60 [1979]: 159). Several copyists' manuscripts with expression marks in Schumann's hand survive, although the autographs from which they were copied do not. These include: Berlin, Deutsche Staatsbibliothek, Mus. ms. autogr. Schumann 29 (*Intermezzi*, Op. 4; the first Intermezzo is in a copyist's hand with all expression marks in Schumann's hand; the rest of the MS is autograph); Düsseldorf, Heinrich-Heine-Institut, MS 71.126 (*Fantasiestücke*, Op. 12, and *Etudes Symphoniques*, Op. 13); Paris, Bibliothèque nationale, MS 311 (*Myrthen*, Op. 25; thirteen of the *Lieder*); and New York, Pierpont Morgan Library, Cary Collection (*Drei Gesänge*, Op. 31; in Clara Schumann's hand with all expression marks in Schumann's hand). The autograph of the *Fantasiestücke*, Op. 88 cited in n. 31, appears to be an unusual case. The manuscript is dated 1842, but the copy of the score was not made until years later: it is in the hand of Karl Gottschalk, Schumann's Dresden copyist, and presumably dates from early 1850 (Op. 88 was published in November 1850; see Hofmann, *Erstdrucke*, p. 193). Gottschalk's copy (New York, Pierpont Morgan Library, Morgan Collection; the manuscript also includes string parts in the hand of another copyist with additions in Gottschalk's hand, and, on one pasteover, in Clara Schumann's hand) contains numerous corrections and additions in Schumann's hand, but the original layer of expression marks is in Gottschalk's hand. It is perhaps significant that in his years in Dresden (1844–50) and Düsseldorf (1850–56) Schumann no longer inserted all expression marks into copyists' manuscripts, but instead added to and modified material already copied from the autographs.

33. E.g., Berlin, Deutsche Staatsbibliothek, Mus. ms. autogr. Schumann 38 (G-minor Piano Sonata, Op. 22), and Mus. ms. autogr. Schumann 20 (F-sharp-minor Piano Sonata, Op. 11, finale).

34. E.g., Vienna, Gesellschaft der Musikfreunde, MS A-285 (F-minor Piano Sonata, Op. 14, draft of the scherzo published in the second edition); MS A-286 (*Humoreske*, Op. 20, sketch); sketches and drafts for various works in two collections of loose sketch leaves in Berlin, Deutsche Staatsbibliothek, Mus. ms. autogr. Schumann 35 and 36.

35. Schumann explained his use of pedal indications in a footnote on the first page of musical text of the first edition of Op. 11: "The authors [Florestan and Eusebius] use the pedal in almost every bar, according to circumstances required by the harmonic units. Exceptions, where they wish the pedal not to be used, are marked with ⊕ ; then, when the indication 'Pedale' reappears, the constant use of the pedal resumes." See also Schumann's letter of September 21, 1837, to Adolf Henselt (Erler, *Robert Schumann's Leben*, 1:126). For a discussion of Schumann's pedal indications and Clara Schumann's disregard of them in the Schumann *Gesamtausgabe*, see Boetticher, "Neue textkritische Forschungen," p. 67.

36. New York, Pierpont Morgan Library, Heineman Collection; facsimile in Hermann Abert, *Robert Schumann*, 3rd ed. (Berlin, 1917), facing p. 72. This leaf (oblong format, three systems; the facsimile in Abert is misleading since it presents recto and verso as a single page containing six systems) is inscribed by both Schumann and Clara Wieck ("Bescheidend doch mit Liebe unterschreibt sich Clara Wieck"). Clara's inscription appears to have been written with the same pen and ink as the rest of the leaf. Perhaps this leaf, dating from August 18, 1837, during the time when Robert and Clara were reunited after their long separation, might serve as evidence that their renewal of contact with one another was not limited to correspondence. (But see Schumann's letter to Becker of August 26, 1837, in Erler, *Robert Schumann's Leben*, 1:121.)

37. Düsseldorf, Heinrich-Heine-Institut, MS 71.126, a manuscript in the hand of a copyist with almost all expression marks in Schumann's hand.

38. Leipzig: Breitkopf & Härtel, February 1838. See Hoffmann, *Erstdrucke*, p. 29.

39. A similar situation obtains in the sources for the *Fantasie*, Op. 17. The opening theme (right hand, bars 1–12) is completely phrased in Schumann's autograph (see the facsimile cited in n. 31). In the *Stichvorlage* (Budapest, Széchényi Library, Mus. Ms. 37; see Pl. II in Walker, "Schumann, Liszt and the C major Fantasie"; the manuscript is in a copyist's hand with expression marks in Schumann's hand) the phrasing slurs were omitted, and they are not present in the first edition (Leipzig: Breitkopf & Härtel, 1839).

40. *Photogramm* in Vienna, Österreichische Nationalbibliothek, PhA 1273 (the manuscript had been in the collection of Louis Koch).

41. Some works of the 1830s—e.g., all three piano sonatas—survive in multiple fair copies. Other works, including Opp. 17, 13, and 12, survive in one or more autograph fair copies and in a copyist's manuscript with Schumann's additions and corrections. In these multiple manuscripts Schumann both refined details and made major structural revisions (see Roesner, "Schumann's Revisions").

42. *Robert Schumann: Manuskripte, Briefe, Schumanniana. Katalog Nr. 188. Musikantiquariat Hans Schneider* (Tutzing, 1974), p. 178. On September 21 Schumann wrote to Henselt that he had just finished the *Davidsbündlertänze* (see above).

43. October 13: "Für Friese an den Davidsbündlertänze corrigirt . . ." October 14: "Am 14ten (Sonnabend) heiter aufgestanden. Den ganzen Morgen an den Davidsbündlertänzen corrigirt—sie dann an Clara geschikt [*sic*] mit offenem Briefe—" (Tagebuch V. Zwickau, Robert-Schumann-Haus). I would like to thank Dr. Gerd Nauhaus of the Robert-Schumann-Haus for providing these quotations. Cf. Boetticher (*Klavierwerke*, p. 163), who reads the first two words of the entry for October 13 as "Zu Hause" and interprets the passage as a reference to Schumann's correction of the manuscript. Boetticher (ibid., p. 163, n. 12) also cites an entry for October 27 dealing with the correction of proofs for Op. 6, but Nauhaus communicates that Op. 6 is not mentioned in the diary for that day. If Schumann sent his manuscript to Clara on the 14th (she was about to embark on a concert tour of Dresden, Prague, and Vienna), he likely would not have been able to read proof against it on the 27th. The probability that Schumann sent his autograph manuscript to Clara on the 14th is strengthened by her letter to him of November 19: "How then do you know that I cannot endure your *Davidsbündlertänze*? Up until now I have not yet had time to devote two hours to them alone in peace, and one needs that. To decipher [*entziffern*] such a document [*Schrift*] is only held in reserve for me" (Litzmann, *Clara Schumann*, 1:146–47). Is it likely that Clara would have used the words *Schrift* and *entziffern* in this context unless she were referring to the document itself? Clara's letter comes in reply to Schumann's letter of November 8 in which he asks her why the *Davidsbündlertänze* please her so little and requests that she play them often at 9 P.M., the hour they had reserved for thinking of each other during their separation. See Boetticher, *Schriften*, p. 153.

44. Robert Friese, the publisher of the *Neue Zeitschrift für Musik,* was not a music publisher; presumably his engravers were not particularly skilled in music engraving. The following quotation from Schumann's letter of December 9, 1837, to Karl Kosmaly refers to musical examples in the text of an article, but perhaps it also reflects the situation at Friese's establishment: ". . . with the sole request, however, to include as few *musical* examples as possible, for you have no idea what unspeakable trouble that causes in the printing shop." See Erler, *Robert Schumann's Leben,* 1:131.

45. The *sf* in the right hand in bar 72 (bar 4 of Ex. 4) is in the *Stichvorlage* and was obviously overlooked by Schumann in his proofreading of bars 1–8.

46. See Boetticher, "Neue textkritische Forschungen," p. 71.

47. Is it possible that the young Schumann may have proofread at the piano? His admonition in 1851 to Carl Reinecke not to proofread the four-hand piano arrangement of Op. 97 at the piano, because too much can be overlooked, may have been based on personal experience. See Erler, *Robert Schumann's Leben,* 2:153–54.

48. See Boetticher, "Neue textkritische Forschungen," p. 53, and *Klavierwerke,* p. 8. See also Berthold Litzmann, ed., *Clara Schumann—Johannes Brahms: Briefe aus den Jahren 1853–1896* (Leipzig, 1927), 2:200–2, 238f.

49. See, for example, the letters published in Erler, *Robert Schumann's Leben,* 2:22f., 55, 63, 72, 75–76, 90, and 157. (Most of the letters to publishers printed in Jansen, *Briefe: Neue Folge,* are abridged.) For a discussion of the extensive unpublished correspondence between Schumann and his publishers, see Wolfgang Boetticher, "Robert Schumann und seine Verleger," in Richard Baum and Wolfgang Rehm, eds., *Musik und Verlag: Karl Vötterle zum 65. Geburtstag am 12. April 1968* (Kassel, 1968), pp. 168–74. Schumann's ever-present concern that the format, title page, typeface, and other details of an edition reflect its musical contents is discussed in Hofmann, *Erstdrucke,* pp. xxviii–xxxi.

50. Boetticher, "Neue textkritische Forschungen," p. 69, n. 179.

51. This suggests lack of concern (or perhaps haste or carelessness) rather than a deliberate change. New details such as those in Book I, No. 3 (discussed above) suggest reinterpretation without direct reference to the parallel passage.

52. MS A-282. Facsimile of title page in Hofmann, *Erstdrucke,* p. 410. For a brief discussion of this source see my review of Boetticher, *Klavierwerke,* op. cit., p. 162.

53. For some interesting speculations see Boetticher, *Klavierwerke,* p. 164.

54. March 1835. See Hofmann, *Erstdrucke,* p. 21. The musical text in this edition was not engraved but hand-drawn and printed by lithography.

55. Erler, *Robert Schumann's Leben,* 1:112–13, 115.

56. In a letter to Clara of February 6, 1838 (Boetticher, *Schriften,* p. 167), Schumann says that he gave the dances to Friese because the few *Groschen* paid by the music publishers were not worth speaking about. But given the short amount of time between Schumann's completion of Op. 6 and its going to press, we cannot asume that Schumann tried very hard to have the work accepted by a music publisher. It seems more logical to suppose that Schumann responded to Friese's request for a work. Jansen (*Die Davidsbündler,* p. 43) states that Schumann himself paid the costs of engraving Op. 6, an assumption based, perhaps, on Schumann's later attempt to sell the plates and ca. 170 unsold exemplars to Hofmeister. See Schumann's letter of November 5, 1842, to Hofmeister (Jansen, *Briefe: Neue Folge,* p. 434), where the composer mentions that the work is not known because Friese, unlike the music publishers of the day, is not a music dealer.

57. See Erler, *Robert Schumann's Leben,* 1:248.

58. Gerd Nauhaus informs me that there are no letters from Schumann to Friese listed in Schumann's *Briefverzeichnis* for the years 1837–38, and only one letter from Friese to Schumann (November 9, 1837). The *Briefverzeichnis* does not record the contents of this letter.

59. "Mein lieber Redakteur! Die Davidsbündlertänze sind fertig [und] u.[nter] a.[nderem] die Besteller ausgegeben; ich hoffe dass ich als Waffenträger des Königs mit der goldnen Harfe meine Geschäfte *gut* besorgt habe u.[nd] dass der Psalter meines Davids wie ein ewiger Ton um den Ringkreis der Mutter Erde wallen werde, bis er des Ursängers [?] Davids historisches Alter erreicht. . . ." I would like to thank Dr. Nauhaus for his transcript of this letter.

Friedhelm Krummacher / *Mendelssohn's Late Chamber Music*

For the English translation I am greatly indebted to Evan Bonds (University of Virginia, Charlottesville).

1. Among these are Eric Werner, *Mendelssohn: A New Image of the Composer and his Age,* trans. Dika Newlin (London, 1963), rev. as *Mendelssohn: Leben und Werk in neuer Sicht* (Zurich, 1980); Georg Knepler, *Musikgeschichte des 19. Jahrhunderts* (Berlin, 1961), 2:747–70; Carl Dahlhaus, ed., *Das Problem Mendelssohn* (Regensburg, 1974); Matthias Thomas, *Das Instrumentalwerk Felix Mendelssohn-Bartholdys: Eine systematisch-theoretische Untersuchung* (Göttingen, 1972); Friedhelm Krummacher, *Mendelssohn—der Komponist, Studien zur Kammermusik für Streicher* (Munich, 1978); H.-Kl. Metzger and R. Riehn, eds., *Felix Mendelssohn Bartholdy* (Munich, 1980).

2. See, for example, Donald Mintz, "The Sketches and Drafts of Three of Felix Mendelssohn's Major Works" (Ph.D. diss., Cornell Univ., 1960); Matthias Thomas, "Zur Kompositionsweise in Mendelssohn's Ouvertüren," in *Das Problem Mendelssohn,* pp. 129–48; Reinhard Gerlach, "Mendelssohns Kompositionsweise," in *Archiv für Musikwissenschaft* 28 (1971): 119–33; idem, "Mendelssohns Kompositionsweise (II)," in *Das Problem Mendelssohn,* pp. 149–67; Friedhelm Krummacher, "Über Autographe Mendelssohns und seine Kompositionsweise," in Carl Dahlhaus et al., eds., *Kongressbericht Bonn 1970* (Kassel, 1971), pp. 482–85; A. Kurzhals-Reuter, *Die Oratorien Felix Mendelssohn Bartholdys* (Tutzing, 1978); R. Larry Todd, "Of Sea Gulls and Counterpoint: The Early Versions of Mendelssohn's *Hebrides* Overture," in *19th Century Music* 2 (1979): 197–213; idem, "An Unfinished Symphony by Mendelssohn," in *Music & Letters* 61 (1980): 293–309; Douglass Seaton, "A Study of a Collection of Mendelssohn's Sketches and Other Autograph Material: Deutsche Staatsbibliothek Berlin Mus. Ms. Autogr. Mendelssohn 19" (Ph.D. diss., Columbia Univ., 1977).

3. I am grateful to the Biblioteka Jagiellońska in Kraków for permission to examine the sources and to Ludwig Finscher (Heidelberg) for assistance in obtaining microfilms. I was unable to examine the article by H.-G. Klein, "Korrekturen im Autograph von Mendelssohns Streichquartett Op. 80. Überlegungen zur Kompositionstechnik und zum Kompositionsvorgang," in C. Lowenthal-Hensel

and Rudolf Elvers, eds., *Mendelssohn-Studien* (Berlin, 1982), 5:113–22, which appeared after the present study had gone to press.

4. Friedrich Theodor Vischer, *Aesthetik oder Wissenschaft des Schönen* (Stuttgart, 1857), p. 1054f. (the fourth installment, *Die Musik,* includes contributions by Koestlin, sections 767–832); Ferdinand Hand, *Aesthetik der Tonkunst* (Jena, 1841), 2:386ff.

5. Carl Dahlhaus, *Die Idee der absoluten Musik* (Kassel, 1978); idem, *Grundlagen der Musikgeschichte* (Cologne, 1977).

6. Carl Dahlhaus, *Die Idee der absoluten Musik* , pp. 91–104; Friedhelm Krummacher, "Kunstreligion und religöse Musik: Zur ästhetischen Problematik geistlicher Musik im 19. Jahrhundert," *Die Musikforschung* 32 (1979): 365–93.

7. Georg Friedrich Wilhelm Hegel, *Ästhetik,* ed. Friedrich Bassenge (Berlin, 1965), 2:319ff.; Adolf Nowak, *Hegels Musikästhetik* (Regensburg, 1971), p. 179ff.

8. See *Briefe von Felix Mendelssohn-Bartholdy an Ignaz und Charlotte Moscheles,* ed. Felix Moscheles (Leipzig, 1888), p. 111 (letter of February 7, 1835); and *Felix Mendelssohn Bartholdy: Briefe aus den Jahren 1833 bis 1847,* ed. Paul and Cécile Mendelssohn Bartholdy (Leipzig, 1875), p. 1f. (letter of March 4, 1833).

9. *Felix Mendelssohn Bartholdy: Briefe,* p. 346f. (letter of October 15, 1842).

10. Regarding Mendelssohn and Bach see Eduard Devrient, *Meine Erinnerungen an Felix Mendelssohn-Bartholdy und seine Briefe an mich* (Leipzig, 1872), p. 114 (letter of July 13, 1831), and Felix Mendelssohn Bartholdy, *Reisebriefe aus den Jahren 1830 bis 1832,* ed. Paul Mendelssohn Bartholdy (Leipzig, 1869), p. 97f. (letter of December 18, 1830). Regarding Mendelssohn and Beethoven see L. Dahlgren, ed., *Bref till Adolf Fredrik Lindblad från Mendelssohn, Dohrn, Almquist, Atterbom, Geijer, Fredrika Bremer, C. W. Böttiger och andra* (Stockholm, 1913), p. 19ff.

11. Examined more fully in Friedhelm Krummacher, "Zur Kompositionsart Mendelssohns: Thesen am Beispiel der Streichquartette," in *Das Problem Mendelssohn,* pp. 169–84, and in Metzger and Riehn, *Felix Mendelssohn Bartholdy,* pp. 46–74.

12. Discussed in detail in Krummacher, *Mendelssohn—der Komponist,* p. 96ff.

13. Julius Eckhardt, ed., *Ferdinand David und die Familie Mendelssohn-Bartholdy* (Leipzig, 1888), p. 204 (letter of January 26, 1844).

14. Charlotte Moscheles, ed., *Aus Moscheles' Leben: Nach Briefen und Tagebüchern* (Leipzig, 1873), 2:162, 280. About this edition see Friedrich Hofmeister, *Musikalisch-literarischer Monats-Bericht* (February 1851), p. 23.

15. Concerning the finale see Krummacher, *Mendelssohn—der Komponist,* p. 365ff; p. 297f. for the first movement and p. 411ff. for the slow movement.

16. Georg Knepler, *Musikgeschichte des 19. Jahrhunderts,* 2:770; Ernst Rychnowsky, "Aus Felix Mendelssohn Bartholdys letzten Lebenstagen," in *Die Musik* 30 (1908–09): 141–46 (especially p. 143, with the letter from Moscheles to Joseph Fischhof of November 7, 1847).

17. Julius Eckhardt, *Ferdinand David und die Familie Mendelssohn-Bartholdy,* p. 204; Sebastian Hensel, *Die Familie Mendelssohn 1729–1847* (Berlin, 1879), 3:20 (letter of August 12, 1843).

18. Charlotte Moscheles, *Aus Moscheles' Leben,* p. 200; Rychnowsky, "Aus Felix Mendelssohn Bartholdys letzten Lebenstagen," p. 143; Felix Moscheles, *Briefe,* p. 282 (letter of October 5, 1847).

19. See Krummacher, *Mendelssohn—der Komponist,* p. 459ff.

20. Ibid., p. 231ff., for the variations.

21. Ibid., p. 325ff., for the first and last movements, and pp. 418ff. and 263ff., for the inner movements of Op. 80.

William S. Newman / *Three Musical Intimates of Mendelssohn and Schumann*

The able research assistance of Penny Schwarze, doctoral candidate in musicology at the University of North Carolina, is gratefully acknowledged. Mention should be made here of an excellent related article by Johannes Forner, "Mendelssohns Mitstreiter am Leipziger Konservatorium," *Beiträge zur Musikwissenschaft* 14 (1972): 185–204. It emphasizes not the individual artistic achievement of Mendelssohn's associates, as in the present article, but their substantial cooperation in building up the new Leipzig Conservatory.

1. One indication is the absence of works by Loewe in current (1982) American recording catalogs, although there is a good representation of his ballades in current German catalogs. The ballades have fared better, recently, in dissertations.

2. See, for example, the studies cited in notes 5, 14, 15, and 25, below.

3. As by Maynard Solomon in "On Beethoven's Creative Process: A Two-Part Invention," *Music & Letters* 61 (1980): 272–83.

4. The figures in this paragraph come from Günther Stiller, *Johann Sebastian Bach* (Berlin, 1970), p. 30; the *Brockhaus Encyclopedia* (17th ed.), under the respective cities; and P. T. Bradford, H. Williams, and R. B. Carter, eds., *Comprehensive Atlas,* 3rd ed. (Boston, ca. 1844).

5. As a gauge of taste, Johannes Forner compares how often various composers were heard, in "Mendelssohns Mitstreiter am Leipziger Konservatorium," pp. 191 and 203–04.

6. Moritz Hauptmann, *The Letters of Moritz Hauptmann,* ed. A. Schöne and F. Hiller, trans. A. D. Coleridge, (London, 1892; rep. New York, 1972), 1:240, 243.

7. See the list in *Die Musik in Geschichte und Gegenwart.*

8. *The Letters of Moritz Hauptmann,* 1:174–75.

9. See Philip L. Miller, *The Ring of Words* (Garden City, N. Y., 1963; rep. 1966), p. 102.

10. *The Letters of Moritz Hauptmann,* 2:144.

11. Robert Schumann, *Gesammelte Schriften,* ed. Martin Kreisig, 5th ed. (Leipzig, 1914), 1:109, and 2:383–84.

12. Vol. 42, cols. 677–78.

13. See W. S. Newman, *The Sonata in the Classic Era,* 3rd ed. (New York, 1982), pp. 388–90.

14. Charlotte Moscheles, ed., *The Diaries and Correspondence of Ignatz Moscheles,* trans. A. D. Coleridge (from the German of 1872; New York, 1873, rep. 1970). Two Ph.D. dissertations have added to our knowledge of Moscheles's life and works: Ingeborg Heussner, "Ignaz Moscheles in seinen Klavier-Sonaten, -Kammermusikwerken, und -Konzerten" (Universität Marburg-Lahn, 1963); and Carolyn Denton Gresham, "Ignaz Moscheles: An Illustrious Musician in the Nineteenth Century" (University of Rochester, 1980).

15. Cf. Lilia Nitschkova-Goleminova, "Schumann—Moscheles—Paganini, Berichtigungen zur Biographie Robert Schumanns," in *Die Musikforschung* 31 (1978): 16–28. (However, the possibility must be allowed that the "question" grows out of Wolfgang Boetticher's earlier attempts to discredit Mendelssohn's and Moscheles's relations with Schumann, especially by withholding or downplaying some of the evidence.)

16. *The Diaries and Correspondence of Ignatz Moscheles,* p. 353.

17. *The Letters of Moritz Hauptmann,* 2:212.

18. *The Diaries and Correspondence of Ignatz Moscheles,* p. 357.

19. Ibid., p. 357.

20. Ibid., p. 251.

21. An undated, inexact list appears in *The Diaries and Correspondence of Ignatz Moscheles,* pp. 421–28.

22. See *The Diaries and Correspondence of Ignatz Moscheles,* pp. 259–61.

23. *Revue et gazette musicale de Paris,* November 23, 1845 (for Paris) and June 28, 1846 (for London); *Allgemeine musikalische Zeitung* 49 (1847), cols. 691–92; *Neue Zeitschrift für Musik* 26 (1847): 41–42.

24. A full study of David, his playing, and his works is lacking. The short article in *Die Musik in Geschichte und Gegenwart* seems to be the fullest, best balanced account to date. The chapter in La Mara's *Musikalische Studienköpfe,* vol. 3 (Leipzig, 1878, pp. 55–80) is an unmitigated panegyric; the section in Andreas Moser's *Geschichte des Violinspiels,* 2nd ed. (Tutzing, 1967), 2:209–11, includes curious underevaluations.

25. Now lost, the letters were copied by Werner Schwarz at the Berlin Staatsbibliothek in 1929 and 1930; thirty-two letters were published by him in "Eine Musikerfreundschaft des 19. Jahrhunderts," in *Saarbrücker Studien zur Musikwissenschaft* 1 (Kassel, 1966): 282–303.

26. "Eine Musikerfreundschaft des 19. Jahrhunderts," p. 292.

27. See the list in *Die Musik in Geschichte und Gegenwart.*

28. On this realization, see Imogene Horsley in *Journal of the American Musicological Society* 23 (1970): 545–46.

29. Vols. 2–3 (November 13, 1867, to March 4, 1868).

Marcia J. Citron / *Fanny Hensel's Letters to Felix Mendelssohn*

1. *Catalogue of the Mendelssohn Papers in the Bodleian Library, Oxford*, vol. 1 (Tutzing, 1980). I would like to express my appreciation to Miss Crum for permitting me to examine the page proofs of her catalogue when I first studied the letters at the Bodleian in the summer of 1980.

2. Sebastian Hensel, *The Mendelssohn Family (1729–1847)*, trans. Karl Klingemann, 2nd ed. (New York, 1882), 1:82–84.

3. Karl Mendelssohn-Bartholdy, *Goethe and Mendelssohn*, trans. M. E. von Glehn, 2nd ed. (London, 1874), p. 50.

4. Ignaz Moscheles, *Aus Moscheles' Leben*, ed. Charlotte Moscheles (Leipzig, 1872–73), 1:93; Henry Chorley, "Mendelssohn's Sister and Mother," in W. A. Lampadius, *Life of Felix Mendelssohn Bartholdy*, ed. and trans. William Gage (New York, 1865), pp. 210–11. Felix relates Chorley's praise in a letter to Fanny of Oct. 24, 1840 (Depositum Berlin 9, Mendelssohn Archive, Staatsbibliothek Preussischer Kulturbesitz, Berlin).

5. Among her approximately four hundred compositions are piano works and lieder, but also works for chorus and orchestra. Several reviews of her few published compositions appeared in the *Neue Zeitschrift für Musik* 26 (1847): 14, 38, 89; 27 (1847): 50; and 28 (1848): 15, 88. See also the review "Ueber die Claviercompositionen von Fanny Hensel," in *Allgemeine musikalische Zeitung* 49 (1847), cols. 381–83, and my "Lieder of Fanny Mendelssohn Hensel," *The Musical Quarterly* 69 (1983): 570–94.

6. For a first attempt to catalogue the sources, see Rudolf Elvers, "Verzeichnis der Musik-Autographen von Fanny Hensel in dem Mendelssohn-Archiv zu Berlin," in *Mendelssohn Studien* 1 (1972): 169–74; and idem, "Weitere Quellen zu den Werken von Fanny Hensel," in *Mendelssohn Studien* 2 (1975): 215–20.

7. Two recent unpublished studies are Victoria Sirota, "The Life and Works of Fanny Mendelssohn Hensel" (D.M.A. diss., Boston University, 1981); and Carol Quin, "Fanny Mendelssohn Hensel: Her Contributions to 19th-Century Musical Life" (Ph.D. diss., University of Kentucky, 1981).

8. Sebastian Hensel, 1:viii–ix. Of course, many of Fanny's letters originally in the Green Books could have been removed, as many others were, by Felix, who liked to give letters away as gifts (usually as *Albumblätter*), and by his grandson Albrecht, who as a later owner of the collection may have put some letters up for sale (see Felix Mendelssohn Bartholdy, *Briefe an deutsche Verleger*, ed. Rudolf Elvers [Berlin, 1968], pp. xxiii–xxiv). Smaller collections of Fanny Hensel's letters are preserved in West Berlin, New York, and Washington, D. C.

9. Mendelssohn, *Briefe an deutsche Verleger*, p. xxv.

10. Rudolf Elvers, "Felix Mendelssohn Bartholdys Nachlass," in Carl Dahlhaus, ed., *Das Problem Mendelssohn* (Regensburg, 1974), p. 43.

11. See Fanny's letters throughout 1837 in the Green Books, and Felix's numerous letters to the family from February 1837, as well as letters dated May 29 and June 8, 1837 (New York Public Library collection).

12. Green Books letter (henceforth GB) Vol. 5, No. 7; January 5, 1836.

13. New York Public Library letter of June 24, 1837. It is incorrectly dated June 2, 1837, in Felix Mendelssohn Bartholdy, *Briefe aus den Jahren 1830 bis 1847*, ed. Paul and Carl Mendelssohn Bartholdy, 3rd ed. (Leipzig, 1875), 2:88–89.

14. A view already proposed in the secondary literature. See, for instance, Jack Werner, "Felix and Fanny Mendelssohn," in *Music & Letters* 28 (1947): 303–37; and Eric Werner, *Mendelssohn, a New Image of the Composer and his Age*, trans. Dika Newlin (London, 1963), pp. 76–77.

15. The work referred to is the *Sonate écossaise*, Op. 28.

16. Letter from Felix to Fanny, Jan. 30, 1836 (Depositum Berlin 3, 10); the published version in Mendelssohn, *Briefe . . . 1830 bis 1847*, 2:72, contains several alterations in spelling and wording.

17. Nos. 17–20 in this version; Nos. 13–16 in the final version. See Arntrud Kurzhals-Reuter, *Die Oratorien Felix Mendelssohn Bartholdys* (Tutzing, 1978), pp. 59–60.

18. Part of No. 21, "Gott sei mir gnädig" (No. 17).

19. No. 22 (No. 18).

20. Part of No. 23 (No. 19).

21. No. 24 (No. 20, with this text modified).

22. Pauline Schätzel Decker (1811–1882), Berlin soprano, a singer of opera and oratorio.

23. Piano edition issued by Simrock in November / December 1836, and by Novello [1836].

24. "Der du die Menschen," No. 11 in the first version, does not appear in the final version, but was published posthumously as the second of the *Zwei geistliche Lieder*, Op. 112.

25. Part of No. 35 in the final version.

26. The excluded soprano aria is "Der du die Menschen"; the soprano aria in F is part of No. 26, the alto aria part of No. 12.

27. Part of No. 13.

28. Fanny herself had presented the Berlin premiere of the oratorio at one of her Sunday musicales, on Jan. 22, 1837 (GB 6, No. 5; Jan. 20, 1837).

29. Carl Friedrich Rungenhagen (1778–1851), from 1833 successor to Zelter as director of the Singakademie, having competed successfully against Mendelssohn for the position. See Werner, *Mendelssohn*, pp. 227–33.

30. Edward Grell (1800–1886), assistant conductor at the Singakademie under Rungenhagen. Felix's description appears in a letter to Fanny of January 13, 1838 (Depositum Berlin 2).

31. Karl August Lichtenstein (1767–1845), active in Berlin opera and theater as manager, producer, and conductor. "Mache dich auf" is No. 14.

32. Probably Georg Abraham Schneider (1770–1839), active in Berlin theater and pedagogy.

33. Probably Hubert Ries (1802–1886), violinist in Berlin orchestras.

34. Fanny's refusal would have won the approval of Felix, who in fact never used the instrument in his works.

35. The invitation from the Singakademie for Felix to conduct the performance is dated Nov. 20, 1837 (GB 6, No. 119). See also Felix's letter to the family of Nov. 13, 1837 (NYPL).

36. The work could be the *Sonata appassionata* of ca. 1829.

37. Piano Trio in E major, Op. 83.

38. Variations on a theme from *Robert le diable*, as identified in the *Allgemeine musikalische Zeitung* 39 (1837), col. 388.

39. Charles-Auguste de Bériot (1802–1870), Belgian violinist and composer; Moritz Ganz (1806–1868), cellist and composer.

40. The aria in B-flat is "A te, fra tanti affani," written for tenor. But another aria, "Fra l'oscure ombre funeste," for soprano, is written out in Fanny's hand in MA Ms. 71 (undated) in Berlin.

41. Karl Möser (1774–1851), Berlin violinist (concertmaster) and pedagogue.

42. This piece is perhaps located in a *Sammelband* in private possession; see Elvers, "Weitere Quellen," p. 216.

43. For instance, in his conversation with Eckermann of March 11, 1828; see J. P. Eckermann, *Gespräche mit Goethe*, ed. H. H. Houben (Wiesbaden, 1959), p. 514.

44. Letter from Felix to Fanny of Nov. 14, 1836 (Depositum Berlin 3, 15).

45. Mendelssohn was deep at work on his oratorio *Elijah*.

46. *Sechs Lieder für eine Stimme mit Begleitung des Pianoforte*, Op. 1.

47. *Gartenlieder: Sechs Gesänge für Sopran, Alt, Tenor und Bass*, Op. 3.

48. An edition of the letters in German with English translations is forthcoming from Pendragon Press.

Ralph P. Locke / *Mendelssohn's Collision with the Saint-Simonians*

The present article is an expansion and rethinking of the Mendelssohn pages in my dissertation "Music and the Saint-Simonians: The Involvement of Félicien David and Other Musicians in a Utopian Socialist Movement," 2 vols. (University of Chicago, 1980), pp. 156–65. (My book based on the dissertation, *Hymns for the Temple of Peace: Music, Musicians, and the Saint-Simonians*, is forthcoming from University of Chicago Press.) I should like to thank the following persons for their generous help and advice on the present article: Margaret Crum, Rudolf Elvers, Jane Fulcher, Philip Gossett, the late Dorothy V. Hagan, Jessie Ann Owens, Nancy B. Reich, Douglass Seaton, Jurgen Thym, and R. Larry Todd.

1. Locke, "Music and the Saint-Simonians," chaps. 2, 4, 7, and 8, and appendices 1, 2, and 5 (the surviving scores); cf. *The New Grove Dictionary of Music and Musicians*, s.v. "David, Félicien,"

and my paper forthcoming in the *Report of the International Musicological Society's 13th Congress (Strasbourg)*.

2. Locke, "Music and the Saint-Simonians," pp. 105–8, 131–56, 165–78. The section on Berlioz (pp. 165–78) summarizes and complements my previously published article "Autour de la lettre à Duveyrier: Berlioz et les Saint-Simoniens," *Revue de musicologie* 63 (1977): 55–77, and 64 (1978): 287. On Liszt, see my article "Liszt's Saint-Simonian Adventure," *19th-Century Music* 4 (1981): 209–27, and 5 (1982): 281.

3. Eric Werner was the first to make substantial use of many of the original letters, in *Mendelssohn: A New Image of the Composer and his Age*, trans. Dika Newlin (New York, 1963). His account of Mendelssohn's months in Paris (pp. 185–89) is still unsurpassed, but it deals with the Saint-Simonian episode only very briefly.

I wish to express my gratitude to the Bodleian and New York Public Libraries and the Bibliothèque de l'Arsenal for kindly permitting me to transcribe—in person or from films or photocopies—the previously unpublished and incompletely published letters cited here. (See nn. 11, 14, 18, 20–25, and 41–47.)

4. The discussion of the Saint-Simonian movement in the present article is based in large part on four classic and comprehensive studies: Sébastien Charléty, *Histoire du Saint-Simonisme (1825–64)*, 2nd ed., rev. (Paris, 1931); Henri-René d'Allemagne, *Les Saint-Simoniens: 1827–1837* (Paris, 1930); George G. Iggers, *The Cult of Authority: The Political Philosophy of the Saint-Simonians* (The Hague, 1958); and Frank E. Manuel, *The Prophets of Paris* (Cambridge, Mass., 1962), pp. 101–93 and 328–34, reprinted with slight revisions in Frank E. Manuel and Fritzie P. Manuel, *Utopian Thought in the Western World* (Cambridge, Mass., 1979), pp. 590–640 and 855–58.

5. On the movement's slogans, see Henri Fournel, *Bibliographie saint-simonienne* (Paris, 1833), pp. 111–17. On the derivation of Marx's related slogan (". . . to each according to his *needs*"), see Manuel and Manuel, *Utopian Thought*, pp. 696–716.

6. Saint-Simon, *Catéchisme des industriels* (published 1823–24), in *Oeuvres de Saint-Simon et d'Enfantin* [and of other Saint-Simonians], 47 vols. (Paris, 1865–78; repr. Aalen, 1963–64), 37:3–4 (hereafter cited as *Oeuvres*).

7. Stendhal, for example, was scornful; Rouget de Lisle, one of the few early exceptions, actually wrote a song for Saint-Simon. (See Marguerite Thibert, *Le Rôle social de l'art d'après les Saint-Simoniens* [Paris, 1927], p. 24; Herbert J. Hunt, *Le Socialisme et le romantisme en France* [Oxford, 1935], pp. 23–24, and, on Rouget de Lisle, Locke, "Music and the Saint-Simonians," pp. 28–37.)

8. [Léon Halévy and others], *Opinions littéraires et politiques* (published 1825), in *Oeuvres*, 39:207. This is an unusually early statement; the idea truly flourished a few years later, e.g., in the tenth session of *The Doctrine of Saint-Simon: An Exposition, First Year, 1828–29* (published 1830), ed. and trans. George G. Iggers, 2nd ed. (New York, 1972), pp. 156–57. (French text in *Oeuvres*, 41:267–70.)

9. Emile Barrault, *Aux artistes: Du passé et de l'avenir des beaux-arts. (Doctrine de Saint-Simon)* (Paris, 1830), pp. 77–79; cf. pp. 20–22. See also Barrault's sermon "L'Art: Paganisme, Christianisme, Saint-Simonisme" (Salle Taitbout, 1 May 1831), in *Oeuvres*, 44:160–90. The pages on art in the "first session" of the *Doctrine, First Year* may also have been written by Barrault.

10. *Tableau synoptique* (a large poster), reproduced in d'Allemagne, *Saint-Simoniens*, between pp. 96 and 97. Cf. *Oeuvres*, 42:354–56.

11. Mendelssohn to his father Abraham, February 21, 1832, in *Briefe aus den Jahren 1830 bis 1847*, ed. Paul Mendelssohn Bartholdy and Carl Mendelssohn Bartholdy, 6th ed. in one vol. (Leipzig, 1889), p. 248. All page references to the *Briefe* are to the "Erster Theil," a republication (differently paginated) of the *Reisebriefe* (1862). I have based my translations of letters included in the *Briefe* on those of Lady Wallace (Mendelssohn, *Letters from Italy and Switzerland* [Boston, ca. 1863]). Translations of unpublished letters and other sources are mine. The original texts of all cited passages from unpublished or incompletely published letters can be found in appendices 1, 4, or 5 below, or in Locke, "Music and the Saint-Simonians," pp. 157–59, 162–65.

12. Mendelssohn to his sister Fanny Hensel, September 2, 1831 (*Briefe*, p. 200).

13. Mendelssohn to Fanny Hensel, April 20, 1825 (Sebastian Hensel, *Die Familie Mendelssohn*, 18th ed. [Leipzig, 1924], 1:167–69). Cf. letters of September 2, 1831 (Auber is "commonplace and trivial"), February 15, 1832 (Paris's "fashionable music" has not changed in seven years), and February 21, 1832 ("mediocre music" is performed and extolled)—*Briefe*, pp. 200, 243, 249.

14. Mendelssohn to his father, December 11, 1831 (unpublished, New York Public Library). Hiller recalled his early friendship with Mendelssohn in *Felix Mendelssohn-Bartholdy: Briefe und Erinnerungen*, 2d ed. (Cologne, 1878). Gustave d'Eichthal had known Felix in 1824–25 while serv-

ing an apprenticeship in Abraham Mendelssohn's banking house in Berlin (Barrie M. Ratcliffe, "Saint-Simonism and Messianism: The Case of Gustave d'Eichthal," *French Historical Studies* 9 [1976]: 489–90). A friendly letter survives from Abraham and Felix Mendelssohn to Gustave d'Eichthal (May 3, 1825, Bibliothèque de l'Arsenal [Paris], No. 15032/75). In 1829 d'Eichthal's brother Adolphe played host to Felix and translated into French Felix's letter of thanks to the Philharmonic Society (see their correspondence in the Bodleian Green Books).

15. On Jews in the movement, see Frank E. Manuel, *The New World of Henri Saint-Simon* (Cambridge, Mass., 1956), pp. 344–47; J. L. Talmon, *Political Messianism: The Romantic Phase* (London, 1960), pp. 77–81; and Barrie M. Ratcliffe, "Some Jewish Problems in the Early Careers of Emile and Isaac Pereire," *Jewish Social Studies* 74 (1972): 201–2.

16. D'Eichthal and Rodrigues were both "Pères du collège"—the highest rank in the movement except for that of "Père suprême" (Charléty, *Saint-Simonisme*, bk. 2, chap. 1, pt. 2, p. 78). Rodrigues, in fact, held a position of reverence within the movement as the only member still active who had known Saint-Simon well; in the winter of 1831–32 his title was "Chef du culte" and he was the movement's most active fund-raiser (ibid., bk. 2, chap. 3, pt. 1, p. 132, and pt. 4, pp. 152–53). Hiller's involvement is documented in Locke, "Music and the Saint-Simonians," pp. 154–56.

17. E.g., letters of December 19, 1831 (*Briefe*, p. 217), December 20, 1831 (*Briefwechsel mit Legationsrat Karl Klingemann* [Essen, 1909], pp. 88–89), and January 11, 1832 (*Briefe*, p. 227).

18. Mendelssohn to his father, December 11, 1831 (see n. 14). He also reported that he teased Gustave d'Eichthal, Hiller, and Léo (Hiller's banker cousin) by announcing with mock seriousness that he was a *doctrinaire* in politics. The *doctrinaires*, Guizot among them, had been moderate and constitutional royalists during the Bourbon Restoration—the mildest possible opposition. Their program was now corpulently embodied in France's bourgeois monarch, Louis-Philippe.

Mendelssohn complained in other letters about the endless political chit-chat, some of which surely referred to the notorious Saint-Simonian movement (December 20, 1831; December 28, 1831 [Hiller and Léo again, disguised by the editors as one individual: "L. ."]; January 14, 1832—*Briefe*, pp. 218–19, 222; 226; 231–32). And on December 20, 1831, he expressed to his sister Rebecka his astonishment (or mock horror) that he had sat amid "actual Saint-Simonians" (including his friend d'Eichthal?) while viewing a session at the Chamber of Deputies (*Briefe*, p. 222).

19. Mendelssohn to Karl Immermann, January 11, 1832 (*Briefe*, pp. 227–28).

20. Lady Wallace translates these last words freely but perceptively as "and even that one, by some private hand of course" (Mendelssohn, *Letters*, pp. 329–30). The Prussian government had outlawed distribution of even faintly leftist literature.

21. Mendelssohn to his family, January 14, 1832 (Bodleian Library; *Briefe*, pp. 232–33). My transcription of this letter and of the letter of January 22, 1832 (appendices 1 and 4) differ significantly from the previously known versions. The editors of the *Briefe* not only made substantial cuts in Mendelssohn's text but also changed (or misread) a number of words and even added phrases of their own. In addition, they disguised d'Eichthal and Rodrigues by replacing their names with the misleading abbreviations "A. ." and "P. .". In secondary matters (e.g., spelling and punctuation) I generally follow the editorial practices of the editors of the *Briefe*. "U. sey" and "drüber," for example, become "und sei" and "darüber," and Mendelssohn's frequent commas are often replaced by more specific marks. But the words, for the first time, are his own.

22. Mendelssohn to his family, January 21 [recte 22 or 21–22], 1832 (Bodleian Library; *Briefe*, pp. 235–36). The transcription in appendix 4 incorporates important corrections; see n. 21.

The score which Mendelssohn mentioned in this letter was probably a copy of the published edition (1825), not the manuscript. Whether Mendelssohn was being serious about the troops having seized the score is unclear; he was (as he admitted) joking when he wrote that he would have to play the piece in the courtroom and that only the slow movement, because it was the only one written in moderate tempo, was exempt from government suspicion. ("Juste-milieu" was a term used to refer to political moderates, i.e., supporters of Louis-Philippe; "mouvement"—which Mendelssohn humorously equated here with allegro—meant liberal or progressive, e.g., the opposition leader Adolphe Thiers. See Locke, "Music and the Saint-Simonians," p. 162, n. 68; cf. Werner, *Mendelssohn*, p. 63.) If Mendelssohn in fact performed the Quartet at rue Monsigny, the Saint-Simonian leaders probably liked its serious, Germanic style (see Locke, "Music and the Saint-Simonians," pp. 68–74) and also the fact that it was dedicated to Goethe. The B-minor Quartet surely held strong Parisian associations for Mendelssohn, because the dour Cherubini had examined it during Mendelssohn's visit in 1825 and given his grudging approval (Werner, *Mendelssohn*, p. 25).

23. Unpublished letters in the New York Public Library: February 28, 1832, to his father: "This evening I'm going with Eichthal and Lanjuinais to see a new tragedy by Delavigne, *Louis XI*"; April 2, 1832, to his brother Paul: "Everyone here is looking forward to seeing you—Eichthal, Franck,

Hiller, etc."; April 11, 1832, to his sister Rebecka: "Even Eichthal agrees that at the moment nobody is thinking about business matters."

24. Felix Mendelssohn to his father, February 13, 1832 (unpublished, New York Public Library); the letter also reports that Olinde's cousin Edouard Rodrigues has been very friendly and has asked about Mendelssohn's father.

25. Mendelssohn to Michel Chevalier, February 19, 1832 (Bibliothèque de l'Arsenal, Fonds Enfantin, No. 7759/38). The transcription in appendix 5 constitutes the first complete publication of this letter. The letter has not, to my knowledge, ever been cited in the Mendelssohn literature, even though an abbreviated version was published over fifty years ago by d'Allemagne (*Saint-Simoniens,* p. 182). My transcription reproduces Mendelssohn's text with no silent corrections.

The letter is marked up in several hands other than Mendelssohn's. Under his signature, someone has added the words "Rue le pelletier." At the top someone has written "Globe [the word "correspo." is crossed out] *Supprimé. 3342,"* indicating that the letter was scheduled for publication in the *Globe,* under the rubric "Correspondance," but then suppressed, presumably with the approval of P. Cazeaux, one of the paper's several editors-in-chief, since "Caz." is written in large letters across the page.

26. This may be what Werner had in mind when he dismissed Mendelssohn's criticisms of the Saint-Simonians as "immature" (*Mendelssohn,* p. 186). Another of Mendelssohn's objections—that the placement of people according to their ability (what the Saint-Simonians called *capacité* or *vocation*) would stifle all natural incentive to work—probably stemmed from a fear that the Saint-Simonian leaders would decree arbitrarily (judge coldly, as he put it) which individuals were more "capable" and therefore deserved greater responsibilities and rewards.

27. "La Parisienne" was the battle song of the July Revolution of 1830. It was long thought (wrongly) to have been composed by Auber. Mendelssohn despised it (letter of September 2, 1831; *Briefe,* p. 200).

Pierre-Jean de Béranger was the most popular author of political chansons in France in the 1820s; he was twice imprisoned by the Bourbons for propagating republican and Bonapartist ideas. The ancient Greek poet Tyrtaeus wrote verses to spur the soldiers of Sparta to victory.

28. The "liberté" in Rodrigues's injunction to painters seems to refer to Delacroix's barebreasted *Liberty Leading the People* [into battle] (1831); Rodrigues seeks instead portrayals of women persuading men to lay down arms.

29. Félicien David later composed a Moses oratorio (*Moïse au Sinaï,* 1846), to very detailed specifications from Enfantin.

30. The Saint-Simonians began building an amphitheater-like "temple" at Ménilmontant in July 1832, and David composed a piece for the occasion, later incorporated (with new words) into his *Christophe Colomb* (1847).

31. This and the speech by Barrault (appendix 3) were both delivered publicly on November 27, 1831, and published in *Le Globe* the next day and in the brochure *Religion saint-simonienne: Cérémonie du 27 novembre* (Paris, 1831); the passages quoted are from the brochure, pp. 11 and 16–18. Both speeches were reprinted in *Religion saint-simonienne: Recueil de prédications,* vol. 2 (Paris, 1832), and later in *Oeuvres,* 4:203–39, and 45:220–57. Rodrigues gave Mendelssohn twenty copies of a shorter brochure containing only his own speech (*Religion saint-simonienne: Appel* [Paris, 1831]; ten thousand copies were printed; see Fournel, *Bibliographie saint-simonienne,* p. 83).

32. See Locke, "Music and the Saint-Simonians," pp. 76–78.

33. See n. 31.

34. *Begrüssung* (*Humboldt* Cantata), unpublished; snippets of Rellstab's text are quoted in Karl-Heinz Köhler, *Felix Mendelssohn Bartholdy* (Leipzig, 1966), p. 58.

35. On the hierarchy, see Charléty, *Saint-Simonisme,* bk. 2, chap. 2, pp. 61–78. On confession, see the tenth session of *Doctrine,* ed. Iggers, pp. 157–59; and *Oeuvres,* 4:173–76.

36. Mendelssohn's complex and profound attachments to his Jewish roots and his Lutheran beliefs are laid bare in Werner, *Mendelssohn,* pp. 28–44; see also pp. 83, 238–39, 283–85, 416–17, and 452–54.

37. For detailed accounts of the investigation and the resulting courtroom proceedings, see Charléty, *Saint-Simonisme,* bk. 2, chaps. 3 and 4, and *Oeuvres,* vols. 7, 8, and 47.

38. Manuel, *Prophets of Paris,* pp. 151–58, 185–89 (Manuel and Manuel, *Utopian Thought,* pp. 615–19, 635–38), and E. M. Butler, *Saint-Simonian Religion in Germany: A Study of the Young German Movement* (Cambridge, England, 1926).

39. On the "question de la femme" and the November schism see Charléty, *Saint-Simonisme,* bk. 2, chap. 3, pt. 1, pp. 125–36.

40. Enfantin to his mother, August 1831 (*Oeuvres,* 27:197, 201–2).

41. Duveyrier to Arlès-Dufour, August 18, 1842, forwarded to Mendelssohn by the latter with a friendly cover letter, August 26, 1842 (Green Books, Bodleian Library).

42. Mendelssohn's letter to Duveyrier (October 13, 1842) is lost, but his objections are clear from passages in Duveyrier's letters back to him, November 28, 1842, and November 6, 1843 (Green Books, Bodleian Library).

43. Duveyrier's letter, just cited, of November 28, 1842. The word "met" *(rencontrés)* is conjectural; a section of the letter, including the signature, was snipped out, presumably for a collector. Verdi and Tchaikovsky later wrote successful operas based on Schiller's *Jungfrau.*

44. Duveyrier to Mendelssohn of November 6, 1843, cited in n. 42. Cf. Mendelssohn to Immermann, January 11, 1832 (*Briefe,* p. 230).

45. Arlès-Dufour to Mendelssohn, November 3, 1843 (Green Books, Bodleian Library).

46. Duveyrier to Mendelssohn, May 7, 1845 (Green Books, Bodleian Library).

47. Enfantin to Mendelssohn, May 7, 1845 (Green Books, Bodleian Library); his emphasis. Enfantin also reminded Mendelssohn that he had met the composer (and his father) in 1822 [in Switzerland?] and the composer again in 1825 "chez Rodrigues."

Jon W. Finson / *Schumann and Shakespeare*

1. Robert Pascal, *Shakespeare in Germany, 1740–1815* (Cambridge, England, 1937), p. 1.

2. For the following account, I have relied heavily on Pascal (see n. 1), on Friedrich Gundolf's classic *Shakespeare und der deutsche Geist* (Berlin, 1922), and on Rudolph Genee, *Geschichte der Shakespeare'schen Dramen in Deutschland* (Leipzig, 1870).

3. Pascal, *Shakespeare in Germany,* p. 2.

4. Ibid.

5. See Pascal's list, ibid., pp. 191–99.

6. Ibid., p. 40; all translations, unless otherwise noted, are my own.

7. Ibid.

8. Ibid., p. 48.

9. Ibid., p. 48–49.

10. Ibid., p. 82.

11. Ibid., p. 85.

12. Ibid., p. 99.

13. Ibid., p. 141; Pascal notes that this passage is sometimes misattributed to Friedrich Schlegel.

14. See Gundolf's commentary on Schiller especially, *Shakespeare und der deutsche Geist,* p. 285ff.

15. Anton Friedrich Justus Thibaut, *Ueber Reinheit der Tonkunst,* 3rd ed. (Heidelberg, 1851), pp. 3–4.

16. Robert Schumann, *Tagebüchern. Band I, 1827–1838,* ed. Georg Eismann (Leipzig, 1971), p. 230.

17. Paula and Walter Rehberg, *Robert Schumann. Sein Leben und sein Werk,* 2nd ed. (Zürich and Stuttgart, 1969), p. 12ff.

18. Leon Plantinga, "Schumann and the *Neue Zeitschrift für Musik,*" in Alan Walker, ed., *Robert Schumann, the Man and his Music* (London, 1972), pp. 164–65.

19. Schumann, *Tagebüchern,* p. 128.

20. *Ibid.,* pp. 351–53; not all of the plays on the list are by Shakespeare.

21. The contents of these early sketchbooks are partially described in *Robert Schumann, Manuskripte, Briefe, Schumanniana. Katalog Nr. 188. Musikantiquariat Hans Schneider* (Tutzing, 1974), pp. 76–83; No. 40 in this catalogue received the designation "Schumann 13" in Bonn; No. 41 is "Schumann 15."

22. We do not know the exact date of the last lesson; see Schumann, *Tagebüchern,* pp. 409–10.

23. Rehberg, *Schumann,* pp. 77–79.

24. Schumann, *Tagebüchern,* p. 128.

25. Ibid., p. 411.

26. Robert Schumann, "Ferdinand Hiller," in *Gesammelte Schriften über Musik und Musiker,* ed. Martin Kreisig, 5th ed. (Leipzig, 1914), 1:44.

27. See the discussion by Edward A. Lippman, "Theory and Practice in Schumann's Aesthetics," *Journal of the American Musicological Society* 17 (1964): 314–23.

28. Eric Sams, *The Songs of Robert Schumann* (New York, 1969), p. 33.

29. Schumann, *Gesammelte Schriften,* 2:155–56.

30. This chronology comes from Schumann's own *Haushaltsbüchern,* Deutsche Staatsbibliothek, Berlin Mus. ms. 1175, III, 50v–51r.

31. Ibid., 61r.

32. Ibid., 72r.

33. Ibid., 72v.

34. See the letter to Peters recorded in Schumann's *Briefverzeichnis,* Robert-Schumann-Haus, Zwickau, 4871 VII C, 10 A3, p. 543, No. 2168.

35. Ibid., p. 561, No. 2307.

36. Alfred Dörffel, *Literarisches Verzeichnis der im Druck erschienenen Tonwerke von Robert Schumann,* Supplement to *Musikalisches Wochenblatt,* 1 (1870): 30.

37. This letter is in the possession of the Staatsbibliothek Preussischer Kulturbesitz, Berlin, Ms. ep. R. Schumann 24; it is also reprinted in *Robert Schumanns Briefe. Neue Folge.* ed. F. Gustav Jansen, 2nd ed. (Leipzig, 1904), p. 373.

R. Larry Todd / *Mendelssohn's Ossianic Manner*

1. Cited in W. Jackson Bate, *Samuel Johnson* (New York, 1975), p. 521. See also Johnson's comments in *A Journey to the Western Islands of Scotland,* ed. R. W. Chapman (London, 1930), pp. 106–8.

2. Friedrich Schlegel, *Dialogue on Poetry,* trans. Ernst Behler and Roman Struc (University Park, Penn., 1968), p. 60.

3. J. G. Sulzer, *Allgemeine Theorie der schönen Künste,* 2nd ed. (Leipzig, 1793; repr. Hildesheim, 1967), 3:634.

4. Ibid., 3:636.

5. See Rudolf Tombo, *Ossian in Germany* (New York, 1901), p. 87f.

6. See Helene Toussaint, "Ossian in Frankreich," in *Ossian und die Kunst um 1800* (Munich, 1974), pp. 97–138.

7. Examined in H. Quittard, *"L'Uthal* de Méhul," *La Revue Musicale* 8 (1908): 295–300; and David Charlton, "Ossian, Le Sueur and Opera," *Studies in Music* 11 (1977): 37–48; also, Aubrey S. Garlington, Jr., "Lesueur, *Ossian,* and Berlioz," *Journal of the American Musicological Society* 17 (1964): 206–8.

8. See Preston A. Barba, *Cooper in Germany,* Indiana University Studies 21 (1914): 56–57; and, more recently, J. K. Brown, "The Tyranny of the Ideal: The Dialectics of Art in Goethe's 'Novelle,' " in *Studies in Romanticism* 19 (1980): 229–30.

9. Carl Shaeffer, ed., *Lenaus Werke* (Leipzig, 1910), 1:105.

10. Karl Klingemann, ed., *Felix Mendelssohn-Bartholdys Briefwechsel mit Legationsrat Karl Klingemann in London* (Essen, 1909), p. 45. Lea was probably reading one of the *Leatherstocking Tales,* such as *The Pioneers* or *The Last of the Mohicans,* which began to appear in translations during the 1820s.

11. Stendhal, *Life of Rossini,* trans. R. N. Coe (Seattle, 1972), p. 387.

12. The stylistic indebtedness of Cooper to Scott has frequently been examined. See in particular, George Dekker, *James Fenimore Cooper, the American Scott* (New York, 1967), passim; and Donald Davie, *The Heyday of Sir Walter Scott* (London, 1961), pp. 101–65. For an attempt to link Cooper with Ossian, see Georg Friden, *James Fenimore Cooper and Ossian* (Uppsala, 1949).

13. *Sechs schottische National-Lieder* (Leipzig, 1977). The autograph of the folksongs is preserved in the Brotherton Collection of the University of Leeds.

14. Described in Johnson's *Journey,* pp. 134–48.

15. Washington Irving, "Abbotsford," in *The Works of Irving* (London and New York, n.d.), 3:522.

16. Including "Kelvin Grove," "Auld Robin Gray," and "Lord Muira's Strathspey."

17. See Martin Butlin and Evelyn Joll, *The Paintings of J. M. W. Turner* (New Haven, 1977),

1:180–81, and the extensive literature cited therein; and Gerald Finley, *Landscapes of Memory: Turner as Illustrator to Scott* (Berkeley, 1980).

18. Reproduced in Sebastian Hensel, ed., *The Mendelssohn Family (1729–1847)*, trans. Karl Klingemann, 2nd ed. (New York, 1882), 1:208.

19. At the Bodleian Library, Oxford. For a facsimile, see my "Of Sea Gulls and Counterpoint: The Early Versions of Mendelssohn's *Hebrides* Overture," in *19th Century Music* 2 (1979): 205.

20. Hensel, *The Mendelssohn Family*, 1:202–7. The letters are dated August 7 and 10, 1829.

21. Thomas Pennant, *A Tour in Scotland* (Warrington, 1774), 2:262.

22. *The Lord of the Isles*, canto 4, section 10.

23. Discussed in Todd, "Of Sea Gulls and Counterpoint," pp. 199–201.

24. See the fascinating study by Roger Fiske, "Brahms and Scotland," in *The Musical Times* 109 (1968): 1106–11. As Fiske demonstrates, there is a marked similarity between this melody and the opening of Mendelssohn's *Scottish* Symphony. Fiske's recent book, *Scotland in Music: A European Enthusiasm* (Cambridge, 1983), which includes much of interest to the reader of this essay, unfortunately appeared after the present volume went to press.

25. Further details are in my "Of Sea Gulls and Counterpoint," p. 198.

26. See especially Louise Leven, "Mendelssohn's Unpublished Songs," *Monthly Musical Record* 88 (1958): 206–11; German trans. in Gerhard Schumacher, ed. *Felix Mendelssohn Bartholdy* (Darmstadt, 1982), pp. 37–43.

27. Mendelssohn would meet Alexis in October 1833 in Düsseldorf. See Lionel Thomas, *Willibald Alexis, a German Writer of the Nineteenth Century* (Oxford, 1964), pp. 56–57.

28. See Mendelssohn's letter of April 25, 1829, in *Letters of Felix Mendelssohn to Ignaz and Charlotte Moscheles*, trans. Felix Moscheles (London, 1888; repr. New York, 1970), p. 11.

29. Letter of February 15, 1833, Felix Mendelssohn Bartholdy, *Briefe an deutsche Verleger*, ed. Rudolf Elvers (Berlin, 1968), p. 25.

30. *Uhlands gesammelte Werke*, ed. Hermann Fischer (Stuttgart, n.d.), 1:53.

31. " 'Unsre Kunst heisst Poesie': Om Niels W. Gades Ossian-ouverture," *Svensk tidskrift för musikforskning* 53 (1971): 73.

32. Macpherson's poems, of course, were largely inspired by a tradition of Ossianic ballads. The evidence is reviewed in R. P. Fitzgerald, "The Style of Ossian," in *Studies in Romanticism* 6 (1966): 32–33.

33. The chronology of the symphony has yet to be reconstructed in full, partly because the surviving MS sources are scattered, and partly because its composition overlapped that of the *Italian* Symphony, finished in 1833. Some of the sources are examined in Douglass Seaton, "A Draft for the Exposition of the First Movement of Mendelssohn's 'Scotch' Symphony," *Journal of the American Musicological Society* 30 (1977): 129–35. See also Eric Werner, *Mendelssohn: A New Image of the Composer and his Age*, trans. Dika Newlin (London, 1963) pp. 417–20.

34. Probably coincidental, since Mendelssohn's sketch of 1829 had already determined the A-minor tonality.

35. *Allgemeine musikalische Zeitung* 45 (May, 1843), col. 342.

36. Hensel, 1:198.

37. Irving, 3:523.

38. Canto 2, section 1.

39. Though it was included in the short catalogue compiled by Julius Rietz for the second volume of Mendelssohn's *Reisebriefe* (Leipzig, 1861).

40. Henry Phillips, *Musical and Personal Recollections during Half a Century* (London, 1864), 2:237–42.

41. Ibid., 2:258; M. B. Foster, *History of the Philharmonic Society of London, 1813–1912* (London, 1912), p. 199.

42. Foster, p. 199.

43. *The Poems of Ossian Translated by James Macpherson, Esq.* (New York, n.d.), p. 311.

44. Described in Daniel Ternois, "Ingres et le 'Songe d'Ossian,' " in Georg Kauffmann, ed., *Walter Friedlaender zum 90. Geburtstag* (Berlin, 1965), pp. 185–92; Toussaint, "Ossian in Frankreich," p. 127ff., and Henry Okun, "Ossian in Painting," *Journal of the Warburg and Courtauld Institute* 30 (1967): 352–53.

45. *The Poems of Ossian*, p. 284.

46. For facsimiles of this and "Le Songe d'Ossian," see Daniel Ternois, ed., *Tout l'oeuvre peint d'Ingres* (Paris, 1971), plates 22 and 23.

47. *The Poems of Ossian*, p. 285.

48. Phillips, 2:239.

49. *The Poems of Ossian*, p. 321.

50. Other portions of Phillips's correspondence to Mendelssohn are also in the Green-Books Collection and are catalogued in Margaret Crum's extremely useful *Catalogue of the Mendelssohn Papers in the Bodleian Library, Oxford*, Vol. 1 (Tutzing, 1980).

Index of Principal Names and Works